THE HORSE CATCHERS

TRILOGY

BOOK ONE

When the Horses Came

AMANDA COCKRELL

AVON BOOKS ◆ NEW YORK

This is a work of fiction. Names, characters, places, and incidents either are the product of the author's imagination or are used fictitiously. Any resemblance to actual events, locales, organizations, or persons, living or dead, is entirely coincidental and beyond the intent of either the author or the publisher.

AVON BOOKS, INC.
1350 Avenue of the Americas
New York, New York 10019

Copyright © 1999 by Book Creations Inc. and Amanda Cockrell
Published by arrangement with Book Creations Inc., Canaan, New York,
Lyle Kenyon Engel, Founder
Library of Congress Catalog Card Number: 98-93784
ISBN: 0-380-79549-3
www.avonbooks.com

First Avon Books Printing: April 1999

AVON TRADEMARK REG. U.S. PAT. OFF. AND IN OTHER COUNTRIES, MARCA REGISTRADA, HECHO EN U.S.A.

Printed in the U.S.A.

WCD   10 9 8 7 6 5 4 3 2 1

For my mother,
Marian B. Cockrell

INTRODUCTION

COYOTE WILL EAT ANYTHING, AND SO OFTEN ENOUGH HE chews a hole in time. It is on days like that that we may see people we think we remember, grinding corn in whitewashed houses or fishing in a cold river, back when things were not written down but told aloud, grandmother to granddaughter, father to son. In "real" time those days have frozen into stories told around a fire or recited by academics in papers weighed down by an accretion of footnotes. But here, now, they flow like water around Coyote's four gray paws, cavorting, telling their lives, shouting them loud enough for us to hear.

Pretend that you are kneeling, peering through the hole, and see a blanket on the loom, or Grandmother Spider in the angle of a roof beam, catching breakfast. Coyote trots across your vision, thinking one last new animal into the world. (If he didn't think of it, he will take credit for it.)

This is when myth is born, when the gods step into the human world, leaving holes behind to mark their passage. It is what makes magic, that open door. Rising through the hole like smoke, the story will dance itself into existence with Coyote, taking on one skin of the many possible ones.

And thus you will not find in the Red Earth people a portrait of any real pueblo, modern or historical, or in the Buffalo Horn people a real tribe of the plains, although one tradition has it that the first horses came up from the bottom of a river to a Kiowa chief named Long Arrow. Rather they are a composite of life as it might have been in those places at that time. I have chosen this approach for a number of reasons.

First, the coming of the Spanish laid what has been called a "fault line" across the history of the Southwest, so it is hard to tell which ways of doing things belong to the old times and which have been altered or scarred or rearranged by the intruders. In addition, the Pueblo peoples are intensely private about their private business, and for excellent reasons. A true rendering of any one pueblo's ceremonies and religion would be difficult to achieve and a bad idea anyway. And finally, the peopling of the West by Horse and his children did not happen quickly. I have written only a story of human people's first meeting with First Horse as it might have been. Mythology has its own landscape to play itself out in.

So bend down a little more and see what is being woven on the loom. Watch the pattern that emerges from a pair of russet hands—a new animal, unnamed as the animals were when the people first came up into this world along the trunk of a pine tree. But look closely. How many hands are on the loom? Is it only one man's (for among the Red Earth people the men are weavers) or many? Are there eight and have they grown black and gray, ever so lightly furred?

Look closely if you want to see Grandmother Spider, her great gray backside moving across the pattern, her eight arms shifting warp and weft. The new animal moves, shakes its head, startled to find itself here. Grandmother sees a pair of yellow eyes in the corner of the pattern. She didn't weave them there, but she beckons gracefully anyway, and a coyote trots across the world. The new animal sees Coyote and dances on its strange, uncloven hooves. Grandmother Spider nods.

When Grandmother weaves something into the People's world, it is Coyote who sets it moving.

Coyote grins, tongue lolling out. Listen and he will tell you how it all came about. His own version, anyway.

PROLOGUE

Bone Song

THIS IS THE WAY COYOTE TOLD IT, WHEN HE SAT DOWN beside the fire. The horses had been snorting on their picket line all night. You could just see their eyes gleam. It was one of those star-shot nights when anything might fall out of the sky and you would see it coming a long way off.

The air smelled like frost and green wood burning, and there was a feel to the night the way there is when the seasons shift, and everyone had been talking about horses.

The wood was smoky, and he beat the smoke away from his face with his hat. The hat was dark felt, grease-stained and ragged at the edges, with the stars showing through the tears. His nails were long and dirty, and his face was wrinkled, the color of sand. It was hard to say how old he was. He crossed his boots, one ankle over the other, and leaned back against the bumper of the pickup truck, propping his elbows on the edge of it.

"I will tell you about the first horses," he said, so they listened. "When people first came, folowing the big animals, we had horses then. But those all died with the camels and the mastodons and the big dire wolves. Maybe they ate too

4

many of them. Then a long time after that we had horses again.'' He thought about it. ''It might have been over at Tucson.''

''Tucson?'' one of the kids said, thinking of car dealers' lots shining in the sun and 7-Eleven signs.

Coyote shrugged. ''Maybe it was near Taos, then. Maybe it was farther south, too.'' These things don't matter to Coyote. In the desert everything talks to him. ''Anyway, there were some horses,'' he said, scratching behind his ear, ''that the new people brought back here, which is why we got horses again, and have horses today. Those new people tied them by their heads to a line, and something came by and let them go.''

''What?'' The boy was maybe twelve, eyes like nickels in the moonlight, just beginning to understand what might come out of an autumn night.

Coyote grinned. ''Something,'' he said offhandedly. ''A storm maybe . . .''

This is how that would be: The storm comes suddenly, the way storms do in the desert, making a noise to show it is there, filling the dry washes with roiling mud, cracking open the sky. The air is white for an instant with splintered tines of lightning, then dark again, the thunder filling in the place where the light has been, rumbling the earth beneath the surface. The horses feel it in their hooves. They are afraid and stand on their hind legs and snap their ropes. They run into the storm, their hooves drumming the wet ground . . .

''The next day someone came and caught some of them,'' Coyote said, waving away any other questions. ''But the rest kept running.''

Beneath the ground are the old bones, brittle outlines of horses who lived here when saber-toothed tigers and woolly mammoths lumbered through the night. The bones feel the hooves in the grass above them and sing an old bone song to them. The horses hear it.

"They were separated in the storm," Coyote said, remembering it. "Puma ate one of them, and one fell and broke its leg, and someone else ate that one." He looked thoughtful. "But there were some left. After a while they were thirsty, and hungry as well because the grass was bad that year. They looked for food, and that is how they found human people."

He thought for another minute. "It could have been anyone. Maybe they called themselves the Red Earth people."

Any people of the desert are Red Earth people. That is all there is out here.

"Anyway, it was some of them and some of the buffalo hunter people," Coyote said. "They changed the world." He stopped to pare his dark nails with his belt knife. His fingers were long and bony, and he wore a black leather jacket with silver conchos on it, very showy, and a silver belt buckle. "It takes power to keep the world moving," he said. "If things stopped changing, the world would stop spinning, and then it would all fall into the sky."

There was a snuffling and snorting on the picket line. The trail guide stuck her head through the tent flap and squinted at them. "The red roan's got loose again," she said, exasperation in her voice. "And who are you talking to out there?"

The tent flap slaps closed behind her, but the story stays in the air, limned in moonlight, phosphorescent as old bones. It starts itself over again, layer on layer, always new with each telling . . .

The horses snort and shuffle on their picket lines, ears pricked to the wind. The smells on the air are new to them; everything in this land is new, raw as new rope. They nose the ground for the last grains of feed as the wind rises. The sky is darkening over the red mountains, leaching the color out of them. Lightning crackles over the crest, and the low boom of thunder follows it. The horses switch their tails and toss their heads, pulling at the rawhide ropes, ears swiveling, nostrils flared. Their heavy hooves dance uneasily on the ground, fear of the storm and the unknown prodding at them.

It is only one of Coyote's children coming along a dry wash, curious about these new creatures. He stops under the lip of the wash. Above him he can see the animals dancing on their picket line, bigger than deer. These are new animals. His gray ears stiffen, and he cocks his head, studying them. Whatever they are is too big to eat. He thinks about that. Too-Big-to-Eat might eat you. These things work both ways. Coyote tastes the air cautiously. They smell like grass eaters, but something around the fire beyond them eats meat; he can smell that, too.

Coyote sniffs again and inches upward, scrabbling out of the wash, his paws digging like a badger's. There is something new out there, and it needs looking at. It is Coyote's job to inspect new things.

The storm walks down the mountain, blowing the wind toward him, away from the new animals, and now Coyote smells leather rope, of which he is very fond. Coyote will eat anything he can chew. He likes rawhide rope, and shoes, and the edges of tents. He likes grasshoppers, honey, woodrats, prairie dogs, dead buzzards, cloth, horned toads, acorns, peccaries, porcupines, turtles, melons, bumblebees.

Coyote flattens his belly along the grass and wriggles forward, his nose to the ground. The strange animals haven't seen him yet. He finds a pile of their droppings and stops to sniff. Very pleasant. He rolls on his back, working the smell into his coat. To catch a coyote you can bait your trap with food, but something to wallow in or something strange and new works better.

He is under the horses' feet before they see and smell him. They are not from the wild; they have not been wild in a long time. He might be a dog, they think, shifting nervously on their heavy feet. In this wild country he might be anything, but he is little and he isn't biting them. Lightning splits the sky open right above them, and thunder booms. Coyote doesn't care; he's biting a piece out of the rawhide rope that runs through all their halters and fastens to a ring in the ground.

The horses pull at the rope as the thunder cracks again. Coyote likes the smell of the new animals. Their young might be good to eat. But he doesn't care for the smell of the crea-

tures at the fire beyond the picket line. They are making sounds he has never heard before, which is intriguing, but tonight Coyote has some sense. He grabs his loose length of rawhide and runs away before the horses can hear him thinking about eating their young.

The storm breaks the night open like an egg. The horses rear, trailing their loose end of rope. The rain comes in torrents, as if someone has upended a bucket. Roiling brown water fills the wash. The horses run away into the rain, scrabbling and sliding in the mud along its banks.

1

Dreaming of Horses

OUT OF BREATH SAW THEM IN A DREAM. THEY RAN through his sleep like water flowing or the booming of a night-hawk—something big, unseen in the desert, looking for him. He woke up feeling that if he turned his head quickly enough he would catch them.

"I saw something," he said to his mother, Red Bean Vine, as she ladled maize mush onto a hot clay griddle. His stomach tightened at the smell. These days the Red Earth people were always a little hungry.

"There is a lot to see," Red Bean Vine said placidly.

"No, I mean I dreamed something. Something talked to me."

Red Bean Vine sighed. Out of Breath always thought he knew more than anyone else. "You are young," she said. "We have priests to dream things for us, and they are busy now." Then she thought that was unkind, so she said, "What do you think you saw?"

"I don't know," Out of Breath said, disquieted. "It told me it would change the world." He had just realized that. It

9

hadn't actually spoken, but the sound had been painted on his dream like a pattern forming on a loom.

Red Bean Vine made a noise between her teeth as she flipped the maize cake with a flat piece of bone. "Well, if it can bring rain, then Turquoise Old Man will be glad to hear of it." *And if it can't, don't trouble him with it.* That last was unspoken but unnecessary.

"It didn't say anything about rain," Out of Breath said, thinking. He wasn't sure what it *had* said.

Red Bean Vine sighed. Maybe if his father hadn't died. Maybe if she had taken another husband. Out of Breath was like a wild squash—anything might grow from his blossom. Her own father has been a trader who had settled among the Red Earth people with Red Bean Vine's mother. Not really a solid man. You always thought he might turn to smoke, and finally he did, and wandered on to who knew where. The Red Earth people thought Out of Breath was entirely too like him.

Out of Breath ate his maize cake, still thinking about what he had seen in the desert of his dream, a terrible beauty, moving fast. His stomach growled, but there wouldn't be any more this morning. He knew better than to ask. For two years now the rain had come sporadically, and the bean vines had withered. When the people of the valley peeled back the pale green husks of the maize, there were worms underneath that had come from nowhere, eating their way from some other world into this one. Turquoise Old Man and Squash Old Man had asked the kachinas about it, but they couldn't say. They had met with the headmen of the other cities along Water Old Man's course to talk about it, and even at the trade fair at High Up City.

The deer and the antelope had grown more wary, and on the last hunt, even Out of Breath, who had been the one most likely to run down a deer since the summer he had turned twelve, two years ago, had thought that they must have vanished through whatever door had opened to let the worms in.

He stood up, discontented, knowing there was work to do, the thing that had talked to him from the desert still whispering in his left ear. It was easy to listen to it, easier than to make himself want to hoe the bean field and clean the water channels, easier than to want to finish the blanket on his loom. He took his bow from its shelf and hefted it, but it was not a day to hunt. There was a proper day for everything. Out of Breath dug his fingernail into the smooth mud of the shelf. His mother had plastered it herself, and the finish was so hard he could barely dent it. He had felt the same way talking to her about his dream.

"Stop that and go see to the beans," his mother said over her shoulder without even looking.

Out of Breath put the bow back and patted the dancing deer painted on the wall beneath the shelf. He liked the way they were always in midair. The Red Earth people were never in midair.

As he scrabbled in the basket where he kept his clothes, his mother said, "Don't wear your good shirt."

After a while Out of Breath emerged reluctantly in an old shirt, the cotton worn soft with washings. He climbed down the ladder from his mother's second-story house, and the scrawny turkeys pecking in the courtyard gobbled at him. He scowled at them and stamped his foot. "You are stupid," he told them. "Hoo!" The turkeys fluffed their feathers, affronted, and gobbled loudly. Out of Breath let them alone before his grandmother came out of the house waving a spoon at him. There was always someone to pay attention to what he was doing. Beneath his mother lived his old Grandmother Owl Ears; his mother's sister, Green Melons; and her husband, Armadillo. Above them lived his Uncle Calabash, his mother's brother, who wore a skirt and hadn't married. Out of Breath thought about telling Uncle Calabash about the dream, but he suspected Uncle Calabash would say what Red Bean Vine had said.

The people of the valley were farmers, and if you were farmers there were ways of doing things that did not change, that could not change. Out of Breath could understand that, but just now he felt like a bee in a hive, buzzing busily about its honey while some giant hand with a bag was lowering itself carefully out of the sky.

He turned in a slow circle, craning his neck at the people on their roofs, knowing they were watching him, disapproving, thinking he ought to be in the bean field by now. All around him the Red Earth people's city rose up like the sides of a bowl, golden and red and blinding white in the morning sun, the biggest city in the great valley of Water Old Man. The plastered walls were as smooth as river stones, and in some places the women had mixed straw into the final coat of mud to make it gleam. Ladders led from one flat roof to the next. They stair-stepped two and three stories high around the court-yard, the Squash people's houses on the north of the stream and the Turquoise people's on the south. A footbridge took you across from one side to the other. Half the year the Squash people's Squash Old Man led the city, and the other half it was Turquoise Old Man. In bad times the two met with all the men in the underground kivas and talked about what to do. Out of Breath was a man now, since last year, and met with the other men, but very young men were expected to keep quiet. When you were old enough to marry and could weave a blanket flawless enough to please a bride, then it would be proper to talk.

He watched his neighbors come and go on their roofs. Among the Red Earth people there was no such thing as your own business. For instance, everyone knew that Weaver and his wife should behave like respectable people now that they were married, instead of staying in their house all day, legs-in-the-air. (Out of Breath could hear giggles.) And everyone knew that Wants the Moon, on her roof shelling beans, was almost too old to marry by now and that it was her own fault because she had a bad reputation for being willful. (She was Turquoise Old Man's father's cousin, and not of his clan, so *he* could have married her and was supposed to but wouldn't, she was so bad.) Everyone knew that Out of Breath was too like his grandfather with the wandering foot, and Red Bean Vine had been advised to reason with him (Red Earth children were never beaten) until he saw that this was so, because any-one with a grandfather like that had to be careful. Out of Breath sighed and dug his toe in the dirt.

Uncle Calabash came out on his roof with a sack of new clay for making pots. He looked as elegant as always, his black hair wound into elaborate knots on either side of his head, the way Out of Breath's mother wore hers. His skirt was embroidered in red and blue and yellow, and the blanket around his shoulders was knotted with a fringed red sash. He flapped his skirts at Out of Breath. "Go on! Shoo! Take care of the beans, and the beans will take care of you."

Out of Breath trudged across the footbridge. Beyond the city were the maize fields, the bean fields, cotton, pumpkins, gourds, and squash, watered by channels cut from the river. There was still enough water in the river, in Stream Young Man who flowed south into Water Old Man, to water the fields, but the worms came anyway, and the beans turned ashy and wilted. Borers in the squash vines withered the stems, and the squash rotted.

Turquoise Old Man was in the bean field, turning a pod between his fingers. He frowned at Out of Breath and pointed at the other young men and boys already hoeing the muck and old grass from the channels. "It is unfortunate when young men cannot get up before the sun."

Out of Breath ducked his head, polite. "I had a dream," he said. "I think it may have been important."

"The beans are important," Turquoise Old Man said. "Young men's business is not to lie about dreaming dreams. I know the kind of dreams young men have in the morning."

"It wasn't that kind of dream," Out of Breath protested. "It was a dream about the world."

Turquoise Old Man frowned at the beans in his hand. They looked dusty, as if someone had painted them with gray clay. He moved stiffly down the rows, and Out of Breath could see that his bones were hurting this morning. He trotted after. "There was something in the desert that wanted me to find it," he said. "Something that would change the world. That was what it said."

Turquoise Old Man lifted his gray head from the gray beans and narrowed his brows so that they came to a point over his nose. "Go and clear the channels. If there are dreams to be had, they will be had by old men who dream them properly, and not by young men who do not want to get up in the morning.''

Out of Breath felt his eyes sting and glared angrily at Turquoise Old Man's back for making him cry and look foolish. He stalked over to the rest of the boys and chopped at the channel with such a vicious bite that he cut a notch in the side and had to fill it back in. "I had a dream," he said to Canyon Wren. "It was important, but old Knock-Knees wouldn't listen. I will go to Squash Old Man at noon. There is something south in the desert I am supposed to find."

"I wouldn't," Canyon Wren said. "Squash Old Man is talking to that trader who came last night. *He* says there are monsters in the south this year."

"It isn't monsters," Out of Breath said stubbornly.

Canyon Wren looked thoughtful. "The trader says he has seen a man who has seen a man who has seen them. They have shiny skins, like mica, and they throw fire."

"Hmmph. He has seen the kachinas," Out of Breath said.

"Maybe you saw them in your dream."

Out of Breath thought about that and didn't like the idea. The thought of talking personally to the kachinas made his skin itch. Last year when he had become a man and the old men had told him their secrets, he had found out that the kachinas at the kachina dances were men inside kachina masks. When you danced a kachina, the kachina came, and went inside you while you danced. That seemed to him even worse than the idea of the kachinas coming on their own, which was what the children were told. Out of Breath didn't want a kachina inside his skin.

"They weren't kachinas," he said. He wasn't sure when *it* had turned into *they*, but now he thought of whatever it was as *them;* more than one. Something had said he should find them.

"Maybe it *is* monsters," Canyon Wren said cheerfully. "Maybe you are a new hero who is going to kill them."

Out of Breath tucked his tongue between his teeth and dug his hoe into the channel. There was no point in arguing with someone like Canyon Wren who never thought about things, never wondered why the sun didn't singe the sky or where bugs went in the winter.

When the sun was overhead, he went to find Squash Old Man and left Canyon Wren eating an onion and a bowlful of fried peppers out of his basket. Squash Old Man was sitting in the sun in the courtyard, looking as if he were asleep, chin to his chest, his breath fluttering his blanket fringe. Out of Breath sat down at his feet and waited for him to wake up.

Squash Old Man kept his eyes shut.

Out of Breath fidgeted, watching the sun. He coughed loudly. He stood up and sat down again, rattling his wooden hoe on the ground. The courtyard floor was hard as stone, dirt packed down by generations of feet.

Squash Old Man snored.

Out of Breath squinted at him. "It is a shame that Squash Old Man is asleep," he said. "There is a bug in his nose."

Squash Old Man's fingers slapped his nose. He opened his eyes and glared at Out of Breath.

"With respect, Uncle," Out of Breath said quickly, before Squash Old Man could tell him to go away, "there is something important to tell you."

"Is it a message?" *From someone important?*

"No, Uncle, it is something *I* have to tell you."

Squash Old Man lifted his brows. "Have you found the hole in the sky where the worms are coming through?" he asked, his voice heavy with sarcasm.

"No, Uncle. It was a dream. I have dreamed a dream."

There were two kinds of dreams: the ones you dreamed alone, that only mattered to you, and the ones the kachina and medicine societies had, all the men together in the kivas with the chiefs of the societies to tell them how to dream their dream, and afterward what it meant. Squash Old Man's snort made it clear that Out of Breath's dream was of the first sort.

"Something is going to change the world," Out of Breath said importantly.

"Undoubtedly," Squash Old Man said. "Undoubtedly. But not soon, I think. There has been all the change we need since we came into the upper world. The gods have given us maize and clay pots and the bow to hunt with, which our ancestors did not have. There is nothing else to want. So go along now and take care of the beans.''

Out of Breath lost his temper. "The beans are moldy!" he said. "If the old men know so much, why are the beans moldy?" Then he ran away before Squash Old Man could say anything.

All afternoon Out of Breath thought about it, while whatever it was talked in his ear. It breathed on his neck, caressed his cropped hair seductively with soft lips. He looked south, beyond the pumpkin field with its dry vines and the cotton that was the only thing growing properly this season. You couldn't eat cotton. His stomach growled. There was still food in the storerooms, but the Two Old Men were cautious about doling it out. Maybe food was what was waiting for him in the desert. Maize Girl had brought them maize once, in the far-off times. Why not new food?

"I am going to go find out what they are," he said to Red Bean Vine that night, when he had licked the last dollop of stew from his bowl. Red Bean Vine was a good cook; she could make even wild onions and ground squirrel taste good. But Out of Breath's stomach growled for deer meat and thick maize bread fried in back fat. Still, he surprised even himself.

"Go where?" his mother demanded. "Find what?" She looked out the window at the stars. The black night was everywhere outside. Within the city the lighted windows glowed like squares of sun taken inside for the night to keep them safe.

"To the south," Out of Breath said before he could change his mind. "Where my dream said. I am going to find out what was in my dream."

"You will find Coyote," Red Bean Vine said. "He will eat you."

"He will not eat *me*," Out of Breath said with the assurance of youth. He crossed his fingers, though, and put a pinch—although imaginary—of his stew on the fire, lest Coyote think he had been disrespectful. Coyote was old and powerful, besides being unreliable. You didn't want him at your campfire.

"Something will eat you," Red Bean Vine said. "You will be stolen by the Outsiders." The Outsiders had come from the north in the Ancestors' time and taken some of the People's land. They had no cities of their own and raided the People's sometimes. That was why most outer walls had few windows and doors. Everything faced inward, to the safety of the courtyard. "You have been talking to that trader," Red Bean Vine said. "I should have married again so you would have a man to teach you discipline."

"The trader says it is monsters," Out of Breath said scornfully. "There aren't any more monsters in the world." He was stubborn now, his resolve made real with the words. "I am going."

"Don't think I will give you any food to take with you," his mother said.

In the morning everyone knew that Out of Breath had been disrespectful to Squash Old Man and was going into the desert because he had had a dream and gone crazy. It was that grandfather, the Red Earth people sighed, shaking their heads. He hadn't liked to farm, and he had played the flute too much. With a grandfather like that, what could you expect?

Wants the Moon said maybe there *was* something in the desert, but nobody listened to *her*.

Uncle Calabash gave him a new pair of shoes he had made, with white shells and blue beads sewn on the toes.

"Not because you are right, but because your old ones are worn out and you will burn your feet in the sand without these." He tucked a gourd with a piece of honeycomb in it into Out of Breath's pack and shook his head dolefully. "Something will eat you, and we won't even have your body to bury."

Red Bean Vine gave him a journey bag with a handful of beans, a few cakes of maize, and a skin bag of water and told him he was lucky to have that much. And when he came back he must apologize to Squash Old Man for being a mannerless boy. Her eyes were red with crying, but Out of Breath wouldn't change his mind.

"I was not mannerless," he said. "Squash Old Man never listens. And then he says one is mannerless."

"Only the buffalo hunters go out by themselves and see visions," Red Bean Vine said. The buffalo hunters were shiftless people with no towns.

Out of Breath looked uncomfortable. He had tried to have the dream again last night, but nothing had come. He thought of telling Squash Old Man he was wrong and decided he would rather something ate him in the desert. "It wasn't a vision," he said.

He set out across the courtyard with his journey bag and his bow and arrows over one shoulder. He wore a loincloth and an old shirt, with a blanket across his shoulders to pad the pack and to wrap himself up in at night. Everyone shook their heads and rolled their eyes as he passed. Out of Breath could hear the bee-buzz of their murmuring. The People had always lived in hives. The Ancestors had lived in the red sandstone cliffs in houses you had to climb the cliff walls to get into. You could still see the hand- and toehold trails they had cut up the canyon walls. Even now, flat on the ground, they were enclosed, encapsulated, safe within their houses, their kivas. Experimentation was not encouraged. Travel was unheard of, except to hunt or go to the trade fair twice a year at High Up City. Traders would bring you what you wanted—red and green feathers, spotted cat skins and greenstone from the south, shells from the Endless Water in the west, buffalo skins from the buffalo hunters on the plains—and give it to you in exchange for maize meal and pottery and cotton cloth. No need to go elsewhere. The hive buzzed as the Red Earth people shook their heads at Out of Breath.

Only Weaver and Wants the Moon seemed to have nothing to say. Out of Breath could see Weaver inside his doorway, kissing Quail, his wife. They both stopped kissing and smiled at Out of Breath as he passed. Those two were always in a good mood and still not behaving as proper people.

Wants the Moon was sitting on her roof again, painting

black and white pots. She painted better pots than anyone but Uncle Calabash. She looked amused and half lifted a hand to him, but Out of Breath knew that she always looked amused, which people didn't like because it offended their dignity, no matter how beautiful her pots were. Out of Breath gave a half wave back to her to be polite. He had never noticed Wants the Moon much before, except to hear the gossip about her, since she was six years older than he and would have been married by now if she wasn't as stubborn as a peccary. He thought she cocked her head as if she were listening to him as he went by, but it was hard to see with the sun in his face. It had just come over the mountains to the east and up over the top of the highest house in the town, and the mud walls glowed red-gold all around her as if she were sitting in the middle of a honeycomb. Honey-warmth poured out of it, rubbing away the night chill.

Out of Breath decided not to think about where he would sleep tonight. He set out past the bean fields, where the other boys were working, and ignored the looks they gave him. At the edge of the field he scratched his head. Someone should tell him where to go now, but nothing did. Well, then. He turned southwest for no better reason than that it would put the sun at his back, and followed Stream Young Man.

In a while Stream Young Man turned southeast, and Out of Breath left him. It was easy walking in the morning, and his new shoes felt light on his feet, as if they might walk a little above the trail if he let them. They went south past Old Horned Toad Canyon toward the blue mountains and the black desert beyond that was made when the world was young and fire came out of the ground. A hawk soared on the thermals overhead, and far away, over a stand of cottonwoods, the buzzards had found something interesting. Out of Breath spread his arms, wishing he were a bird. Beside the trail, the sage grew dusty green and the yucca spread its spiked leaves. A barewood tree cast its contorted shadow on the ground, like an old basket with the weft sprung loose and a horned toad looking out of it. In the spring the tree would burn with pink flowers, but now its naked limbs bore only shadows and grasshoppers.

Out of Breath left the trail and the dry grasses whispered under his feet. *This way,* they said. *This way.*

At noon he ate one of the maize cakes his mother had given him, and the honeycomb, and refilled his waterskin at a stream. The water burbled clear over the stones. He took off his shoes and let it wash his toes. A yellow and black butterfly danced past him on the wind, and Out of Breath put his shoes back on and followed it. It might lead him somewhere, he thought— to *them,* whatever they were. He had the sense of something waiting, around a boulder or a stand of trees. Chasing it was infinitely more pleasant than hoeing the irrigation channels in the bean fields. Red Earth people were never idle; to sit under a tree and play the flute was suspect. Out of Breath took his flute out of his pack and played it as he went, giving the butterfly music to dance to. It wasn't until the sun was halfway down the sky that he wondered how far he was from home.

The sky seemed wider than it had above the city. Out of Breath wondered if it had stretched. He had gone beyond the roads that led to other valley cities. He thought about what his mother had said about finding Coyote instead of something fine, and he thought he saw him, yellow eyes at the corner of the horizon, gray paws on the blue cloth of the sky. Out of Breath screwed up his eyes until Coyote went away.

There were hardly any trees in this place, and a cool breeze blew out of the stretched sky. *I will have to build a fire at night*, Out of Breath thought, and when he found some deadwood he slung it in his blanket over his back, afraid there wouldn't be any more.

By sunset he had come to a dry country of red sandstone and yellow tufa cliffs, with the sky dark blue overhead shading into flame in the west. Out of Breath had hunted over this country, but not alone. Alone, the land spread like the sky, unending, moving faster and faster into the distance, broken only by the rough teeth of the mesas. Out of Breath felt as if he were at the bottom of a bowl, a very small piece of un-identified something in Thought Woman's cookpot.

He had been following a dry wash, and when the dark came down suddenly like a hide over a cookfire, he scrambled under

an overhanging lip of the bank and peered out. He made a
fire with a handful of dry grass and the slow-burner of sagebrush bark he had nursed along the trail from home in a clay
bottle and teased the wood into flame. Whatever *they* were—
whatever had told him to come here, whatever was going to
change the world—would see his fire and come and find him,
he thought. He ate another maize cake and drank most of the
water in his waterskin. He settled back, still a little hungry, to
wait.

In the morning he woke with a crick in his neck from leaning
against the bank all night.The fire had burned down to ashes,
his feet were cold, and his back was stiff. The world had not
changed.

Out of Breath ate the handful of cold cooked beans his
mother had rolled in a piece of oiled cloth for him and looked
unhappily about him. Nothing had come. He couldn't understand why. It had been so clear in his dream. What was he
supposed to do now? His stomach growled. *Hunt,* it said.

"I can't stay here any longer," Out of Breath said to the
thing he was waiting for, in case it could hear him. "I am
hungry."

And the dream was fading. He was not so certain of it as
he had been. But he thought of Squash Old Man—and it was
interesting how quickly Squash Old Man's face could make
him remember his determination. That part was quite clear.

By evening he was still hungry. He had seen deer tracks
and marks of rabbits and peccaries, but they were old tracks
with the edges crumbling in, and now, in this place, no animal
people stirred. There was very little water, either, except for
a sandy hole with coyote tracks around it. Out of Breath lay
on his stomach and drank from it and thought hungrily of the
last maize cake in his pack, which he was afraid to eat now
because he mightn't get anything else.

You could go back home, a voice seemed to suggest inside
his head.

"No," Out of Breath said to whatever it was. He was feel-

ing a little dizzy, and he rolled over and lay on his back beside
the water hole.

Puma will eat you if you stay there, the voice said.

Out of Breath sat up. "There are no tracks of Puma."

The voice made a motion that looked like a shrug. Out of
Breath didn't know how it did that. *This is the only water*, it
said.

Out of Breath stood up. He sniffed the wind. If Puma was
hunting here, no wonder there were no deer. He nocked an
arrow to his bowstring.

The voice chuckled. It was a low, growly sort of chuckle.
Out of Breath smacked his ear with the palm of his hand, and
it went away. All the same, maybe it was better not to camp
here tonight. *I will go back where I was last night, where I
left some wood,* he thought. *And tomorrow I will kill something.* He listened for the voice in his head, but it didn't say
anything back. Satisfied, he set out at a trot for the fire pit he
had left in the dry wash.

Out of Breath didn't like voices in his head, any more than
he liked the kachinas being inside him at dances. Some of the
kachinas were ancestors of the Red Earth people—very powerful or wise or good people might become kachinas when
they died. No one had become a kachina in a long time,
though. Out of Breath thought maybe it didn't happen anymore. He hoped the voice in his head wasn't a kachina. He
saw them in his mind, tall, bird-headed figures with cumber-
some beaks, or pots on their heads with tufts of feathers sticking out. As a child he had run under his mother's skirt when
he saw them. The kachinas had told people to impersonate
them at the dances because in the old days, when the kachinas
really came into the city themselves, they took someone away
with them. Now the men put on kachina masks instead so no
one would have to die.

Out of Breath cleared the ashes of last night's fire and put
the rest of his wood on it. There was nothing to cook, but it
kept him warm, and it would keep Puma away. He wrapped
his blanket around his shoulders and sat with his back to the
bank of the wash. If it rained, the wash would fill with brown

roiling water in a few heartbeats, but there were no clouds. The sky was obsidian, with pinpoints of light in it and a thin moon piercing it like a pin. Out of Breath shivered. He tried to sleep, keeping his ear to the ground just in case, but his head felt strange and his stomach kept growling.

The stars looked as if they were spinning slowly, spiraling across the sky. It made him queasy to watch. Something fell out of them. It had a brush of a tail still spangled with their lights, and the same yellow eyes Out of Breath had seen looking at him out of the afternoon. He held his breath, his heart hammering with fear.

It nosed at the fire and at Out of Breath's pack. *I am sorry,* Out of Breath thought to the kachinas. *I would be happy to have you come into my place.*

It burned its nose on the coals and snorted. Out of Breath closed his eyes, squeezing them tight. You didn't want Coyote in your campsite. You never wanted Coyote in your campsite. Coyote was always hungry, and what he ate was people who had got lost—one way or the other. Out of Breath opened one eye. A gray, hairy shape was sitting across the fire from him, blotting out the stars and the moon. His tongue lolled out between rows of white teeth, and he lifted his back leg and scratched behind his ear.

"I brought you something," he said. It was the growly voice that Out of Breath had heard in his head. Then he was gone, leaping back among the stars. Where he had been, a tall bony figure loomed above the dying glow of the fire. It put its long hairy nose in Out of Breath's face and breathed on him. Out of Breath pressed himself against the bank of the wash and screamed.

2

The Holy Clowns

THE THING JUMPED INTO THE AIR. IT WAS THE COLOR OF dry bones, and when it landed, its feet clattered on the stones of the wash as if they were made of stone, too. It snorted down its long nose.

It was trying to trample him. Out of Breath shrieked again and flung himself upright, staggering sideways along the wash bank. The Thing jumped sideways itself, scattering stones into the fire. It shuffled its bony feet on the ground and blew down its nose again.

Out of Breath and the Thing stared at each other, breathing hard. The sky was beginning to roll toward daylight. There was a thin band of pink in the east, and the sky overhead was threaded with turquoise. Now Out of Breath could see that the Thing was tall and angular, like an elk, but it didn't have any horns. Its tail was longer than Elk's, like a long fringe on its backside. There was more long hair growing along the crest of its neck, and it wore what looked like a piece of old rope around its head. Its feet had hooves, but they looked like rocks: solid, heavy things, with no cleft in them.

When it stayed still, Out of Breath edged a little closer,

fascinated in spite of himself. The wild white Thing was still looking at him. Its eyes were on the side of its head, like a deer's. Its pointed ears, more like a dog's, were swiveled toward Out of Breath. It drew its lips back, baring heavy teeth. Out of Breath backed up again, but he could see that they were grass eater's teeth, not sharp. Still, they were long and as big around as his finger.

Out of Breath considered, his heart hammering in his chest. White creatures were magical. A man who had seen a white deer was always blessed. But sometimes they were ghosts, and of course he didn't know which this one was. He didn't know what it was at all. It made a horrible noise in its throat, like someone saying *huh-huh-huh,* and Out of Breath thought about the kachinas again.

Out of Breath made himself stand still and not run away. The Thing was nosing at his pack, whuffling, its lips pulled back from its teeth. Out of Breath thought about what Coyote had said as he vanished. Maybe this Thing was a new animal come into the world and it was a gift to *him,* to Out of Breath, because he had been the one to dream it. Although of course you had to be careful about what Coyote gave you. Coyote had given fire to people, too, and like fire, most of his gifts could burn you. Out of Breath studied the new animal and wondered if there were more like it, and if you could eat them.

On the other hand, Out of Breath thought, no one else among the Red Earth people had one of these. It would certainly make Squash Old Man pay attention and Turquoise Old Man get his nose out of the beans.

The Thing snuffled at Out of Breath's waterskin now, its lips fumbling, scooting it sideways across the ground. Maybe it was thirsty. Out of Breath looked for something to put water in. The pot that held his slow-burner was too narrow for that bony nose to get into. He picked up the waterskin, marveling at his bravery, and inspected the stones in the wash while the Thing watched him hopefully. Finally he found a big stone with a depression in the middle of it, and shifted it carefully in the creek bed, leveling it. The Thing butted at his shoulder, and he nearly shrieked again.

"Quit that," he said, his hands shaking. "I will give you some." The Thing blew down its nose at him.

Out of Breath poured half his water into the shallow stone bowl, and the Thing stuck its mouth out and sucked it all up in a moment. It licked the wet bottom of the depression with a tongue like a pink fish.

It put its soft lips against Out of Breath's chest and nibbled at his blanket. Its eyes were brown, he saw, with white lashes, and the skin under the fine hairs on its sinewy nose was pink. Out of Breath pushed it away, feeling the heavy skull bones under his palms and the short, soft coat that covered them. "I don't know what you eat," he told it.

The Thing bobbed its heavy head, and he saw again the rope dangling from it, like a piece of dog harness. *It's tame,* he thought suddenly. *Whatever it is, it's tame already.* Like a dog. Maybe it wasn't something to eat. He opened his pack and took out the last piece of maize cake. He put half the cake down on the rock and watched to see what the Thing would do. It scooped up the cake with its lips and teeth and chewed, dribbling crumbs and foam.

Out of Breath stuffed the other half in his own mouth before the Thing could demand that, too. He wondered how much it ate, as big as it was. And if it was his, how he would feed it. "I don't know if I want this," he said to Coyote, who wasn't there anymore.

Out of Breath sat down in the wash to think while the Thing nuzzled his pack, hoping for more food. When it didn't find any, it ate a tuft of withered grass growing from the top of the wash. It was thin, Out of Breath saw now. He hadn't noticed at first because it was so big. But its ribs stuck out under its white hide, and its tail was matted with burrs, which was never a good sign in an animal. Animals kept themselves clean when they could, when they were healthy. He would have to feed it or it would die, he thought. Then after that he could figure out what to do with it. Certainly it was very important and magical, being the only one of it that there was.

Out of Breath stood up and slung his pack on his back. He edged toward the Thing and grabbed the frayed rope that was tied around its head. "Come on," he said, and it came, startling him. He watched it as they walked, his head cocked sideways. Maybe the rope was part of a harness. An animal like this could certainly carry more weight than a dog could. It had little patches of roughened skin on either side of where its bony neck began, like the gall marks a badly tied harness made on a dog.

Out of Breath became more convinced that this Thing belonged to someone else. As he did, he began to wonder if it was someone who might come looking for it, and what kind of someone it might be. It would probably be better to take it home to the Red Earth people right away, he thought, before someone said he couldn't keep it. He had dreamed it, he thought stubbornly. And Coyote had given it to him. (Of course Coyote wasn't above giving people other people's property.)

Out of Breath took the Thing to the water hole where Coyote (or somebody) had suggested last night that he should go home. The tracks were still there, clear in the damp mud.

"Did you give me this?" he asked the tracks, while the Thing stuck its nose in the water hole and slurped the muddy water down its throat.

"Do you like it?" Coyote said, and there he was, across the water hole under a scrub pine, his yellow-gray coat just blending into the sandy ground. The Thing lifted its head and gave him a long look, then went back to the water.

"What is it?" Out of Breath said.

"I don't know." Coyote grinned, his long tongue lolling out.

Out of Breath felt exasperated. He wasn't used to talking to spirits anyway, and he had expected them to have more sense. "Well, where did you find it?" he demanded.

"Oh, south of here. I think." Coyote studied the tip of his tail thoughtfully.

"A long way south of here?"

"Oh, yes."

"Then no one is likely to come looking for it." Out of Breath made that almost a question, and Coyote looked off into the distance as if he had just seen a rabbit.

"Oh, I don't think so," Coyote said, studiously nonchalant. He stood up suddenly and trotted away with a purposeful gait. The next time Out of Breath saw him he was edging through a tangle of mesquite toward the rabbit.

Out of Breath turned back toward the Thing. It stood above the water hole, its muzzle dripping. He tied a piece of rope from his pack to the rope around its head and started north.

His stomach growled, and the sun seemed to swim on the tops of the mountains as if little pieces of fire had got loose from it. His head felt fuzzy. The stones in his path jumped under his feet like horned toads every time he took a step. Out of Breath rubbed his fist across his eyes. He was sleepy and hungry, but he thought that if he slept or tried to find something to eat, the Thing might wander off. Better to keep going until he got home, and then his mother would feed him. He thought about her expression and how Squash Old Man's eyes would shoot out of his head like frogs.

It took all day to get home. When they came to the edge of the bean fields at sunset, Out of Breath stopped and leaned against the Thing's warm shoulder. In the distance he saw someone jumping up and down and waving his arms, and then a lot of voices began shouting at once. The Thing stuck its head in the bean vines and ate a big mouthful, pulling it loose from the vine with a shake of its head. Out of Breath dragged it away.

"I will give you something to eat." He thought it probably needed grass. There was some by Stream Young Man. "Come on." The Thing followed him, chewing.

Out of Breath stopped where Stream Young Man wandered downhill through the fields just outside the edge of the city. The Thing put its head down in the sparse grass. The sun was going down behind the tops of the houses, splashing them red and black. Turquoise Old Man came hurrying across the footbridge and the south courtyard, flapping his hands at everyone who was trying to follow him. No one paid any attention. They all came popping out of their doors, down off their roofs, wading across the stream because the footbridge was already crowded, white clothes gleaming in the dusk, the last of the sun bouncing off shell beads and turquoise necklaces, feathers and coral and polished stones, aprons and loincloths embroidered and painted in red and yellow and green. The Red Earth people were a people who owned much. Hunger was new to them.

Squash Old Man flapped his hands at them, too. "Stay back. Stay back!"

"We want to see it!"

"What is it?"

"It's a monster!"

Dogs followed them, barking.

Red Bean Vine shrieked. "It has my son!"

"I have it," Out of Breath said. "I found it. I told you I would find something."

"Get away from it! It will eat you!"

"ENOUGH!" Turquoise Old Man roared. The Thing started, jumping in the air on all four feet. It landed, snorting at Turquoise Old Man. The people quieted into a hush that flowed across the ground like the purple dusk.

"It does that," Out of Breath said, "if you scare it."

"This is very dangerous," Turquoise Old Man said darkly. "Get back." He turned to Out of Breath. "What have you brought here among us?"

"I found it in the desert, Uncle," Out of Breath said. "I think—" No, perhaps he wouldn't say that. He suspected it was best not to mention Coyote. Anyway, he wasn't sure now that he had seen him. His head was swimming. He lay down and put his face in Stream Young Man and took a long drink. "With respect, Uncle," he said, wiping his mouth with his hand, "this is a new kind of animal that is new in the world, and it came to me in the desert, as my dream said it would. I don't know what it's called."

"It was eating beans," someone said.

There was a commotion and a shoving in the crowd as Grandmother Woodrat stumped past Turquoise Old Man, ig-

noring his orders to stay back. She was older than anyone else
and did what she wanted to. She planted her feet wide apart,
leaning on her stick, squinting dim eyes at the new animal.
"It will eat what we eat," she said. "And there is too much
of it. What is it good for?"

Out of Breath stood up, wavering a little on his feet. The
lighted windows in the city pulsated when he looked at them.
He wished he had taken a big mouthful of beans as he passed,
like the Thing, which was now pulling grass from the stream
bank. "It can carry things," he said. "Like a dog, but more.
It is tame. Look, there are pack marks on its hide."

Uncle Calabash had pushed his way forward, too. Now he
furrowed his brow. Out of Breath thought he was trying to
find a way to agree. "Well, it *could* carry things," he said.
"If we wanted to go somewhere."

"Why would we want to go somewhere?" Grandmother
Woodrat demanded. "We aren't buffalo hunters." She spat
and made a sign with her fingers, because the buffalo hunters
weren't proper people. "Or traders to go pack-on-back." She
sniffed at Out of Breath and then at the trader who was still
in the city and had followed the crowd.

Ignoring her, the trader edged to the front of the crowd to
look at the new animal.

"Have you ever seen something like this?" Turquoise Old
Man asked him.

The trader shook his head, pleased to be important. "Very
likely it came from the monsters that are living in the south."

"It's tame!" Out of Breath said. "It's a new kind of animal.
It's for us!"

The trader shook his head. He wore his hair in long braids
like the people from the north. "That is not something that
belongs in this world. Look at its feet."

"We have gotten along very well so far with the animals
we have," Squash Old Man announced. "This is very ill-
advised. I told you so." He stood next to Turquoise Old Man,
and they looked at Out of Breath as if he had invented the
animal on purpose. "What else does it eat?"

"Maize," Out of Breath said, before he thought better of it.

There was a collective intake of breath.

"That is dangerous."

"It will eat all our food."

"Maybe it is what has been eating *our* maize."

"Those are worms," Out of Breath said.

"Something has brought the worms," Squash Old Man said thoughtfully. "Maybe it is this thing. Maybe the worms are its doing."

"It just got here!"

"We never had one before," Grandmother Woodrat said. "Why should one come now? It's a curse. Very likely a witch has sent it."

Red Bean Vine glared at her. "My son is not a witch."

Grandmother Woodrat smacked her lips. "I never said he was. But things like that don't come out of nowhere." She nodded her head, agreeing with herself.

The animal lifted its heavy head and blew down its nose at her. It made the *huh-huh-huh* noise in its throat, and she stepped backward in a hurry, bumping into Wants the Moon. Wants the Moon steadied her under one elbow as Grandmother Woodrat glared at the animal. "I'm all right. I don't need to be held up."

"Very well," Wants the Moon said, letting go of her so that she nearly fell over. She came closer to the animal and studied it. Out of Breath watched the animal and Wants the Moon looking at each other. No one else paid any attention.

"It might be something to eat," Uncle Calabash said, trying to find some redeeming quality in it. "Are there more of them?"

"I didn't see any," Out of Breath said. "And it isn't to eat. I told you, it's tame."

"So are turkeys, dear," Uncle Calabash said.

"Don't let it come inside," a young woman said. "Keep it away from the children."

Everyone took their children by the shoulders and pulled them back into the crowd as if the Thing had lunged at them.

The children peered at the Thing from behind their mothers' embroidered skirts.

Out of Breath pushed his cropped hair out of his eyes, exasperated. "Yah, you are all fools," he said, stung by what they had said and not caring now if he insulted Squash Old Man again. "I bring you a magic animal and you yammer at me about turkeys and eating your children." He stamped his foot. "*I* haven't had anything to eat, after being in the desert three days finding it. I am hungry."

"And so you should be," Red Bean Vine said with asperity. "Didn't I tell you not to go out there? And you aren't bringing that witch thing in my house."

Out of Breath hadn't thought of that. He didn't think it would go up a ladder anyway. He didn't see his grandmother in the crowd, but he didn't suppose she would let it in, either. Grandmother Owl Ears didn't even like dogs. He looked at Uncle Calabash. People like Uncle Calabash were considered holy, because they were men and women both and so understood things that men or women alone couldn't see. "It's bound to be magic," he said hopefully. "It's white."

"So is a bean worm," Uncle Calabash said. He put his hands on his hips and studied the Thing. "It's very large. I can't think what you're going to do with it." He sucked on one tooth irritatedly. "As if I didn't have enough to do. Weaver's wife is sick, and he is being a crazy person over it. I have a tea brewing for her now."

Red Bean Vine rolled her eyes at her brother. "Then go and brew it and stop encouraging the boy."

"*You* let him go off into the desert," Uncle Calabash said.

"I didn't *let* him."

"Young people nowadays have no manners," Grandmother Woodrat said to her. "They do anything they like."

"Well, a mother ought to be able to reason with a child like that," Old Striped Snake said. He was nearly as old as Grandmother Woodrat and didn't approve of the younger generation either.

"What about *our* children?" a young mother asked, chin out, stubborn.

"What about them?" Out of Breath said. "It eats grass. Look at its teeth."

"Maybe it's like the flesh-eating antelope," his Aunt Green Melons said. "*It* had antelope teeth, I suppose."

"And nobody's seen it since before the Ancestors went up the cliffs," Out of Breath retorted.

Uncle Calabash frowned at him. "Young men without manners never prosper. Now take that thing home—not inside, mind you—and I will think about it. Go on." He gave Out of Breath a shove and smacked the Thing on its rump for good measure. "And you can give it some maize," he told Red Bean Vine. "This grass is not going to be enough for it. It has an appetite like any young man."

Red Bean Vine glared at him, but she hurried after Out of Breath and his new animal. Wants the Moon walked beside them, not saying anything, just running her fingers down the animal's white back as if some secret sign was marked there. Some of the others began to follow them, to make sure it was not going to go inside any of their houses.

Uncle Calabash turned back to Squash Old Man and Turquoise Old Man. "We must consider this animal."

They eyed him dubiously, but he looked determined, and no one liked to cross Uncle Calabash when he was in that mood.

"What do you think it is for?" Turquoise Old Man asked him. The important people, Squash Old Man and the chiefs of the religious societies and the holy clown dancers, huddled around them, excluding lesser souls.

"I don't know," Uncle Calabash said. "I am very startled. I thought the world had stopped changing."

"It is not good for young men to bring change." Bitter Water, who was head priest of the Deer Lodge, stuck his lip out.

"Oh, that is always who brings it," Almost a Dog said. "It is a serious responsibility." The others nodded. Like Uncle Calabash, the men who danced the holy clowns at the Year End ceremonies were to be listened to, having one ear in another world.

"It is almost time for the Maize Dance," Badger said. "And there are worms in the maize, and now this. It may turn the dance the wrong way. We may dance upside down."

"It is hard to know what to do," Uncle Calabash said tactfully. "But more mistakes are made in a hurry than slowly."

"Hmmph," Turquoise Old Man and Squash Old Man said together.

"We will see about it after the Maize Dance," Uncle Calabash said to Out of Breath. The Thing was eating a bowlful of cracked maize in the courtyard, chewing and slobbering foam. All the children had been pulled inside by their mothers, but their russet faces and dark eyes lined the rooftops or peered around the water jars in the courtyard. "Maybe it will go away by itself before then," Uncle Calabash added. He sounded hopeful.

"I don't think so," Out of Breath said. He had tied a big stone to the end of its rope to make sure of that.

Uncle Calabash stirred his potion in a clay pot, squatting by the hearth, his skirt brushing the smooth mud floor. "Weaver's wife is very ill. It came on her suddenly, while you were in the desert." He frowned. "It's hard to say what it is—she has a pain in her belly. All the medicine people have looked at her, but nothing helps. Weaver says it's witches."

"The old grannies think everything is witches," Out of Breath said scornfully.

"Weaver isn't a granny," Uncle Calabash said. "He's a good man whose wife is sick. And you should be respectful to the grannies. We know things." He ground wintergreen in his mortar while he talked, his long hands moving gracefully, around and around. His head on its long neck was bent over the mortar, crowned with elaborate braids with red thread tied into them. Uncle Calabash was really prettier than his mother, Out of Breath thought.

"You aren't a granny yet," he said, smiling.

"I have plenty of children," Uncle Calabash said. "When you marry, I will be a granny." He put the wintergreen into the potion boiling on the fire. It made a scum of foam on the

top that made Out of Breath glad *he* wasn't sick. The rest of
Uncle Calabash's house smelled like dried herbs and soap and
woodsmoke. Uncle Calabash took pride in his house. Sometimes he had a husband, but usually not.

Out of Breath sat cross-legged beside the raised hearth and
watched Uncle Calabash brewing his tea for Weaver's wife.
His collection of healing herbs hung from the ceiling in neat
bundles, stems wrapped in red thread. There were other plants
and potions—to make women's skin smooth and their hair
shiny, and to get a baby—that the women came to him for.
Uncle Calabash's skin was as smooth as theirs. He washed it
every day with yucca soap. A bowl of soap and three bone
combs sat on a shelf beside his sewing basket. Out of Breath
could see that Uncle Calabash was working on a new skirt,
its hem beaded with pink shells and flat pieces of turquoise
and coral. Uncle Calabash always had something to trade for
things like that—his pots were bought by people from other
towns who came especially to bring him a soft deer hide or
an otter skin for them.

Beyond the large main room was a smaller one, where he
slept on a bed of pine straw and shredded maize husks sewn
up in a cotton blanket. The clay around the doorway was
smooth and white and painted with a series of spirals in red
pigment. They joined tail to tail, whirling endlessly around the
doorway. A ladder went up to the roof through the smoke hole.
At the other end, where the main room faced the courtyard,
the door opened onto the roofs, so that you could go from one
end of the houses to the other without ever going down to the
courtyard. Through it, if he craned his neck, Out of Breath
could see the new animal, munching maize, tail swishing flies
from its white back. It was illuminated on one side by the
lights from Grandmother Owl Ears' window, its other side in
darkness, like a piece of the moon. Out of Breath sat back,
contented. It gave him a feeling of being very rich to have the
white Thing tied to a stone outside.

Wants the Moon looked at the white Thing for a long time
before she crept down the ladder from her rooftop, her soft

shoes padding silently along the walkway, then down another ladder and across the courtyard. The moon was up now, half a moon hanging in the black sky, mirroring the white animal below. Wants the Moon bent her head toward it in respect. Despite her name, given for an imperious nature, she knew what she could and couldn't have. The things she wanted, that other women didn't, were all of this world, they were just man things: like the freedom to come and go when she pleased.

She crept up to the white animal and put her hand on its warm flank. It blew through its nose at her and snuffled in the clay bowl as if she might have brought it more maize. She slid her hand along its back, feeling the round vertebrae, spreading her fingers in the coarse hair on its neck. She scratched it between its hairy ears the way she would a dog, and it bobbed its head and snuffled at the blanket tied around her shoulders. Its nose was soft as a child's skin, with a few wiry whiskers sticking out. Its dark eyes caught the moon in little repeats like a reflection on water.

Wants the Moon laid her cheek against the flat side of its head, and then against its throat, where she could hear its blood humming. It turned its head and nibbled at her hair; she could feel its soft lips tasting her. She shivered, terrified, but it just snuffled at her braids, its warm breath a fog around her ears.

All the same, she backed away and studied it again from a distance. The plane of its heavy flank, the water-jar shape of its ribs, the roundness of its hooves, seemed familiar to her somehow, as if she had seen it in some other world and forgotten it in this one.

"What are you called?" she asked it, and it swiveled its ears toward the sound. Dark mysterious eyes, with little moons in them, regarded her. Beyond them seemed to be more moon eyes, reflections like ripples in a pond, a scattering of round stars across the courtyard. Wants the Moon squinted at them and they vanished, a trick of the light. The Thing bent its heavy head toward her confidentially, like a medicine man with secrets to impart. She stepped close again, carefully, and put her hands on either side of the Thing's warm neck, and it told her its name.

Weaver's house was on the Turquoise people's side, and in it Weaver sat with his hands folded in his lap, to keep them from trying to hold his wife still. Bitter Water had told him he mustn't do that when she thrashed in the tangled, damp blankets, and so had Uncle Calabash when he brought her wintergreen tea. "You cannot pull her away from the sickness," he had said. "You will stretch her to breaking. She must loosen sickness's fingers herself." But Weaver kept thinking that if he could hold her still, just pin her in his arms, she wouldn't leave him. Quail moaned and rolled in the bed, clutching her belly with both hands. She had grown so thin, in just a few days, as if something were eating her.

Weaver tucked the blanket around his wife again, gently, for an excuse to touch her. He knew she wasn't cold. It was stifling in the house, with the fires built up to drive away whatever spirits might be hiding in her. It was her bride-price blanket, which he had woven before they were married, a soft, thick one with a pattern of green trees and red mountains, mirroring the ranges that lifted their rough, rocky knuckles above the Red Earth town. The mountains circled the blanket, a bowl to hold home. Weaver smoothed it on her chest, and Quail smiled at him. Her eyes were hollow and glittered in the light that came in the window. She put her hand in his, and Weaver glared around the room, spinning his head quickly, as if he could catch whatever it was that hid there, making his wife sicken.

When he looked back at her, Quail had kicked the blanket off again, whimpering.

Above the river valley, the mountains held leafy canyons thick with willow and alder and chokecherry, where the Ancestors had lived. They had built their houses in the cliffs, cut them into hollows in the walls that climbed sheer above shallow creeks. In morning light the canyon walls would be striped as gaudily as butterflies, red and sulphur yellow and white. Just

now, while Wants the Moon was talking to the new animal
and Weaver's wife clutched her belly with bone-thin fingers,
the mountains were only dim striations in black and gray and
a watcher might have missed one of Coyote's children, scrambling along them to the mesa top. He peered over into the
valley below, ears up, like a child peering off the edge of a
roof. Coyote is curious, always.

Far below in the town he could see the white outlines of
the animal in the courtyard and the white wisps that were
Quail trying to leave through her window. Weaver stood in
front of the window, blocking her, and the wisps battered at
his chest and pummeled his head, but he didn't seem to feel
them. Through Uncle Calabash's window the coyote could see
Out of Breath arguing with his uncle. Wants the Moon was
climbing back up her ladder, her buffalo-hide soles making
little rasping noises so that people in the rooms below turned
over in their sleep and dreamed of snakes.

The half moon grew smaller as it climbed the sky, spilling
starlight out of its ladle. The aspens whispered, and the piñon
pines fanned their needles. The bones under the earth stirred
and cantered through the stone. The people in the Red Earth
town heard them. They got up out of bed and peered through
their windows. Women worried that they had lost something
and counted their needles and cooking pots, and men went to
their looms and found strange threads woven into the weft that
hadn't been there yesterday.

All that night there were too many moons. They reflected
themselves in water jars and wet footprints, in empty ladles
and unfired pots sitting ready for the kiln. They slipped
through cracks in walls and over open windowsills and
through the weave of baskets until no one slept well and the
worms in the maize ears stood on their tails and lifted blind
heads toward the sky.

Uncle Calabash looked out the window that opened away
from the courtyard and watched the moons ripple across the
desert and climb the mesa walls, slipping into the old hand-
and toeholds.

"Wait until after the Maize Dance," he said, maybe to Out of Breath, maybe not.

"Its name is Horse," Wants the Moon said.

Out of Breath looked at her skeptically. "How do you know?"

"It told me."

Out of Breath raised both eyebrows. Wants the Moon looked dreamy, like a half-asleep person, but she wasn't. That was just her face. She had climbed in through his window, and now she looked over his shoulder, watching him weave, which made him nervous.

"Don't stare at me like a lizard," he said.

"You need to know its name."

"I was going to name it myself."

"Well, you can, I suppose," she said doubtfully. "But its name is Horse." She was sure of that. She had heard it quite clearly, a soft whisper that unwound itself in the darkness, uncoiled like a leaf; said, *I am here.* "It was saying it in its throat," she said. "Under the skin."

That was where the blood was, where the life was kept, so he supposed she must be right. He felt irritated somehow that it hadn't been he who had heard the white animal speak its name. "I suppose that is a good thing to know," he said, irked.

Wants the Moon smiled. It was pleasant to tell a man something he didn't know. She went on down the roof past Red Bean Vine's rooms, up the ladder, across two more flat roofs, and into her own house.

The house felt empty, as if someone who had been there had left. She wished she could have the white animal in it. It was a fine house, even the old grannies had to say that. Wants the Moon had plastered the walls herself, with a smooth red finish, and painted dancing suns on them. Why should she care if no man would come live in it with her and tell her what to do every day when she woke up in the morning? It was foolish to wish for something that would only make you angry soon. That was what Wants the Moon's mother had said, although she hadn't meant not having a husband by it. But she had been a willful woman in her own right, and *her* husband the same, and they had fought constantly, their voices harsh as crows, shrieking and tearing at each other. They had died three winters ago of the lung sickness, both of them together, locked in battle to the end over whose fault it had been.

Everyone had thought that then certainly Wants the Moon would take a husband, would tire of loneliness and be a proper woman. Bitter Water had told Turquoise Old Man that now he should take her a blanket, that she would be more biddable now. But Turquoise Old Man (who wasn't really old) had found a woman who had been biddable to begin with, and taken *her* a blanket, and it was too late to change his mind. Then everyone said behind their hands that that was a good thing; a woman like that would never make a good wife.

So Wants the Moon had made her house the way she wanted it, and bought her own blankets in exchange for the pots she made—everyone was happy enough to buy those—and she went to the trade fair at High Up City by herself every year, without a man, and when she was there sometimes she made a trade-fair marriage with some man for a few days. She knew better than to bring one back to Red Earth City.

But the white animal was something different. It sang in her blood, just under the skin, as if her cheek and hands were still pressed to its throat. It made her want to dance, a Horse Dance that no one had ever danced before; climb on the white animal's back and dance with it, prancing through the long grass, white as smoke, like the holy clowns who danced the maize in each summer.

The holy clowns came up out of the kivas one by one, ghostly as pale morning light. Out of Breath thought as always that he could see through them, and then, when they got closer, decided that he couldn't. It was hard to be sure. They circled the courtyard, weaving themselves like mist through the people, cavorting, spinning, one foot raised high, maize husk headdresses whispering the name of the maize. Slowly they encompassed the Red Earth town, wove a basket of blessing around it.

Out of Breath watched solemnly. On the other side of the dance ground he could see Wants the Moon, her fingers pressed to her mouth. She looked as if she longed to leap from the ground and follow. It didn't matter that under the white rags and the maize husks was Almost a Dog, dancing past him close enough to touch. Today he was more than a man, other than a man, a blessing on two feet.

The holy clowns met at the center of the courtyard, spirit emissaries from the Turquoise kiva and the Squash kiva, arms waving now, great excitement, miming important news. Runners separated from them, going east, west, north, and south, vanishing into houses and underground into the kivas again, reappearing moments later, white as quartz under the blue sky. The kivas were holes in the earth, with ladders descending into their dark recesses, opening into underground chambers where the old men took council with the kachinas. Out of them might come anything, news from the spirit world. The kachinas had come out last night, circling the town on their long legs, beaked heads bobbing. They would come into the houses and dance, and if you entertained one, you were blessed and terrified.

This morning the holy clowns rose from the kiva holes like sacred smoke. They drank from a gourd that the runner from the north had brought out of the Squash kiva and waved their arms, waving spears and bows now, jumping into the air, preparing to drive off the enemy who had come to raid the maize stores. They lunged left and right, and the small children giggled. One of the clowns scooped up a sack of maize and held it to his chest, frowning furiously, while another tried to pull it away from him, mimicking the greed that divides a people and makes them unready to meet the enemy.

The holy clowns were lesson bringers. The citizen who transgressed village mores found himself mercilessly ridiculed. Two more clutched each other dramatically, in passionate embrace, and the whole audience chuckled. Out of Breath grinned. Weaver and his wife were being lectured for their behavior. The holy clowns put their black-and-white-painted heads together, identical inane faces of lust, maize husks sprouting from their ears, and hopped in a circle on one foot. It didn't matter that Quail was likely dying. The message was still important. It might even be that it was unregulated conduct that had made her sick in the first place. Another clown ran from the center of the cluster and circled the couple on all fours. Out of Breath stiffened. The clown scuttled like a spider, but Out of Breath saw the long white tassel sewn to his backside. The white clown stopped, reared up, and snorted down his nose.

Out of Breath looked about him uneasily, while all the people's dark eyes looked back at him, but the clowns leaped suddenly in the air and ran back into the kivas.

A ripple whispered through the people in the courtyard, Out of Breath and his animal forgotten for now as quickly as the clowns had held them up to be thought about. Now it was time to dance the maize home, and the ripple flowed into the dance, men and women in separate lines, spiraling around each other, weaving the harvest between them. The women danced barefoot, taking fertility from the earth, giving it to the maize. White cloth, knotted over one shoulder and belted in red, spun out like petals as they whirled. Long hair flowed around them, loosed from its braids, floating on the sun, and headdresses of thin wood and bright feathers made them taller than the men, stately, like deer. All around them the maize whispered, in baskets on dancing backs, in bundles carried by the holy clowns, weaving in and out of the lines.

Out of Breath saw his mother, Red Bean Vine, and Aunt Green Melons dancing with the married women, and Wants the Moon in the line of unmarried girls, older and taller than most of them, her bare feet tracing the pattern of the drums, red-feathered headdress bright against the green maize in her basket. They sang together, trying to dance the worms out of the maize, dance them back through whatever hole in the sky they had come in by. Out of Breath had seen Wants the Moon this morning talking to the white animal tethered beyond the dance ground, feeding it cut grass. He was willing to believe she could talk to the worms.

Out of Breath's short kilt was embroidered in red and green and black, belted with a heavy sash, a fox skin dangling from the back. He could feel it slap against his legs, in rhythm to the rattles tied below his knee, dancing down the line, dancing in the maize.

Flute song lifted the dance above the drums, above the hard-packed dance ground, notes rising in the blue and gold sky like birds. It carried maize on it, ripe and golden in green ears, and the people danced it home, circling, spiraling, gathering in. It was a singing magic older than the Red Earth town, older than the Ancestors' cliff houses, as old as the humpbacked flute player who some people said had brought the maize from the south in the far-off days, and whose likeness the Red Earth people still carved into the rock of sacred caves in respect. He had brought flute music, too, other people said, although in some drawings the long flute looked more like his penis. He was someone you talked to when you wanted things to grow.

Out of Breath felt the dance pick him up, lift him on its magic so that his feet moved just a little above the ground like the flute player's, the long-distance traveler, and the deer-foot rattles drummed like hoofbeats. He thought he saw the white animal dancing with the rest of them, its pale mane flying, but its hooves made no sound on the packed earth. Then it was gone again, nothing more than wisps of white mist floating over the dance ground, and he could see its real self, tethered by his doorway, white against the tan houses and munching cut grass.

It gave him an uneasy feeling between his shoulder blades that the holy clowns had decided to notice it. He wondered what Wants the Moon thought, and what it said to her. Then he tried not to think about that, because it was not right to think of anything but the maize during the Maize Dance. Anything might make it go away, make the worms come, eating their way into existence. He concentrated, furrowing his brows, dancing harder. The lines spiraled around him, singing with the voice of the maize. It took them three circuits of the dance ground before the other sound fought its way through the blue air to them, howling like coyotes from Weaver's house.

3

Horse Says His Name Again

QUAIL WAS DEAD. ANYONE COULD HAVE TOLD WEAVER that, but he stood hugging her body to him, trying to talk her back into the world. The grandmothers and the headmen of the medicine societies and three of the holy clowns filled the rooftop outside Weaver's third-floor house and tried to tell him, but he just glared at them stubbornly while Quail hung from his arms as if he had killed a deer. Uncle Calabash tugged at her gently, but Weaver tugged back.

In the courtyard the Red Earth people were finishing the Maize Dance because that was not a thing that could be interrupted. Out of Breath craned his neck while he danced, trying to see what was happening on Weaver's roof. Weaver was still howling, and the noise made the hair stand up on Out of Breath's arms. It was not a good thing to happen in the middle of the Maize Dance, and he could tell that no one else liked it, either. Squash Old Man's mouth was folded into a frown like a shriveled flower. Turquoise Old Man growled something to Cat's Tooth, his sister's son, who had become a man last winter and already was taller and wider than most of the Red Earth men. Cat's Tooth slipped out of the dancing

45

line and ran toward Weaver's house. Weaver belonged to the Turquoise people, and he was embarrassing all of them. His wailing rose over the rooftops and pounded on the sky, pursuing Quail's spirit. If he kept it up, he might catch her, and that wouldn't be good.

"Quiet down or we'll tie you up," Cat's Tooth growled at Weaver, his snaggletooth pushing his lower lip aside. He shook Weaver by the shoulders.

Uncle Calabash detached Quail's body while Cat's Tooth pinned Weaver's arms. Uncle Calabash laid her on the bed and said over his shoulder to Cat's Tooth, "There's no need to be rough with him."

"Then make him be quiet." Cat's Tooth bounced on the balls of his feet, getting ready to knock Weaver over. He curled his lip. "He'll spoil the dance. Turquoise Old Man says to keep him quiet, and how else do you think we're going to do it?"

Uncle Calabash nudged Cat's Tooth out of the way and put his arm around Weaver's shoulders. "Come along, dear. Let the women get her ready to leave. She has to leave now. I'll give you something to drink." He talked softly, the way he would to a child.

Weaver shook his head. They could see the whites of his eyes all around his pupils like a crazy person. "No. That's my wife. I have to keep her here with me."

"She's dead, you stupid turkey!" Cat's Tooth told him.

"You keep a respectful tongue," Uncle Calabash said. He looked straight at Cat's Tooth for a long time until Cat's Tooth shrugged and sat down on the floor.

"Come along." Uncle Calabash edged Weaver to the door. The others' eyes followed them down the ladder and along the edge of the dance ground to Uncle Calabash's house. They looked worriedly at Quail's body. None of this was any good. Death and crazy people in the middle of the Maize Dance would make something awful happen. Already they could feel it, hopping around out there in the maize field, like a dark toad. Three crows lit on the rooftop over their heads, squawk-

ing raucously, sharp-beaked, feathers shiny as obsidian. *Awk!*
they said and lifted themselves up over the roofs, circling the
dance ground below.

The uneasiness hung over the town like dark oil where the
crows had been. Its smudge hung across the red dip of the sun
in a band of dark feathers. More crows had lined up on the
edges of the rooftops. When the women went after them with
brooms, they just circled in the air, *awk*ing, and lit again.
Sometimes they would fly down and stab their beaks at the
garbage in the midden or at toads that suddenly everyone was
finding in the shadows of the water jars.

Weaver was in Uncle Calabash's rooms upstairs, sleeping
now; Uncle Calabash had given him something to keep him
from shouting her name. It was not a good idea to say the
name of the dead so soon because it might call them back.

In Weaver's house, Quail's sisters and aunts had washed
her body, and the rest of the family had buried her before it
was full dark, sitting up and facing east where she would think
about being dead for three days, until they brought her food
and a string to mark the way to the Skeleton House. (Only
children were buried with the string pointing home, so that
they could come back and be reborn.) On the fourth morning
her spirit would get up from the grave outside the town and
follow the string, leaving her breath body behind. Someone
would have to watch Weaver until then, everybody thought.

Long after it was dark, Out of Breath got up and went to
his window. He could see the white animal eating grass in the
courtyard below and some dark shadow rolling along the
ground, lit by lamplight from his Grandmother Owl Ears' window, as if something were walking around it. He and Wants
the Moon had fed the animal just after the dancing while the
town watched them suspiciously, as if the animal had had
something to do with Quail. Almost a Dog, the holy clown's
paint scrubbed from his face, had stared at it and sighed, until
the skin itched between Out of Breath's shoulders and a brown
toad had hopped suddenly out of the pile of grass, startling
them all and making the animal blow down its nose.

"Horse," Out of Breath said experimentally to the white

animal. That was what Wants the Moon had said its name was. Out of Breath sniffed and drew his eyebrows together at that. If it was going to tell its name to anyone, it should have told it to him. He said "Horse" again anyway, rolling the sound around on his tongue.

Every time he said the new name, the shadow on the ground moved a little, but Horse, if that was who it was, didn't seem to notice. Out of Breath didn't think it was Horse's shadow. In a while he saw that the shadow was leaving footprints: moon-colored and shiny, like false water in the desert, a wedge-shaped pad with four oval toes. Each footprint sparkled on the dark ground and then sank into the earth. Out of Breath leaned on the windowsill and stared. While he watched, the footprints bunched themselves together and leaped up, rising in the black air like shooting stars.

The crows flew off the rooftop with a heavy flapping of wings. They circled and vanished, squawking, while the footprints' arc slowly faded in midair. Out of Breath heard something land on the floor behind him. When he spun around, Coyote was sitting there, poking his gray nose into Out of Breath's bedding to see if there was something to eat in it.

"Go away!" Out of Breath hissed. "Before my mother sees you." He thought now that the old men had been right— things like this should be seen by old men in kivas.

"People see me all the time," Coyote said. "Your spirit isn't right with the world if you can't see me."

Out of Breath eyed him apprehensively. No one wanted to see Coyote. He didn't want to now, but he didn't know how to make him leave. No one ever drew Coyote, in their wall paintings or on their pottery, because no one wanted him to come. And besides that he smelled bad, and Red Bean Vine was a meticulous housekeeper.

Coyote stretched out by the fireplace as if he were somebody's dog. "After all," he said, yawning, "how could I teach human people to hunt if First Hunter couldn't see me?" His mouth gaped open, wider and wider, and Out of Breath found himself yawning, too. Coyote closed his jaws again with a snap. Out of Breath straightened his shoulders in a hurry. It might not be a good idea to get sleepy.

"It was time for me to bring human people something else new," Coyote said.

"It says its name is Horse," Out of Breath told him.

"I hadn't named it yet."

"Well, that is what it says its name is. It told the woman."

"Oh, very well." Coyote sounded annoyed, too, but he scooted closer to the fire so that it warmed the matted fur on his belly. "I don't suppose you have anything to eat?" he said. "Toads leave a taste in my mouth." He licked his muzzle, long red tongue exploring. Out of Breath could see pointed teeth, like stars, on either side of the tongue.

Out of Breath thought. It was rude not to feed a visitor, and in this case it might be dangerous since Coyote ate anything. He crept into the storeroom and grabbed a handful of dried deer meat, nearly their last. He slipped out again quickly before his mother, who had ears better than Rabbit's, could hear him. He held the dried meat, hard as wood, out to Coyote. Coyote ate it in one gulp. He looked thoughtful, brought it up, chewed it another time or two, and swallowed it again.

Out of Breath looked nervously at the door to his mother's room, but there was no sound but a gentle snoring that grew louder after a moment. Coyote seemed to be expecting Out of Breath to do something else, or to say something. "How did you teach human people to hunt?" Out of Breath asked him, to be polite. In any case, if Coyote wanted to stay, he would stay.

Coyote folded his front paws, one over the other. "I will tell you how it was," he said.

Out of Breath sat down on his bed to listen. Coyote was always claiming to have done great things. Sometimes he lied, but sometimes his stories were true.

"When the world was new," Coyote said, "First Young Man was coming along one day . . ."

He was a nice young man, although not very much smarter than rocks, and he was not a good hunter. In fact, he was hungry all the time because he was so bunglesome that he never caught anything but worms. When he chased the deer, they ran away from him, and he fell down. When he chased Bear, Bear led him into beehives, and the bees stung him. When he chased rabbits, they laughed at him. He lived with his grandmother, and they were hungry because he never caught any game.

First Young Man met a coyote coming along one day, but he didn't try to shoot it with his bow or even say bad names to it. He was too hungry. He just kept on following some rabbit tracks, trying to catch a rabbit. The tracks went into a thicket and got mixed up with some other tracks that First Young Man couldn't read, and he stood there scratching his head. While he was thinking, two coyote pups tumbled out of the thicket and wriggled into a hole under some rocks.

While First Young Man was still trying to make heads or tails of the rabbit tracks, the old coyote that he had seen on the trail appeared in front of him. The coyote wore a ragged coat and a slit in one of his big ears, and he had a sack of rabbits over one shoulder.

"Ho, Bunglesome," the coyote said. "How is it with you?"

First Young Man opened his eyes wide. "Did you talk just now?"

"Why not?" Coyote said. "Did you let me go by this morning without shooting at me?"

"Why not?" First Young Man said. "You don't taste good. And in any case, I never hit anything."

"You let my cubs go without shooting them, either. Do you know me?"

"No," admitted First Young Man.

"Well, I know you. You are a good sort even if you are a bungler who lets the whole forest know you are coming along. Step inside with me and I will teach you some things."

"Step inside where?" First Young Man looked at the hole under the rocks. His foot would fit inside it, maybe.

"In here," Coyote said, and he disappeared through the hole.

First Young Man put his foot in the hole to see what would happen. There was a rumbling noise under the earth, and the ground opened up. First Young Man fell through it into a passage with a door at one end. He could just see Coyote's tail disappearing through the doorway, so he followed.

"Old woman!" Coyote shouted. "We have company."

A little old coyote woman appeared. She had a long gray snout and yellowy-gray fur and a black tip on her tail. "Come in," she said. The pups were rolling on top of each other with their brothers and sisters. She shooed them away. "Mannerless! We have company." They rolled into the corner, biting each other. The room had fine blankets on the walls and floor, and a hearth with a fire crackling in it at the center. The smoke went up a smoke hole.

Coyote stretched, front paws extended, belly to the ground, and his skin split down the front. He stepped out of it and hung it on a peg on the wall. First Young Man could see now that he was a little old man with a shock of gray hair. He had old, pale scars in the russet skin of his face and hands and going down inside his shirt, and there was a piece still missing out of one ear.

The little old coyote woman kept her skin on, but she brought out bowl after bowl of buffalo stew and ribs of deer meat and hot ears of maize and rabbit pie. The smell filled the whole room, and the pups scrambled up and raced for the dishes. The coyote woman smacked them away until she had filled a bowl for First Young Man. Then she fed the pups. They gobbled their food, splashing it on their noses and biting each other's ears.

The food was delicious. First Young Man had never eaten anything so good. When she filled his bowl again, he ate some more.

"Well," the old coyote man said, "it is clear you know how to eat. The problem is that no one has ever taught you to hunt. Meet me tomorrow and I will do that. Bring prayer sticks with you."

First Young Man went home to his grandmother. Coyote had given him two rabbits to take with him, which made the old woman very happy. She cooked them for dinner. All night

*the young man sat up making prayer sticks, tying them with
bright string and feathers. In the morning he went to meet
Coyote. It had snowed overnight, and the land sparkled. First
Young Man's breath hung in the air. He was rather hoping
that Coyote would give him some of the coyote woman's stew
for breakfast, but Coyote just set out on the trail.*

*"Lesson number one," Coyote said. "The lighter the stom-
ach, the lighter the foot. A hungry hunter can smell the game.
Never eat in the morning."*

*First Young Man sighed, but he followed Coyote down the
trail, trying to smell game in the wind.*

*"Next lesson," Coyote said. "When you take someone's
body, you have to give something in return. You can't expect
something for nothing. Offer the person you have killed, and
his kind, prayer sticks."*

First Young Man patted the prayer sticks in his shirt.

*At the bottom of the first valley they came to, they found
fresh deer tracks in the melting snow. "Now, it is your business to look at these tracks," Coyote said. "These were made
by the leader. You can see that because they have been
chipped into by the tracks of those following him. This will be
a big buck and worth hunting between the two of us. See how
these tracks are melted a little at the edges? That means he
came by here a while ago. When you see that the tracks are
sharper and less melted, then you had better walk as if you
were stepping on eggs, because the deer will be listening behind some bush up the valley."*

*First Young Man nodded solemnly. His stomach was growl-
ing. He wondered if the deer would hear that.*

*"I will leave you sometime along the trail," Coyote said.
"When I do, don't yell for me as if you had lost your mother.
Just keep on following the trail until you see that the grass in
the bottom of the tracks hasn't straightened up yet. Then sit
down and sing."*

"Sing?"

*"Like this." Coyote sang softly, "Deer, deer, I see your
footprints. I come following you.*

"When he hears that, he will be charmed by it and puzzled.

He will hesitate, and that will give me time to run around to the head of the valley before he gets there. Deer going home travel in canyons the way you do in pathways. When you have gone a little farther, sing again. I will hide where a ravine branches out from the main canyon. When the deer sees you coming, he will run, but I will be there before him, and we will drive him up the side canyon. Then you sing again, and I will run ahead of him up the canyon again.''

First Young Man scratched his head, trying to keep track of all this.

"When he sees me," Coyote said, "he will turn around and see you. Then he will lower his head to meet you, and I will run up and nip his heels."

"Lower his head," First Young Man said. "Then you nip his heels."

"When he turns around to me, he will put his side to you," Coyote said, "and you will shoot him with your arrow just back of where the gray hair changes color behind the shoulder."

"Behind the shoulder," First Young Man said.

"Have you got that straight?" Coyote asked. "Because if you don't, he will run right through you, antlers and all, and then it won't matter whether you catch anything."

"I think so," First Young Man said, wondering if he did. *Stop, sing. Chase him up the canyon. Shoot him behind the shoulder.*

"Now, this is most important," Coyote said. "When he falls, you are to go to him and throw your arms around him and breathe his breath. You say, 'Thank you, my brother. Today I have drunk your sacred life.' Do you understand all that now?"

"Yes," First Young Man said. "The words of my uncle lodge in my heart."

"Let's hope so," Coyote said.

So they set off on the trail of the buck, and it all happened as Coyote said it would. When the deer turned to face him in the ravine, First Young Man drew his bow, and when Coyote ran out and nipped the deer in the heels, the deer turned his *flank to First Young Man. First Young Man loosed his arrow. Somewhat to his surprise, the arrow flew straight and sank into the buck just behind where the hair changed color at the shoulder.*

First Young Man ran to the buck, threw his arms around the buck's neck, and drank his last breath. Then he planted a prayer stick so that other deer would come to the place and not be afraid.

Coyote was beside himself with pride. "Ho! I have taught you how to hunt!" he chortled, chasing his tail and jumping in the air. "Today I have made First Hunter out of Young Bungler. The four-footed people shall be your friends forever, and I have made this so. Remember that it was I who taught you. Now, then, let's skin it."

Coyote showed First Young Man how to skin and dress the deer, gulping down the offal hungrily while First Young Man wrapped the deer in its hide for carrying.

"From now on you will hunt alone or with your own kind," Coyote said, licking his muzzle, "but you will remember to favor those who taught you."

"I will, Uncle," First Young Man said earnestly.

"You must beware, of course, of the sorcerer," Coyote added. "The wizard-coyote, like me yet unlike me. He will try to trick you."

"I will beware," First Young Man said, wondering how to tell them apart.

He took his leave of the coyote, and after that it was just as Coyote had said. First Young Man became a famous hunter, the greatest of all his people. Always when he killed a deer he remembered to leave the blood and the offal for his uncle and his uncle's children. And when something stole his turkeys in the night, or someone ate the green corn from his storehouse, he knew that it was not his friend Coyote, but the wizard-coyote, as he had been warned.

The story hung in the firelight. Out of Breath could still see the buck and First Young Man and a shadow that might have been Uncle Coyote but was fading into the gray ears and paws on the other side of the hearth. Coyote looked pleased.

"I never heard of a wizard-coyote," Out of Breath said. The wizard-coyote sounded very much like the one across the fire from him.

"Oh, I assure you, I am much imitated," Coyote said modestly. He tucked his tail around his paws.

Out of Breath looked at the story. It still seemed to be happening. "I think there's more," he said.

"No, probably not," Coyote said, but the story didn't go away; it was still hanging in the fire smoke. Coyote blew at it, but it coiled itself in the air, snakewise. "Oh, very well," he said.

Out of Breath could see the snake. He thought Uncle Calabash had told him this story, too . . .

Rattlesnake was caught under a rock that had slid down the mountain in a heavy rain, pinning him. He was most angry about it, thrashing his head this way and that, but he couldn't free himself. Slowly he grew tired and lay with his head in the mud, glowering, when a duck walked by.

"Brother Duck," the rattlesnake called. "Move this rock so that I can get free!"

The duck was in a good mood, since the rain had filled the creeks and brought out a great many nice bugs, but he was suspicious. "How do I know that if I free you, you won't eat me?" he asked.

"I promise I won't eat you," the rattlesnake said earnestly. "It wouldn't be right to eat someone who has helped me."

"Well, in that case," the duck said, "I will move this rock for you."

The duck shoved the rock, and it rolled off the snake. In an instant the rattlesnake was coiled to strike. "It has been a long time under that rock," he said, "and I am very hungry. You're just what I want for my breakfast."

"That isn't fair!" the duck protested. "I have just done you a good deed. And furthermore, you said you wouldn't eat me."

"A good deed is always repaid with evil," the rattlesnake

said, rippling his coils. *"Hold still. It will be less unpleasant for you if you don't try to get away."*

The duck found it very hard to look away from the snake's slitted eyes, but he managed to squawk, *"Good deeds are repaid in kind!"*

"Yah," said the rattlesnake. *"Everyone knows otherwise."*

"Well, I don't," said the duck desperately. *"We must find a judge to decide if that's true."*

"Oh, very well," said the rattlesnake, who did not like being made to seem in the wrong, *"but you'll see."*

So they went along, the snake keeping a close eye on the duck, until they came to an old dog who was digging grubs out of a hollow log and eating them. He was very thin, his ribs showing through his matted coat, and his eyes were rheumy with age.

"Here is a very old person, and so a most sage one," the snake said. *"Ask him if good is not repaid with evil."*

The duck asked the dog what he thought, and the dog shook his head sadly. *"Look at me. All my life I hunted for Man. I guarded his house, and I ran down the fleet-footed deer and rabbits. I played with his young and let them pull my ears, and now what thanks do I get for it? Now that I am old and slow, he turns me out to fend for myself and kicks me away from his fire."* The dog sighed mournfully. *"Good is always paid back with ill usage."*

"You see?" said the snake, coiling himself up.

"That is a prejudiced witness," said the duck. *"Although a very sad story. We need an impartial judge."*

"You will see," the rattlesnake said, swaying his wedge-shaped head. *"You will ssssssee."*

A coyote came trotting along, and the snake said, *"Tell me, brother, is not good always repaid with evil?"*

The coyote looked at them with interest. *"It depends, I suppose,"* he said, trying to figure out what was going on. *"Explain yourselves."*

The duck explained the situation while the coyote scratched behind his ear with his back foot and kept an eye on the rattlesnake. *"Before I give you a decision,"* the coyote said when the duck had finished, "I will have to see exactly how it all happened. Show me where you were when you freed the snake."

They took him to the rockslide, and the coyote studied it. "I will have to see exactly where the snake was caught," he said.

The rattlesnake was willing to demonstrate, since he was sure that the coyote was going to rule in his favor. He was certain that the coyote would have eaten the duck himself and so would declare it the proper thing to do. He slithered up the rocks and pointed with his rattles at the stone that had pinned him.

"Hmmm." The coyote scratched behind his ear again. "How were you lying, exactly?"

The rattlesnake stretched himself out to show him.

"Let me place the rock where it was so that I get the complete picture." The coyote rolled the rock onto the snake and stood back. "Like that?"

"Exactly like that," the snake said.

"Good," the coyote said. "Stay there for a moment." And he pounced on the duck and ate it.

"That isn't fair!" the snake protested, thrashing his head furiously.

The coyote licked green feathers off his nose. "Well, you said that good is always repaid with evil," he pointed out.

"I never did you any good!" the snake said. "And neither did that duck. That was my duck," he added.

"Certainly you did," the coyote said. "You brought me a fine lunch." And with that he bit the snake's head off carefully, from behind, and ate the rest. He took the rattles home for his cubs to play with.

Coyote appeared to be pretending that that story had been about another coyote entirely. He was very busy with a flea at the base of his tail. When he had finished with that, though, he said, "If you're going to annoy the snake people, make sure they have a rock on them."

"What do you mean by that?" Out of Breath asked him.

"I mean you had better find something to do with that fine new animal I gave you, or your people in this town here will kill it. These people don't take well to change."

"That wasn't change, with the rattlesnake," Out of Breath protested. "That was trickery."

"They are very similar," Coyote said.

"Well, I don't know what to do." Out of Breath didn't know what Coyote was talking about, either, and his head felt muddled.

"Figure out what it's good for."

"It can pull a load, but nobody wants to take anything anywhere. They said so."

"Yah bah. They'd be happy enough to bring an elk home. Or a buffalo."

"There aren't any buffalo. And Elk is hard to find too, lately."

"You aren't thinking!" Coyote said crossly. He yawned again, and Out of Breath yawned, and when he opened his eyes, Coyote had gone.

It was light outside. Out of Breath scrubbed his eyes with his fist. Gold light was pooling over the dance ground from the east. He pulled his shirt over his head and sniffed. His mother was frying bread on the kitchen fire. Out of Breath padded hungrily into the next room.

Red Bean Vine clucked her tongue. "You were awake all night talking to yourself," she said. "You probably kept Grandmother up, too. You know how lightly she sleeps. And Weaver howling from upstairs. I don't know how anyone is going to get anything done today."

"Weaver?"

"Didn't you hear him?" Red Bean Vine asked, exasperated. "Yammering and crying, until I suppose your uncle gave him something else to drink, to quiet him."

"No, I didn't hear him."

"Well, you were lucky. He wants to go and get that poor woman out of the ground. He says she's not dead. We're going to have a time with him, I can tell." She flipped the bread on the flat clay griddle. "It's all the unsettlement here. It's affected his mind."

Out of Breath watched her hungrily. "What unsettlement?"

Red Bean Vine threw up her hands. "Worms and moths! Crows! That *Thing* you brought home!"

"It's a horse," Out of Breath said. "It told Wants the Moon so."

"And stop running around with her! She's too old for you, and she won't make a proper wife. You know what people say about her!"

"I'm not going to marry her!"

"Well, then, stop going around with her, or Turquoise Old Man will make you. He wants her to marry somebody."

"He doesn't want her to marry *him*."

"That was a long time ago. He has another wife now, so there's no chance of that." Red Earth men rarely married more than one wife, and this one wouldn't have stood for it. "So you stay away from her."

Out of Breath shrugged. He had never thought of Wants the Moon in that way—other than that, at his age, he thought of all women that way, most of the time. As soon as his mother took the bread off the griddle, he stuffed his piece in his mouth, burning his tongue. Then he ran onto the roof and down the ladder to the courtyard before she could ask him why he hadn't taken his hoe.

When he got to the ground, the white animal wasn't there. He said bad words under his breath and went at a trot in the direction it had gone. He found it with Wants the Moon, standing in the shallow water of Stream Young Man.

"What are you doing with my horse?"

"Giving it a drink," she said. She looked as imperious as ever, dark brows lifted haughtily. "We have to find out what we can do with it, what it is for."

"I was going to say that." Out of Breath wasn't sure how the horse had become her animal, too.

"I have an idea," Wants the Moon said. "I have been thinking."

"What have you been thinking?" She was older than he was, which meant he had to be polite.

"It's very big," she said. "I think you can sit on it."

"On the horse? You mean, as if you were a pack?"

"I think so. It could take you a long way if you did that."

"You could fall off," Out of Breath said.

"You could fall off a ladder," Wants the Moon said disgustedly. "I think it could carry you on its back the way Duck carried Rattlesnake across the river the time that Coyote settled their quarrel."

"Duck didn't carry Rattlesnake across the river," Out of Breath said. "He rolled a stone off his back."

"Well, that's not the way my grandmother told it," Wants the Moon said.

Out of Breath wasn't sure who had told him the version he had just heard. "What happened at the end of that story?" he asked her.

Wants the Moon looked exasperated. "Coyote decided for the rabbit. He got the snake to let them take him back across the river so Coyote could see how it all happened, and then they left him there. Don't you know anything?"

"I'm not sure anymore," Out of Breath said. Any story he heard lately seemed prone to change. Maybe *he* would be someone else tomorrow.

"Well, I'm sure of this," Wants the Moon said. "Let's try it."

"Who's going to get on him?" Out of Breath wondered if Horse's story were telling itself, too. Then he might be the Vanished Man, taken into another world by an animal no one had ever seen before. Or would ever see again. They would just disappear over the horizon.

"You're smaller than I am." Wants the Moon gave him a scornful look. "I will get on it if you won't."

"No. I'll do it." Out of Breath felt his fate upon him. "You help me. How will I tell him where to go?"

"I thought of that." She unwrapped two lengths of yucca rope from her waist and tied them like dog leads on either side of the harness on the horse's head. He didn't seem to

object. They led him across the stream to the farther bank
where the ground was flat, and Wants the Moon bent and
cupped her hands so that Out of Breath could put his foot in
them.

"He seems very high," Out of Breath said.

Wants the Moon boosted him up without answering, and
Out of Breath found himself facedown over Horse's back,
smelling his warm horse scent. Horse started walking. Out of
Breath grabbed Horse's mane, while Wants the Moon ran after
them. Out of Breath pulled his leg up over Horse's back and
sat, clutching a handful of hair. He shifted his weight uncomfortably. Horse had grown fatter, but he was still bony. Wants
the Moon tugged on Horse's head, and he stopped.

"Here." Wants the Moon handed Out of Breath the lines
she had tied to the harness, one on each side of Horse's head.
He pulled on one experimentally, and Horse turned that way.

"I told you!" Wants the Moon did a triumphant dance step
in the grass and Horse snorted and swerved sideways, and Out
of Breath found himself hanging on one side again, his heel
barely hooked over the ridge of Horse's backbone. Wants the
Moon giggled and pushed him back up, her hands on his backside.

Out of Breath wrapped his arms around Horse's neck. Horse
put his head down and cropped grass. Slowly Out of Breath
sat back up. The ground seemed very far away, but Wants the
Moon was chortling behind her hand, which was insulting. Out
of Breath put on his most dignified face and said to Horse,
"Take me somewhere." He pulled Horse's head up with the
ropes, and Horse ambled forward.

Out of Breath felt Horse's muscles move under his white
skin, felt the salt sweat dampen his hide. After a little while
it began to feel like being part of Horse. Out of Breath's veins
flowed into Horse's veins; his ligaments coiled out from his
skin and knotted themselves with Horse's. *This is what he is
for,* Out of Breath thought. *This is what you do with him.* They
had left Wants the Moon behind, sorry no doubt that she had
let Out of Breath try it first. He wondered what would happen

if Horse ran. It would be like riding on the wind. Out of Breath
tapped Horse with his heel, and Horse broke into a bone-
shattering trot. Out of Breath's ligaments unknotted themselves from Horse's like hands letting go. He clutched Horse's
withers and pulled on the ropes, biting his tongue as he
jounced and bounced.

Horse slowed to a walk again, and Out of Breath bent his
head, gasping. Maybe it took practice. He tightened his knees
around Horse's middle. "Go on," he said, teeth gritted. "Go
fast."

Horse leaped into the air and lumbered across the red earth
and the dry grass. Out of Breath hung on. This was not as bad
as the trot. It was a rocking gait that didn't send his teeth
through his skull. He leaned forward, and Horse flowed over
the ground like water.

Out of Breath looked around him as they ran. The children
who had been sent to scare the birds and rats from the maize
field had gathered in a clump to goggle at him, and the women
stopped washing their clothes in the creek and stared. A white
shirt, unnoticed, floated downstream like a cloud. Horse's
hooves drummed on the hard earth, shaking it, and Out of
Breath heard an answering murmur under the surface, down
in the stone, and a clattering on the wind.

Out of Breath and the horse ran. A lizard sunning itself on
Weaver's wife's grave scuttled off in a fright and was eaten
by a red-tailed hawk whose notice was attracted by the movement. A woodrat that had come out of his nest in a cactus
patch dived back in to tell his wife about it, and the hawk's
shadow floated over the spot where he had been. A troop of
peccaries that had come to root in the melon patch flung up
their tails and galloped off, snorting.

The earth rattled. Things began to turn over—baskets of
sewing on shelves, water jars in the courtyard, pots drying on
roofs. The crows that had moved into the town rose in a flock
from the maize field and flew off, flapping over the mountains
to tell the Bean Canyon people about it. In the Red Earth City,
Turquoise Old Man and Squash Old Man and the priests and
grandmothers and medicine men all came out of their houses

and out of the squash rows and out of the kivas where they had been talking to the kachinas, and waited with Wants the Moon for Out of Breath to ride up. Uncle Calabash was trying to keep Weaver from putting mud in his hair and eating rocks, but Grandmother Owl Ears came, leaning on a stick, with Aunt Green Melons and her husband, Armadillo. Red Bean Vine came, drying her hands on her apron and glaring under her brows at Grandmother Woodrat, who mumbled about witches under her breath. Almost a Dog sniffed the air, balanced on the balls of his feet.

Out of Breath saw them gathering, a white cloud puffing itself together on the edge of the courtyard, clogging the way into the town. He could run through them on Horse's hard hooves; he could scatter them like dry vines. He pulled on the ropes and Horse slowed, first to a jolting trot and then to a walk, blowing down his white nose.

"Ho, Six-Legged!" Wants the Moon made an elaborate gesture of respect to Out of Breath on the horse. Her eyes gleamed.

"I will be Six-Legged now," Out of Breath said, grinning. Wants the Moon had given him a fine new name, as befitted an occasion like this. He took a deep breath to take the name inside himself and smiled at her to thank her.

Squash Old Man pushed her out of the way. The trader from the north was just behind him, eyes darting over Squash Old Man's shoulder. The trader held out his hand, middle finger crossed over the next one.

"This is an ill thing," Squash Old Man said. "I have been thinking hard about it, and now I am certain." He nodded at the trader. "This man here has seen these things in the west."

"He has seen a man who has seen a man who has seen things," Six-Legged said. He wrapped the name around himself firmly. "And he said they have shiny skin. And two legs. This Horse has four legs and it is white, which is magical, but always well-intentioned. Ask Almost a Dog."

Almost a Dog had stopped sniffing, but he shook his head regretfully. "It is very hard to tell. There is something in the air here now. It smells off, like an egg that's turning. I don't know."

"It's that animal," Grandmother Woodrat said. "It's making Weaver crazy. Everyone could hear him howling last night."

Grandmother Owl Ears nodded at Six-Legged. "I hardly slept. Ask your aunt."

"Weaver's wife dying made him crazy," Six-Legged said.

"Very likely it is that animal that has brought the sickness, then," Squash Old Man told him. "We have talked about it, and we do not want it here."

Six-Legged's fingers tightened on the ropes in his hands. He looked down at them all from Horse's back, stunned. "It's a new animal!" he said.

"We do not need new animals," Squash Old Man said.

"It's dangerous!" Grandmother Woodrat sucked on her side teeth.

"Everyone will get sick!"

"And what about the children?"

"I don't want that thing near my house!"

"That is not a good new name for you," Grandmother Owl Ears said to Six-Legged.

"Look at him on its back. It isn't natural."

Six-Legged looked at Wants the Moon. She looked mad enough to chew rocks, like Weaver. "Yah! You are all stupid!" she said. She stomped over to Horse. "Give me your hand," she told Six-Legged.

He goggled at her for her language to Squash Old Man and the rest, but he held his hand down. She grabbed it and pulled herself up on Horse's back behind him. She drummed her heels against Horse's ribs.

Horse flung his head up and leaped forward, scattering the old men and grandmothers. Women screamed and swung their children into their arms. Horse's hooves clattered on the hard dirt of the courtyard.

Six-Legged pulled Horse's head around, turning him back out of the city. He could feel Wants the Moon's arms tight around his waist, her legs clamping Horse's hairy sides behind his. He gave Horse his head, and they flew past the bean fields, past the melon patches with their round green moons, past the stunted maize and the worms chewing their way through the green ears. They followed the course of Stream Young Man, hooves biting half moons of grass and mud from the bank, flinging them in the air as they passed. The crows, which had been circling their way back from the Bean Canyon people's city, saw them and swooped over their heads, cawing.

Wants the Moon tightened her arms around Six-Legged's waist. Her long black hair welled out behind them like a comet's tail, streaming sparks from its ends. Horse's hooves left the stream bank and clattered on the hard red earth, in the scree of stones where Old Horned Toad Canyon cut through the dry hillside, through the littered dry leaves of mesquite and cottonwood and willows, past the white flames of yucca bushes and a green lizard sunning himself on white stones. They raced up the canyon, hooves thudding on a deer trail, ducked their heads as low-hanging branches raked their faces. Six-Legged could feel the salt sweat on Horse's flanks and Wants the Moon's breath in his ear.

Horse's white haunches gathered and lifted them into the air, leaping in rabbit jumps. Hooves drummed the air, booming like Nighthawk's wings, lifting them above the dusty tops of scrub oak, higher than the high mountains where the piñon pines grew, racing on the thermal currents with Hawk and Condor, bowling them out of their leisurely spiral, a flap of squawking feathers. They were a ribbon on the sky.

At the end of the canyon there was nowhere else to run, and Horse slowed, flanks heaving. Six-Legged pulled him to a stop. His own legs felt watery. A pool, nearly dry in mid-summer, held the sharp edges of deer tracks around it in the caked mud. Horse put his muzzle down in the stagnant water. Six-Legged laid his head on the side of Horse's neck and felt him swallow, deep gulps of water like the sound of hoofbeats.

Wants the Moon unclenched her hands slowly from around Six-Legged's middle. When he turned to look at her, her hair was a wild tangle around her face. Her eyes glowed, and she shook with excitement.

"That is what he is for!" she said. "To fly. Like being a bird."

Six-Legged nodded, breathless.

Wants the Moon swung her legs back and forth along Horse's flanks. She ran her hands across his hairy white backside. "We have to take this horse somewhere else," she said. "Or they will kill him. You saw them."

Six-Legged was getting a crick in his neck from turning around to talk to her. He slid down from Horse's back and slid the rest of the way out of the sky with a thud, remembering. "You insulted Squash Old Man."

"They'll kill it," she said again.

"Coyote said they wouldn't kill it if we figured out what it was good for," Six-Legged said, hopeful.

Wants the Moon stopped swinging her legs. "*Who* said?"

Actually that wasn't exactly what Coyote had said. He had said Six-Legged ought to find something to *do* with Horse or the Red Earth people might kill it. And Six-Legged didn't like mentioning that he had been talking to Coyote. "Nobody," he said.

"Well, don't talk to . . . Whoever, anymore," Wants the Moon said. "It isn't safe. And we found what it was good for, and they didn't like it. We have to leave. How long will it take you to pack your clothes and your bow and steal some food?"

"What?" Six-Legged goggled up at her.

"Well, we can't change the world if Squash Old Man kills this horse."

Six-Legged knew that she was the only one besides himself in the Red Earth City who *wanted* to change the world. But *leave?* "You mean leave the city?"

She folded her arms. "We should find out where this horse has come from."

"How did you get to be the Person Who Decides Things?" Six-Legged asked. "*I* found it."

"It told me its name."

He thought about that. Names were important, and knowing names gave you power. But he felt as if Hawk had picked him up in his talons and was taking him somewhere, whether he liked it or not. He had just been somewhere. She hadn't. She didn't know how big things were outside. "Where would we go?" he asked her.

"To find where he comes from, so we can find another one."

"How do you know there is one?"

"There must be a female," Wants the Moon said. "Just look at him—he has a bigger one than Elk's. What is that for if there's no female?"

Six-Legged didn't know. He imagined himself telling his mother that he was going with Wants the Moon to find Horse Woman. He thought it might be easier to just go. And he wondered what was wrong with a woman who wanted to change the world. That was for men, if it was going to happen at all. But Wants the Moon was sitting on the horse, and she didn't look as if she were going to get off.

"It was nearly full moon last night," she said. "We'll go tonight before Squash Old Man can decide anything. And before Weaver's wife gets up out of her grave. I don't want to meet *her*."

Six-Legged sighed. He would argue with her later when the stubbornness had worn off. How would they know where to look for another horse? He pulled himself up on Horse's back and made Wants the Moon give him the reins. Squash Old Man and Turquoise Old Man would change their minds when they had thought about it. They hadn't actually said anything about killing it. He would tell them Coyote had given it to him, he thought with satisfaction, and then they would be afraid to.

There was still a crowd of people in the courtyard when they rode back. They parted to let Horse through, and Six-Legged, pleased, thought that they had decided they were fools. He nodded gravely at Squash Old Man and Turquoise Old Man to let them know that he understood.

Turquoise Old Man grabbed Horse's ropes. Squash Old

Man had a knife in his hand, an obsidian blade like black water.

Wants the Moon drummed her heels in Horse's ribs. Six-Legged kicked out at Turquoise Old Man. Horse lifted himself on his hind legs, towering over Turquoise Old Man. Wants the Moon and Six-Legged slid down his backside, landing hard in the courtyard. Six-Legged picked up a rock and threw it at Horse's rump.

Horse reared again, kicked out, and ran, leaping over Stream Young Man like a white deer, trailing his ropes behind him. They heard his hooves thunder along the stream bank and crash through the maize field.

Wants the Moon picked herself up from the ground. She was crying. "You are wicked fools," she said, sobbing, and ran away from them all, her feet making spatters like rain on the courtyard floor.

Turquoise Old Man looked at Six-Legged. Six-Legged hunched his shoulders and turned away. Turquoise Old Man cleared his throat. "That was not a good animal to have among us," he said.

4

Otter Water

THE NIGHT WAS BIGGER THAN THE BOWL OF THE VALLEY. The darkness went on and on, the mountains diminished in the blackness. Wants the Moon was still weeping, but silently, as they walked. Six-Legged wanted to put his arms around her and comfort her, but he thought she would hit him if he did. She was folded in on herself like a box. The full moon gleamed on the whispering dry leaves of the maize and on the white bolls of cotton ready to pick. The cotton floated in the field like the moon's children.

They had seen Horse's tracks along the stream bank, but then lost them in the maize. It was hard to see. Horse was probably gone, Six-Legged thought drearily. He would have to go back to being Out of Breath, who always walked. He went on, propelled by anger. He had had a fine, magical horse, and Squash Old Man had taken it away. He hoped Squash Old Man withered and blew away like the maize and that peccaries came and ate him. He wanted to go away from this place, away from where nothing new and magical could come without someone wanting to kill it, away from where the world wanted always to stay the same, and rot in its field.

Wants the Moon sniffled and scrubbed a hand across her eyes. Six-Legged reached out and took her other hand. They trudged on. Weaver's wife's grave was far behind them; it didn't seem to matter now if they met her. She was only a ghost. *They* had owned something from another world, and they were looking for it.

When they saw him, finally, they thought it was only more cotton, or moonlight on stones. Then Horse switched his tail, took shape, arching his white neck against the obsidian sky, bobbing his white head, waiting for them to come and untangle his ropes from a mesquite bush.

The desert was not as large with Horse walking beside him, Wants the Moon on Horse's back. She sang softly to Horse, and her voice made a cup around them, holding back the desert sounds, the whisper of hunting snakes, the silent wings of owls, the shriek of a mouse in owl talons. Six-Legged counted over in his head the things they had taken, crept back in the night for, and hoped it was enough. The Red Earth people, like all the people of the great valley of Water Old Man, were not travelers. When you had a city with gleaming walls and fields full of maize and melons and beans and peppers, why would you travel? That was what Six-Legged had always thought. He had been on hunting trips of three, sometimes ten days. What did you pack for a trip into the next world? He was sure now that was where they were going.

He had taken his bow and all the spare arrows he could find, because chipping arrowheads took time. He had taken dried meat and two big sacks of maize from the storeroom and a bagful of onions, peppers, and beans; two shirts and leggings and a heavy blanket; waterskins and a basket for cooking (pots were too heavy and broke easily); a bag with willow bark, wintergreen, yarrow, juniper berries, and a gourd full of pitch stolen from his mother's medicine stores; spare shoes; a buffalo horn with slow-burner in it; spare rope and skinning knives and cutting knives and spoons and bowls and endless things that he had thought of at the last moment and stuffed into his packs while his mother slept. His packs

and Wants the Moon's were slung over Horse's back behind
her, so only one of them could ride him at a time. Six-Legged
didn't know what she had brought, or stolen.

They had crept in and out of the city in the dark, dragging
their packs bumping and thumping through the courtyard,
waking dogs who had to be shushed, tiptoeing past the houses.
Six-Legged's mother hadn't waked, and no one had called out
to them. Six-Legged thought that maybe the city didn't want
them, would not wake at their leaving. They were dangerous
now, and accursed. Wants the Moon had just left her house
and everything in it that she couldn't take. Someone else
would move into it if she didn't come back.

Horse hadn't seemed to mind the packs. They had tied them
under his belly to keep them from slipping and found out later
that he had held his breath to make his stomach big, and when
he let it out, all the ropes were loose. A pack slid under his
belly, and he stopped, kicking at it while Wants the Moon
clung to his back.

"He knows things," Six-Legged said, tightening the ropes.
"About packs. He was tame already, so there must be more
of him."

If there weren't, where would they go?

The sun came up, puddling the mountains with fire, and
they slept, yawning, with Horse tethered to a cottonwood tree.
At noon they went on again, afraid that Squash Old Man might
send someone after them. Last night they had followed the
road that went to the Bean Canyon people because it was easy
going. But news traveled fast between the cities of the valley,
and if they stayed on that road, someone was sure to tell
Squash Old Man where they were. So they turned off the Bean
Canyon road where a deer trail ran into the foothills, and at
night they found water and a place to camp.

Six-Legged had found that Horse would stay if they tied his
rope to a piece of deer antler driven into the dirt, and they
tethered him in a patch of grass. Six-Legged put up a brush
hut while Wants the Moon made a fire with the slow-burner.
She put a flat stone in the fire and spread maize meal on it to
cook. It was almost like being at home with his mother except

for the sky over them and Wants the Moon's flame-colored left breast, gleaming in the firelight where her blanket had slipped from her shoulder. She hadn't seemed to notice. She yawned and stretched, and when she had eaten her share of the maize cake, she said, "This won't last long. You'll have to hunt for something tomorrow."

Six-Legged nodded, trying not to look at her breast, until she rolled herself in her blanket and went to sleep. Horse snuffled at the ground, pulling up grass with soft lips. Six-Legged heard them both breathing in the still night.

In the morning they watered Horse in the stream, splashing their faces in the cold, clear water and trying to grab the minnows that zipped along the bottom over rocks thick with orange moss. Water striders skated across the surface where the current eddied into a shallow pool under a willow. A dragonfly hummed over it on shining blue wings. Wants the Moon snatched up an unwary turtle sunning itself beyond the fringe of willows and put it in a basket to cook for dinner. She grinned over her shoulder at Six-Legged.

They moved Horse's tether to a new patch, and while he ate, they tried to decide where to go next.

"I found him," Six-Legged said, gnawing a piece of dried meat, nearly the last of it, and trying to tear the end off between his back teeth. "My dream told me to go south."

"There's nothing in the south but desert and black rock," Wants the Moon said. "If there are more horses, they will have to come north to look for something to eat."

"Then they will be coming from the south," Six-Legged said. "That is where that trader told everyone the monsters were, so *something* is in the south."

"Do we want to meet monsters?"

"You said you weren't afraid."

Wants the Moon licked the last shreds of her share of the meat off her fingers. "We should have thought about this before we left." She folded her arms, thinking. "What is it that we have to do?"

"Find another horse," Six-Legged said. "Find something to eat, too, soon."

"Then where is the best place to hunt? A horse will go where the deer go. They eat the same things."

Six-Legged wondered how she could be so sure there *was* another horse. Maybe they were only telling themselves that. He thought about deer instead, which had grown scarce in the valley but most likely were still in the high country to the northeast. The Red Earth people didn't usually go that far, but they didn't usually have a horse to ride, either. And if he and Wants the Moon were searchers, then they couldn't search by staying in their own valley. Going north seemed to make as much sense as going south. Coyote might have got Horse from anywhere. "We might catch a deer in Snake Canyon," he said. "They water there this time of year sometimes."

"All right," Wants the Moon said, now that she had won. "You can ride Horse today. It's your turn."

When they had loaded their packs, they turned away from the roads that ran between the cities of the valley. There was nothing now that they wanted at the ends of those. They climbed together, following the deer trails, north and east, toward the slopes where the piñon pines grew and a high tableland lay beneath bloodred mountains. They foraged as they went, scavenging turtles and camas bulbs and wild greens and cress from the stream. Six-Legged killed a rabbit and some ground squirrels, and once they dug a badger from its hole with sticks. It chased Wants the Moon up a tree before Six-Legged killed it. They ate it greedily, always hungry.

They cut grass for Horse or staked him out on a long rope to graze. Higher up the mountain they had to find him berries and piñon nuts to eat and discovered that he wouldn't eat bark like the deer. He ate a lot. When they came to grass, they stopped for several days so he could eat.

Wants the Moon and Six-Legged looked at each other often, to reassure themselves that they were not alone in the wildness around them. When they heard the coyotes' warbling howl in the valley below, they sat very close together. They were not of a wandering people, and the wildness was wilder than they had thought. Once they saw a band of people going to the trade fair at High Up City and hid from them, worried now that they were being hunted. It was being wild like the wild rabbits that made them afraid, Six-Legged thought, but he didn't know what to do about it.

When they looked back toward where they had come from, they could still see the blue and purple mountains in the southwest and the jagged-toothed blue peaks to the west, beneath which the Red Earth people's city and all the others of their kind nestled in the foothills and canyons, below the red stone cliffs, banded in yellow and green and white and black, where the Ancestors had carved their houses. Even in these times, the Outsiders who had come from the north wouldn't go there. They thought the ghosts of the Ancestors would eat them. Six-Legged felt like a ghost himself now, bones wandering the mountains. He wouldn't go back, he thought stubbornly.

The days were getting shorter. It was still summer, but the ground squirrels were dragging pinecones into their burrows, and the snakes in Snake Canyon were slow and unwary. That made them dangerous and easy to step on, so they watched the trail carefully. There were no more horses, though, or their strange half-moon prints in the ground.

"We are going the wrong way," Six-Legged said. Wants the Moon ignored him. "What are they doing at home, do you think?" he asked her.

"What they always do," she said. She was stitching up a hole in Six-Legged's buckskin leggings with a bone needle and sinew thread. She had brought cotton thread with her, too, he had discovered, and pins and everything else to mend their clothes or make new ones if he killed a deer and they tanned the hide. She seemed to expect him to do that.

"They are the way they always are at home," Wants the Moon said. "The old men tell everyone how to live, and the old women make sure they do it. Bah." She bit through the end of her thread with sharp front teeth.

Six-Legged decided that she might be happier here in the wild, but when he thought about home, he thought that his mother would have given him up by now. It would be time to pick the cotton and card and spin it. He remembered the blanket unfinished on his loom. Maybe she would marry again, and some other man would finish it. He sniffed, feeling sorry for himself.

"There were deer tracks at the spring this morning," Wants the Moon said. "We need more meat."

"Then you can come and help me!" Six-Legged snapped. "If you want a deer."

"All right," Wants the Moon said placidly, as if women hunted deer every day.

He got her up before first light and prodded her onto the trail, still yawning. They found tracks quickly enough, a buck and three does, but Horse made so much noise that they could hear the deer break through the scrub ahead and go flying up the canyon. Six-Legged swore. Woman magic was always more powerful than hunting magic. He should have known.

Wants the Moon dug her heels into Horse's flanks. Horse lunged up the canyon after the deer while Six-Legged grabbed at his mane to keep from falling off. Wants the Moon handed him his bow, an arrow nocked to the string. Six-Legged let go of Horse to take it and fell off. He landed on the rocks and lay there with his whole body hurting while Wants the Moon brought Horse around in a circle. She slid off his back and peered at Six-Legged.

"Are you all right?"

"No, I am dead, and you are a crazy woman. You have to stop doing that."

"We have to practice this," she said. "I think you should sit behind me."

"Well, I don't."

"That way I can guide Horse and you can shoot the deer. Get up."

"The deer are in the next world by now." Six-Legged got up slowly, feeling his bruises, shaking his leg gingerly to see if it was broken. He limped over to Horse, who was placidly eating thistles. "And you have mucked up the trail."

Wants the Moon bent and peered at the deer tracks, overlaid with Horse's hooves. "There are people's feet here, too," she said.

"Those are yours," Six-Legged said.

"They are not. I just got off Horse. And they are bigger than mine."

"Then they are mine." He bent to look at them. They weren't his. There were five people's prints, going up the canyon after the deer. Where were they now? Six-Legged looked around nervously. The gray-green shadows of the aspens rustled, full of mysterious, impenetrable shade. "Maybe Squash Old Man has sent someone."

Wants the Moon was squatting by the footprints. "They aren't our people," she whispered.

"Then they are Bean Canyon people," Six-Legged said, but the hair stood up on the back of his neck. "Or Blue Mesa people."

"What would they be doing up here?"

"Then they are High Up City people." Six-Legged nocked an arrow to his bowstring.

"And that is why you are going to shoot them?" Wants the Moon was whispering, but it was an urgent, fierce hiss like a snake's.

He didn't answer. The woods were still. Even the deer could no longer be heard in the brush. They had gone far up the canyon, or they were frozen, too, waiting.

"Our people don't make their shoes this way," Wants the Moon said, catching the whispered words between her teeth. "None of the valley people do."

Six-Legged reached his right hand out for Horse's reins and looped them around his arm. A magpie squawked in the aspen leaves and then was quiet. The sun filtered through the trees in yellow bands, and they could see a patch of blue sky above the treetops, floating on the canyon rim. A little breeze rustled the leaves. Six-Legged half drew his bow.

Horse flung up his head suddenly, ears swiveling, nostrils wide. "Get on his back!" Six-Legged said to Wants the Moon.

This time she listened to him. She swung herself over Horse's back and gathered up the reins, flicking them loose from Six-Legged's arm. Horse danced nervously, ears pricked.

Six-Legged braced himself and watched the trees, waiting for something to come out of them. A branch cracked ahead beside the deer trail, and he spun toward it. He could feel the fear run down his arms and coalesce into the arrow nocked between his fingers. Something was stalking him, had been diverted from its pursuit of the deer by their presence. Not a puma; something on two feet that left shoe prints. High Up City people would have shown themselves.

The magpie saw that the human people were hunting their own kind. It had seen the first ones go up the canyon after the deer, and then the others come behind them. Now the first humans had turned back, stalking the others. The magpie could feel their slow steps in its feathers. It was curious, and so it put its bird thoughts in one of them, to see what it would be like.

The stalkers peered through the scrub and branches. Magpie could see blurred shapes on the trail below them and five bodies here in the trees beside him, counting the one with the torn ear that Magpie was in just now. They had heard something blundering and thrashing in the brush below them in the canyon and hidden. That was wise until you knew what was on your trail. But now they could tell it was only two people of the enemy cities, who couldn't even keep quiet in the woods. There was something with them, maybe a big dog. Half an Ear and his brothers nodded at each other silently, sizing up opportunity. Magpie could feel their acquisitiveness. It was not unlike being hungry. Half an Ear's people knew they were the only True People in the world and that the city dwellers were only for killing or taking for slaves. Magpie wrestled with that idea, and it grew easier to think it while he was in the human person's thoughts, but still, it made his brain itch. Half an Ear motioned to his brothers, and Magpie moved uneasily in his head. There was blood in there now and teeth and a smell of weasels. Half an Ear and his brothers screamed like cats. Magpie flew out of them again, diving upward for the sunlight at the top of the canopy.

*   *   *

They came out of the shadows in a run, howling unintelligible words, two from ahead and three others from behind. Six-Legged loosed the arrow he had nocked and drew another. One of them fell, cursing him, hand clapped to his thigh, long hair spilling out of its feathered pins. *Outsiders.*

Six-Legged had seen an Outsider man the Blue Mesa people had captured once, and two dead ones who had raided the Red Earth City when he was a boy. He had seen them in his dreams and childhood warnings to children who strayed too far from town. Grandmother Owl Ears had told him about them, how they were not human people at all but had fanged teeth like Puma and ate blood and city people's babies.

He shot another arrow and hit no one. They kept coming.

"Get up!" Wants the Moon shouted and held her hand down to him. An arrow nicked his shoulder. He didn't know whether the Outsiders wanted to catch them or kill them. Maybe they didn't know, either. But being an Outsider slave was worse than dying. He let fly one more arrow and they slowed, dancing from side to side, wary. They would be on him in ten strides. Horse pranced frantically on the path. Wants the Moon pulled at Six-Legged's arm, and he turned and jumped for Horse's back. Wants the Moon pulled him up and spun Horse in the trail, and they thundered toward the men who were coming up behind them. As he straightened up, Six-Legged saw them raise their bows. One stepped across the trail, bracing a spear against his thigh. Horse plunged on, and the man with the spear turned and ran, flattening himself against a tree as the trail narrowed. He must have felt Horse's hot hide in his face, and Wants the Moon raked her nails across his eyes as they passed. The Outsider grabbed at their legs, but Six-Legged beat at him with his bow until he let go.

More arrows hummed around them. Six-Legged managed one shot back as they went by, clinging to Horse's ribs with his knees, drawing the bow past his ear. Horse plunged through the trees, floundering in thickets of scrub. Wants the Moon turned his head back toward the canyon mouth as the branches whipped their faces.

Three peccaries rooting under the trees snorted and flew out from beneath Horse's feet. Six-Legged could hear the men running after them, their words like birds screaming, or bees, unintelligible and angry. The deer trail was narrow and full of stones. The men behind them could go as fast as Horse. Six-Legged swayed on Horse's rear, trying to keep his balance while the wind blew dust in his eyes. He turned and loosed an arrow at them again but didn't hit anyone. Ahead, where the canyon mouth opened into a high valley, was flat ground. There Horse could run, if he didn't break his leg here first. They drummed their heels in Horse's ribs, and he leaped over a log across the trail and landed, stumbling, floundering in a scree of rocks. The hunters bayed after him.

Horse slithered down an incline, nearly on his haunches. Stones rattled under his hooves. Six-Legged waited to feel the arrow in his back. The howling behind them was like hunting coyotes. He nocked an arrow at the men who seemed to him now to be running on four legs, gray and dusty in the sunshine. The arrow disappeared in the light.

The canyon widened. The trickling stream at its center pooled into a water hole before it flowed out past a clump of greasewood into a sandy wash. Wants the Moon set Horse toward the wash, and he jumped it while the men behind them clambered across. As she bent low over Horse's neck, Six-Legged gave up trying to shoot and wrapped his arms around her waist, clutching his bow and quiver to his side.

Horse flew. On flat ground he ran as he had run in Old Horned Toad Canyon, when they had run from Squash Old Man. They felt the air lift them, cool on their faces, knew they were birds in the air. Six-Legged looked over his shoulder to see the men behind him driving their legs hard to keep up, falling behind. He laid his head against Wants the Moon's back and let Horse climb the sky.

They ran until the flames of the low sun began to burn their faces. Then Horse slowed, put his hooves on the earth, and stood puffing and blowing down his nose, his flanks heaving. By now the hunters were gone, not even specks in the distance.

They were somewhere, suspended in the dusty light, bound by their two legs to travel the old, slow road.

"They will track us," Six-Legged said.

Wants the Moon pointed at a stand of cottonwoods across the valley. He nodded. They moved toward it at a walk now, weary and wet with the sweat of fear. There was flowing water under the cottonwoods, flat and shallow. They got off and walked Horse down the middle of it, ankle deep, splashing bright drops in the air.

They went a long way down the stream and then circled back to their camp. There was no question of staying in it. The Outsiders would backtrack and find where they had come from. Six-Legged stuffed their belongings in the packs while Wants the Moon tied a blanket on Horse's back to keep them from galling him.

"You ride," Six-Legged said, hefting a pack up. "I walk faster."

She nodded and led Horse up to a fallen log to climb on his back. They set out, going in water when they could, moving northeast quickly while the sun went down at their backs.

"There were only two of them," Half an Ear said sullenly. The magpie perched above him, listening. "They weren't worth catching."

"Bah, you are worthless puppies," the chieftain of the Outsiders said. He glared at the five. "We teach them to fear us, and now you let two go to tell their kind that the People of the Wind are only puppies after all, who cannot catch a ground squirrel. Yah! Go and be ashamed of yourselves."

Half an Ear kicked a stone. "They rode on a white deer with no horns," he said. "They ran away from us on it."

The chieftain of the Outsiders folded his arms, and a woman over in the darkness by the midden pile giggled. Half an Ear spun around to glower at her.

"A white deer with no horns?" The chieftain looked at the five with growing disgust. "Yah bah, why have I had sons? Go and tell your mothers you have been fermenting cactus while you were supposed to be doing man's work and have seen drunken visions.''

"It wasn't a vision," the youngest brother said. "It shot arrows at us."

"And how did it hold its bow?" the chieftain asked with elaborate sarcasm. "In its hooves?"

"*It* didn't shoot," the middle brother said. "The man shot."

"One man, and a woman. With a white dog, probably. And you couldn't catch them. Go in your tents and be ashamed until morning." The chieftain stalked toward the fire, where his wife was cooking a deer haunch. "Your son is an idiot," he said. He pulled a piece of fat off the haunch and ate it. "It is not good hunting in this place."

The magpie went back to follow the two people with the animal it had never seen before. He saw them kill a deer, an old one that they had barely beaten the coyotes to. They were looking for a winter camp and watching the sky uneasily as the air grew colder around them and turned hard and brittle with ice.

Magpie saw them stake Horse in a meadow to graze and make themselves a brush hut that caught fire when they tried to stay warm in it. They came running out, shrieking and dragging their blankets and packs. They built another fire and rolled themselves in their blankets beside it. Magpie shook his head. That would never do. Puma was in these hills. A person needed a nest with some defenses to it. Something in a high tree, so to speak. Other people were always hungry.

The tawny shadow that eased along the ground thought so, too. It had never seen anything like the white animal, but it could tell by the smell that you could eat it. It slunk closer, belly to the ground, the black tip of its tail twitching.

Horse flung up his head, ears swiveling, nostrils wide. He screamed and reared on his hind legs, jerking at his tether. Six-Legged flung himself out of his blankets, knife in his hand. Horse bucked, screaming and yanking at the rope until the stake came out of the ground. He ran, trailing it after him like a snake. Six-Legged saw a tawny shape bunch itself and leap through the night after him.

"Get up!" He kicked Wants the Moon, who was already scrambling from her bed, and stuck the pitch torch they had used the night before into the dying fire. It blazed up, and Six-Legged and Wants the Moon ran after Horse and Cat.

They stumbled through the night, plunging through scrub oak and foxtail grass, calling to Horse. Six-Legged carried his bow in his other hand, and Wants the Moon had a hunting spear and a half-burned branch from the brush hut. The only thing Cat was afraid of was fire.

Where the land sloped up into a grove of scrub oaks, Six-Legged grabbed Wants the Moon by the arm and jerked her to a halt. She stared at him, breathing hard, until he pointed. "There!"

They could see Horse, a white ghost shape in the scrub, his tether and stake caught in a young oak tree. He was frantic with fear, trampling and thrashing among the bushes. They looked around wildly for Cat, tawny as the dust and dry grasses. He could be anywhere. He could be behind them.

Six-Legged eased forward, his bow slung on his back now, his knife in his hand. Horse lunged and snorted. "Be still!" Six-Legged hissed at him. He could feel Wants the Moon at his back, and then something else.

The great tawny shape leaped at them. They spun, holding out the torch. Wants the Moon swung the branch over her head, whirling out a great spiral of sparks.

Cat slowed, snarling, and Horse thrashed in the scrub behind them. In the torchlight they could see the yellow glare of Cat's eyes and the maddened glow of Horse's.

"Yah! Get back!" Six-Legged shoved the torch at Cat. Cat spat and lifted one great paw, claws unfolded, batting at them. Six-Legged shoved the torch at him again. Wants the Moon whirled the branch over her head until the end glowed red, then threw it. It singed Cat's hide with a shower of sparks, and he roared. Six-Legged gave the torch and his belt knife to Wants the Moon and nocked an arrow to his bow. He loosed it, heart hammering, but it went wide, cutting a red welt down

Cat's flank. Cat howled, balanced between anger and fear of the torch.

Wants the Moon cut Horse's tether, pulling him away from the tangled branches, wrestling to hold him. With his rope in one hand, she waved the torch at Cat again with the other while Six-Legged nocked a second arrow. Cat spat and roared one more time, then turned into the brush as the arrow clipped his ear. They ran the other way, clutching the torch.

"He is not very smart," Wants the Moon said.

Six-Legged looked with disgust at Horse, calm now, munching grass by the ruins of their camp. "He is stupider than a horned toad," he said. "Being smart is not what he is for. Running is what he is for. We will have to remember that."

At the start of the Snow Moon they came to some caves in the high hills and found one big enough for them and Horse. The talus slope caught the low winter sun, and there was a stream just below and piñon pines to gather nuts from. They found bones and bits of flint that said that people might have been here once, and other bones and droppings that said that Bear had, too, but now no one was using the place but the otters under the bank—they looked carefully all the way to the back of the cave with a torch to be sure—so they made beds of pine branches and blankets. Wants the Moon dug rocks out of the earth to make a fire pit and hearth.

"This is how the people lived before they lived in the cliffs," Six-Legged said. "Maybe here in this cave." He thought he could see marks on the walls where they had made it bigger, and he imagined them, dressed in skins, with baskets full of wild greens and berries, waiting for Maize Girl to come and show them the way to plant maize and build cities. He could see one of them in the firelight, combing her hair with a bone comb. Behind her was a man with a flute and a pack on his back.

"We will have to find graze for Horse," Wants the Moon

said, and the figures vanished. "When it is frozen, we will have to dig it out of the snow."

"Are we going to stay here all winter?" Six-Legged asked, although he knew the answer. You couldn't travel in the winter. You could stay here or go home.

Wants the Moon smiled. She had found clay to make pots with, and she was patting one into shape. "It is a good place. Someone lived here."

"Puma most likely," Six-Legged said to be surly. But he could see her outlined by the light of the woman with the comb, as if they were the same.

"You can cut me some wood tomorrow," Wants the Moon said, "and I will make a kiln and fire these. Then we won't have to cook in baskets."

She was happy. She was like a girl child playing house, Six-Legged thought, with her own cave to be mistress of and no one to tell her how to be, and himself for a husband to cut wood. But there wasn't any maize or beans or melons. They would have to gather piñon nuts and berries like those people in the shadows of the cave, and hunt. He wondered if she had thought of being hungry, or dying here.

In the morning it snowed, the first snowfall of winter. They looked out from the cave mouth at a crystalline world, changed and inscrutable under the snow. As they watched, an otter came out of the landward door of his den and poised at the top of the slope, looking around.

"Good morning," Six-Legged said to him.

The otter looked at him, whiskers twitching. *Good morning*, he thought back. Then he launched himself down the slope, sliding on his belly, flipping this way and that, making a snake-shaped path to the stream. He landed in a cold spray of water.

Six-Legged grinned. Another otter head popped out of the bank, and he told it good morning, too, to make sure it knew he wouldn't eat it. The otters had been here first, and it was their bank. It would be bad manners to hunt them. They would know where the fish lived, and if he was polite, they might tell him. Where there were otters, there would be fish.

The second otter sat on its haunches, surveying the white world. Then it launched itself down the path while the first one scrambled back to the top in a flurry of snow. Two more came out and wrestled each other to the bottom, rolling over and over, paws and black tails thrashing, sending up showers of snow.

Six-Legged cut himself a handful of bare shoots growing above the stream and began to make himself some snowshoes. It would be fine to be an otter, he thought, and slide on the snowbank all day.

Be an otter, the otters said to him.

Wants the Moon came out of the cave and put her pot in the sun to dry. Good clay came from drying raw mud from the riverbank, pounding it to powder, and mixing it with sand. She was experimenting with this first pot. They would know more when they had fired it, she said, once Six-Legged had dug her a kiln. Then she took note of his snowshoes.

"That's good," she said approvingly. "It will be easy to track in this snow."

Eat fish, the otters said to him.

"I thought I would fish," he said.

"You can fish any day."

"Horse won't like the snow."

"Did I say to ride Horse? I am going to ride him, and take a basket to cut grass for him and greens for us. There are probably bearberries on this slope, too. It's the right sort."

Six-Legged wondered how she knew what the right sort of slope was. The valley people rarely ventured this high.

"I had a grandfather from High Up City," she said, as if answering his thoughts and as if that meant that knowledge ran in the blood, with where to find bearberries.

"I thought you wanted me to dig you a kiln," he said.

"You can dig me a kiln when you have hunted."

Eat fish, the otters said, but Six-Legged gave up. He lashed the snowshoes together with thong from the deer's hide and began to lace it back and forth across the frames to make a netting. He could see the scars left where someone had sharpened his spearpoints on the rock by the cave mouth. No doubt he had had a woman standing over him, too, telling him to hurry with it. He tightened the thong with his teeth. "When I have finished these," he said.

She seemed satisfied with that, and in a while he saw her riding on Horse's back, bundled in blankets and deerskin leggings, a pair of harvest baskets slung across Horse's rump.

Six-Legged took his bow and quiver and began to scout along the creek bank for tracks, leaving his own round prints like bear paws behind him. The otters had churned up the snow around their den, but beyond it the surface was marked with prints of quail feet and rabbit feet and the delicate hooves of deer, traceries of direction and purpose, of unknown lives lived mysteriously just out of sight. Six-Legged began to follow the deer.

A sleek head popped up out of the water and dived back down. He knew that otter dens always had an underwater tunnel as well as a back door in the bank.

Where are the deer? he asked, and the head popped back up.

Going home to sleep, the otter said. *You haven't called them.* It waggled its whiskers.

Six-Legged thought about that. He broke some twigs off a bush and found the branches brushed with shredded wool left by the sheep that lived on the high peaks. Six-Legged turned the wool in his hand. It was old and damp with snow, and there were no tracks to be seen. Sheep hadn't been here since summer. They were mysterious animals, elusive and canny, with thick shaggy coats and curving horns, and they jumped from crag to crag on the mountains, eluding hunters. Six-Legged knew a man who had fallen off the mountain and died, hunting sheep. The wool was a gift, he thought—from the otters, not the sheep. He tied it in tufts to the twigs and made prayer sticks to call the deer, who were similar animals with horns and split hooves. That was how magic worked. Like called to like. Maybe they *would* find Horse his Horse Woman, Six-Legged thought, easing his way silently along the deer trail, his snowshoes whispering on white feathers. If he could talk to otters, anything might happen. Or maybe he was only going crazy, like Weaver, from too much time in the wild land.

The deer had gone up a narrow ravine thick with piñon pines and cypress. He came on them suddenly, surprising them and him. They bolted, tails up, their thin legs flying among the stones and snow, kicking up a white shower as the otters had. Six-Legged drew his bow and took aim at the flying shapes. He loosed the arrow, and one tumbled down, legs thrashing. It tried to rise and he nocked another arrow and shot again, cursing. It was ill luck to leave a wounded deer to run off. Ill luck and hungry luck, too. The deer flopped in the snow and shuddered. Six-Legged thought of Coyote's story and ran to it. He stopped short, making sure that it was dead, that the pointed antlers were still, and then he put his arms around its warm neck and tried to breathe in whatever was being breathed out—life, magic, deer knowledge.

"Thank you, brother," he told it dutifully and pushed the prayer sticks with the sheep's wool into the snow.

Dragging the deer back through snow was heavy work. He thought once of leaving it and going for Wants the Moon and Horse, but wolves or coyotes might come and steal it, or even Puma. So he tugged it along the trail by its antlers, bumping and thumping and slithering on the frozen ground, and thought about hot deer liver fried on a stone in Wants the Moon's fire pit.

The sun was low when he got back to the cave; the snow lay along the ridge like liquid fire, running with red and pink and orange flame. He dragged the deer to the ground in front of the cave. Wants the Moon came hurrying out with a skinning knife.

"This is a fine one. Oh, and a fine hide." She set to work, chattering. "We'll tan it, and then we'll have a tent to live in in the spring, like the buffalo hunter people."

Six-Legged sat on a rock, catching his breath, and wondered how long she thought they were going to travel. Forever, maybe.

"We can use hide for all our clothes, just the way the Old Ones did." She slit the back legs expertly up the inside. "And we can make spoons with the bones, and rattles with the

hooves. It isn't right that we haven't danced for the kachinas."
She eased the hide away from the skull, knocking the antlers
loose at their base. "Get me a bowl."

Six-Legged sighed and stood up. He didn't want to live the
way the Old Ones had; he wanted her to cook some of the
deer, any of it. He got her a bowl, still unfired, and she cracked
the skull open with a wedge and put the brains in the bowl to
tan the hide with later. "Cover them with snow and put them
in the cave so nothing gets them," she said, looking at the
otter tracks on the bank.

Six-Legged put the brains in the cave and found Horse in
there eating grass. He went back and slit the deer's belly open
and took the offal down the bank for the otters.

They were still chasing each other in the snow, and he
thought they had something else to say to him, but he couldn't
hear it. Maybe they were saying it to each other and it was
only their faint otter-thought echo that he heard. He stood a
long time watching them. Their dark shapes flowed along the
snow like black water, rolling and tumbling each other over,
sliding down the hill on their bellies. He tossed the deer offal
down the hill, and they plunged through the snow to it. They
gobbled some of it down and dragged the rest into the water,
diving for their tunnel. The last one turned on the edge of the
snow and looked up at him. *Thank you, human person,* it said
and flowed off the bank into the stream, otter water.

Six-Legged yearned to follow them, to swim through icy
water up into the warmth of a grass-lined den, to nest with
warm brothers and twine his back and paws around otter sisters sleek with dark fur and soft whiskers. Instead he stood in
the dusk, hungry and uncertain. Something talked to him
through the cold, and whoever it was smelled of green leaf
buds and spring frogs sleeping under frozen mud.

Finally, when the otters didn't come out again, he trudged
back up the hill.

When Wants the Moon had dressed the deer out to her own
satisfaction and had made Six-Legged come and help, she built
up the fire in the cave and put a haunch on it, speared on a

stick and propped on the antlers. The smell made Six-Legged's mouth water. He cooked the liver on a hot stone because he couldn't wait. He handed a piece to Wants the Moon, and they ate it with their fingers, greasy and dripping, and then cleaned them in the snow.

The world rippled with starlight, with moonlight, watery white as shells. Otter light, Six-Legged thought. Wants the Moon smiled at him over her shoulder, her teeth very white in her face, her eyes a little slanted, which was what gave her the dreamy look that made her look biddable when she was not. She was shivering, and when they went inside, Six-Legged opened his blanket and pulled it around them both. They sat by the fire while the meat cooked and the otters came back out on the bank to watch them.

"They will steal from us," Wants the Moon said. The otters sat on their haunches by their back door tunnel, whiskers twitching.

"They showed me the deer," Six-Legged said. "They're going to teach me to fish."

If Wants the Moon thought that was an odd answer, she didn't say so. When the haunch was cooked, they ate until they were sated and hung the rest in a tree with a rope. They gobbled handfuls of tart, wrinkled berries and the winter greens Wants the Moon had foraged for, boiled with wild onion and hot stones in a basket, and drank melted snow. They washed again, plunging hot greasy hands into the icy bank, scrubbing their mouths with snow. Wants the Moon went around the side of a big rock to piss, and Six-Legged watched her dark legs making otter patterns on the white snow. He turned away quickly when she looked back at him.

Horse was still in the cave, luminous in the snow light that came through the opening. They decided to let him stay, since he had pissed once already that evening and maybe he wouldn't do it again and flood them. Puma might come sniffing around that deer.

"You are too stupid to stay outside," Six-Legged said to him companionably, full and stupid himself now, with his arms full of blankets.

Horse blew down his nose and settled on the cave floor, front legs tucked under him. Sometimes he slept standing up. Six-Legged wasn't sure how he did it.

Still holding the blankets from his bed, Six-Legged looked uncertainly at Wants the Moon. It was too cold to sleep alone, the bone-chilling cold that asks for another person's warmth. He looked at her yearningly, and she moved over in her own bed and made room for him. Six-Legged wrapped all the blankets around them both, and tucked her head into his shoulder. He had grown over the autumn, and he was taller than she was now. He could feel her breast against the tips of his fingers and held them very still, hoping she wouldn't notice.

Wants the Moon closed her eyes, but he didn't think she was sleeping. He thought it might be hard to sleep when she could feel that he had gotten hard and was pressed against her leg, but he didn't know what to do about it. His cock did what it wanted to, with no encouragement from him. Sometimes he felt that it was an entity of its own, and he only followed it around.

Wants the Moon opened her eyes and closed them again in a slow blink, squeezing them lazily shut. Her red-brown throat rippled in the firelight like wet fur. He could see how she would be under the blankets, sleek and sinuous, twined against him, soft-pawed. Six-Legged moved his fingers a little, just enough so that they were lying on her breast, as if he hadn't noticed he was doing that.

Wants the Moon wriggled closer, eyes still closed. Holding his breath, he slid his other hand around her other breast and then down her belly, burrowing through the blankets to bare warm skin. Half his mind waited for her to leap up screaming and hit him; the other half was lost in the otter dance of his blood.

Horse's sleepy breathing filled the cave, vibrating on the same note as theirs. He was a luminous ghost shape in the shadows, suffused with a pale light of his own. Six-Legged felt Wants the Moon's cold fingertips trace his spine and ribs, slide between her belly and his, and close around his cock. He burrowed his hand deeper in the blankets and slid it between her legs. His face was burning. This was what the air had been saying to him, what the otters had talked of in their silent otter-thoughts, what lay curled in green buds and sleeping frogs in the heart of the earth. Now he no longer thought she might hit him, but was only struck with wonder at his good luck.

Wants the Moon shifted her legs, turning under his hand, and wrapped silken, damp arms around his neck. She let him push her knees apart, leaning over her, breathing hard. He looked down. His cock stuck out in front of him like a sentinel, or a bird's long beak. He thought it probably glowed. His fingers found soft, moist folds. It was like putting them in his mouth.

He slid into her, while Horse snored and the otters circled the tree outside, their black shapes churning up the snow, try-ing to think human thoughts and know how to get the deer down.

5

Horse Woman

BITTER WATER'S DAUGHTER WOLF EYES HAD MOVED INTO
Wants the Moon's house with Canyon Wren. He had brought
her a blanket in the fall, and she had gone to grind maize at
his mother's house, and then they were married. Everyone
watched them to make sure they behaved like decent people,
not like Weaver and Quail, but Wolf Eyes knew what was
proper. She plastered over Wants the Moon's walls with a new
coat of pale mud, and every morning she went to grind her
maize with the other women in the houses next door while
Canyon Wren worked at his loom.

With the troubling animal gone, Red Earth City settled itself
like a dog in the sun, hungry still but dreaming its life in
familiar patterns. Yet something was moving under the surface, under the husk, and people woke at night listening, or
stopped to squint at the white and straw-colored walls and try
to decide what looked wrong.

Maybe it was Weaver, who still howled at night and sometimes had to be tied up. Maybe it was the way Red Bean Vine
kept looking over her shoulder, as if Out of Breath would
come back. Maybe it was just that Aunt Green Melons had

wanted Wants the Moon's house for *her* daughter (who was almost old enough to marry) and spread her vexation around: Grandmother Owl Ears' house was so crowded with Aunt Green Melons and her husband and their children; there was more room in Wolf Eyes' mother's house; the new couple could perfectly well have lived there. Aunt Green Melons told everyone this until Red Bean Vine snapped at her that you couldn't keep a perfectly good house empty for a year while some people looked for husbands for their daughters.

No one but Uncle Calabash could do anything with Weaver. He sat in Weaver's house, holding Weaver's hand and talking softly to him while Quail's ancient grandmother, who had lived with them, stumped around the rooms, burning the supper and complaining of the cold, because Weaver had not made any blankets for her this winter.

Weaver's face was flushed as if he had a fever and at first everyone thought he was going to die, too. But he didn't get sick, only crazier, and once they stopped him from trying to dig up his wife's grave. That was when Bitter Water and Almost a Dog and Uncle Calabash decided to take Weaver into the kiva and see what the gods could do with him. They made him a bed and burned sage and resin and fanned the smoke across him. They built up the fire and poured water on hot rocks to make steam. They waited to see what rose from him in the heat.

When Weaver wakened, they took him up into the cold air and put him to bed again in his own rooms. The grandmother stuck out crossed fingers at him, and Uncle Calabash slapped her hand away gently. "That is an ill thought."

Uncle Calabash sat down by Weaver's bed with a piece of embroidery to occupy him, red thread stitched neatly into white cloth. The old grandmother relented and sat down beside him.

"The end of this world is coming," she said, nodding her head busily.

Uncle Calabash chuckled. "How are you so certain?"

"Worms," she said, folding her lips. "Monsters." She looked at him sidelong. "That thing your nephew brought."

Uncle Calabash nodded. "These things are hard to discern. Maybe when Weaver wakes up, he will tell us. Maybe he has seen it where he has been."

"I've seen it all," the grandmother said. "The end of the world is coming."

"Oh, not before spring comes," Uncle Calabash said placidly. He set another three stitches, delicate traceries of scarlet cotton. "I want to buy a shell necklace at High Up City, the kind that are all pink inside, to wear in the spring. With red shoes." He smiled dreamily. "I will bring you a headdress with macaw's feathers in it, and all the old men will want to marry you." His voice was soothing, and he stroked Weaver's forehead as he talked. The grandmother nodded in her chair, and a thin snore bubbled between her lips.

When Weaver awoke in the morning, he got up without a word, sat down at his loom, and started threading the heddles through the warp threads that had hung, gathering dust, since Quail got sick.

Uncle Calabash didn't say anything, just watched him setting up his pattern and put his finger to his lips when the grandmother looked as if *she* was going to say something. He pulled her into the next room. "He'll be all right now. Let him weave. He'll make you something to keep you warm."

Uncle Calabash went home, crunching across the new snow in the courtyard, and told his sisters about it over a bowl of hot gruel. They nodded their heads with relief. Having a crazy person in the town was dangerous. It attracted all sorts of spirits you didn't want.

"It was that wife of his," Green Melons said. "She didn't know how to behave. It wasn't natural. No wonder she died."

Red Bean Vine didn't say anything. If her brother could have brought back the boy who used to be Out of Breath, she would have been happy.

Uncle Calabash put an arm around her shoulders. "He goes where he has to go," he said. "That is his fate."

Red Bean Vine sniffled, and Green Melons sniffed back.

That was another one who didn't know how to behave, but of course she wouldn't criticize her sister's child.

Grandmother Owl Ears popped through the kitchen doorway. "The sun's up," she said. "You don't expect me to do everything myself." Her gray braids stuck out from her head, and she looked more like a burrowing owl than ever.

Green Melons' daughter, Swallow, stood behind her, looking sulky, and Swallow's brother, Flitter, capered from one foot to the other, his flute in his hands. "I'm going to play for you," he said. "Grandmother says I'm to play for you."

"Very well." Uncle Calabash winked at Red Bean Vine. They followed their mother into the storeroom, where she kept the family hoard of maize. Dusty sunlight came through the three high windows in a sheet of cold light, bending as it hit the floor. The storage jars were stacked against one wall, the grinding stones set into a trough down the center, worn smooth with years of use. The jars were not full, not the way they should be, brimming with dried red and gold kernels, and the grandmother screamed and stomped her feet at a mouse that ran from the mouth of one of them. Another bad year and the people would have to think about moving their city. Uprooting like a tree torn from its bank in the wind. It had been done before, of course.

Here in the storeroom it was hard to think of that, where the grindstones were built into the floor, set into the hardened clay, five in a row for a mother and her daughters and her granddaughter. Uncle Calabash settled himself at his, and Swallow flopped herself next to him with an elaborate sigh. This was a place to think about solidity, about the family stretching backward through mothers and grandmothers, forward through daughters and granddaughters, always here, always in this place. Here you thought to the rhythm of the grinding while Flitter sat cross-legged on the floor and played his flute.

It was soothing, Calabash thought, to be in your mother's house, bent over the third grindstone from the end with the handstone in your palm, the way you had done ever since you were old enough to remember, ever since you woke up one

morning and thought that you were a girl, that that was what
you wanted to be. It was still a pleasure to pass the meal from
one sister to the next, grinding it finer and finer, until it was
a soft dust that would coat your fingers. You didn't notice that
your knees hurt and your back ached. The music rolled the
stones back and forth, rolled your arms with them.

It was well to be mindful and grateful for having maize to
grind, Red Bean Vine thought. The worms had left enough to
get by on, even if another bad season would see them living
hand to mouth like the wandering people with no cities. Was
that where her boy was, wandering under an open sky? Clouds
closed over the sun again, thick as gray cotton, and the squares
of light on the floor vanished, seeping into shadows. Red Bean
Vine shivered.

Grandmother Owl Ears was so old that her back hurt
whether she was grinding maize or not, and the world was
clouded all days, so it made no difference to her. What mattered was grinding meal with your daughters, in the house that
your mother and grandmother had lived in before you. It was
a shame that the boy had gone off with that woman and the
monster from the desert, but he would have gone off and married soon enough anyway. Sons left, but daughters stayed
home, and their husbands took care of you. Owl Ears was
content that her only son had decided to be a daughter. Let
some man bring him a blanket instead of the other way around.

Green Melons thought that now that Weaver was sane
again, no doubt he would be bringing a blanket to some other
girl. There was no reason it shouldn't be Swallow. Weaver
made more beautiful cloth than anyone else among the Red
Earth people and sold it at the trade fair at High Up City for
anything he wanted. He had bought that wife who died a necklace of turquoise and red feathers and a blanket of fox skins.
There was no reason Green Melons shouldn't be his mother-
in-law next time.

Swallow thought about the boys she had seen at the winter
solstice, when the sun turned around and everyone danced it
back toward spring. She had hidden behind the rain jars to
watch them, the firelight rippling on their bare shoulders like

red water. They were different now, not the boys she had played with in the creek and thrown moss at. Their bones were green, elongated and full of some power that made her want to follow them and touch their shoulders and their shorn hair.

Feet pattered on the walkway below, and someone huffed up the ladder against the outer wall. Quail's grandmother stuck her head down the hole in the roof, and Flitter's flute song faltered. "Come and stop him!" she howled at Uncle Calabash. Her wispy hair looked as if she had pulled at it with both hands.

Uncle Calabash got up from his grinding stone and brushed the meal off his hands, a fine shower of pale dust. He peered up at her. "What is he doing, Grandmother?"

"He's weaving monsters!"

Uncle Calabash scratched his head, speckling his black hair.

"In the pattern," the grandmother said. "I saw it. He's put that animal in the pattern. He's crazy. It will come and eat us all."

Grandmother Owl Ears stood up, too, grimacing as her knees protested. "Go and stop him," she said to Calabash.

Uncle Calabash went across the courtyard again, following his own fading prints through a flurry of new snow. Weaver's sanity looked like prints in the snow to him, too—here one moment, gone the next. He was sitting at his loom when Calabash huffed up the ladder and in the front door. The grandmother was far behind, scurrying across the courtyard wringing her hands, muffled in three blankets so that she looked like a round bird. They could hear her agitated chirping through the white veil.

Calabash looked at the loom. The pattern was barely started, but he could see the thing's ears, and in any case Weaver had drawn it on his wall. It leaped among the red and black suns and arrows that decorated the west wall as if it had jumped through them.

"That is not a good idea," he said to Weaver to see if Weaver could hear him.

Weaver nodded as if in agreement but went on shifting the heddles, pulling threads through the warp. The bottoms of the ears appeared as if they were dropping down from the sky.

The grandmother came puffing along, her nose red with the cold. "What did I tell you?" She sneezed. "The end of the world. In a blanket."

Calabash went to the horse on the wall. He scratched at the fresh paint with his fingernail. Weaver flung himself out of his seat and closed his hands around Calabash's neck while the heddles rattled together on the loom. Weaver's eyes glittered, his lips were parched with the fever that had just left him, and bright tears streaked his face. Calabash thought that now the sickness was in his skin, his muscles, down to the bone. It wouldn't be sweated out.

He turned away from the wall, carefully, and pulled Weaver's fingers loose from his throat.

"Go away," Weaver said. "That's my horse. Don't touch it."

The grandmother howled and crossed her fingers at him, middle finger over forefinger. Naming things always brought them. It was ill luck for Wants the Moon to have asked the thing's name in the first place.

"You don't want it in your house," Calabash said gently.

"Go away," Weaver said.

Calabash went, with the grandmother following him, still howling. They put her to bed in Grandmother Woodrat's house. Then the men went in a delegation to Weaver to show him that he was making a mistake. When he picked up an ax handle and waved it at them, they left.

"He is crazy," Bitter Water said. "He will make something bad happen."

"Maybe he is mad instead," Almost a Dog said. There was a distinction. Crazy people were evil. Mad ones were merely touched by the spirits in ways that ordinary humans couldn't understand. It could be hard to tell the difference.

"If we go back, he will stop weaving and finish making that ax instead," Calabash said. "We should let him alone."

"You are the one who said to come and reason with him," Bitter Water said. People like Calabash were touched by the gods, too, neither man nor woman, a person between worlds, and so possessing unusual wisdom.

"That was before the ax."

"Well, we can't keep him tied up," Almost a Dog said, addressing the practical issues.

"What about that blanket?" Bitter Water asked. He didn't like the idea of the horse forming in the air on Weaver's loom.

"Let him weave his blanket, and we'll give it to the kachinas," Turquoise Old Man said. "Would that work?" He looked hopefully at Almost a Dog.

"Whatever is in his head," Almost a Dog said, thinking, "he may dance it out at the equinox. Many people go crazy in the winter."

The other men grunted and looked at the sky. That was easy enough to do, going crazy in the winter, when it looked as if nothing would ever grow and you would never be warm again. Snow turned to muddy slush in the courtyard, and the bare brown stubble in the fields looked like someone's unearthed bones. If it was a bad enough winter, women took to scrubbing their kitchen walls until they wore the plaster away, and middle-aged men whose backs were beginning to hurt them were found staring out their windows, arms folded, waiting to die. That was why the Red Earth people danced the sun along its path at the solstice and the equinox—to be sure it came back.

"We will leave him alone till spring and see what happens," Turquoise Old Man decided. "Maybe he only needs a new wife."

There were a number of mothers who thought that, besides Green Melons, but Weaver never came out of his house long enough to appreciate their daughters. All winter he stayed inside at his loom, the old grandmother said when she finally went back there. "He cries," she said. "And weaves that blanket."

At the equinox they danced the Spring Rain Dance, and the Turquoise People gave the governance of the city back to the Squash People for the summer. Turquoise Old Man gave

Weaver back to Squash Old Man, who didn't know what to do with him either.

Then in another moon, after the Bean Dance, no one had time for Weaver, not even to try to drag him out of his house to work in the fields. It rained, but the rain brought the worms with it again. All but the oldest women left their grinding stones and cookfires and went out with the men to pick worms from the bean sprouts and the new maize.

Swallow watched the boys, bending to the hills of beans, smashing the small green worms between their fingers. It was warm, and she wasn't wearing anything much—none of the younger children ever did unless they were cold—but she was suddenly conscious of her new breasts and the new hair that her body was growing, on her legs and between them and under her arms. The sun felt like a hand on her back, and she had a sudden urge to lie down and roll in it, in the space between the beans, scratching her back with the sand. She picked a worm off the beans and stared at it before she closed her fingers on it. It was bright green, like the bean shoots. Maybe it was part of the beans, some bad part that had worked itself loose from the good part. Everything was like that, Uncle Calabash said, everything was half and half, light and dark, birth and death, rain and drought. That was the circle of life; without one, you couldn't have the other.

One of the boys flung a smashed worm at her, and it stuck to her shoulder. Swallow forgot the circle, screamed, and brushed it off. She chased him through the bean hills, pelting him with sand. The spring sky wheeled over them like a plate of turquoise, and a mockingbird that had been dipping above their heads, watching, dropped down in the rows to pick up the crushed worms.

On a day like this it was hard to be fearful of anything, and when the Red Earth people saw Weaver blinking in the sun, his new blanket around his shoulders, they sighed with relief and called him into the bean field with them, patting him affectionately. Here he was outside again after a dark winter. The sun had warmed the craziness out of him. Spring tended to do that, and no doubt it would soak any dangerous magic from the blanket as well.

He looked wobbly on his feet, so they sent him to sit with Old Striped Snake and beat on a clay drum to give them a rhythm to work by. But after a while he put down his drum and stood up, staring at the sky. He was thin; the blanket draped around his shoulders looked as if it enclosed a length of ladder. He saw what they were doing and began to pick worms himself, holding each one in his palm and staring at it before he threw it to the ground. The mockingbird hopped behind him.

"Smash them before you throw them down, Brother," Almost a Dog said. "What the bird doesn't get will crawl back in the beans."

Weaver didn't seem to hear him. Almost a Dog beckoned to a small girl. "Follow him, child, and step on the ones he throws down."

She cocked her head at Weaver and began to follow in his footsteps, right foot raised high, stamping down hard, then the left, then the right, tongue between her teeth. The Red Earth people chuckled and went back to their own bean hills.

Weaver went in a straight line through the field, not looking to either side. He picked the worms that stood on their tails in his path, passed unseeing by the rest twining like green shoots among the bean tendrils. The child followed him, and other people began to move in where he had passed. He wasn't doing any good, but no one would tell him so. It was enough to have him out in the sunshine in the field after a winter with his heart underground. Now he could give that blanket to a new bride, and she would get him to weave antlers into it and make it a deer. It only took small changes to set a pattern straight. The Red Earth people knew the pattern, and gently they nudged the recalcitrant into it. They smiled at Weaver affectionately as they came behind, picking the worms he didn't see.

Weaver went faster than anyone else, and so he came to the end of the field alone, with the other people far behind him. At the edge he stopped so abruptly that the child bumped into

his backside. He didn't seem to notice her. She peered around
the brown and white blanket that hung from his bony shoulders to see what he was looking at.

The sun gave the shimmer of water to the new green shoots
in the maize field, just beginning to rise like thick grass from
the ground. Beyond the fields were flowers, the brief desert
blooms that come out of nothing and last a few days so that
for a little while the world is painted blue and yellow and
scarlet. The child thought at first that he was looking at the
flowers; she heard his breath indrawn in a deep whistle like
someone just learning to breathe again. Then she saw what
was glowing in the sun at the edge of the field, fire-outlined
and dark against the blue and yellow blossoms: a red-brown
animal with hide the color of skin, its head among the new
shoots of maize.

The child turned and ran howling back to her mother, floundering over the bean hills. Weaver stepped out of the field into
the rows of maize, walking straight toward it.

The animal lifted its head as he came. It looked at him with
large dark eyes, the sun and turquoise sky reflected in them.
It was emaciated, with ribs poking through a ragged coat that
fell from its hide in tufts. It bent down again to eat vora-
ciously, slobbering down the pale green shoots, biting them
off where they sprang from the ground. Weaver put his hand
slowly to the rotting rope around its head, touched the warm
red skin. It lifted its bony nose and butted him in the chest,
leaving slobber down the brown and white threads of the new
blanket. Weaver smiled.

He tugged at the rope, and the animal left the maize and
followed him. He was still smiling, walking carefully through
the hills of beans while the horse's heavy hooves dug up the
soft ground behind him, unseen.

Squash Old Man and Bitter Water met him, with the Red
Earth people converging behind them like a flight of black-
birds across the bean fields.

"Take it away!" Squash Old Man shouted, waving his
arms. "It's trampling the beans."

The horse threw its head up, jerking the rope free.

Bitter Water planted himself in Weaver's path, barring his way. He was afraid of the animal, but he stood his ground.

Weaver smiled again. He rubbed the red-brown nose, coiling the rope softly into his hand again. The animal quieted and nuzzled his ear. "She came back from the Skeleton House," he said. He beamed at them all and started around them through the field. The animal followed him, her hooves making round dents in the soft earth. They could see it was a female now when she stopped to hike her tail and piss, leaving steaming puddles in the moon-shaped prints.

"Stay here!" Squash Old Man bellowed as the Red Earth people wheeled across the field to follow them, but no one paid him any attention. They were afraid of the animal, but they crowded as close as they dared, so that they encircled a second, empty circle and enclosed it, as if Weaver walked in a bubble. Squash Old Man followed because it was his duty, with Bitter Water dancing furiously beside him on the edge of the bubble.

Uncle Calabash pushed through them, ignoring Bitter Water, and came into the empty space around Weaver and the horse. It felt like being inside a spell, with walls of magic shimmering between himself and the world. Bitter Water grew quiet in respect; there were places that Uncle Calabash could go that other men could not. His red and white skirts whispered around his ankles, and his elegant doeskin shoes printed the mud beside the horse's round moon prints. Uncle Calabash remembered Out of Breath riding the white horse and thought that something rode on this one's back, too, but he couldn't see it. He bent his head to listen instead. In the silence now he heard Weaver whispering softly to the horse, talking into its red ears. "I will make you a bed with my new blanket on it, the one I wove for you. It's a new bride blanket. I made it to bring you back. I know. I will make you bean cake and flatbread to eat, and turkey stew with squashes."

They crossed the narrow footbridge that ran over Stream Young Man, the horse picking her way carefully, and crossed the courtyard to Weaver's house. His house was on the second story, with the old grandmother underneath. Weaver led the horse to the grandmother's first-floor door, tugging at her rope. "I will need to live here now," he said over his shoulder to Uncle Calabash and Squash Old Man. Inside they could hear the old grandmother screaming and the rattle of a ladder as she climbed her way out of the room onto the roof above.

"She is too old to climb ladders all the time," Uncle Calabash said to Weaver.

The grandmother put her head over the edge of the roof. "Drive it away! It will put a spell on us!"

"It's your granddaughter," Weaver said, smiling. "It's Quail coming home."

The grandmother screamed, crossing her fingers at him. Some of the Red Earth people had heard Weaver, too, and they began to repeat it to those who had not, while the grandmother scolded and danced on the rooftop, shaking her finger.

Weaver pulled the blanket from his shoulders and laid it across Red Horse's back. "See what I have made you?"

"You mustn't take her in there," Calabash said gently, reasonably.

"It's her house," Weaver said. "But she can't climb a ladder. She has big feet now." He ducked through the doorway and tried to pull Red Horse after him.

Red Horse balked, snorting at the room, musty with winter damp, at its darkness and strange smells.

"Come on." Weaver pulled at the rope. Red Horse laid her ears back.

Weaver smelled the bread the grandmother had been cooking and snatched it from the hot griddle. He held it out, and Red Horse whuffled at it and took a step forward, her long teeth reaching for it. She was hungry. And now she dimly remembered that once there had been a stable, with grain in a box. Weaver backed inside. Red Horse followed, tail whisking, red fire disappearing into the dark house.

The Red Earth people's voices rose in furious protest, an ascending flight of shouts that fluttered around the rooftops. The crows came back with them, preening their dark feathers. Calabash could see the words among them, feathered with anger, mating with the crows. Anything might come out of their nests. They lined the rooftop while the grandmother and the Red Earth men and women shouted more into the air. Green Melons' face was contorted, lips pulled back from her teeth. "Witch monster! Go back where you came from!"

Weaver didn't listen. He smiled at his wife, who was eating bread. She whickered and looked at him hopefully. He gave her some dried squash, and she ate that, too. He spread the new blanket on the bed.

It was hard because she didn't like to stay inside. Weaver made the bed for her, but Quail wouldn't lie on it. Instead she stood with her head stuck out the door. He made all of Quail's favorite dishes. She ate the bread and bean cake, but not the turkey stew, even when he tried to feed it to her with a spoon. But she ate a great deal, and the beans gave her gas.

"Maybe you will need to get used to food again," Weaver said, but she didn't answer him. She flicked her long red tail at the flies that lit on her rump.

The old grandmother crept down and tried to drive Quail out of the house. Weaver had to chase her back up the ladder. She clung to the top rung, screeching that he was crazy, that he had brought monsters home.

"It's your granddaughter Quail." Weaver kept trying to explain that to her, but she didn't understand.

"I don't want ghosts in my house." The grandmother made signs with her hands. "And stop saying her name. She will come back."

"It is all right," Weaver said soothingly. "She has a new body now. The white monster made her sick, so at the Skeleton House they gave her *its* body to wear. See how now it is skin-colored like a person?"

"You are crazy," the grandmother hissed at him from the top of the ladder.

"I will comb your hair the way I used to," Weaver told Quail as the grandmother climbed out onto the roof. He could hear her rummaging and banging things on the floor above them. He got Quail's bone comb and began to run it through the matted hair on her ribs. Big tufts of winter coat fell away, and she leaned into the comb, enjoying herself.

"Do you remember how I used to comb your hair?"

Red Horse sighed and blew air out through her soft lips. The firelight made her sleepy, and she had eaten her fill for the first time in weeks. Memories of snow and hunger and big cats that stalked her through the mountains faded into drowsiness. She braced her knees and closed her eyes while the human person scratched her ribs.

Weaver looked at his wife. When he squinted his eyes in the firelight, turned his head just to the right degree, he could see Quail under the red hide. Her dark eyes were covered by Red Horse's long lashes, and the white bones of her face were fused in the long bony nose. Her hips were the gaunt bones of Red Horse; her blood ran through the new body, animating it. If he gave her the things she had had in her old life, she would come out of this body and put her own on again. That must be how it would be.

When he had combed the loose hair out, he went to the storeroom and got the last strips of dried deer meat that hung on the walls. The grandmother had taken the sacks of meal and baskets of onions and beans, dragging and hauling them up the ladder with her to the house above, but she didn't have enough teeth for dried meat.

Weaver held the strips out to Red Horse, and she nosed them and turned away.

He tried to think what to do, what would make her happy. "Should I hunt for us tomorrow? It is a good moon to catch rabbits. You like rabbit haunches roasted with onions."

Red Horse looked out the window at the low sun on the courtyard, where a pile of half-grown puppies tumbled each other over in the dust and a turkey cock paced importantly back and forth, his wattles bright red, gobbling to his hens. There had been a place like this once, but it had been before the boat on the water, before the storm that scattered them from the picket line. Before. Red Horse closed her eyes again. Her memory was always a bright image of now, surrounded by fading pictures of other nows jumbled one on the other the way humans stored things in their dreams.

Weaver sighed and closed his hand around the deer meat.

Tomorrow he would cook it for her in a stew. He would feed it to her until she learned to eat again.

The grandmother peered through the smoke hole in the roof. She could see Weaver talking to the animal while its heavy feet dug up her floor and it left its droppings on the yucca mats. The grandmother whimpered and crawled backward from the smoke hole. She stood painfully, pulling herself upright against the wall, and scurried along the roof.

6

The Grandmothers

SIX-LEGGED WOULD HAVE STAYED WHERE THE OTTERS WERE if Wants the Moon hadn't been infected with a spring restlessness when the snow melted.

She thought if they stayed any longer he would be an otter himself, sleek and supple but with whiskers about his nose and smelling of fish.

"She wants to go away," Six-Legged told the otters, sitting on their bank.

Women are like that, a young otter said to him. *Always wanting to move their houses.*

The otters would like him to stay, he thought. He had made a fish weir to catch fish, and the otters stole from it. When the snow melted, they made slides in the slick spring mud and showed Six-Legged how to use them, slithering belly-down from the top of the slope to land with a great splash in the cold water. But Wants the Moon didn't want to be an otter, and these days he liked to please her.

They kept track of the turning moons and the sun's path with marks on the cave wall, and when the deer went down the mountain to browse in the new grass, Six-Legged and

Wants the Moon went with them on Horse, a travois tied behind him. Horse didn't like the travois at first. It bumped behind him when he walked and he thought it was chasing him, so he ran. When it ran, too, thumping and banging on the ground, he kicked it to pieces. So they started again, with a piece of rope trailing behind him, and then a blanket, and then, when he would let the blanket follow him, the travois made of sticks and hide. Finally they cajoled him and petted him and told him that he was Most Beautiful and Most Strong, and he let them load their packs on it.

Six-Legged practiced hunting from Horse's back. By Snakes Waking Moon he could guide Horse with his knees and leave both hands free to draw his bow, although sometimes he still fell off, and sometimes Horse ran under a low-hanging branch and knocked Six-Legged off, just to amuse himself. But he was strong, and he could run down a deer, and he could smell water. They found that if they gave him his head and he was thirsty, he would take them to water.

Spring filled the air with a soft, wet scent like fruit that made everything come out of its burrow, whiskers twitching, nostrils flared to catch the air. It became easier to keep bellies full. At dusk a peccary grunted out of the woods to nose at their packs, and Six-Legged chased it on Horse, trying to nock an arrow while it wove between the trees, tail up and snorting. When he had cornered it against a rockfall, he was glad of Horse's hooves. Peccaries had a temper. He thanked it as he killed it, but he didn't think it appreciated that the way the deer did.

They headed away from the hunting runs of the Red Earth and other valley peoples to where the plains ran eastward in a sea of grass into the buffalo hunters' country. Wants the Moon said that was where a horse would come if there was another one. Six-Legged doubted now that there was, but at night when she let him get under the blankets with her, he didn't care. They had been all winter on their own and hadn't died, so there was no reason to think they would die now that spring had come. And less reason to go home, where someone would take Horse, and Wants the Moon, away from him.

They saw no villages on the plain, but there were signs that people had camped by the river they were following—the marks of old fires and bits of flint chipped from arrowheads scattered along the bank under cottonwoods and sycamores. The river courses were the only places where trees grew here. The trade trail that linked their own people with the buffalo hunters ran through this vast grassland and followed the river for a while. Six-Legged thought that if they stayed on it, they might come to people. Neither of them was sure what would happen if they did come to a village. The people here were not really human, not like the people of their home valley. It might be that, to be prudent, they killed newcomers.

Six-Legged tried to teach Horse to track, like a dog, but that didn't work. He could smell water and things that wanted to eat him, but he wasn't interested in deer.

"He doesn't care what people eat," Wants the Moon said. "That isn't his work. Eating grass and running is his work."

"Then we need a dog," Six-Legged said. "We need something whose work is smelling deer."

The next day Six-Legged met a porcupine and killed it and brought it back to camp so that he could trade the quills for a dog if they met any people.

They argued the wisdom of that at dusk while Wants the Moon pulled the quills out of the porcupine and the river burbled by below them. They took one side and then the other because they didn't really know, but it was something to keep them occupied. While they argued, Horse threw up his head and whickered through his nose.

That generally meant that something was out there that he was interested in, and Six-Legged got up slowly and put his hand out for his bow. Horse's ears swiveled toward the east, cupped to catch sounds Six-Legged couldn't hear. Six-Legged motioned Wants the Moon into the shadow of the trees, and she pulled up Horse's stake and took him with her. They melted into the shade, leaving only his white hide to gleam through the dappled leaves like pieces of shell.

The ripple of the water lapped through the stillness. Six-Legged held his breath, trying to be part of the water and wait

for whatever it was. He narrowed his eyes into the dusk and
looked toward where Horse had aimed his ears. Something
was coming through the foxtail grass above the river, where
the rolling grassland sloped down into the flat alluvial plain.
He could just make out a man, or a person anyway, with three
dogs and a travois. Two of the dogs pulled the travois, and
the other paced at the traveler's side, ears pricked. While Six-
Legged watched, the dog stopped short and stared through the
dusk at him.

The traveler stopped, too, reaching around behind him for
an arrow from the quiver on his back.

Six-Legged cupped his hands. "Good journey to you!" If
the man was a trader, which he looked like, he would speak
the valley people's language.

The traveler lowered his bow, peering at Six-Legged. Six-
Legged trotted up the slope toward him. The dogs raised their
hackles, and the man spoke sharply to them. Six-Legged could
see now that the man had a pack on his back as well as the
bundles that loaded down the travois. He wore red feathers
tied in his hair and a heavy necklace of blue stones and white
shell. There were holes in his earlobes with shell spirals
through them. He had three sashes around his waist, of the
kind the valley people made, one embroidered in red spirals
and two painted with green and yellow suns. A trader, most
surely, showing off his wares.

"Have you come from the buffalo hunters?" Six-Legged
asked him. All traders spoke a smattering of the valley lan-
guages as well as the buffalo hunters' talk and the speech of
the coast. This one was beginning to go gray in his hair, which
meant that he had been foot-on-trail for years.

"Where have you come from?" the trader asked him suspiciously.

"We are from the Red Earth people." Six-Legged motioned
Wants the Moon out of the trees so the trader could see there
were two of them. "We are traveling just now."

The trader looked as if he wanted to ask why—valley people didn't travel—but that would be rude. "I have been in the

camp of Hole in the Sunset, among the Buffalo Horn people,"
he said grudgingly.

"You are welcome to share our camp," Six-Legged said.
He looked sideways at the trader's dogs, wondering if he
might sell one of them. The dog at the trader's heel looked no
more than six moons old, young enough to switch his alle-
giance to a new human.

The trader nodded his thanks and made a gesture of respect
at Wants the Moon. She smiled at him, and then Horse walked
out of the trees, trailing his tether.

The dogs raised their hackles and began to bark, and the
trader's mouth opened in the round shape of an egg. He
backed away up the slope again, shouting at the dogs, reaching
for his bow.

Six-Legged flung himself at the man's ankles, grabbing at
leggings and pack, wresting the bow from his hand. The man
kicked at him, shrieking. The dogs snarled around him, and
Six-Legged beat them away with the bow. The man clambered
to his feet, scrabbling back up the slope, hands digging frantically in the grass for purchase.

He ran away, the loose dog yelping at his heels, while Six-
Legged stared, puzzled now. The travois dogs backed off and
followed him, bumping the travois up the slope. A pack fell
off and rolled back down, spilling open in the grass. Wants
the Moon ran out to get it.

"He was afraid of Horse," Six-Legged said, turning the
man's bow over in his hands.

Wants the Moon, practical, was inspecting the pack. "There
is a buffalo robe in here," she said. "And a very good deerskin."

"Why should he be afraid of Horse?"

Wants the Moon was still unrolling the pack, rummaging
among obsidian arrowheads and bone combs, necklaces of
pink shell. Six-Legged grabbed Horse's lead and swung himself onto his broad white back. "Where are you going?" she
asked.

"To catch him."

Wants the Moon pulled the pack into her lap. "He left it here."

"I want to know why he ran away." Six-Legged put his heels in Horse's side and urged him up the slope. He could just see the running man in the dusk, going westward along the riverbank with the dogs behind him. His pack bounced on his back, and the load on the travois was beginning to shift dangerously. He looked over his shoulder when he heard the hoofbeats, and his face stretched with terror.

Horse clambered to the top of the slope, and Six-Legged bent over his neck and kicked him into a gallop. Horse's hooves thundered along the ridge. The man ahead of them turned and ran away from the river, floundering in the scrub brush and buffalo grass. His dogs had gone in the other direction with the travois, leaving a trail of spilled packs behind them.

"Come back!" Six-Legged shouted at him, but he only ran harder, gasping for breath, gulping air. The loose dog disappeared in the distance, wailing.

Six-Legged leaned down from Horse's back. He could almost touch the man's pack now. He snatched at it, and the trader stumbled, legs thrashing. Six-Legged clung to Horse's withers. The pack slid from the trader's shoulders as he picked himself up again and ran. A sobbing sound came from his throat and rose to a whistle as he gulped in air. Six-Legged righted himself as Horse came even with the running man again. The trader turned a terror-stricken face over his shoulder, eyes glazed with exhaustion. Six-Legged grabbed at his hair, and then dropped from Horse's back on top of him. The trader went down in a frantic jumble of arms and legs. Six-Legged held him down and sat on him while the trader bucked under him, saucer-eyed with fear.

"Stop it," Six-Legged said. "Hold still." He pinned the trader's wrists with his hands and shifted his weight so that his knees dug into the trader's thighs. Horse had slowed as Six-Legged dived off him and now had come back to nose through the spilled pack. Six-Legged had spent much time teaching him to come back when someone fell off him.

The trader had gone rigid and was chanting something up at Six-Legged in a language Six-Legged didn't know. "Be quiet." Six-Legged prodded him in the belly with one knee, and the trader exhaled a *yoop* of air and was silent.

"Why did you run away?"

The trader swiveled his head to look along the ground at Horse. "Eeeehhh!"

Six-Legged shook him. "We aren't going to hurt you. Why did you run away?"

"I will give you what's in my packs," the trader said. "Don't let it eat me."

"It eats grass."

"Don't let it throw fire."

Six-Legged narrowed his eyes at the trader, wondering if the man was crazy and if that was why he wandered around by himself. "It hasn't got any fire. What would it throw it with?"

"You are a sorcerer," the trader said. "I have great respect for sorcerers. If you will let me go, M-Most Wise, I will give you my packs."

"My wife already has one of them." Six-Legged didn't think she would let it go.

"Oh, she can keep it." The trader closed his eyes and moaned. "I have seen such things before. They threw fire and made it thunder when there was no rain. They had two heads, but they didn't come apart."

"You saw animals like this one?" Six-Legged shook him. "Stop moaning and tell me, or I will let him eat you."

"These had two heads," the trader said, licking his lips. "I am trying to tell you, Most Wise, but I am frightened."

Six-Legged relaxed his grip a little. Out of the corner of his eye he could see Wants the Moon coming. He bent over the trader warily, ready to grab him again if he struggled. "Tell me what you saw. Tell me where."

"South. South toward the Sun people. The Spotted Cat people."

"What did you see?"

"Monsters. Like that one. Two of them. With two heads each."

"What did they do?"

"They made a storm. They made thunder. I told you. They threw lightning at us. We were very frightened and ran away." He sobbed, rolling his head to one side, cheek flat in the dirt, to look at Horse. "Let me go, Most Wise. Most Wise Woman." He looked pleadingly at Wants the Moon, standing over him.

"This fool says he has seen a horse, but it had two heads," Six-Legged said.

"Where was the other head?" Wants the Moon asked him. When the trader didn't answer, she prodded him with her toe.

"Above the first! A round head like a calabash. It glowed." Wants the Moon snorted.

"Maybe he saw someone riding it," Six-Legged said. "But he says it made thunder and threw fire." He didn't like that part. It sounded too much like kachinas or Coyote or someone you didn't want to fool with.

"Let me go, Most Wise," the trader said again. His teeth were chattering.

"You can't sit on him all day," Wants the Moon said. "Where does he say he saw this horse?"

"South. Near the Spotted Cat people."

"That's a long way. Do you think we should go there?" They looked at each other dubiously. The Spotted Cat people were even more alien than the buffalo hunters. They built cities, it was said, and drank blood. "I don't want to go there," Wants the Moon said.

Six-Legged got off the trader. The man was up in an instant, scrabbling in the dirt until he was balanced on his fingertips and the balls of his feet. He crouched low to the ground, watching them.

"We won't hurt you," Six-Legged said.

The trader hesitated another moment. Suddenly he leaped to his feet and ran. They stood still and watched him dodge through the grass like a rabbit until he was gone.

Six-Legged and Wants the Moon looked at each other again.

"I think he comes from the Endless Water people," Six-Legged said. "The Ones Who Live at the Coast. He had shells in his ears."

"All those people are crazy," Wants the Moon said. "They live too close to the edge of the world." It might be easy for sanity to fall off the edge. Or other things to climb up over.

They surveyed the litter of spilled packs. Wants the Moon began to pick them up. The trader might run until he got to the coast; most certainly he wouldn't be back for whatever he had lost.

In the nearly full dark Six-Legged thought he saw a pair of yellow eyes peering at him from the buffalo grass. *I brought you a new present*, a voice said in his head. *There are useful things in his pack.*

"Many thanks to you," Six-Legged said hurriedly. He wondered if Coyote would eat the trader, now that his dogs were lost, but he was afraid to ask.

Wants the Moon kept gathering up the trader's things, her arms full of blankets and long strings of eagle feathers. She upended a basket, woven tightly enough to cook in, and put it on her head to carry it. "Stop talking to that!" she hissed and hurried away toward the fire, where the embers made a red hole in the darkness, big enough to step through and leave the night on the other side. She pulled it around her until it made a room and sat counting her booty in it.

Coyote watched her from the edge of the darkness and then set out west at a trot. Maybe he would turn south, after he had caught up with the trader, and see what these things were that shot fire.

In Red Earth City, Quail's old grandmother went from house to house, telling about the ghost animal in her living place and how her son-in-law had gone crazy. If someone gave her food or hot willow tea for her bones, she stayed longer and told them how the ghost animal walked the floor at night, moaning in a ghost voice, and how her son-in-law fed it all her meal.

She came to Grandmother Owl Ears' house at midday and

told the story to Red Bean Vine and Green Melons and Green Melons' children.

"Maybe he is mad," Red Bean Vine said, remembering her own son and how she would take him home again, crazy or not. "Maybe the spirits have done this to him and he is holy."

"Then the animal would be holy, too," Green Melons said, "and it is not." She folded her lips.

Swallow looked sideways at her mother. She knew Green Melons had thought that Swallow ought to marry Weaver and that now Green Melons was angry and resentful about it. Swallow had picked out her own boy, from a house on the Squash People's side. She didn't want Weaver, even if he stopped being crazy.

"If he had married again, this wouldn't have happened." Green Melons looked pointedly at the old grandmother.

"He thinks he *is* married again," Flitter giggled. "That's what's wrong." Grandmother Owl Ears stared at him until he put his hand over his mouth.

Quail's old grandmother smacked her lips over the mush that Red Bean Vine had given her. "My grandson-in-law became crazy with grief for my granddaughter," she announced. "He won't marry again." Green Melons' daughter was too young for Weaver, and a flighty girl anyway.

"Maybe the thing *is* his wife? Could that be?" Red Bean Vine looked at all of them. They shifted uncomfortably. That would mean ghosts in the city, drifting transparently through the white walls, coming to rest in places they had known. Where there was one ghost there would be more. When something punched a hole in the wall between the worlds, matter flowed through it until it was patched.

"The men are going to talk to the spirits about it in the kiva," Flitter said. "Canyon Wren told me."

"And you are not to tell people what is going to happen in the kiva," Grandmother Owl Ears said. "That is for grown men." She scooped mush into her mouth with two fingers. "But now that you have started, you can say when they are going to do it."

"Canyon Wren said tonight," Flitter said. "He said they

had to do something fast because old Grandmother Woodrat dreamed her soup bones got up and talked to her." Actually he had heard his father talking to Canyon Wren while he just happened to be in the same room behind a water jar. He chuckled. "Grandmother Woodrat talks to rocks, anyway."

"And maybe they tell her something worth hearing," Grandmother Owl Ears said.

"Will they take my grandson-in-law into the kiva again?" Quail's grandmother asked. She looked crafty. If they did, she could chase the ghost thing out of her house while he was gone.

Almost a Dog and Bitter Water tried to take Weaver, but he picked up the ax handle again and shouted at them, so they let him alone. They could consult the spirits about him without his actually being there. It might be easier.

The priests of the Deer Lodge and the Sun House Lodge and the chiefs of the holy clowns gathered with Turquoise Old Man and Squash Old Man and all men who were related to Weaver in some way, through blood or ritual. Uncle Calabash came because although he was a woman, he was also a man.

The women had cleaned the Turquoise kiva until it sparkled, then gone away again up the ladder, leaving only the spiderweb that clung beneath the high part of the roof, in the shadows where the light never went, because when Grandmother Spider comes into a kiva it is wise to let her stay. The men went down the ladder then and sat in a circle underground, around the fire pit. Bitter Water's tame eagle sat on its perch in the stream of light that came from the roof, its yellow eyes glowing. The men beat their hands on a hollow log and sang their questions.

After a while the kiva grew darker inside, and the questions rose to the roof with the smoke of incense and the steam of water poured on hot stones. The smoke gathered itself into a dark cloud. They watched it, slowing the singing, and when they were wet with sweat they could see the web in the smoke, stretching itself through the kiva roof to the roof of the sky, with Grandmother in the center of it, eight dark, supple legs splayed on the corners of the world.

Their voices hushed to a murmur; the drumbeats slowed to the tap of fingertips. They swayed in the steam and the smoke while Bitter Water talked to the grandmother of the world, because Weaver belonged to her.

"Tell us how we may unknot this man from his ghost," Bitter Water said.

The thought ran through their minds—it wasn't their thought—that there were ghosts in the old-time, and stories of how they came back to their families and lived there. "That is one thing in stories," Bitter Water said. "It is different in the now-time, giving people bad dreams about bones."

"It may not be a ghost." The voice came to them like the thought, through ripples of space, flung back and forth along the cloth of the sky. Only Bitter Water understood its words.

"Then what is it?" he asked.

"That man has gone out of my care," Grandmother Spider said. She dangled from the spokes of her web above their heads. Everything that is woven or knotted or braided or twined, or people who do that work, belongs to Grandmother Spider, but she is not in charge of crazy people. They are Coyote's. She tried to tell the Red Earth men that, but human people are stubborn.

"Tell us how we may take away this ghost animal," Bitter Water said to her again.

Grandmother Spider swung her black and gold body slowly, back and forth across the world, leaving a white line like lightning behind her. "The animal is already being woven into the lives of human people. One of my webs lasts a long time, but not forever. There is always a new web. You live in the days when the new web is spinning."

"What will happen to us?" Bitter Water asked.

"For that you will have to ask Coyote," Spider said. "But he won't know. When he gets caught in a web, he thrashes it to pieces in getting loose, and then no one knows what will come, until the new one is built."

"What are we to do, Oldest?"

"What you want to," Spider said. "It doesn't matter."

* * *

The Red Earth people stood in the center of the dance ground in the morning sun. They formed a tight knot, like an unopened flower, out of which a few tendrils splayed from the men on the outer edges, who were restless with waiting.

Bitter Water sat at the center of the milling crowd with Flitter's father, Armadillo, and beat on a drum. The sound made the people vibrate like bees.

The children watched them from the windows and the rooftops, leaning over the white mud walls. Every so often the men shouted up at them to go inside, but they didn't move. Quail's grandmother stood on her roof, her face tight with satisfaction. In the courtyard below, the people began to shout, flinging one angry name after another at Weaver's door. The children shouted with their parents: "Weaver! Weaver! Go away!"

The sound roared through the courtyard, banging off the walls, clambering through Weaver's windows, growling and heavy. He saw it come in, feathered and beaked like a kachina no one had seen before, and he ran outside. Red Horse followed him through the open door. When the sound beat at her ears, she laid them back and bared her long teeth.

Weaver faced the people in the courtyard, squinting into the sun. He saw Calabash off to one side of them, not apart but not with them, shaking his head sadly. Green Melons and Grandmother Woodrat were at the front, fists clenched, their faces screwed up with anger.

"Go!" they shouted at him. "Go away!" Red Bean Vine had tears in her eyes, but she was shouting, too. They began to throw rocks. It didn't matter what they did—Grandmother Spider had said so—so they would do this. If Weaver was Grandmother's, then she would take care of him.

Swallow threw a rock that thudded into Weaver's shoulder. He staggered, looked around him at angry, empty faces. They closed in on Weaver and the horse, driving them toward the footbridge and the gap that opened between the houses of the Squash people and the Turquoise people, out into the bean fields.

A rock went over his head and bounced on the ground in

front of him. Another hit Red Horse in the rump, and she screamed and reared, lunging for the stream. Weaver grabbed the rope around her head and clung to it as she dragged him across, splashing muddy river water in his face, soaking his shirt and breechcloth. His feet slipped on the mossy rocks, and the stream rose to his armpits. He floundered, afraid to let go of Red Horse's rope, afraid of the rocks and the howling Red Earth people behind him.

He stumbled up the far bank and turned once to look back. Green Melons had a rock in her fist. She threw it, and it hit him in the chest, knocking his breath out in a sharp, exploding gasp. He tried to inhale and his lungs burned. More stones flew around him. Red Horse fought at the end of her rope, ears back, heavy head swinging from side to side like a snake's. Weaver pulled at the rope while the rocks showered down on them. She fought him, afraid of the rocks, pawing and rearing in a blind panic. Mud and grass flew out from under her hooves.

Weaver saw the wide, dark eyes, the foam flecking her muzzle. "What will we do?" he asked her, weeping.

She swung her rear, plunging between Weaver and the rocks. For an instant she stilled, trembling, and he heard her say, quite plainly, "Get on my back, Husband."

Weaver flung himself over her withers, clutching her mane, facedown, as she spun and galloped through the gap between the Red Earth houses. He swung his right leg over her back and buried his face in the wild red mane.

7

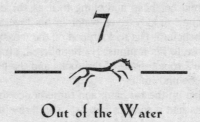

Out of the Water

WEAVER LET RED HORSE CARRY HIM ACROSS GRAND-mother's web, unafraid as only the mad can be. Wherever she stopped running, he slid from her back and ate the things she found for him: sweet green grass and white grubs that were living in a dead log. At night he talked to her beside the fire that he built. Sometimes she changed shape for him and wore her old body, shaking out her long black hair in the firelight. "I will stay with you," he told her, his stomach cramping from the green grass. "I will build us a house. Yes." He nodded to her while she flung her head up and stared out into the night.

Six-Legged and Wants the Moon camped along the river and looked out at the night, seeing more than Weaver saw and maybe less than Red Horse. They were of a people who never wandered, and despite his trader grandfather's trail foot, Six-Legged had lately begun to feel the world growing larger around him again. There was something new in the night wind that made Horse lift his head and snort, his moon feet moving restlessly. They had all felt it since the trader who had talked about the Spotted Cat people had run away.

"Maybe that man saw the monsters the other trading man talked about," Wants the Moon said. "Do you think these horses are theirs?"

"We don't even know if it is 'these' horses," Six-Legged said. "We have only seen one."

"Are you a monster's horse?" Wants the Moon asked the white shape dozing under a whispering cottonwood.

Horse had grown quiet, and now he didn't stir.

Six-Legged shifted apprehensively, watching the shadows. "I don't think we speak horse language," he said. If Horse had come from another world, that wouldn't be surprising. And if he had, what else might have ridden in on his back?

Turn it loose, a voice said.

Six-Legged snapped his head around. He could just see a gray shape, the glint of a yellow eye, in the shadows beyond the protective circle of the firelight.

"What?" He would make it prove it was there, if it was going to come and talk to him.

Coyote moved his nose and the tips of his paws into the firelight. "Turn it loose," he said again.

"You will eat it," Six-Legged said. Wants the Moon looked at him oddly. He didn't think she could see Coyote.

"Probably," Coyote admitted.

"But you brought it."

Coyote looked uncomfortable. "Some of my ideas are better than others."

Six-Legged started to ask him what he meant by that, but the gray snout and the paw tips vanished. Horse was still dozing, the firelight staining his milky coat pink, like a sunset on water. Six-Legged moved closer to Wants the Moon, snuggled up against her to shut out the night, nuzzling her ear until she let him under her blanket with her.

Coyote moved away into the trees, climbing the night air until he could look across the rolling grassland to the red sandstone cliffs in the west and the yellow desert and black volcanic lava flows to the south. Something burned on the horizon there like the lights the northern coast people saw in the sky. Jagged lines of red and yellow and bursts of shiny stuff like

bits of the sun and moon compressed into things. Coyote had
seen a drinking cup made of something shiny as mica. His
hairy ears pricked up with curiosity at the same time that he
wished he hadn't brought the human people the new animal
that had come out of the lights. Of course he had had to,
because that was how things were in the world; that was his
job, bringing new things. But the world was running beside
Horse now to something so different that it made even Coyote
afraid.

He looked into the sky and howled until Grandmother Spider came out along the spokes of her web, hanging from the
Great Bear, and asked him what the matter was.

"I want to put it back," Coyote said. "Can I put it back?"

"What good would that do?" Grandmother asked him. Her
great dark body swung across the sky, leaving a comet trail
of moonlit rope behind her.

"Much good," a deep, furred voice said from the plains.
"For us, much good." Coyote looked down and saw Buffalo
standing on a canyon rim to talk to them, his horns upcurved
like the moon. "The human people will hunt us on that horse.
They will eat us."

"They are supposed to. And it isn't that," Coyote said fretfully, even though he had just finished telling the human people to turn the horse loose and let *him* eat it. There was more.
He could see it being born in Grandmother Spider's web. The
part of Coyote that lived in the world looked up at her, whimpering.

"No web is forever," Grandmother said.

Coyote tucked his tail between his legs. The sky over him
looked deeper and blacker than before.

"Let him put the horse back where he got it," Buffalo said
to her. "Then the world will be as it should be."

"No," Coyote said. He shivered, but he could feel himself
putting on changes like a new coat. Coyote is killed all the
time, but he never dies. All the same, it is painful.

"Then what will happen now?" Buffalo asked, pawing the
ground. "Will you let this horse-thing hunt us?"

Grandmother Spider deftly wove a weft thread under the

warps. She could tell that Buffalo thought Horse was what was changing the world, because Buffalo can't see any farther into the future than human people can. Just now, of course, for Buffalo, that was true, so she said to him, "Horse will speak to you about that in the tall grass. And you will have things to say to Horse, also."

"I will not speak the horse-thing's talk," Buffalo said stubbornly.

"You both have hooves," Grandmother said. "And eat grass. Horse will hear you when you speak."

"We need to go to the buffalo hunters' camps," Wants the Moon said. She was bathing in the river with a ball of yucca soap. The morning sun caught her skin and polished it until it gleamed like wet stone. Six-Legged was watching her upturned breasts and not listening. "Did you hear me?" she demanded.

He smiled at her. "No."

She straightened up and faced him, hands on hips. "We can't stay here in the wild any longer. We have to take Horse to the buffalo hunters. He will talk to Buffalo there. I dreamed that. You are not the only one who has dreams."

"They will kill us as likely as not." Six-Legged watched the way drops of water in the dark hair between her legs caught the light.

"They don't kill traders." She tossed the soap onto the bank and bent again to wring out her long hair. "We will take them the things we got from that man who ran away."

"He had just *come* from the buffalo hunters," Six-Legged pointed out, forced to pay attention. "And *we* aren't traders. Then they will make slaves of us." He argued not entirely for argument's sake. This morning, with the sun on the river and on the buffalo grass, the world looked safe again. It was hot, and they and Horse had plenty to eat. Yesterday they had found three turtles in the river. It was only at night that whatever it was came out of the darkness and frightened him.

"Everything will happen as likely as not," Wants the Moon said scornfully. "They will be glad to see us as likely as not.

I had a grandmother who was captured from the buffalo hunters. I can still talk some of their talk. Maybe they will like that."

"And maybe they will be angry because we stole your grandmother," Six-Legged said.

"We will bring them back someone," Wants the Moon told him. "I am pregnant."

Six-Legged stared at her. Now that he looked, he could see that her belly was rounder, and her breasts had got bigger. He grinned, looking at them. "I wondered why they were growing."

"If you could see beyond the end of your cock"—Wants the Moon pointed at it where it stuck out from under his breechcloth—"you would have thought of it. I haven't bled in two moons. I am not going to have a baby in the wild like the Outsiders, or a wolf." She waded out of the water and wrapped her skirt around her, tying the sash around her waist, covering the curve of her belly. A hot wind rippled the grass, hotter even than at home, and neither of them had worn much clothing, but now Six-Legged thought she wanted to cover the baby. He wasn't sure why.

"There will be women with the buffalo hunters."

"Oh." Six-Legged supposed that was important. He thought of the baby being born with no one there but him, and a little pulse of fear fluttered in his throat. It was easier to put a baby inside than to take it out. He imagined it nestling there, no bigger than his thumb. When it had to come out, it would be bigger.

Wants the Moon didn't seem to be paying attention anymore to what he was thinking. She was stuffing their belongings in the packs, methodically, balancing them for weight, talking to Horse while she did so. "You will run down the buffalo for them, and they will be glad to have us live with them. When the buffalo hunters see you, they will help us find your woman, and then there will be two of you, and then more."

More horses, more people. Small people born of himself and Wants the Moon. Six-Legged began to feel proud of him-

self, and important. He loaded the packs on Horse and told
Wants the Moon to ride.

"Where?" she said.

Six-Legged turned in a slow circle. The plains stretched
limitlessly to the horizon, north, south, and east, rippling with
grass like the Endless Water. The buffalo hunters lived on the
edge of a sea of grass and fished in it for the buffalo. He and
Wants the Moon could follow the marks of the trade trail that
went along the river, Six-Legged thought, and see where that
brought them. He had heard that the buffalo hunters had a
midsummer camp where they took hides to trade for baskets
and shells and turquoise. It would be easy enough to see where
that had been, if they found it, and to wait there.

"The trade trail," he said.

That was easy enough at first, but when the traders' path
left the river, it sank into the buffalo grass without a ripple.
There were landmarks, things to look for like mountain peaks
and river bluffs and hills with cairns of stones, but Wants the
Moon and Six-Legged didn't know them. No voice from his
trader grandfather or the man whose goods they had put in
their packs came to whisper in his ear. No words sang in her
head from her buffalo hunter grandmother, stolen from these
plains. The grass flowed away like a soft cat skin stretched
over the land. Wants the Moon thought she could hear its
blood running just under the surface, the faint tremor of a
heartbeat below ground.

Wants the Moon knew now why her people didn't travel.
If they went east, they would come to this sea of grass and
stand transfixed with fear, afraid it would swallow them up.
A burning wind blew across it by day, and at night their teeth
chattered with the cold. One morning they came to the top of
a bluff and saw, spread out like the shadow of a moving cloud,
a herd of buffalo. Their dark shapes flowed across the yellow-
green grass by the thousands, a moving carpet of animals,
shaggy heads and moon-curved horns, humpbacked and mysterious. Six-Legged and Wants the Moon huddled at the bluff
top and watched them, afraid to put their small selves in the
path of those unnumbered hooves.

Wants the Moon thought it must have been the tremor of the buffalo that she had heard in the ground. She pressed her hands flat against her belly. At night she tried to hear the baby instead, listening with her head cocked toward it, hoping it would tell her where to go. Six-Legged looked at her oddly. But the only sound she heard was hunting coyotes warbling in the low hills that humped like buffalo backs from the ground to the north. The plains looked flat only from a distance. In the midst of them, they threw up rolling hills and bluffs, and unexpected rivers flowing at the bottoms of chasms cut through the earth. More than once, following Horse's nose for water, Wants the Moon and Six-Legged stopped as the ground dropped suddenly away beneath them, sheer cliffs slicing down to the hidden river below.

"This isn't a trail!" Wants the Moon said, nearly crying, when they came to a bluff that had been invisible no more than ten paces from its edge. "And it's where we turned back this morning."

"No, it's not," Six-Legged said.

"It is." She leaned her forehead against Horse's mane, pounding her thigh with her fist.

Six-Legged scouted along the edge of the bluff like a dog, sniffing the air. A jumping mouse skittered out from under his feet and disappeared in curving bounces down the side of the cliff. A small shower of pebbles followed it. Six-Legged lay down on his stomach and peered over the edge. Something used the trail the mouse had followed, but the something was small. He saw old buffalo droppings on the ground. Why would buffalo come here if they couldn't get down to water? He peered over the edge again, looking for the white scatter of bones—sometimes the buffalo hunters drove a herd off a cliff and butchered the dead and dying at the bottom. But he could see only the green canopy of trees along the water's edge, bordering the swift flow of the river. On the other side the bank rose in a series of shallow ridges studded with wind-bent scrub and stones. He decided that the buffalo must come here to drink, and thus there must be a way down from this side.

Six-Legged stood up and waved his arm to Wants the Moon to follow him. She shook her head stubbornly. He trotted away from her anyway, picking his way along the bluff's edge while she sat with arms folded. The grass was chewed with the marks of many hooves. Six-Legged nearly fell when the ground sloped suddenly away, in steep curves cut with the marks of hooves. He stuck his fingers in his mouth and whistled, turning back again. "It's a buffalo trail!" He saw her scrub her hand across her eyes and kick Horse forward, following him.

The trail was steep, pushing them forward, ready to tumble them end over end. *Go down!* it said with its plunging slope. Six-Legged thought of the otter slide. Then he thought of thousands of buffalo flowing down the canyon side. He got behind Horse. If Horse fell, it wouldn't do much good to be in front of him. Horse jolted down the trail with Wants the Moon swaying on his back, fingers wrapped in his mane, and the travois bumping behind him.

Near the bottom the angle grew less steep and the trail widened, the ground churned by thousands of hooves. Horse sniffed the air suspiciously, but whatever else he could smell, the water lured him on. Wants the Moon's mouth ached for it. There was only a little puddle left in the waterskins, warm and slimy and stale. Her hair hung lankly down her back, her hairpins long lost. To keep it off her neck, she had tied it in a knot and wrapped a thong around it, but it slowly slid loose and stuck to her neck and back. Her skin was gritty, dry with the hot wind. She wanted to plunge her whole self in the river and soak the water through her skin.

Horse lumbered down the last slope, through the stand of green scrub that bloomed along the river's edge. Wants the Moon yelped as nettles brushed her thighs, and Six-Legged pulled his blanket around him. They blundered on through the nettles and a stand of cactus. Horse picked his way through the stones of the riverbank. The current was cold and a damp spray hung above the river channel like mist. Wants the Moon took deep breaths of it. At the water's edge she slid off Horse's back and knelt by the shallows, balancing herself on the rocks.

She plunged her hands into the water, splashing it on her face, sucking it down her dry throat. Horse stuck his muzzle in the water beside her.

Six-Legged drank his fill and stopped himself before the cold water gave him stomach cramps. He tugged Horse's head out of the river. Wants the Moon was standing in the current now, water flowing past her hips, her long black hair plastered to her wet back. Six-Legged shaded his eyes with his hand and squinted into the afternoon sun. Somehow they had turned around and were facing west, but he thought the river bent and unbent and if they wanted to go east they would have to cross it anyway. It was like a shaman's charm, a knot that had to be untied to make another binding.

"How deep is it?" he called to her.

"You can see," she said. "I don't know, in the middle."

"I think the buffalo cross. You can see where the trail comes out on the other side."

"It's not moving very fast." Wants the Moon tested her weight against the current. "I think we could swim it."

"What about the packs?"

"Tie them to Horse."

"Can Horse swim?"

They considered him. Horse lifted his head and pricked his ears at something across the river. No one had ever asked him to swim. He swished his tail at the flies that settled on his rump.

"Anything can swim," Six-Legged decided. "If the buffalo cross here, it's either shallow enough or they swim." He untied the packs from the travois, tied them all on Horse's back, and led Horse into the water.

Mossy stones in the riverbed shifted underfoot. Horse slithered on them, and Six-Legged kept a tight grip on his lead. They waded farther into the current, feeling the cold flow around their legs. The water was icy, like falling from summer into snow. Wants the Moon ducked her head under again and flung it back, her long wet hair spraying them with droplets. The water was up to her waist now, but the bottom was sandy and the walking easier. They bent upstream against the current, taking careful steps. The empty travois drifted downstream, its traces tugging gently.

The river bottom vanished. Wants the Moon floundered, thrashing her feet, finding nothing. She sank under the current and surfaced, sputtering. Six-Legged had grabbed hold of Horse's withers. Horse stood with his head above the water, snorting, his legs braced. Six-Legged held out his other hand to Wants the Moon, and she stretched her fingertips toward him, the current pulling at her, tugging her downstream.

Six-Legged lunged for her hand and caught her by the thumb. He pulled her toward him, and she kicked her feet in the water, trying to swim.

"Hoo! It's deep here!" He pulled her closer until she could get a grip on Horse's mane.

Wants the Moon spit out water. Horse stretched his head and neck above the current. She couldn't find the bottom with her feet. The packs were all under water. Horse began to toss his head, scrabbling for footing. The current caught the travois and the packs and lifted him off his feet.

"Go," Six-Legged said, prodding Horse in the ribs. They clung to him as he headed into the channel. The water dragged at the travois, and Six-Legged cut the traces. They tumbled downstream on the current.

Horse paddled his legs, fighting the current, with Six-Legged and Wants the Moon clinging to his neck. They were chilled through now, and Wants the Moon could feel her fingers going numb. The river roared in her ears. She kicked her feet, trying to help Horse fight the river's flow as it pulled them downstream. If they went too far, they would get caught in a canyon where the river had cut deep into soft rock and straight sides rose from the water's edge, with no strip of shore to climb out upon. She was sure they had seen it downstream and had peered despairingly over the sheer cliffs. If it wasn't another river. The sky was burning around the sun, turquoise flowing into flame, and it made her eyes water. The river shore rushed past them on the other side, too far away to reach. The packs, soaked through, dragged them down, reaching for the river bottom.

There were people on the shore. Wants the Moon saw them
suddenly, going along the far bank, a hunting party with spears
and bows. As the river swept them nearer, one of the men
turned. He shouted, and they all spun around and goggled at
her, eyes and mouths round as eggs. She floundered in the icy
water, kicking. Six-Legged was gasping and spitting water.
Wants the Moon pulled her belt knife loose and sawed at the
packs with it while the water ran up her nose and wrapped its
arms around her legs.

Six-Legged had his knife out, too, but he hesitated. "We'll
never find them again!" he gasped.

"Cut them!" Wants the Moon said, teeth gritted, and he
cut at the ropes of the other pack.

The waterlogged rope was hard to cut, and the obsidian
blade was stubborn underwater. It turned from the rope and
cut Wants the Moon across the knuckles. She hacked furiously
at the fibers. On the bank she could see the hunting party
running just ahead of them, shouting words she couldn't hear
above the river. Six-Legged's pack slid free, and then hers
was almost loose, tumbling in the water beside her, caught by
a thread of rope. It banged into her shoulders, bumping and
shoving her under, and she grabbed the rope and cut it
through. A smaller pack still trailed from Horse's pack harness—she cut that loose, too, not trying to save anything now,
giving it to the river before the river ate them. The river was
going to eat something. They grabbed Horse's mane and spit
out water as he paddled for the shore, bobbing in the current
now like a monstrous duck.

Long Arrow of the Buffalo Horn people stood on the shore,
breathing hard, staring at the apparition in the water. Huge and
three-headed, it floated on the current, its center head a white
oblong pitted with dark eyes and nostrils like a buffalo skull.
The smaller heads on either side might belong to human spirits—or to otter heads, or carp from the river. There was no
saying. Long Arrow stopped and held a hand up to his hunters.
They had not been able to outrun the thing, and it behooved
a brave man to stop and meet it face to face. It was rising
from the shallows now, a bony white beast with a wild fall of

hair along its head and neck. Long Arrow said a quick prayer
to Badger, who was his guardian spirit, and made a gesture of
respect to the thing in the water.

It lunged from the shallows, blowing down its nose and
shaking itself like a dog, loosing a spray of water. Long Arrow
saw now that it had only one head, although that one was
dreadful enough. The other heads belonged to something that
had taken human form, a man and a woman. Long Arrow
squinted to see if he could see water people or river otters
under their skin, but he couldn't. The sunlight glinted on their
wet bodies and on the white thing and the river behind them
and dazzled him. He made another gesture of respect to them
and waited to see what would happen. His men were cowering
behind him. Out of the corner of his eye he saw Bull Calf
trying to tiptoe backward.

"Come back!" Long Arrow snapped without taking his
eyes off the white river thing.

Bull Calf stopped in his tracks and edged reluctantly back
into the group of hunters.

The water spirits stopped at the edge of the shallows, dripping, looking at Long Arrow while he looked at them. The
woman spirit stepped forward, and the white creature followed
her.

"This is Horse."

Long Arrow put his hand behind his ear to tell her to say
it again. She might be speaking his language, but the words
were funny.

"This is Horse," she said again. "The river brings him to
you." He thought that was what she said.

Long Arrow thought some more. Water spirits were ancient,
very old in their magic. They brought men powerful things,
and sometimes visions of the future. You should take what
they brought. He stared at the human people. This time, for a
flashing moment, he thought he saw wet otter skin under the
russet skin of the man. The woman's skin didn't change.

"Come," he said to them.

The woman said something to the man, and they followed
him, leading the white thing.

8

What Hears You When You Shout

'THIS IS A MISTAKE,' SIX-LEGGED SAID.

There were buffalo hunter people ahead of them and behind them, closing them in. The nearest ones kept looking over their shoulders at Horse and making signs with their fingers. A black hunting dog started to bark at Horse, hair standing up in a ruff on its back, until one of the men shouted at it and smacked it.

"They think we're enemy people," Six-Legged said.

Wants the Moon shook her head. "I told him we swam the river to show them Horse. They're taking us to their headman so he can welcome us."

"He's as likely to tell them to kill us," Six-Legged said pessimistically. "How do you know what they're doing?"

"I understand their talk. I told you that." The men behind her broke into an argumentative conversation. "Well, some of it," she said.

"I lost my bow in the river," Six-Legged informed her.

"They would have taken it away from you anyway, I expect."

Six-Legged didn't say anything else. They had to go somewhere, so he supposed it might as well be here. He eyed the buffalo hunters curiously as they walked. They were all men, and they wore their hair long down their backs, tied with thongs into two bundles. Their only clothes were a skin apron, front and back, that hung from a thong around the waist, and skin shoes, made all in one piece, without a sole. Fascinatingly, some were tattooed, the kind of thing you might expect from wild people who lived in tents. Six-Legged had never seen any up close. Bands of dark dots and swirls of unknown significance decorated their chests, forearms, and faces.

"Why do they mark themselves like that?" he whispered to Wants the Moon.

"I don't know," she whispered back. "Grandmother from the buffalo hunters had marks like that on her forehead."

They went up a trail that wound away from the river and across a ridge of scrub trees and more nettles. Someone had cut back the nettles, and Six-Legged thought they must use this trail often, maybe to wait for whatever animals came to drink at the river. The wind had let up and whispered gently now in the dry buffalo grass. The grass crunched under his feet—he had lost his shoes in the river—and now and then a grasshopper whirred away from his bare toes. His heart hammered under his skin, but there was nothing to do but keep walking.

On the other side of the ridge the land was stony, like old bones poking through the earth, and they wound their way down among them to a flat, endless plain that went to the horizon, with a line of trees cut across it. From above, the trees were a swift curve as if someone had painted them there with a brushstroke. Descending, he could see the outlines of skin tents among the trunks, and his nose twitched at a drift of woodsmoke. The dog pricked up its ears and ran ahead of the rest toward the camp.

"We will take you to Hole in the Sunset," Long Arrow announced, turning to talk to them over his shoulder. Wants the Moon thought that was what he said.

The buffalo hunters hurried the Red Earth people and their horse across the grass, which was marked now with the tracks

of many people and dogs. Children and women and men came
out of the trees to gawk at them, and in a moment a man with
a buffalo-hide blanket over his skin apron pushed his way
through them. He was broad in the shoulders and long-legged,
with wild spirals tattooed in blue-black on both cheeks. Eagle
feathers were tied into the leather thongs that bound his hair,
so he was most certainly a person of importance—Hole in the
Sunset, Six-Legged supposed, assuming that Wants the Moon
actually understood one word in three of these people's talk.
It sounded like magpies to him.

The rest of the camp clustered around Hole in the Sunset
while the leader of the hunting party explained things to him.
He was clearly the headman. Six-Legged let his eyes stray to
the others.

The small children were mostly naked, as children among
the Red Earth people were, but the women wore skin dresses
that reached from their necks to above their ankles. Some of
them were tattooed, too, on the parts that showed. Their hair
was braided or hung loose like the men's. They all stared at
Horse openmouthed, and then at Wants the Moon's cloth skirt
and blanket and painted sash, and at Six-Legged's breechcloth.

"The river spirits came out of the water where the buffalo
trail is," Long Arrow was telling Hole in the Sunset. "The
woman spirit told me they have brought us this creature. I
don't know what it is."

Hole in the Sunset studied Horse, and then Long Arrow.
Long Arrow had done a brave thing to bring the creature back
to camp, so it would not be becoming for the chieftain to gawk
like a fool. Accordingly, Hole in the Sunset kept his mouth
closed while he thought, but he found it hard to take his eyes
off the white monster. Any animal that came up from the river
was a gift of the spirit world. And a white one was doubly
magical, whatever it was. Also, whatever it was, Hole in the
Sunset didn't know of any other chieftain of the buffalo people
who had one, so no doubt the spirits had marked him as a
man who was favored.

Hole in the Sunset felt pleased with that, but not surprised.
Weasel, who had come to him on his vision walk, had told

him that he would have a magical life. Now it appeared to be beginning. Hole in the Sunset put his hand on Horse's white hide, marveling at the sleekness of it, the rose tint of the inner nostrils, the delicate, leaf-shaped ears. He beamed at Six-Legged and Wants the Moon. "I thank the spirits of the river for this most wonderful gift," he told them, more than satisfied.

"He's thanking us for it," Wants the Moon whispered to Six-Legged.

"We aren't giving it to him!"

"He thinks we are."

"Well, we aren't!" Six-Legged said. "Tell him so!"

Hole in the Sunset clapped a hand on Six-Legged's shoulder. Six-Legged jumped.

"Of course there is nothing that this poor person owns that could please so great a spirit, who comes from the depths of the river," Hole in the Sunset said in the voice that signified excessive respect and politeness. "But nonetheless the Buffalo Horn people wish to honor you for your gift."

"He's going to give us a present," Wants the Moon hissed as Six-Legged looked at her frantically for translation.

"This poor man has a daughter," Hole in the Sunset said, "White Buffalo." Looking proud and crafty, he beckoned her from the crowd. "And a niece," he added as an afterthought— one could, perhaps, take two birds with one arrow—"whose name is Wind in the Grass." The girls stood side by side, smiling. They were young, with long legs like does and great waterfalls of black hair. They stared at Six-Legged curiously.

The Buffalo Horn people nodded approvingly to one another. It was a crafty move to marry the chieftain's daughter to the river spirit. That would bring the band good fortune. And to add Wind in the Grass—well, that was generous, as befitted a chief. The chieftain's sister Lark, mother of Wind in the Grass, had made an unfortunate marriage to a lazy man. Nonetheless the chieftain was fond of his sister. She was a woman with broad, flat feet and a round, dispirited face, as if life had squashed her, and she smiled mistily at Hole in the Sunset and straightened her daughter's hair.

"He's giving them to you!" Wants the Moon said, outraged.

"Really?" Six-Legged looked at the girls with growing interest.

The Buffalo Horn people nodded their heads again, gratified. The river spirit accepted the gift. That was good. Only Angry in the Morning scowled and folded his arms, but that was understandable. He was supposed to have married White Buffalo himself.

Angry in the Morning's mother put her hand on her son's arm. "Behave yourself," she whispered. She thought White Buffalo too pleased with herself. How did you teach a daughter-in-law to wait on you properly when she was the chief's child? "It is her fate now to be wife to the river spirit," she said with secret pleasure.

"The river spirit already has a wife!" Wants the Moon said. She thumped her chest. "I am the wife of the river spirit!"

"That is fine," Hole in the Sunset said. "Now you will have two other wives for company, and to do your work. And the river spirit will have two young human wives to please him as well as his old spirit wife. That will be well."

Wants the Moon bit her lip and glared at Six-Legged. He grabbed her by the wrist. "Don't start anything!" he hissed at her.

"Tell him you don't want those women!"

"I don't speak his language," Six-Legged said. "Anyway, they're a gift." You didn't turn down a gift; that was insulting, insulting enough to start wars. It had happened before.

"Then I will!"

Six-Legged tightened his grip on her arm. "Tell him I am grateful." He squeezed his fingers tighter until she nodded.

"We are grateful for your fine gift," Wants the Moon said balefully.

Hole in the Sunset beamed as his daughter took the river spirit away with her to the new tent he had given them. Wind in the Grass trailed behind, carrying her clothes and cooking baskets. The old wife stood to one side, arms folded, but she would come around, Hole in the Sunset thought. She was going to have a baby—that made women cross, but she would be glad of two more wives when the child came. All was as it should be. He turned to look at Horse again. It was tethered to a stake, cropping grass as if it had always lived among the Buffalo Horn people. One could ride on its back, Long Arrow said. Tomorrow the river spirits would show him how to do that.

"You are not eating with your husband and his new wives." Angry in the Morning bent over Wants the Moon's shoulder, as she stood, arms crossed and cursing, on the edge of the feast firelight. Inside its red circle, beside the chieftain, Six-Legged sat with an arm around each girl, squeezing their breasts and eating baked turnips and quail. Wants the Moon spat on the ground.

"It is not right that the woman of the river should be neglected thus," Angry in the Morning said slyly.

Wants the Moon narrowed her eyes. "It is not right that the man of the Buffalo Horn people should begrudge his woman to a powerful spirit who has given his band a great gift."

Angry in the Morning made a gesture of respect and backed away. Wants the Moon watched him go, her eyes slitted. White Buffalo's laughter bubbled like water from her place at the fireside. Wants the Moon stalked toward the tent that Hole in the Sunset had given her, kicking stones out of her path.

It was a fine tent of softest buffalo hide, painted with running buffalo, their horns curved like bows, and a bright sun spreading its rays through the sky. It seemed a wild, strange place to live, unlike a house, but it was very fine. A lucky place. Any man would like a tent like that, even with an *old* wife, and it would serve Six-Legged right if he came to see her in it and found it occupied.

She watched Angry in the Morning skulking around the edges of the firelight, too. She didn't trust him, though. He had yellowy eyes like a rattlesnake. If he thought she was going to do Six-Legged a bad turn to suit him, he was mistaken. Wants the Moon sat down in her new tent to think.

*   *   *

Six-Legged squeezed his fingers around White Buffalo's round, melon-shaped breast, wiggling it through her soft cowhide dress, and she giggled. She had small spirals tattooed on each cheek, barbarous and seductive. He wanted to see where else she was marked with that alluring ornamentation. Wind in the Grass, on his other side, didn't have any tattoos, but he put his arm around her, too, so she wouldn't feel left out. The man called Long Arrow was singing some kind of song and gesturing at Horse, glowing whitely under the trees. Someone had given Six-Legged a tart drink of mashed berries that made his head buzz, and he beat time with three fingers on Wind in the Grass's shoulder blade. He wondered apprehensively where Wants the Moon had gone but decided it might be better to let her temper cool by itself. And it was hard to think with a girl in each arm, when one of them—he peered down, trying to decide who—was slipping her hand under his breechcloth. The hand was withdrawn, and Wind in the Grass and White Buffalo put their heads together across his chest, whispering. They smiled winningly at him, pointed at Long Arrow, said something he didn't understand, and dissolved into giggles when he looked from one to the other. (Wants the Moon could have told him that Long Arrow was also named for what was in a different quiver altogether, and that Six-Legged was being compared to him. But Wants the Moon was in her tent thinking.)

Six-Legged stood up unsteadily, and the girls each took one arm and guided him toward their new tent. The moon filtered like fine sand through the trees, and in the distance, across the grass, he could see it shining on the stalks that rippled in the night wind. It had got into his blood, he thought, and made it hum like a bee. It had got into his cock, which stood out nearly straight in front of him, following his new wives down the path to their tent.

In the morning, Wants the Moon was sitting cross-legged in front of her own tent when Six-Legged got up before dawn to piss. He peered at her in the dusky light, wondering if she was going to start cursing him, but she only smiled placidly, nod-

ding her head to show that she saw he was there. No one else
was awake yet after the feasting, but Wants the Moon's hair
was combed and coiled into neat knots at the sides of her head,
and she had stuck sprigs of yellow flowers in it.

"You're awake early," he said, yawning. He was careful
not to get too close.

"It's a fine morning." She smiled at him again, enigmatically.

Six-Legged eyed her suspiciously. She didn't say anything
else, and he went on down the path to the place where the
men went, itching in the middle of his back. When he came
back, she had gone inside her tent. He stumbled into his own,
sleepily scratching, and burrowed between the warm bodies of
his wives. Something was wrong, he thought, but it fluttered
in the peripheral vision of his mind, just out of sight. He burrowed deeper under the buffalo robes, and as his blood began
to wake up, it slipped entirely out of reach.

Hole in the Sunset stood in front of his tent and stretched.
A fine morning. The sun was a fat pink glow on the horizon,
and his wife was coming up the path from the stream with a
water basket on her head. (The Buffalo Horn people were travelers. Clay pots were for people who stayed still.) Her name
was Porcupine, she was a round woman with a broad bottom
and nearly all her teeth, and she was a good wife. He smiled
at her affectionately.

Porcupine pursed her mouth in a worried knot as she waddled up the path. "That new thing is gone," she said.

"My new horse?" Hole in the Sunset started down the path
at a brisk walk—it was beneath his dignity to run—and in a
few strides he could see that she was right. There was no white
hide glowing in the pearly dawn light. Hole in the Sunset
roared a question there was no mistaking, and the Buffalo
Horn people tumbled out of their tents.

Six-Legged sat up, his heart hammering, and pushed Wind
in the Grass aside.

White Buffalo had already stuck her head out the tent flap.
"Father says his horse is gone," she said.

Six-Legged caught the word *horse* and stumbled out of the

tent, tying his breechcloth and looking for where Horse should be. He swore. Horse had a way of slipping his tether if it wasn't properly knotted, but Six-Legged had been careful. Now he would have to send for Wants the Moon because Horse would come when she called him, and he wouldn't for Six-Legged.

Six-Legged looked around at the Buffalo Horn people, and at Hole in the Sunset, who was shouting and waving his arms. He couldn't think of a way to talk to them, so he stalked to Wants the Moon's tent and pulled the flap open without asking, which was rude, but she wasn't there. He swore again, vicious words in his own language about other people's excrement.

Hole in the Sunset had stopped shouting. Six-Legged turned around and saw Wants the Moon sauntering down the path they had followed yesterday to the camp. Horse walked behind her, swishing his white tail and snuffling at her hair with his bony white nose.

She stopped in front of Hole in the Sunset long enough to let him observe that Horse wore no tether.

"Where did you go with my horse?" Hole in the Sunset demanded.

"I went to get him for you," Wants the Moon said carefully. The more she talked with these people the more they sounded like her grandmother, and the talking became easier. "You can see that he follows me." She paused and cocked her head toward Horse's, as if listening. "But he is angry."

"Angry?" Hole in the Sunset looked perplexed.

"Who am I?" Wants the Moon demanded of him. Six-Legged watched her suspiciously, trying to understand.

"You are the river spirit's wife," Hole in the Sunset said.

Wants the Moon folded her arms across her chest. "I am also from the depths of the river. And you have not done *me* any honor."

"I have given you a new tent!"

"You have not given me what you have given the man. That is why the river animal is angry, because you have insulted *me*. If your people do not treat me with respect and give me what they give the man, it will go away again."

Hole in the Sunset peered at her. "You want wives?" There *were* warrior women who took wives of their own, but they generally didn't have husbands, too. It might be possible, but he thought he ought to talk to the shaman. Elk Walker had gone to the mountains at the start of the new moon to talk with Elk and cut curing plants with his apprentices, and he hadn't come back yet. People like warrior women and soft men were the shaman's business because they crossed into two worlds.

Wants the Moon looked exasperated. "No. I want new husbands. You gave my man two beautiful young wives. I want two beautiful husbands."

The Buffalo Horn people gawped at her. The two young wives giggled, and Six-Legged wondered what was happening. Porcupine Mother glared at the girls, who clapped their hands over their mouths.

Wants the Moon stamped her foot. "I want two young men."

"You already have a husband," Hole in the Sunset said.

"Women don't have two husbands, much less three," Bull Calf said.

"Two more would make three. It is not permitted," Hole in the Sunset told her.

"I am not a woman. I am a river spirit, like the man." She pointed at Six-Legged, who didn't know what to do. "I will go away because you have insulted me, and the horse will follow me." She turned as if she was going to do that, and Horse whickered and started after her, nuzzling at the flowers in her hair.

Hole in the Sunset coughed.

Wants the Moon looked over her shoulder.

"It is true the river spirit woman is not a human woman," he said, making a concession. The rules might not apply. Certainly spirits were known to have even heartier appetites than humans. He looked at his young men doubtfully. Several of them had begun to preen, brushing their long black hair with their fingers, striking a pose to flex their muscles.

"We might wait until Elk Walker comes back from the mountains," Hole in the Sunset suggested. "He will know how these things are done maybe."

"If you think the shaman's magic is more powerful than mine, maybe he will find you another horse," Wants the Moon said angrily.

Porcupine Mother laid a hand on Hole in the Sunset's arm. "It is true there are beautiful young men among our people," she murmured, looking at the ones who were brushing their hair.

Hole in the Sunset saw how it was. How true, he thought, and how wise was Porcupine. Sometimes these dilemmas presented opportunities. There was, for instance, Sunflower, whom all the young girls were fighting over. And Blue Racer, who was too pleased with his reflection in the water. Just the young men to marry a river spirit.

"It is true, Most Astute," he said to his wife. "And do you think that I should give this spirit the young men she asks me for?"

"Well, a woman would think so," Bull Calf muttered. "Women don't have any morals."

Porcupine sniffed. No wonder no one wanted to marry Bull Calf. Even Blue Racer, who was so vain, knew better than to insult women. "I think it is an excellent idea that you have thought of, Husband," she said to Hole in the Sunset.

Another wedding required another feast. That went without saying. Six-Legged's wives bustled about cooking turnips and camas bulbs and a mush of the maize for which the buffalo hunters traded skins to the people in the cities to the west. Dried buffalo meat was soaked and cooked, and a hunting party went out after rabbits, inviting Six-Legged along with gestures and smiles. He went, perplexed, unsure what was going on. When they came back to the camp, the young men were laughing and pushing Blue Racer and Sunflower, making crude jokes that were easily understood from the gestures that accompanied them. Long Arrow said something, pulled his cock out, and waved it at them, and they fell on the ground laughing. Six-Legged saw Wants the Moon sitting outside her tent, in a fine new dress of white buffalo cow skin sewn all over with porcupine quills and shell beads, with her hair freshly washed and his wives braiding it into the style the Buffalo Horn women wore.

"What have you done?" he demanded.

"Why do you want to know?" she asked airily.

Wind in the Grass giggled and pointed from Six-Legged to herself and White Buffalo. Then she pointed at Sunflower and Blue Racer and Wants the Moon.

Six-Legged's jaw dropped open.

Wants the Moon looked at him, satisfied. She patted her new braids, stood up, and went inside her tent.

"It isn't decent!" Six-Legged shouted after her. "That's my baby!"

Elk Walker, the shaman, came back from the mountains in time for the feast. He blinked when he saw Horse and scooted inside Hole in the Sunset's tent to talk. He was an old, thin man, with hair gone completely gray and cut in wispy tufts so that it stuck out from his head like grass. His apprentices walked around Horse in a circle, staring, touching his white hide with the tips of their fingers. When Elk Walker emerged, he went straight to Horse and laid the flat of his hand on Horse's flank. He crouched, put his ear to Horse's chest, and listened. Then he stood up and looked at the sky. Hole in the Sunset followed him out of the tent, and Elk Walker nodded at him.

"You are right," Elk Walker said solemnly. "This is a new story being told among our people. We are the time of legend. Us. Now. People will remember us."

Hole in the Sunset nodded, satisfied. That was what mattered, that you were remembered.

Elk Walker turned to look at Wants the Moon, standing with her two husbands in her finery, and Six-Legged, stomping back and forth outside his tent, grumbling. "You will want to be careful of those two," he murmured. "They are dangerous. Spirits always are."

"They came with the horse," Hole in the Sunset said.

*　　　*　　　*

Wants the Moon liked the way her white buffalo hide dress fell in soft folds over her knees. The baby hardly showed yet. That was good. Maybe one of these boys would put another one on top of it. That would serve Six-Legged right. Blue Racer and Sunflower sat one on either side of her, feeding her bits of rabbit meat and scoops of maize mush with their fingers. Their faces glowed in the firelight, casting their bones into high relief. She wondered what would happen now. She felt like the otters, launching herself from the top of a precipitous slide, hurtling toward the water. The fire made her face hot. The old shaman had sprinkled her hair with maize meal, and her young husbands had made up their beds in her new tent.

Wants the Moon stood up. "Stay," she said to the young husbands, the way she might to dogs. Then she walked unsteadily into the woods to piss. When she came back, they were waiting for her.

"We are honored," they said to her.

"Our children will be very powerful," they said to her.

"This one also," they said, stroking her belly.

"It is a lucky thing to have such a wife," Sunflower told Blue Racer. "People will remember us even when the world has changed. We will be the Young Men Who Married a Spirit."

Six-Legged's wives tugged at his arms as he stood glaring after Wants the Moon. "Come to bed, Husband." They pulled at him, chirping inducements in words he didn't understand. It was like living with a flock of birds. The wives were like wrens. The shaman who had come down out of the mountains squawked like a crow. Hole in the Sunset's laugh was the faint *hoo-hoo* of a burrowing owl in the distance. No one spoke things Six-Legged could understand but Wants the Moon, and she was in her new tent legs-in-the-air with *two* men. Six-Legged balled his hands into fists. The night wind blew in his ear and told him how he was hard done by.

*　　　*　　　*

Wants the Moon woke in the morning with her young husbands snoring on either side of her, their thick black hair splayed out like river water on the buffalo hides. Their skin was bare of the tattooing that marked the older men, and they smelled of woodsmoke, the yucca soap they had washed with, and the sage leaves that were interwoven with the bedding underneath the buffalo robes. Wants the Moon prodded Blue Racer with her foot.

"Get up. It is morning."

He yawned and smiled at her, wriggling his torso up out of the tangled furs. Sunflower sat up, too, and squinted against the sun that slitted past the edge of the tent flap. The light inside the tent was gray-gold and thick with the sun and the heavy movement of the wind outside. The edges of the tent rattled with the wind.

Sunflower sniffed the air. "The buffalo will be moving." He shoved Blue Racer playfully. "Tomorrow I will bring back a new buffalo skin for our wife."

"You caught it in your dreams," Blue Racer said, "galumphing all over the bed and snorting. I heard you. In the daylight, *I* will kill the buffalo. You can help."

They grinned at each other. Today, now that Elk Walker had come home, was the day the men would break camp to follow the buffalo. In a few days the women would follow, too, and butcher the kill after the hunters had driven the great humpbacked beasts over the buffalo leap. Hole in the Sunset and Long Arrow had been watching the buffalo all moon as the herds wandered slowly toward the high bluffs where they could be stampeded.

Sunflower and Blue Racer stretched their arms and legs. This was what a man lived for—to race Buffalo with the wind in his hair, dance just in front of Buffalo, teasing him on, dancing past the horns, until Buffalo hurtled into blank air, surprised and pawing the wind, and the hunters stopped at the edge, stopped just in time. It was not an easy thing to do. Sometimes the hunter went with Buffalo, spinning down to rocks, impaled on Buffalo's curved horns. That was what made it worth doing, worth dancing the hunt out around the

fire afterward. A man who made first kill or otherwise distin-
guished himself could tattoo his triumph on his chest and face
and earn the privilege for his wife and daughters, too.

Sunflower tied his skin apron around his waist and began
daubing the hunting paint on his chest, dipping his fingers into
a buffalo horn of white clay. Blue Racer watched him lazily.
He could dress and paint himself in half the time it took Sunflower, who was a perfectionist and did everything twice. He
reached for Wants the Moon instead, but she smacked his hand
away and stood up, pulling her new buffalo-hide dress over
her head. Blue Racer watched her, disappointed. Once he had
put on the hunting paint he couldn't have anything to do with
women until after the hunt. Woman magic was too strong; it
overrode hunting magic.

Wants the Moon knew that perfectly well. Women were
powerful because they bled every moon and didn't die of it.
Even without the hunting paint Blue Racer should know better
this morning.

"Sharpen your buffalo arrows instead," she scolded him,
"while I go and get water. Then I will cook, if you have not
eaten everything in the baskets already." They were young
men with appetites. Late at night they had been hungry.

Now they looked abashed. "Yes, Most Wise." Blue Racer
began to look for his loincloth, tangled in the buffalo robes
on the spirit wife's bed.

The wind whirled around her feet as Wants the Moon
stepped out of the tent, blowing dust and stalks of dry grass
with it. The fierce sun had shrouded itself with a gray-yellow
light. Six-Legged glared at her out of it.

"What have you been doing?" he shouted at her.

Angry in the Morning, loading his packs in front of his own
tent, laughed loudly and shouted something at him.

Six-Legged whirled around. "Keep your face shut!" he
yelled.

Angry in the Morning laughed again.

Six-Legged's wives came up the path from the river with
water baskets on their heads. "Don't listen to him," White
Buffalo told Six-Legged complacently. "He is always in a

temper in the morning. He is only jealous." It was very nice to make Angry in the Morning jealous, she thought. It made her feel important.

Six-Legged ignored her and turned back to Wants the Moon. "Slut," he said loudly in the language of Red Earth City.

"Follows-His-Cock," Wants the Moon said back to him. "Sticks-It-in-Anything."

"You brought us here," Six-Legged said. The wind whipped up a spiteful little gust around his feet. "It is your fault if the chief wants me to have his daughter."

"And his niece and any other ugly girl he doesn't know what to do with," Wants the Moon said.

"At least they are good wives and content with one husband. Now you have shamed me." He folded his arms across his chest.

"Shamed *you!* Shamed *you?*" Wants the Moon started for him, her fingers balled into fists. "I am carrying your child, and *you* go off with other girls and leave me to look like a fool—and *I* shamed *you?* I just want what you have, what is good enough for you, since you think you are a river spirit now, or I will tell the chief that you are only a stupid boy who found the horse in the desert, and maybe it's somebody else's horse, anyway, and maybe he will kill you!" She was nearly in Six-Legged's face now, shouting in it, the wind boiling around them both in a dark cloud. The sun had gone behind the clouds that roiled in the sky, and the light shone a queasy gray-yellow across the wind-whipped grass and the trees, turning the leaves upside down, ghostly white.

Angry in the Morning put his packs down, and Six-Legged's wives clung together, whimpering. Hole in the Sunset came from his own tent, with Elk Walker scurrying behind him.

"I told you they were dangerous," Elk Walker said. He went to Wants the Moon's tent and spoke urgently to the Young Husbands. They shook their heads, with eyes as uneasy and quick as birds. They didn't know what to do either.

"Something will come out of the river and get you!" Wants

the Moon screamed. "For lying and being greedy!"

"*You* told the chief of these people what we were. *You* thought of that, Most Untruthful." Six-Legged spat the words out at her.

"You liked it enough! You liked it while all the girls were for you! Yah! Stick it in a knothole!"

"I'd just as soon stick it in a beehive as in you!" Six-Legged roared back. "Slut Old Woman! Rattlesnake Old Woman!"

"Old?" Wants the Moon drew back her fist and smacked him in the ear. Six-Legged grabbed her by the shoulders and pushed her while she kicked at him. He let go with one hand to cuff her across the mouth. She sank her teeth into his palm.

"Slut!" he howled at her again, slapping her head with his other hand.

The Buffalo Horn people watched, horrified, as the wind roared around them. An argument between spirits was dangerous to be around; they could see sparks rising from their faces. The sky was dark now, but there was no rain in it. Elk Walker fought his way through the wind toward them. He took Wants the Moon by the arm, fingers gripping her like claws. The wind lifted the tents and tilted them sideways, straining at their pegs. Six-Legged and Wants the Moon turned and snarled at Elk Walker.

"Stop this before you do us damage!" Elk Walker stood his ground stubbornly, pushing his face into theirs.

Six-Legged glared at him, uncomprehending.

"This man has called me names," Wants the Moon said, panting.

"Your names are heard too far," Elk Walker said over the wind. "Too much hears you when you shout."

"Go away and leave us alone," Six-Legged said.

Elk Walker ignored words he couldn't understand. He shook Wants the Moon's arm, turning her to see, dragging her from Six-Legged. "Look!"

Wants the Moon turned her eyes to the horizon and reached her hand out suddenly to clutch Six-Legged's arm. The dark funnel of a tornado boiled along the plain, roaring like an open mouth.

Six-Legged stared. His clenched jaws parted in terror, and his heart pounded behind his breastbone. The tornado's heart was impenetrable, black as fear. Wants the Moon and Six-Legged stood in the wind and stared.

"Did we do that?" Six-Legged whispered.

Yellow eyes looked at them out of the storm. *Maybe,* said the eyes.

9

The Black Wind

RED HORSE TOSSED HER HEAD IN THE RISING WIND, TEETH bared against whatever was in it. Weaver clung to her neck. The air howled around them, carrying sticks on it, and small toads, and tufts of feathers. The endless grass lay flat along the ground. The spear that Weaver had made spun around in the wind and whirled away. Red Horse lunged in the air, trying to follow it. Weaver wrapped his hands in her mane, and she flew after the wind.

Along the base of the low hills where they had come in their flight were caves wind-carved from the soft red stone and the yellow tufa. Weaver could see them like dark mouths waiting behind the curtain of wind, ready to swallow them. He had been afraid of them this morning. Now he thought they might keep him from blowing into the sky. The wind had come for Quail, he thought, out of the skeleton place to try to take her back. He called her name, sang to her sobbing until the red ears swiveled back to listen and she slowed. Weaver slid off her back and pulled at her lead, stumbling toward the caves while the wind roared louder. A tree went by, uprooted, and Weaver and Red Horse struggled against the wind that

152

wanted to pick them up, too, and hurl them into the sky.

The air had grown dark, and the storm was like a hand trying to lift him by his hair. Red Horse's eyes were wild, ringed with white, stones held against the sun. She plunged up the slope to the caves, her hooves thrashing, floundering and staggering on the loose scree while the blowing sand stung their eyes.

The voice of the whirlwind bellowed behind them. Weaver heard it talk to him while he cowered against the dark wall of the cave. Red Horse heard it, too, and reared, thrashing in the stony darkness, hard hooves clattering against the rock. Weaver clung to her lead, calling her his wife's pet names, calling her Quail and his Morning Light and his Soft Feathers, but she didn't hear those names; she only heard the storm's voice. Her hooves exploded and landed in his belly, and he doubled over, gasping. She kicked again and flung him against the cave wall.

Outside the storm howled, *I am here. I am. I am.*

Weaver clutched his belly, trying to breathe through the pain and the storm's roar, sucking in air through aching lungs. His stomach heaved. When he brushed his bare legs, blood came away on his hands, warm and viscous. His skin was cold, clammy as the stones at the back of the cave. He shivered, wrapping his arms around himself, rocking back and forth, weeping.

The wind whirled through the cave, carrying small branches and the body of a shrew. The scrap of fur splattered on the cave wall and fell, sticky and boneless, on Weaver's shoulder. He flung it away from him, shrieking. Red Horse was lumbering through the cave now, frothing and terror-stricken, galloping in circles. She thudded past him, hooves clattering on stone, as he scrambled out of her way. He rolled himself into a ball, frozen against the cave wall.

For an instant the storm grew quiet. The air paled, thick with fear but suddenly still, perched precariously on the edge of the wind. Weaver lifted his head, which had been buried between his knees. Red Horse stood trembling, her legs planted far apart, braced, eyes wide. He stood on shaking legs, reached to touch her muzzle.

"It's gone away," Weaver told her. "It's gone away without you."

She flinched from him, quivering. The roaring began again with the trailing edge of the storm, the wind shrieking and rolling stones down the hill. Darkness closed around them like a hand. Weaver flung his arms around his wife's neck, but she reared and hurled him into the stones. His head and ribs thudded against the cave wall as the storm's voice pummeled him. He slid to the floor, sinking deep, out of the roaring into a sticky blackness in his head while Red Horse galloped in endless circles around the cave, her eyes a mad glitter of fear.

The eye of the storm glowed a sulfurous yellow through the dark gray air, like something brought up from the earth. It picked up trees and rolled boulders down the mountainside. It tossed men into the air and inhaled their tents, flinging them over the horizon. It made frogs and fish fall in the desert, sucked up from streams in its path. It shredded the doings of two-legged and four-legged people and spat them out in places forever changed. Woodrat cowered in his house in the cactus, and Owl was snatched from her perch and sent careening, wings battered, rolled over and over in the air.

The storm sucked up anger, shook it loose from people to feed itself. Woodrat's wife left off scolding him and shivered in the corner of their den while the storm took their quarrel and spun it into the black wind. The otters buried their noses in their paws under the bank, piled one on top of the other in an otter heap. The wind drank the porcupine's disgruntlement, the badger's temper, and tossed them, empty, into the air. The peccaries heard it coming and snorted with fear, scurrying for their dens under the trees. The storm came upon them and lifted the trees away. When they squealed at it, it snatched up their fury and their snouts together and threw them into its pack. It spun around and around on itself, blacker and blacker, and flung the buffalo herds like pebbles into the emptiness of the plains, scattered like rain.

The Buffalo Horn people had run when they saw the dark whirlwind put its finger down from the clouds, but it came swiftly, darkening the plains and spitting lightning from its core. It veered to follow them as if they were buffalo to be driven, roaring in their ears and snatching people away into the sky. Mothers clutched children to them, terrified, while the wind took the smallest by the other hand and tore them away. It pulled up tents and toppled trees, wrapping everything around itself and spinning until the world was dizzy.

Angry in the Morning tried to hold his tent down, and the storm picked him up with it and threw him into a tree. The Young Husbands had cut the ropes of their tent and tried to take it with them, to save it. Now they rolled themselves in it, holding Wants the Moon between them, to hold it down. The wind pulled Porcupine's buffalo robe from her shoulders and took Elk Walker's medicine bag and upended it, carrying it away over the trees in a shower of carved charms and holy bones. The buffalo robe sailed away on wings spread like Great Condor's.

Six-Legged crouched over White Buffalo and Wind in the Grass, trying to shield them from the debris that flew this way and that from the camp—beds and hides and coils of rope, bags of meal and tent poles like flying spears. A turkey tumbled by, upside down, and a dead badger landed in the rain basket that had stood outside Hole in the Sunset's tent, flattening it.

Lightning forked through the black wind. Wants the Moon trembled in the Young Husbands' arms. She felt it trying to lift her, swallow her whole. When she opened her eyes, she saw the eye of the storm. This was where the heart of the world lived, she thought. Not in the peaceful slow dance of new grass and ripe maize, the slow shift of seasons, but in this, the wellspring of terror, the dark pinpoint that held all power. This was where Coyote truly dwelled. As she thought of him, she saw him shed his gray, matted coat at the heart of the storm and step clear of it in a skin made of the lightning.

Wants the Moon buried her face between the Young Husbands' chests again, her teeth chattering. She felt them all sliding across the ground, tent and all, the stones digging into her bare arms. A tree shrieked and crashed down. Wants the Moon heard its voice as it was split open.

Horse remembered the storm that had come when the gray dog animal had let all the horses loose. This storm was like that one, and the air was thick with the gray animal's smell. Horse pulled at his rope, afraid of the wind and breaking trees. Lightning spat out of the black air. The wind whirled him around, and he reared, pawing at it with his hooves while the two-legged people ran through the wind screaming. The rope stretched taut and snapped. Horse whirled, the rope flying around his head. The eyes of the storm were spitting fire, and its mouth was open to eat him, more fearsome than Big Cat. He ran, plunging through the camp, and the rain and wind swallowed him up.

Weaver woke to find Red Horse snuffling at his face. Her muzzle was flecked with dried foam, and when he moved, she hurtled backward from him, hooves scrabbling on the stone.
    Weaver looked around him. They were in the cave, not dead. Sunlight filtered through the cave mouth, blocked with a tumble of uprooted trees and a dead peccary blown there by the storm and caught in the branches of a piñon pine. Weaver sat up carefully and edged his way outside through the splintered trees without moving them. He thought they might be all that had kept Red Horse in the cave all night. The air outside was silent and birdless, the landscape blasted as if the giants of the old days had come walking down the valley, flattening trees and uprooting mountains.
    It didn't take her, he thought. *It could have, while I was sleeping.*
    Weaver scratched his head. Could it be that the storm had not come for Quail after all? He edged his way down the tumbled slope. If the storm had not come to take Quail away, then perhaps it was a message. Storms like that had something to say, if their language could be deciphered. Weaver looked at the trail it had left down the valley, as clear as if someone

had dragged a giant travois along the ground. A storm road. Perhaps he was supposed to follow it.

Quail was in the cave, snuffling at the tangled branches. She would be hungry. He would have to find her grass. It would be easier, he thought, when she was a human person again and could eat human food. On the other hand, then he couldn't ride on her back. Perhaps it was better this way.

Weaver rummaged among the broken stones on the scree below the caves. Huge chunks of soft sandstone had been pulled loose and lay like cracked pots all around. The cliff face was a new raw face, sheared away just outside the cave mouth. Weaver pulled his knife from his belt, the only weapon he had left now, and climbed back up the slope. The stone was soft and easy to carve, like dry yucca root. Weaver dug the blade into it, cutting a curving line for the neck and back, a wild fall of hair for the tail. He gave her legs, dancing up the cliff face, and a bird beside her to show who she had been. He had no loom to weave on, to tell whatever it was that had sent the storm that he would obey. He would use stone instead, to show he understood, that they had been here but were gone on now.

Wants the Moon was not entirely sure she was alive when the storm quieted. She opened her eyes slowly. She was still clinging to Sunflower in the tatters of their tent, but Blue Racer was gone, pulled away from them by the wind. The Buffalo Horn people staggered around the place where their camp had been, eyes dazed, like people who have been awakened in the night. The shiftless father of Wind in the Grass lay chest down in the mud, his head twisted around like an owl's, staring blindly up at the sky. His wife, Lark, stared back at him blankly, as if she didn't know what to do with him, blood from a cut on her cheek running down the front of her sodden dress. Angry in the Morning was pinned under a felled tree. He gritted his teeth as Long Arrow and a huge young man named Bear Paws tried to get it off him. His mother circled around them, wailing and wringing her hands. Wants the Moon saw Blue Racer kneeling beside Angry in the Morning and talking to him quietly while they hacked at the tree. Blue Racer's back was gashed open and smeared with blood.

The camp was a sea of mud and broken things. Everything was smashed or taken by the wind; jagged stumps of trees stuck up out of the ground like spears. Wants the Moon looked for something to carry water in. She saw her cloth sash tangled in a branch, pulled it loose, then stumbled over the downed branches and soaked it with water in the stream. On the way back she found the body of a child, half buried in the mud. She picked it up gently and carried it with her. A woman came out of the trees, weeping, her face covered with mud and blood. She wailed when she saw Wants the Moon and took the child from her. Sunflower took the wet sash and began to clean the blood from Blue Racer's back.

Wants the Moon heard Wind in the Grass and White Buffalo sniveling over Six-Legged, who sat in the mud, not moving but apparently alive. She went over to him. Wants the Moon looked at the young wives, and they left.

"We did this," she said somberly.

"I think so." Six-Legged closed his eyes.

"Where is Horse?"

"I don't know."

Wants the Moon sat down in the mud beside him and watched Sunflower. The woman was still wailing over the body of her child. Three more children were missing, carried off by the wind. Bears Paws' brother had been found with a tent pole driven clear through his body, and Old Grandmother Onion Digger had had the breath blown out of her. She lay against a tree, lifeless and flat as a deflated bladder.

Hole in the Sunset stood with his arm around Porcupine, who was weeping into his chest. Elk Walker limped through the camp, silently counting the dead and missing. He had lost his staff and medicine bag and leaned on a broken cottonwood branch instead. Two of his apprentices were seeing to the injured; the third was dead, smashed head first into a boulder by the stream. A half-grown buffalo lay on its back in the middle of the camp, dead eyes staring, tongue stuck out between its teeth. The Buffalo Horn people walked around it as if it were a rock in their way until Porcupine wiped her eyes and called to three of the other women to help her skin it.

"I am ashamed," Wants the Moon said to Six-Legged.

"We are ashamed together."

"I am sorry I hit you and called your wives ugly."

"I am sorry I called you a slut."

They looked at each other miserably. Elk Walker came and stood over them. They looked up at him.

"The buffalo will be scattered now," he said. "It will be a long time before the herds can be hunted. This one will not last us long." He gestured at the half-grown one that the women were cutting up, weeping as they skinned it.

Six-Legged hung his head.

"Without buffalo meat and buffalo fat our people will starve," Elk Walker said relentlessly. "Our women will not carry their babies, and the young children that are already here will die."

Wants the Moon bit her lip. Tears spilled out of her eyes. "We are sorry," she said. "We didn't know."

"Some magic is too great for the people to live among," Elk Walker said. "Or to live among the people. That's what Uncle told us a long time ago."

"Who is Uncle?" Wants the Moon asked.

"He is just Uncle," Elk Walker said. "Our people's Uncle."

Wants the Moon remembered Old Grandmother talking about Uncle. He was always very hungry and not to be trusted, but he told the people the truth. She wondered if that was Uncle she had seen looking out of the storm. She had thought it was Coyote, but maybe they were the same. "What can we do?" she asked.

"You brought us the horse thing," Elk Walker said. "Then you took it away again."

"That was the storm," Wants the Moon said. "It was frightened."

"We are frightened also," Elk Walker said. "And some of us are dead. And the buffalo are scattered with the horse thing."

"If we find Horse, will the buffalo come back?"

"Uncle will know about that," Elk Walker said. "Probably. You will have to go and talk to him."

Wants the Moon looked around the broken camp. The Buffalo Horn people looked back at her, their dark eyes accusing. *You came among us and let your magic loose, and it has killed us,* they said.

I don't have magic, Wants the Moon thought. *It was a lie.* Perhaps the lies you told became real if you weren't careful. Old Grandmother had said that, too.

"We will go and find the horse," she said. "We will undo what we have done."

Elk Walker nodded once at her, his face expressionless. He gave her a grunt that might have been approval or might have been a warning. "If you meet Uncle, tell him we are still his children," he said.

10

Uncle

THE STORM HAD CUT A PATH THROUGH THE WORLD LIKE A woman cutting flesh with a knife. Inside the path the world was broken. Outside it, all was as it had been, but the path was very wide. It took Wants the Moon and Six-Legged three days to walk to the edge of the path, while Wants the Moon explained to Six-Legged what they had done and what Elk Walker had said. At dusk the first night they made camp on a slope where Six-Legged had found some flint. He sat chipping arrowheads with a rock at the fire that Wants the Moon started from sticks with no slow-burner and no fire drill, rubbing them until her hands blistered.

"I never heard of Uncle," Six-Legged grumbled. "These people don't know anything. Is Uncle like a kachina?"

"I don't think so," Wants the Moon said. She was cutting a fire drill now and plaiting a slow-burner of sagebrush bark. Now they had nothing again, not even Horse. She thought that the Buffalo Horn people could have given them some food and slow-burner and arrows that they had found in the mess of the camp, but they hadn't. The prairie was alive with grasshoppers, maybe blown here by the storm, and Six-Legged and

161

Wants the Moon had caught some of those and roasted them in the fire. Wants the Moon looked at the prairie and shivered. The sky overhead was black and speckled with cold stars, and she kept seeing, out of the corner of her eye, something watching her from it. "I don't think we should talk about their Uncle," she said.

"Well, I'm hungry," Six-Legged said. His stomach growled.

"Don't talk to Uncle about eating things," Wants the Moon said crossly. "That is like telling you-know-who." She put the slow-burner away and rolled up in her blanket.

Six-Legged noted that she had left her fine new doeskin dress behind and wore her old cloth skirt and blanket, torn from being dragged through the downed trees by the wind. His young wives had sobbed and hung onto him and finally, when Elk Walker had shouted at them, had sent him off with nothing much either. That seemed to be part of what they had to do—get by with nothing, since they had left the Buffalo Horn people with nothing. That was what Wants the Moon had said. Six-Legged edged closer to the fire and butted his head against her back, and she let him get under the blanket with her, but he didn't do anything else and neither did she.

In the morning they caught more grasshoppers, and Wants the Moon found a prairie dog hole that looked like someone was still in it. She sat quietly by the hole with a rock until it came out, blinking at the desolation. When they had picked the bones clean, they started across the grass, not really knowing where was best to go. Wants the Moon called to Horse and whistled between her teeth for him, but he didn't answer. The storm had blown all the tracks away. Neither one said what they both knew. If they didn't find him, they couldn't go back, and if they didn't go back, they would die.

At night they came to some trees, and Six-Legged made a bow from a broken cottonwood sapling and strung it with the prairie dog's guts. He cut some arrows out of serviceberry shoots and feathered them with twigs tied on with threads picked from Wants the Moon's skirt. Then he made a spear, and they practiced shooting the arrows and throwing the spear, pretending that they were not children of the cities, that they could live the wild life of the wild lands even without a horse to carry them or any of the things they had taken with them from home.

The featherless arrows wobbled and went wide. Wants the Moon hacked off her long black hair with Six-Legged's belt knife and tied it into a fishnet and a line to snare rabbits with, but she caught only a turtle dug from the mud at the bottom of the churned-up stream. They pried it open and ate greedily, scraping the shell clean. By the third day they were eating ants and grass, and their stomachs heaved them up again. Wants the Moon's lips were blistered with the heat that had returned like a breath from a kiln, and Six-Legged's eyes were swollen and crusted with the blowing dust.

At last they came beyond the storm's path to the edge of a dry lake bed. The rain there had turned the salt grass newly green, and it gleamed like water. As they came over a rise, they saw that in the distance the grass was filled with sandhill cranes, pacing in leggy troops, fanning their great white wings, heads bobbing. Wants the Moon put her hand on Six-Legged's arm, and they stopped, licking their lips, staring hungrily.

They slid carefully down the slope to the edge of the salt grass, and Six-Legged motioned Wants the Moon down. They began to wriggle forward on elbows and knees. The grass got in her nose, and Wants the Moon froze, hand clapped over her mouth, convulsed with the effort not to sneeze. Six-Legged slithered past her, the bow and arrows in his hand.

Wants the Moon pressed her finger under her nose until the sneeze subsided. Then she crawled after Six-Legged, but he had stopped, too. He heard her coming and put out a hand to keep her back. Beyond them the grass rippled with the passage of another body. They peered at it and saw the flash of gray ears and the brush of a dust-colored tail tipped in black.

The coyote eased forward another arm's length, wriggling on its belly. The cranes didn't seem to notice. Their heads were all turned the other way, necks stretched out, watching something else. Six-Legged lifted himself a little out of the grass to look.

Beyond the cranes, on their other side, a second coyote danced in the salt grass. It ran in circles, leaping into the air, turning flips. Tongue hanging out, it flung its body this way and that, leaped up and snapped at the sky, fell back and rolled over, waving its legs in the air.

It was entirely comical, and Wants the Moon giggled. Six-Legged dug his fingers into her arm, but the coyote flattened in the salt grass just ahead had heard her. It looked over its shoulder at them, ears just above the grass, yellow eyes peering through the green blades. The eyes met hers and she froze. The coyote stared at them for a long moment, thoughtful. Then it slunk on.

Six-Legged hung on to Wants the Moon's arm. "Wait."

They crouched, watching, while the second coyote enlarged its dance. It hurled itself into the air, turned flips, and pranced on its hind legs. The cranes stretched their necks out curiously. It wasn't close enough to be a danger, so they watched, long legs like reeds growing out of the salt grass, white-clothed, attentive as people at a clown dance. The clown coyote spun in a mad spiral, tongue lolling out.

The first coyote edged closer. After a moment Wants the Moon and Six-Legged followed it, leaving a respectful space between them. When it was only a few spear-lengths away, it stopped, and they saw its hindquarters and the black tip of its tail twitch. As the clown coyote gave one last leap, the coyote in the grass shot toward the cranes.

The cranes saw it and scattered, wings beating the air, long dark legs striding the salt grass, awkward as a tangle of tent poles, picking up speed in a slow, ponderous flapping before they could clear the ground. The first coyote grabbed one by the feet and wrestled it down in a flurry of feathers. Six-Legged stood and nocked an arrow in one swift motion. It wobbled through the air, but it pierced a crane through the wing as it rose from the salt grass. The clown coyote had left its antics as soon as its companion rushed the cranes, but it had farther to run. The cranes lifted as it came, and it swerved to catch Six-Legged's while the crane beat its wings frantically against the air, the arrow flopping from reddened feathers.

The coyote grabbed the crane by the good wing. Six-Legged and Wants the Moon ran toward them, Six-Legged beating at the coyote with his bow. "That is my crane! I shot it!" Above them the other cranes filled the sky.

Wants the Moon tried to get under the wings that beat around her head. She clutched the knife in her fist, her arms over her face. The crane thrashed between Six-Legged and the coyote, kicking with its feet. The coyote shifted its grip, sinking its teeth deeper, pulling the wing taut. Wants the Moon got her arm around the crane's neck, the wounded wing pounding at her back, and sank the knife into soft feathers. Blood gushed out, spraying her face. Six-Legged and the coyote were wrestling on the ground now, the crane between them. Wants the Moon kicked the coyote hard in the ribs, and then in the balls. It let go of the crane and turned around to snarl at her, mouth full of feathers. She hit it in the nose with her fist.

"That is our crane!"

The yellow eyes narrowed. She drew her fist back again. Six-Legged smacked the coyote with the bow, then nocked an arrow to the bowstring.

The coyote seemed to think about it. It looked at the crane, flopping in the salt grass, the white feathers staining red, and then toward its companion coyote, who was greedily pulling its own crane apart, tearing chunks out of the feathered breast. The clown coyote stared at Wants the Moon, pale eyes thoughtful. Then it licked a feather from its muzzle and turned away with a disinterested air. They saw it trotting through the salt grass toward its companion, low-slung tail rippling the grass. When it came even with the first coyote, it took hold of the opposite end of the crane, and they tore it in two in a flurry of white feathers and limp black feet.

Six-Legged grabbed their crane by its legs, and they dragged it away with them before the coyote could change its mind. Coyotes wouldn't often tackle full-grown humans, but Six-Legged had the uneasy sensation that these might want something in exchange for the crane. He and Wants the Moon carried it toward the low hills that rose from the other side of the dry lake in a sandy slope dotted with scrub and thistles.

The slow-burner Wants the Moon had packed in a pot made from river mud was still smoldering. Six-Legged uprooted a pile of brush, and they coaxed a flame from the slow-burner. Wants the Moon gutted the crane with the knife and plucked it. They threw the offal down the hillside for the coyotes and put the heart and liver on sticks to cook first. The smell made their mouths water and Wants the Moon's stomach cramp. She felt light-headed and thought that the wing feathers, detached and laid on the ground in an alate arc, their white lengths barred with smears of blood, might rise up in the air on their own, might take a human being with them.

Wants the Moon threaded a bigger stick through the body of the crane, and they balanced it over the fire with each end laid on stones. The air was growing cold as darkness closed in, and they huddled together under one blanket. When the crane was cooked, they ate it as greedily as the coyotes, tearing pieces off with their hands, smearing their faces with the juice. Wants the Moon's stomach cramped again, but she ignored it.

When the meat was gone, they sucked the bones and shared the last of their water. They had made a carrying pot of mud, but it leaked, and what was left in it was clayey and full of grit. They drank anyway and lay down under the blanket. Six-Legged closed his eyes, sated, and snored.

Wants the Moon lay on her back watching the night sky while he rumbled in her ear. Her belly hurt, maybe from eating too much too fast, after only ants and grass. She bit her lip, willing the pain to go away, refusing to heave up what she had eaten. She heard a rustling at the foot of the hill and caught the glint of an eye in the reflected firelight. The coyotes down the hill had ceased to worry at the offal, but she wasn't sure they were gone. Her stomach knotted into a tight ball. She pressed her lips together and stared at the sky. Star eyes looked back at her.

"Are you doing this to me?" Wants the Moon clenched her hands over her belly. She felt teeth gnaw at it.

There was a face among the stars, a man's face, with a long

nose and bushy eyebrows. "I do everything," it said. "It's a lot of work."

"Where is our horse?" she asked it.

"Oh, somewhere. I expect you'll find it if nobody eats it."

"Did you eat it?" A pain ripped her belly, and she doubled up, rolling over on hands and knees, back arched. Turning her head sideways, she looked up again at the Buffalo Horn people's Uncle.

He hung in the sky, sometimes looking like the coyotes and sometimes not. She saw that he had a big club in his hand. The hard pain broke suddenly and left her queasy. Her face burned, and she was wet with sweat.

"You are not well, Daughter," Uncle said.

"Something is biting me," she said between gritted teeth as it started again.

"You try too hard to hold on to things. Now, I know that everything has to be let go of. That is my job in the world, teaching the people how to let go."

"If we let go, we die," she gasped.

"Shall I tell you about that?" Uncle asked. "Shall I tell you how it is?" The face leaned closer, seeming to come out of the sky at her. It wrapped itself around her belly and squeezed. "One day Uncle was coming along," he said.

Uncle is always hungry, and he was coming along with his club over his shoulder looking for something to eat. At last he came to a prairie dog village. They were scampering around their mounds, and they didn't seem afraid of him, but they kept an eye out. Prairie dogs are too small to make more than a mouthful for Uncle, and they knew he usually didn't think them worthwhile. But they were all ready to dart into their holes if he moved. So when he had stood staring at them for a long time, they said most respectfully but a little nervously, "What are you doing, Uncle?"

"Oh, just coming along." Uncle was very hungry, and they looked tasty even if they were small. "Nephews, how would you like to learn a new dance?" he asked them.

"Oh, yes!" said the prairie dogs and wiggled their tails.

"Well, then," Uncle said, "this is how it goes. I'll sing a song and show you. First you have to make a circle around me and stand on your hind legs."

"All right." The prairie dogs scooted into a circle. What fun to have Uncle teach them something new.

"Now," said Uncle, "you'll notice that I sing with my eyes shut. That is part of the dance. And I hit the ground with my club, one, two, three, like that, and every time I hit it, I stamp hard, first with my right foot and then with my left. You must shut your eyes and stamp the same way."

"Oh, yes," said the prairie dogs eagerly, their little hearts beating hard with the excitement of it.

Uncle began beating time with his club and singing:

> "Doggies, doggies, whisk your tails,
>   Whisk your tails, whisk your tails,
>   Just the way I say."

The prairie dogs liked the song very much and sang it over and over, although the sound of the club frightened them a little.

"Very good," said Uncle. "You could sing this on Gathering Day, you sound so good."

The prairie dogs felt warm and delighted. They were obedient little fellows and eager to please.

"Now, shut your eyes tight and stamp hard. Sing very loud now."

The prairie dogs sang for all they were worth, very excited to have been so complimented by Uncle. They squeezed their eyes tight, and their little voices filled the air.

"Better and better," said Uncle. He stamped his feet and sang too: "Doggies, doggies, whisk your tails." The prairie dogs whisked them hard. Uncle stamped his way around the circle and beat time with his club. But now with every beat he brought the club down on a prairie dog's head.

"Doggies, doggies—" THUMP!

"Whisk your tails—" THUMP!

Each prairie dog would squeak, but the other prairie dogs were singing so hard and stamping so loud that they couldn't hear him. They were concentrating very hard on keeping their eyes shut. This went on until one fat little prairie dog, who was getting short of breath, began to think that the dance was going on for a very long time. He opened one eye just in time to see his companions all stretched out on the ground and Uncle's club coming down on his head.

The prairie dog squealed and with a long leap dived for his hole. Uncle was right behind him, but the prairie dog got there first, dived in, and disappeared.

And so there are still prairie dogs in the world, even though Uncle ate his fill of the rest and regretted very much the last fat one who would have had the tastiest marrow of all.

"So you see," Uncle said from the sky, "that is all right. There is always more of everything."

"We aren't prairie dogs," Wants the Moon said between gritted teeth.

"Oh, you're all the same," Uncle said.

The stars whirled around in a spiral, and he was gone. Wants the Moon put her hand over her mouth as her dinner started to come up.

"Hah," a voice said from the other side of the dying fire. The thin sticks of brush had curled to ash. Wants the Moon saw a pair of gray ears and a yellowy ruff. "Don't throw that up," he said. "You'll need it."

Wants the Moon thought she didn't care, but the heaving in her stomach subsided. She was drenched with sweat and shivering.

"You'll catch your death," the coyote said. "I don't know why people don't grow fur." It came over and turned around three times and then lay down next to her, warmth radiating through its rough coat. Six-Legged was still snoring on her other side. She wriggled deeper between them, and the coyote put its head on her chest. "Shall I tell you how it really ended?" he asked. "There are lots of ways to tell a story."

Old Uncle had made a fire and put two of the prairie dogs on a forked green stick. When they were done, he set them aside and roasted two more. He was very hungry, but he had decided to wait until he could eat them all at once. He was just roasting the last two when a gray coyote came up, limping and holding one back paw off the ground.

The coyote looked very sad. "Old Uncle, please give me something to eat," he said. "I am very hungry."

"Hmmph. Go and catch your own." Uncle put the last two prairie dogs on his stick.

"But my leg is broken, and I can't run," the coyote said, whimpering. "I couldn't catch a snail."

"Haw!" Uncle thought that was funny. "Well, then, I'll make you a wager. We'll race for these prairie dogs. Whoever gets around that mountain over there and back first can eat them." Uncle liked to play jokes on people.

"But I told you. I can't run." The coyote looked pitiful, which made Uncle laugh. "And you have such long legs, too."

"Well, well," said Uncle, still enjoying his joke, "I'll tell you what. I'll tie two stones to my ankles. That will even things up."

"Oh, yes," said the coyote eagerly. "That will be fair."

Uncle chortled at the coyote's stupidity and found two big stones to tie to his ankles. He started out with the coyote limping painfully behind him. "Come on!" Uncle called. "Hurry up! Haw!"

"I'm coming as fast as I can," the coyote said, hobbling along.

Uncle loped with great strides; he was taller than the tallest tree, and the rocks hardly bothered him. All the same, when he reached the foot of the mountain, he was a little out of breath. He turned around to look behind him and saw the coyote still hopping along, hardly past the empty prairie dog village.

"Haw!" Uncle said again. "That fool coyote." He went on around the mountain, but the rocks got heavier. There was no sign of the coyote. "I might as well take a little nap,"

Uncle said. He lay down under a tree and sighed with pleasure. It felt very good to stop walking with those rocks.

All the same, he dozed with one eye open, and when he was
rested, he sat up and yawned. "That coyote probably fell down
dead in the sand," he chuckled. "But if not, I had better get
moving. Even a lame coyote can catch up to me if I sit still
long enough."

Uncle went on, feeling much better and listening for the
coyote behind him, just in case. When he came around the far
side of the mountain, he could see the prairie dog village in
the distance and a thin trickle of blue smoke still coming up
from his fire. There was no sign of the coyote on the trail, so
Uncle thought he must have got as far as the other side of the
mountain by now. He picked up his pace a little, looking over
his shoulder. The smell of roasted prairie dog was making his
mouth water. "I can't waste any more time playing tricks on
that stupid coyote," he said. "I'm hungry."

He set off across the valley with great rolling strides. But
when he got closer to the village, he saw that there was something wrong. The mound he had thought was the pile of
roasted prairie dogs didn't look right. It was gray instead of
a nice, roasty brown. And it was moving.

Uncle started to run, the rocks thumping around his ankles.
The mound moved again. The coyote's head stuck up from it,
a bone between his teeth. When he saw Uncle coming, he
stood up, and he stood on all four feet! Then he snatched up
the last prairie dog and streaked as fast as lightning across
the valley, leaving a cloud of dust behind him. Uncle howled.
That coyote was not lame after all, the thief!

Uncle roared again and started after him, waving his club,
but the rocks held him back. The coyote was over the horizon
before Uncle could get as far as the fire. When he came to
the empty prairie dog village, puffing and breathing very hard,
all that was left was a pile of licked bones with not even the
marrow in them. And the only sound was the coyote's bark
hanging in the air. "Thank you!" it said. And then, with a
voice that sounded just like Uncle's voice, "Haw!"

"Well, I don't see any difference between you," Wants the Moon said sleepily. The coyote was warm against her chest, his breath a little cloud of steam in the cold air.

"There's not," the coyote said. "There's not any difference between you and me, either. It's all the same stuff."

"What is?"

"What is," the coyote said. "It's all the same stuff. Prairie dogs, grass, people. Are you going to eat those bones you left?"

"They're from the crane," Wants the Moon said. "So I suppose they're yours." She felt drowsier, tucked between Six-Legged and the coyote, and her eyes kept closing.

"That's kind of you," the coyote said. "I'll take them home later. There's always a little something left in a bone."

Wants the Moon let her eyes close all the way. Six-Legged was right, she thought as she faded into sleep; they needed a dog.

When she woke in the morning there was no one there, but there were gray hairs sticking to her blanket. Her belly ached with a dull pounding as if someone had hit her there, but she didn't want to vomit anymore. She sat up and pushed the blanket away, throwing it over Six-Legged, who was still asleep. When she moved her legs, she felt sticky. The ground under her was crusted with dried blood. Not the crane's. Her own.

Wants the Moon wrapped her arms around her belly and leaned forward, groaning. The blood between her legs was still damp and glutinous. It had soaked into the ground and into her skirt, leaving it stiff where it had dried. She bit her lip, and tears spilled down her cheeks.

"You took it away!" she said, but no one answered her, not Uncle, not the coyote who had kept her warm all night.

Six-Legged woke up to find her snuffling into her fist and scrubbing at her thighs with her bloodstained skirt. "What is it?" he said. And then, "Oh . . ." He backed away from her. That was woman business, and she might be angry at him, too. But he felt sad, because it was his child, someone who wouldn't be now.

Wants the Moon spit in her hand and wiped her skirt against her leg. "I will be all right now," she said, her lips compressed tightly, so that it came out like someone with a toothache. "We will go to the river and get fresh water, and I will wash my skirt." She sounded practical, a housewife making plans to clean.

Six-Legged wondered what she had done with it, how big it had been. Maybe they should take it with them, to bury it properly at home. But where was home, when you lived with wandering people, people who moved every moon? They ought to do something, he thought, so it would know where to go next. He said so, diffidently.

"I buried it already," Wants the Moon said. "It wasn't even a person yet." But she had put a rock on top of the hole. She pushed the ashes around in the dead fire, poking it with her toe to make sure it was out. The crane's feathers were in a bundle tied with a thread from her skirt. The crane bones were gone. "I gave them to a coyote," she said.

Six-Legged stared at her. He wondered if she was wandering in her head. These things sometimes made women crazy. "What coyote?" he asked her.

"Just one who came by."

Six-Legged looked around the dry lake bed, but there was no one there, dancing in the salt grass. He stuffed the feathers and the slow-burner and the fire drill and the waterskin, which was the only thing the Buffalo Horn people had given them, in their pack, and they left the lake bed.

In the next valley they found the watercourse that the Buffalo Horn people called Snake Water, its trees coiled across the grasslands at the foot of a steep bluff. Hole in the Sunset had told them how the land lay, where to find water, but it was hard to see it in your head, Six-Legged thought, even though they had traveled over this country on their way from the cities. Hole in the Sunset had sat down on the ground with them and marked the rivers with bits of string and the mountains with rocks, but it was still hard. Six-Legged's heart hammered with relief when they smelled the water. Sometimes, Hole in the Sunset had said, Snake Water was dry in late summer.

Wants the Moon started to run toward it, stumbling through the knee-high grass and chaparral, the grasshoppers flying out from under her feet. She scrambled down the stony slope to the water's edge and plunged into it, sending spray up around her ankles. The stream was shrunken, only knee-deep, and she lay down to get wet all over, peeled off her skirt, and held it in the current. It floated above the long beards of green moss, blood seeping from its threads.

Six-Legged followed her, cheered by the sight of what appeared to be a fish weir sticking out from the low water. Maybe they could steal someone's fish. Hole in the Sunset had said no one lived out here, if here was where Six-Legged thought it was, but someone could have built the weir and left it. He went down to the water to tell Wants the Moon that and stopped, gaping. On the other bank a horse stood with its nose in the stream. It was a red horse, skin-colored, not their horse, and as it snuffled at the current, a rope trailed from its head into the water. It had appeared like a mushroom after the rain. Out of the trees, maybe. Six-Legged held his breath.

Wants the Moon lay on her back in the current, eyes closed, her shorn hair spreading around her head in a fan. Six-Legged crept to the stream bank. The horse raised its head and looked at him.

"Nice horse," Six-Legged said, stepping softly into the water. "Wait for me, Most Beautiful." The horse pricked its ears toward him.

A howl erupted from somewhere in the trees, and a man crashed out of them, waving a stick over his head. Six-Legged stopped in midstream.

Wants the Moon sat up in the water, then jumped up, holding her wet skirt to her. The man on the bank glared at her, and her eyes opened wide.

Six-Legged stared, too. "Weaver?"

"They drove me away," Weaver said sorrowfully, lowering

his stick. "After she came back." He went to the red horse and laid his head against its flank. The horse swiveled its ears nervously at him.

"I said there would be another." Wants the Moon's teeth unclenched, and her words spilled out, tumbling over each other. "Look, it's a female. I said. I said there was another."

"We have been running," Weaver explained to them. "There was a storm. It tried to take her back again, but I was too smart for the storm, and I tricked it. I know. Yes."

Wants the Moon and Six-Legged looked at each other uncomfortably. She slicked her wet hair back with her fingers and tied her skirt around her waist. "There is a place to go," she said gently to Weaver. "Where they will give many fine presents to this horse."

"Oh, yes," Six-Legged said. He kept his voice low and reassuring. Weaver and Red Horse let their breath out in a sigh.

Wants the Moon and Six-Legged stood in the water and stared at Weaver. Now he was nuzzling his face against Red Horse's hide. "Where did you find her?" Six-Legged asked him finally. How many more were there?

"I told you, she came to the bean field," Weaver said. "She came back."

Back from where? That didn't make any sense, but Weaver had been a little mad when they left and might be even madder now. He looked like one of the buffalo hunters' visionaries, the ones who went off into the desert and ate bugs and saw things. His hair was a tangle of foxtails and cockleburs and probably ticks, and his clothes were torn to tatters, his blanket filthy.

"Was anybody with her?" Six-Legged asked. *Monsters with shiny skin?*

"No, she came by herself. She was hungry."

If she had belonged to the monsters, Six-Legged thought, she was like Horse—she was used to being fed by someone.

"She doesn't like the grandmother's stew," Weaver said. "Or rabbits."

Six-Legged saw the remains of a fire with a ragged carcass

laid across it on a stick. "She's a horse. She eats grass," he said.

"She likes maize," Weaver said.

Six-Legged gave up. "Have you seen my horse? We are looking for my horse."

Wants the Moon waded out of the stream. "Hole in the Sunset might be just as happy with this horse," she said quietly to Six-Legged.

"I want my horse," Six-Legged said stubbornly. "And besides, this one is a female."

She snapped her head around to glare at him. "That is not as good? This one can have babies." The word made her wince, but she bit her lip and the tears stopped.

"Not without the other one," Six-Legged said. "Unless you know something no one else does, Most Knowledgeable."

She broke into ragged laughter. "Maybe they don't do it that way. Maybe we'll have to teach them how, like First Man showing the Mudheads."

Six-Legged smiled at her and touched her shoulder. They waded to the stream bank and came up to Weaver, one on either side. "We'll show you a place where someone will like to see this horse," Wants the Moon said softly, taking Weaver's arm.

Weaver seemed content to go along with them, although he wouldn't let anyone but himself ride Red Horse. They led him in a wide circle, looking for traces of Horse, but he didn't complain. He rode on Red Horse's back, talking softly into her ears, while Wants the Moon and Six-Legged walked beside them.

Once they came on an old pile of round droppings and tried to get Weaver to tell them if he and Red Horse had come this way, but he didn't know.

"He doesn't know where he's been at all," Wants the Moon whispered to Six-Legged.

They shook their heads sorrowfully. At least Hole in the Sunset and his people wouldn't kill him. Mad people were sacred everywhere.

But it was Red Horse who found Horse after all. They stopped for the night where a trickle of water ran down the bottom of a wide wash that was probably full in the spring. They saw tracks of antelope and cats and weasels. In dry country everything drinks from the same dish. And there in the mud at the water's edge was the round, moon-shaped print of a horse.

Six-Legged led Red Horse over to it while Weaver tried to take her rope back from him.

"Stop it!" Six-Legged said. "I want to look at her prints." He pushed Weaver out of the way and handed him Red Horse's rope as soon as he had led her past the print. "Here! Now be quiet."

Six-Legged studied the prints. They weren't the same. Red Horse stuck her nose down in the strange print and snuffled at it like a dog. Wants the Moon was already trotting down the watercourse, following the tracks.

The wind shifted, whirling around itself and then blowing abruptly from the north. Red Horse lifted her head, her nostrils widening. She whinnied, a shrill sound like some huge and unidentifiable bird.

An answering whinny came from the empty air, and she pricked her ears forward. Wants the Moon started to run, her fingers to her mouth, whistling. Weaver grabbed Red Horse's rope to keep her from following.

In a moment they saw him, trotting over a ridge, trailing the tatters of his own rope, his white hide mud-splashed and bedraggled. Red Horse whinnied again, and Horse answered her.

Wants the Moon stopped. If she chased Horse, he would run. He thought it was a game. You had to call him to you. She whistled again, and he trotted toward her. "Oh, muddy and disgusting, Most Disgraceful," she murmured as he picked his way over the stones. "He ran away in the storm. He is lucky he wasn't eaten by cats." She held out her hand and clucked to him.

Horse slithered down the dry edge of the wash, whuffling at her.

"Where have you been, Stupid One?"

He butted his head against her chest.

Red Horse snorted, and Horse looked at her with interest, whickering, forgetting Wants the Moon. She grabbed the frayed end of his rope.

Six-Legged grinned. "Let's see what happens." He started to take Red Horse's rope, but Weaver grabbed him by the shoulder and sent him spinning.

"Ow!" Six-Legged howled, rubbing his shoulder, aggrieved.

Weaver's eyes glittered. "Don't touch her."

"I'm not going to hurt her, Stupid," Six-Legged said. "I want to see if they'll mate."

"No other man may touch my wife. That is not right." Weaver stood between Six-Legged and Red Horse.

"That isn't your wife, that's a horse," Six-Legged said.

Weaver's eyes were wide and glittered like a man who has the fever.

Six-Legged backed away from him a few steps. "That's a horse," he said again.

"That is Quail," Weaver said. "Look at her. She came back from the skeleton people, and when she has been here a little longer she will grow her own skin again. Look at her. You can see her under the animal skin. She is Quail. She told me so."

"That's a horse," Six-Legged said.

Weaver bared his teeth at him and lifted his fist.

Wants the Moon and Horse had come down the wash to them. Wants the Moon took Six-Legged's arm, worried, and Horse pushed his nose into Six-Legged's ear.

"He thinks that horse is his wife," Six-Legged said. "He keeps saying her name."

"Well, quit telling him it isn't," Wants the Moon said uneasily.

"It isn't."

"Do you want him to quit talking about her or not?" Weaver wasn't afraid of his wife's ghost because he was mad, she thought, but anyone else with any sense would be.

"I want to teach her to mate with Horse," Six-Legged said. "What are we going to do now? Do you suppose *he* has—?"

"How do I know?" Wants the Moon snapped. "Men will do anything." She looked at him as if she thought he would, too. But Red Horse didn't look like that would be a safe thing. She danced edgily on her long legs and hard round hooves, trying to pull loose from Weaver's grip.

Horse arched his neck and whickered again, his ears pricked forward.

Weaver pushed Six-Legged farther back. "Don't look at my wife," he said.

"That's a horse," Six-Legged started to say, but Wants the Moon punched his arm. "I don't want her," Six-Legged said surlily instead. He jerked his elbow at Horse, who was pawing at the stones in the wash, digging a hole in the sand with his front hoof. "He does."

"No," Weaver said again.

11

Winter Camp

THE BUFFALO HORN PEOPLE PUT THEIR DEAD UP ON BIERS for the wind to take and cleaned the storm's debris from their camp, stoically parting with the things the storm had wanted.

Wind in the Grass and her mother, Lark, turned her father's head around the right way and closed his eyes while Wind in the Grass wept silently and steadily for her new husband, who had been sent away and might not come back now. Her father's brother, Wolf, married Lark the next day, as befitted the brother-in-law of a new widow. It was his duty, he said, even though the spirit husband of Lark's daughter might not return and then she would be disgraced. Spirits were unreliable; he had said so from the start. Blue Racer and Sunflower, who were mourning their lost wife, heard that and hit him, first one and then the other, hard in the belly, and Hole in the Sunset had to shout at them to be ashamed of themselves before they would stop.

Angry in the Morning had a broken leg, and Elk Walker, the shaman, and his apprentices smeared it with fat and bone-set and tied it between a pair of sticks. Then Angry in the Morning hobbled to Hole in the Sunset's tent with Long Arrow and they talked about what was to be done now. Hole in the Sunset sent scouts to look for the buffalo, and the scouts returned to say that the buffalo had gone, driven by the storm into some other world. Long Arrow took a hunting party to the mountains to look for deer.

Everyone waited to see if the river spirits would come back and bring the buffalo with them. White Buffalo and Wind in the Grass burst into tears again when they thought about it—in less than another moon it would be time to go to Winter Camp, and then their husband wouldn't find them if he came back. That would be all right, Angry in the Morning said, hobbling on his crutch, and White Buffalo said he needn't think she would marry *him* if that happened, then went into her tent to cry some more.

The Buffalo Horn people were loading their dog travoises when Six-Legged and Wants the Moon came back to the camp, bringing Horse and Horse Woman and Weaver with them.

White Buffalo and Wind in the Grass ran out to meet them and flung their arms around Six-Legged, dancing with glee and gawping at Red Horse. Sunflower and Blue Racer were more restrained, as befitted men's dignity, but they grinned from ear to ear, and Wants the Moon accepted their escort gratefully. She could see Hole in the Sunset with Elk Walker and the rest of the Buffalo Horn people waiting for them. She was groggy, weaving with weariness, and clung to the mane on Horse's withers with both hands. Behind her, Weaver rode on Red Horse.

"Who is that?" Sunflower asked her.

"He belongs to the new horse," Wants the Moon said. "So we brought him." The only way to leave him would have been to kill him. He talked softly and steadily to Red Horse as they walked. Wants the Moon wondered what would happen when Weaver learned to talk to the Buffalo Horn people and could tell them this horse was his wife.

She stopped Horse in front of Hole in the Sunset and tried

to stay upright. Elk Walker stumped in a circle around Red Horse, inspecting her.

"This is the mate of Horse, but this man is the only human person who can ride her," Wants the Moon said to Hole in the Sunset, to make sure he wouldn't try and she wouldn't have to worry about Weaver killing him.

Hole in the Sunset frowned. No one had shown him how to ride Horse yet, either. Behind him, Wind in the Grass's Uncle Wolf frowned, too.

"But she will give you many children," Wants the Moon said, hoping Weaver couldn't understand that. "Many horse children and grandchildren."

White Buffalo and Wind in the Grass were still chattering to Six-Legged, one on each arm, telling him all that had happened.

"Be quiet, Daughter," Uncle Wolf said, bustling forward, brushing Elk Walker aside. "These are important matters." He inspected Red Horse up close as Weaver glowered at him from her back. Uncle Wolf looked proprietary. "How many young do these creatures bear at a time?" he asked.

"One!" Wants the Moon snapped. She didn't know, but she didn't like Uncle Wolf. He was as thin and shiftless as his brother, but he was covetous besides. She thought Uncle Wolf had turned the storm to his advantage.

"Our wife is weary," Blue Racer said to Hole in the Sunset, keeping one arm on her thigh where she sat weaving on Horse's back. "It must have taken great magic to bring you this mate for your horse. She needs to rest."

Elk Walker nodded. If the spirits' anger could bring on a storm without their meaning to, their weariness could slow the earth, and so their well-being should be attended to. Uncle had not eaten them, and they had brought the female horse. Therefore their balance was right among the Buffalo Horn people again.

The Young Husbands took Wants the Moon back to her tent, shaking their heads solicitously over her cropped hair, and fed her a bowlful of berries and mush. They patted her and put their hands on her forehead to make sure she didn't have a fever. "We will have many lucky children," they told her when she placed her hands mournfully on her empty belly. "All our children will be lucky children."

"Angry in the Morning and Long Arrow say we will leave the moving-on and hunt on the trip to Winter Camp," Blue Racer said to Sunflower. "You had better go with them then, and I will stay with the travoises and take care of our wife."

"No, you had better go," Sunflower said. "You are a better shot."

"That is not what you said before," Blue Racer retorted. "You said I couldn't hit a buffalo if it lay down in front of me. I heard you say that. I was very insulted."

"Then I am sorry," Sunflower said. "I will admit you are the better shot now."

"It is too late for that." Blue Racer folded his arms. "Most Skillful had better go and hunt deer for both of us."

"While Most Devious lies with our wife and makes another baby," Sunflower said, glowering at him.

"It is not right for a man to prefer lying with his wife to hunting," Blue Racer said. "Now I am insulted again."

"Who said you did? I only said I was sorry I said you were not a good shot."

"You will both go," Wants the Moon told them. "It wouldn't do for people to say my husbands are lazy."

The Young Husbands looked disappointed, but they nodded at each other and said, "Our wife is right. We will do as she says."

Wants the Moon smiled. It was fine to be quarreled over. These young men were not like the men of the cities who had all said she liked her own way too much. The Young Husbands *expected* her to be willful. But willfulness had made the storm come, too. If you lied and said you were a spirit, did you make something happen, so that now it was true? Had Uncle heard her and done that? Wants the Moon lay down uneasily between the Young Husbands and made them lie on either side of her, close, hiding herself behind their warm breath.

The Buffalo Horn people set out at dawn through the wet, shriveled grass for Winter Camp on the high slopes where the sun reached and the winter deer came to browse. They loaded their possessions on travoises pulled by the gray coyotelike dogs who lived with them.

Six-Legged had made a travois for Horse to pull Angry in the Morning, whose leg had not healed yet. He made one for Red Horse, too, but she kicked hers to splinters, so they loaded packs on her back instead. Weaver protested until Six-Legged took him by the throat and threatened to hit him.

"No one is going to hurt her," Six-Legged said between his teeth. "She is only going to carry things. You can ride on her, too, in front of the packs."

That mollified Weaver, and he let them load the rolled skins of tents and baskets full of journey food onto a harness Six-Legged had made for Red Horse. She shuffled her feet and snorted but didn't try to buck it off.

Hole in the Sunset insisted that he ride Horse, as Six-Legged had promised, so Six-Legged showed him how to pull the reins to one side or the other and how to tap Horse with his heel to make him go. Six-Legged and Long Arrow boosted him up, and he settled himself, surveying his band from this new height. He kicked Horse hard with his heel. Horse broke into a trot with Angry in the Morning howling and cursing at the bumps, and Hole in the Sunset fell off.

Horse stopped dutifully.

"This animal does not treat me with respect," Hole in the Sunset said. Long Arrow and Angry in the Morning guffawed.

"It takes practice, Most Wise," Six-Legged murmured.

Hole in the Sunset stuck his chin out. "Then I will get on him again." He jumped as he had seen Six-Legged do, caught his elbows over Horse's withers, and hung, belly-down, kicking his legs, while Horse ambled away.

Hole in the Sunset pulled himself upright and glowered back at Long Arrow and Angry in the Morning. They shushed.

Six-Legged walked behind them, feet blistering, wishing that he had had the foresight to teach Horse to buck other people off.

In the morning, however, Hole in the Sunset discovered that he could not spread his legs far enough apart to get them around Horse again without excruciating pain. He grimaced as Porcupine Mother rubbed his thighs with liniment. Then he gave Horse back to Six-Legged.

"It takes practice," Six-Legged said again, remembering. "Perhaps in Winter Camp."

"No doubt," Hole in the Sunset said with dignity.

He limped beside Elk Walker and Old Grasshopper, whose hereditary right it was to carry the band's medicine bundle, sacred objects rolled in an ancient white buffalo hide. Old Grasshopper, who had seen too many winters, walked unsteadily, and halfway through the morning Elk Walker took the medicine bundle and carried it himself while Old Grasshopper held on to a corner of the yellowing hide. Later they put him on a travois pulled by Elk Walker's apprentices, and he clutched the bundle to his bony chest.

After four days' travel, Six-Legged gave Angry in the Morning's travois to Bull Calf and Bear Paws to pull while he and Weaver rode with the hunting party that broke off from the trail.

There was still no sign of the buffalo herds. They would not be back until spring, Long Arrow said. Their migration pattern had been disturbed; they were like birds at whom someone had thrown a rock. So there would be no buffalo meat to dry and mix with suet and berries to keep the children fat. No thick winter hides to make mittens and caps and robes. In summer, only the best of the meat was kept. It was the autumn buffalo whose every sinew and bone and stringy bite was saved to see the people through the winter. Foolish, Six-Legged thought, not to save in summer, too, the way the People of the Cities did, putting by their meal against a year when the worms came, as they had to the Red Earth town. But he had seen the buffalo covering the plain. When you had that much, perhaps you never thought to save. And what you saved, you had to carry with you. The Buffalo Horn people trailed the herds all year, except in winter.

Now they would have to hunt elk, mountain sheep, and the

red, delicate-legged deer instead, not so plentiful as the buffalo and more wary. That game, too, was scattered since the storm, Long Arrow said, and most of it had gone to the mountains.

Six-Legged had boasted of being able to shoot a bow from Horse's back, and everyone wanted to watch him do it. Weaver could only cling to Red Horse's neck as she galloped, but he would do to help drive the deer, Six-Legged said, if they found any.

Long Arrow had seen antelope prints along the edge of a stream that flowed beneath one of the high bluffs. The bluffs rose unexpectedly from the grassland's floor, like a wall suddenly thrown up.

Uncle Wolf inspected the tracks, and his bony face creased in a smile. "We will drive them with these horses. I will ride on the red one, since the river spirit is married to *my* daughter."

"No!" Weaver appeared to have understood him. Like Six-Legged, he was picking up a few words of the buffalo hunters' talk. He swung around on Red Horse's back and bared his teeth at Uncle Wolf.

"Six-Legged says that this man goes with the new horse," Long Arrow said, exasperated. "Your daughter is not married to the horse."

"Hole in the Sunset has promised me this animal, since he has the white one," Uncle Wolf said.

"No, he hasn't," Six-Legged said, following that and Uncle Wolf's covetous eyes well enough.

"No doubt he will," Uncle Wolf said, unperturbed. "I am your other father-in-law, so it is right."

Six-Legged lost some of that, but Long Arrow pushed Uncle Wolf aside and with gestures told Six-Legged to wait while the hunters set the antelope running. No man could run down an antelope, and Long Arrow privately doubted that a horse could, either, by itself, but they could chase it. The thing to know about antelope was that although they appeared to run in a straight line, they bore always a little to one side, so that eventually they made a great circle. You had only to set your men in the right place to take up the chase. That was what the old men said, anyway, who did not chase antelope themselves anymore these days. In practice, it was not easy.

Six-Legged sat on Horse, swinging his legs and waiting. If they killed an antelope, he might be able to claim the skin. He would give it to Wants the Moon to say he was sorry about the baby. He couldn't give it to either one of his wives because the other one would be angry. Having two young wives was harder than he had thought it would be. They both wanted to be his favorite. White Buffalo was prettier, and she gave herself airs, being the chief's daughter, although Six-Legged had learned that chieftains among these people had limited power. They were leaders, and if no one wanted to follow them, the people chose a new chief. Wind in the Grass, on the other hand, knew several interesting things to do in bed that White Buffalo hadn't heard of. Six-Legged suspected Uncle Wolf of having taught them to her, which would explain why she didn't like him. She hadn't cried over her father either, he remembered.

Six-Legged looked sideways at Uncle Wolf. He was watching Red Horse. When he saw Six-Legged watching him, he strode over to Horse and smiled and nodded at Six-Legged, a shade too friendly, like a man who is trying to sell you a pot that leaks.

"Is my daughter making you a good wife?" Uncle Wolf asked him. "She's a fine young thing." He elbowed Six-Legged jovially in the thigh.

Six-Legged couldn't think of the right words, and he suspected that with Uncle Wolf you wanted to choose your words carefully. He nodded his head gravely instead.

"If she doesn't suit you, I'll beat her for you." Uncle Wolf bobbed his head up and down like a turkey. "They just need training, these girls. When will you teach me to ride the red horse? Hole in the Sunset has promised me that because I am your father-in-law now."

Six-Legged put his heels in Horse's ribs, urging him away so he wouldn't have to answer that. He got Horse between Red Horse and Uncle Wolf.

"Watch and see which way the antelope will run," Six-

Legged said to Weaver. "And then go and wait where it will come around again."

Weaver nodded solemnly and said something into Red Horse's hairy ear. Six-Legged hoped Weaver had understood him. Weaver had learned to hunt among the People of the Cities, who also knew about antelope, but he hadn't been mad then.

Shouts came from up the streambed, and then a crashing in the underbrush. An antelope burst from the chaparral like a shot arrow, springing across the scrub on the bank opposite the bluffs. Six-Legged whirled Horse around, digging his heels into Horse's ribs in earnest now. The antelope leaped across the ground. It was strung with sinew, an animal made of bowstrings, of wind. Running after the antelope on Horse's back was like flying. Six-Legged thought Horse was enjoying it, too. As Horse bent his head low and lengthened his stride, Six-Legged could feel the muscles rippling in his shoulders. This was what Horse was made for, to run. He could carry a pack or pull a travois, but this was his true work. His hooves thundered over the grass, and the wind blew his flying mane into Six-Legged's face.

The antelope was bearing left, hardly noticeably at first, but Six-Legged saw that eventually it would make a great circle around some low hillocks that sprawled beyond the stream. When the hillocks were between them and the bluffs, Six-Legged began to look for Weaver. They shot past a clump of scrub oaks, and Red Horse ran from the trees, hard on the antelope's flank. Six-Legged drew rein and Horse slowed, breathing hard. His neck was wet, and foam dribbled from his mouth.

"It's an antelope," Six-Legged said, patting Horse's shoulder. "And you are a fine horse to nearly catch it." Horse blew down his nose, his shoulder muscles twitching. Six-Legged turned them back the way they had come, walking slowly while Horse's breathing slowed. A little wind came up and stirred the hair between his ears. They crossed the hillocks and settled to wait, resting, the way coyotes do when they are taking turns chasing something. Maybe the coyote people *had* taught men to hunt, Six-Legged thought.

Weaver and Red Horse drove the antelope past where Six-Legged had first taken up the chase, and Six-Legged and Horse ran after it again while Weaver and Red Horse slowed. The antelope was bearing harder to the left now as it tired. The curve of its circle grew tighter, hugging close to the edge of the hillocks. On the other side, Six-Legged gave the antelope to Weaver again. Horse lumbered over the hillocks, breathing hard, and they settled to rest again, but it wasn't long before they heard the thunder of hooves on the hard ground. When the antelope came into sight, it was flagging, its tongue flopping from the side of its mouth, eyes wild, head flecked with foam. Red Horse ran behind it with Weaver clinging to her mane.

Six-Legged drove his heels into Horse's ribs, and Horse shot down the slope. The antelope saw him and veered, but Weaver came up on its right side and it veered back. The other hunters joined the chase now, spilling from their hiding place. Six-Legged saw Bull Calf lumbering through the grass, drawing his bow as he ran. Bear Paws and Uncle Wolf were beside him. Six-Legged hoped they didn't hit him instead.

The antelope had more speed left in it than anyone had guessed. Six-Legged heard Long Arrow shout at them as they passed, and he grinned. The men couldn't keep up, but Horse was gaining on it. Flecks of foam flew back from the antelope's mouth. Horse's back was wet with sweat. Six-Legged unslung his new bow from his shoulder and reached for an arrow from the quiver on his back. The antelope's neck bobbed just ahead of him, and he could hear its labored breathing, wheezing from deep in its chest. Six-Legged gripped Horse with his knees and drew his bow.

The antelope made a frenzied leap through a clump of tall grass, seed heads exploding around it, as Six-Legged loosed his arrow. The antelope stumbled as the arrow pierced its neck. It flung its head back, sending up a shower of blood as it ran, then stumbled again just as they passed Weaver waiting on the edge of the ever-narrowing circle.

The antelope crashed down, back legs flung nearly over its head with the momentum of its fall. Six-Legged leaped off Horse and waited for someone to help him. The antelope was thrashing on the ground, its horns and split hooves slicing the air. The hunters' dogs came up and nipped at the antelope, dodging in and out of the flying hooves. Long Arrow ran up with a rope and looped it around the horns so Six-Legged could slit its throat.

"Thank you, brother," Six-Legged said dutifully to the antelope as he drew the knife across the wet neck that was already soaked with blood and foam and caked with dust. The antelope shuddered and thrashed to stillness.

"That is a good trick," Uncle Wolf said while Long Arrow cut the liver from the belly and handed pieces of it to the hunters. "I think my horse runs faster than yours."

"It's not your horse," Six-Legged said. Uncle Wolf was eating a piece of the liver, the blood running down his chin, just as if he had been the one to kill the antelope. Six-Legged looked to see if Long Arrow had given Weaver some. He had. Weaver was trying to feed it to Red Horse. She threw her head back, and he put his hand on her nose and tried to make her open her mouth. Finally the liver fell in the grass, and one of the dogs ate it.

"He is not right in the head, that one," Bull Calf said.

Long Arrow frowned at him. Bull Calf had a way of saying what other people were thinking when they had decided that it was best to leave it unsaid.

"He thinks that animal is his wife," Lark said to Porcupine as they were clearing out the lodges in Winter Camp. She threw an armful of debris out the door and chuckled.

"Then all the more reason you should keep your husband away from him," Porcupine said severely.

"Oh, I can't do anything with Wolf." Lark didn't sound overly concerned. She had always claimed not to be able to do anything with her first husband, either.

Porcupine thought it would be a long winter sharing a lodge with Wolf. She shaded her eyes and inspected the sky through the open roof. The men had already dug and dragged the old earthen covering and the willow mats away and had gone to cut new beams in place of those that had rotted over the summer. Now she and Lark and their daughters would weave new mats and cut the grass that would go under the new earth roof. In the winter everyone in a family shared a lodge. That meant Lark and Wolf and the girls and their husband and the husband's other wife and *her* husbands. Porcupine saw her sitting outside the lodge, inexpertly lacing willow withes together, and clucked her tongue. And what were they going to do with the man who had come with the new horse? No one had told her that. She supposed *he* would have to come inside, too.

"Why would he marry an animal, anyway?" she asked Lark. "That is only something in old stories. People don't do it nowadays."

"He didn't marry *it*," Lark said. "He had a wife, and she died when the white animal came into their village, Wants the Moon said."

"Did the white animal *kill* her?" Porcupine laid her broom down.

"Oh, no, she died of some sickness. So when the *other* animal came to their village—"

"How many of these animals are there?"

"Wolf says maybe many more," Lark said. "Angry in the Morning says we should go and look for them."

"I don't think that's a good idea," Porcupine said. "We don't know what they may do yet." She knit her brows. Was it a good thing to have White Buffalo married to that man? Angry in the Morning had wanted her, and Porcupine Mother thought White Buffalo had wanted him, too, only they had had a fight. And then the river people had come. Hole in the Sunset had thought it was a fine opportunity for White Buffalo, but Porcupine knew that Elk Walker had told the medicine bundle to watch the river people carefully. What if the new people turned into horses, too? Porcupine Mother had seen the white horse. She didn't want her daughter married to that.

"Anyway," Lark said chattily, apparently not worried about

Wind in the Grass, "when the other animal came, and it was a woman animal, this man thought it was his wife come back. Maybe it is."

Porcupine supposed it could be. Elk Walker thought these new animals were magical, so they *might* be able to be human people. It was very confusing, and the possibilities made her head spin. "Well, no wonder he's crazy," she said. "A thing like that would make any man crazy."

Weaver was sane enough to cut lodgepoles. Six-Legged took him off with Sunflower and Blue Racer to bring back a load of saplings for the roof. Six-Legged had quit being angry over the Young Husbands since he would have to live with them for the winter. Winter had a way of mending quarrels, one way or another. Six-Legged practiced talking to them, wrapping his tongue around the hard edges of this new speech, while they laughed when he got it wrong and clapped him on the back when he didn't. Weaver didn't talk at all, but they treated him respectfully because Wants the Moon had told them to.

The autumn wind had begun to blow the leaves off the trees. The squash seeds that the Buffalo Horn people had planted last spring before they left Winter Camp had made vines and fat yellow squashes, and there were some left that the animal people hadn't got to first. The Buffalo Horn people's way of farming made Six-Legged shake his head: They just put things in the ground and left them. It was like leaving your children to fend for themselves while you went hunting all summer. You were lucky when Coyote left you a few of them.

"That's for the women," Blue Racer said when Six-Legged said something about the squash. "Squash is women's business."

Six-Legged supposed they didn't have time to be good mothers to the squash when they had to carry their real children from camp to camp. The people here did everything backward. The women did the planting and gave the squash what little care it got. They wove baskets. They didn't make pots because pots broke if they were packed on a dog and moved every other moon. No one wove cloth because there was no cotton to weave it with. They wore deerskins or buffalo skins. Everything was measured in buffalo hides: an eight-hide tent, a twenty-hide bride.

Even the earth lodge was measured in hides, although it was built of logs driven into the ground in a circle, inside a knee-deep pit. An entrance corridor extended from the circular pit, and the floor sloped down it to the main lodge. The buffalo hunters built a roof over the lodge out of logs and willow mats and grass, much like the roofs of the cities. But then they packed earth over the roof and walls until it resembled a little hillock in the ground with smoke coming from the smoke hole.

Twenty hides, Hole in the Sunset said proudly, holding up both hands once and then again, and sweeping his arms wide—big enough for the whole family and the horses and dogs. It was warm inside. The earthen roof and walls held the fire's heat, but it made Six-Legged feel as if he were in a badger's den.

His wives seemed to like it, although they complained about Wants the Moon getting the antelope hide, and when they were tired of that they braided and rebraided their hair and squabbled over Six-Legged until Porcupine called them lazy and made them help her pick piñon nuts out of their cones. Wants the Moon, scraping the antelope hide, watched them with a half-hidden smile.

Six-Legged had felt awkward around her ever since they had come back from finding the new horse and Weaver, but he sat down beside her, just outside the lodge door, while she kneaded the antelope's brain into the hide. She had saved it until they got to Winter Camp.

"The babies will be jealous." She smiled at him slyly.

"Don't call them that. They're the same age I am," Six-Legged said grumpily.

"I know." Wants the Moon nodded with obvious sympathy. "If we had stayed home, you wouldn't have married so young, not until you were ready to weave some girl a blanket. Your wife might be young, but you wouldn't be. *Someone* has to be not young."

"And I suppose that was you?"

"Certainly," Wants the Moon said. "*My* husbands know better than to spend their day talking to *that* man, for instance." She nodded at Uncle Wolf, who was speaking earnestly to Wind in the Grass. Wind in the Grass shifted her feet, but she nodded when he talked to her.

Six-Legged growled.

The wind whipped suddenly about their ears, and Wants the Moon looked at the sky. It was gray and thick as a blanket. "Snow soon," she said.

She took her hide inside the lodge. Six-Legged got up to do something about Uncle Wolf, but Uncle Wolf had gone. He was inside, too, talking to Hole in the Sunset and watching the stew cooking on the hearth. He was like a fire that smoked, Six-Legged thought. He blew in your face, and when you got up and moved, he moved, too, and blew in your face over there.

The women had dried the antelope meat and the deer they had killed when they came to Winter Camp, and Porcupine Mother and Lark had boiled a little of it with wild onions and the withered autumn squash. They were trying to make it last. There was a piece as large as his little finger in Six-Legged's bowl. He chewed it greedily while the dogs gobbled their share from the hearth. He heard Uncle Wolf trying to tell Porcupine Mother that his piece was smaller than it should have been.

"When you have killed something, you will have more to eat," she said tartly, and Blue Racer snickered. Wolf took his bowl away sulkily and went to sit by Weaver. Weaver looked at him suspiciously, but Wolf clapped him on the back and nodded respectfully to Red Horse, chewing dried grass.

"Your wife looks very fine this evening," Wolf said.

Six-Legged glared across the lodge at him. "You are not to talk to that man when I am not here," he said to Wind in the Grass.

When the family had eaten, they wrapped themselves in their blankets. The sky darkened early in winter, and there was no point in being awake after dark. Hole in the Sunset and Porcupine Mother had the center bed, near the fire. The rest were laid in a circle against the wall of the lodge. Everyone's belongings were stacked in baskets and boxes between the beds. Six-Legged could hear them all breathing, punctuated by the rattling snore that Hole in the Sunset made. The lodge was stuffy with so many people's breath and the heat of their bodies. The tang of the horses added itself to the woodsmoke and dog smell. Six-Legged's stomach growled.

The snow came down that night, leaving Winter Camp white and mysterious by dawn light, smoke rising from buried hillocks all along the river. Six-Legged looked out the lodge door and thought of the otters in their dens under the stream bank. He wondered wistfully if there were otters here. Probably not. Winter Camp was too clearly human territory. The animal people would have moved out when the human people came back. He went inside the lodge again and began packing up his bow and arrows and the new snowshoes he had made. Snow made game easy to track, and the heavier animals could move only ponderously through deep drifts.

They brought back nothing, though. It was like bringing something, Six-Legged thought, that nothing in your hands. You could almost feel it, hard and inedible. Horse and Red Horse were no help in the snow. They floundered deeper than the deer, and Weaver took Red Horse back and put her by the fire in the lodge and tried to make her drink the tea that Porcupine Mother had made for his cough.

"That man is not right in the head," Porcupine Mother said, and no one argued with her. Hole in the Sunset thought that if Weaver was not right in the head then maybe he would wander out into the snow one day and not come back. Then they could make the new red horse mate with the white one without any argument. Hole in the Sunset went to talk to Six-Legged about that.

"I don't think that will happen," Six-Legged said. Weaver never even left the fire unless Six-Legged made him.

"Then when is the woman horse going to have a calf?" Hole in the Sunset demanded.

"They will decide when they want to do that," Six-Legged

said. "It is a magical horse thing, not for human people to mix into."

"Maybe they don't know how," Hole in the Sunset said. "You could show them." He looked at Wants the Moon, who was sitting a little away from them, listening and pretending not to. Elk Walker said that wasn't a good idea—if the river spirits could make a tornado with their anger, who knew what they would make with that—but Hole in the Sunset wanted a horse calf. "You should show them."

"They know how," Six-Legged said. He had watched Horse trying already, climbing onto Horse Woman's back the way a dog did. She had kicked him, and Weaver had run out of the lodge shouting at them. Six-Legged suspected that when Horse Woman was ready she wouldn't listen to Weaver's shouting. Wants the Moon said Horse Woman was waiting for her season, the way the deer and the buffalo did. Only human people were willing to do it all the time, she said.

"What will happen if Weaver does it?" Six-Legged wanted to know. He waited until Hole in the Sunset had gone before he said that.

"I don't know," Wants the Moon said. "She might have monsters."

"They're already monsters," Six-Legged said.

"Wrong monsters. I don't know." Wants the Moon looked at Red Horse, and Red Horse looked back at her enigmatically. "It wouldn't be a good idea for him to do that," she said.

Winter blew another moon of cold breath down and froze the mountains. Everyone's belly ached. It was growing harder to find grass for the horses, too. Six-Legged and Wants the Moon dug it out of the snow, but it was thin and frozen or half rotted. Weaver kept trying to feed Red Horse his own food, so that neither of them ate. The horses grew gaunter, along with the human people in the lodges. A baby died. The wailing came up from the baby's lodge under the snow like smoke rising from the smoke hole. Six-Legged thought he could see the baby's spirit leaving with the smoke. No babies came to be started that winter, either. Six-Legged waited for his wives or for Wants the Moon to get pregnant again, but no one did. Porcupine Mother said the babies didn't want to come and be hungry.

Elk Walker asked the medicine bundle about it, and the medicine bundle told him the horses would call the buffalo back in the spring. It didn't say how to keep alive *now*. When there was a warm stretch and the snow melted, Six-Legged and Weaver and the Young Husbands took the horses and brought back an old elk, dragging it behind them and shouting with pride. It fed the band for a while, and Six-Legged gave the hide to White Buffalo.

Weaver didn't care about the hide, but Wind in the Grass pouted and began talking to Uncle Wolf when Six-Legged wasn't there. The Young Husbands had a quarrel when the men from another lodge laughed at them and asked why *they* hadn't brought back a hide. The antelope skin that Six-Legged had given their wife began to look larger as she worked on it, larger and finer, and it glowed slightly in the dusty, dim lodge. Sunflower shoved Blue Racer and Blue Racer shoved him back and went to talk with the men from the other lodge. They were beginning to act like soft men, Bull Calf said, chuckling, and maybe they should put on dresses. Sunflower would have hit him if Hole in the Sunset hadn't come to his lodge door and bellowed at them.

Uncle Wolf began to talk to Weaver, murmuring in his ear, and young men from other lodges joined them, telling Weaver jokes and bringing him grass for the red horse and treating her with elaborate respect.

"They are telling him that he should be chief Person With a Horse," Blue Racer reported to Sunflower. "Elk Walker said the horses must talk to the buffalo or we will always be hungry, and they are saying that the river spirits and Hole in the Sunset can't make them do that. Last night Elk Walker dreamed that it takes a lot of horses to talk to buffalo, and Wolf says Hole in the Sunset can't make them have a calf, either."

"I don't like that," Sunflower said, forgetting their feud.

"They are saying that we should go and get more horses

from the People of the Cities, where the crazy one came from."

"The horses came from the Buffalo Trail Water. Long Arrow said so."

"They don't believe that now." Blue Racer thought a moment. "I don't either. Our wife and the river man talk like the People of the Cities. She says there are no more horses, but if they came from our river, why should there be just two of them there?"

"There were only two people at the beginning of the world."

"This is not the beginning of the world."

"Do you think they have lied?" Sunflower looked shocked.

Blue Racer thought some more. "I don't know. She talks to him in the cities' talk, and sometimes I listen. I think they have lied."

"How do you know the cities' talk?"

"Yah, I am not stupid. I have been to trade fairs. If that man can learn our talk by listening, I can learn theirs. I talk to Weaver sometimes. Maybe those people are no more river spirits than you and I are. Weaver says the horses came to the cities."

"*And* he thinks that horse is his wife."

"True." Blue Racer grinned. "It doesn't matter to me. I like being a spirit's husband. Porcupine Mother gives me good food."

"There is no good food."

"Better food, then. But I am going to watch that Wolf. And Bull Calf. He has been talking to Bull Calf, who is as stupid as a groundhog and does what the last person to talk to him has told him to."

"There are more horses in the cities to the west," Bull Calf said to Bear Paws, who lived in the lodge of Old Onion Digger's daughter. "They walked up out of a hole in the ground."

"Where did they come from?" Bear Paws asked.

"Out of the hole," Bull Calf said. "That is what Wolf says the crazy person told him. We ought to have them, not the cities people who squat on the ground and plant seeds and live all their lives in boxes, like prairie dogs.''

''How would we get some?''

''Well, go and take them,'' Bull Calf said. ''The way the river people who came out of Buffalo Trail Water did. That is what the crazy person says, that those people are from the cities, too.''

''Those are river spirits,'' Bear Paws said. ''Long Arrow said so. So does Elk Walker.''

''Maybe they are river spirits from the cities.'' Bull Calf looked irritated. Uncle Wolf hadn't explained it properly.

It didn't matter. Winter was when young men who were cold and hungry in their lodges thought about fighting and a spring war trail. ''*I* want a horse,'' Bear Paws said. ''You are right. We ought to go and take some.''

''Why should cities people have them?'' Bull Calf thought of the other things Uncle Wolf had said. ''They are our enemies, anyway. Let's go and fight them for the new animals. Then we can ride the new animals and find the buffalo. And then *we* will have new hides.''

''And besides,'' Bear Paws said, ''people will sing about us if we fight the cities people.''

''That is what I think.''

That winter, when there was not enough to eat, the idea of horses grew. They were ghost horses, horses-yet-to-come, who put their bony heads in through the lodge doors while people slept, left their moon-shaped prints in the snow, ate the ends of ropes and the last withered squashes, slobbering the crumbs down whiskered lips, so that in the morning men remembered galloping under the earth, bursting upward through grass, and women remembered the pungent scent of sweat-salted hides. *We will come to you,* the horses said, their dark eyes reflecting the wanting, the longing the Buffalo Horn people began to feel for them.

''What are you saying to the young men?'' Long Arrow lifted Wolf by the shoulder and pushed him up against the wall of Hole in the Sunset's lodge with one hand.

"That there are more horses in the cities to the west," Wolf said. "That is only what the new crazy man has told me."

"Why should he tell you? Bear Paws came to me this morning with some tale about a war trail and a vote of the young men. *I* decide when the young men will vote." Long Arrow pushed his face into Wolf's.

Angry in the Morning had been sitting with Wolf, making snowshoes and grumbling. His leg had healed, although he still walked with a limp. Now he nodded at Long Arrow. "The horses live in the rivers there. That is what the new man has told people."

"The new man is just learning our talk," Long Arrow said. "He could mean anything. He called an onion a tadpole yesterday."

"There is only one word for the horse animals," Angry in the Morning said.

"The People of the Cities have learned to call them out of the rivers," Wolf said. He clapped one hand on Long Arrow's arm. "We should go there and get some. And you should lead us."

"But Hole in the Sunset will not let us." Angry in the Morning scowled. He had been chewing on a leather thong to soften it, and it made him look as if he had a mouthful of worms.

Long Arrow loosened his grip on Wolf. Wolf edged around him, sat down again, and clapped Angry in the Morning on the back. "And since when have you listened so mindfully to Hole in the Sunset? Who gave White Buffalo to someone else? Who slighted you in front of all the Buffalo Horn people?"

Angry in the Morning stiffened and glared at Wolf.

"He is still chief," Long Arrow said.

"And he wants a horse calf," Wolf said.

"I am going to talk to him," Long Arrow said. "This is not your business."

"The rivers that flow past the cities are full of these horses," Wolf said. "You will see."

*   *   *

If there was one thing that Uncle liked, it was fighting some-one. And if there was something else he liked, it was causing trouble, stirring someone's stew with a stick. All the young men and old women knew this, and Hole in the Sunset knew it, too. He could feel Uncle in Winter Camp with them when Elk Walker and the Dog Dancers turned the sun around at the solstice. Hole in the Sunset almost saw him one morning, walking along between the lodges with a cloud of shiny insects around his head. There were no insects in winter, so Hole in the Sunset knew who it was. He could feel him in the lodge, too, settling himself by the fire, settling in. He felt hungry.

There isn't any more to eat, Uncle, Hole in the Sunset said to him. *If you will bring us something, we will share it with you.*

Uncle didn't say anything. He just felt hungry. He *was* hunger, dropping like a hide over everyone's head, wrapping himself around them.

After the solstice Six-Legged came indignantly to Hole in the Sunset with a tale that Wants the Moon had heard from the Young Husbands, who had been talking to Wolf.

"There are no horses in the rivers there!" Six-Legged said.

"Would it hurt to go and see?" Hole in the Sunset had talked to Long Arrow, and on the whole they thought it might be a good idea.

"It is forbidden," Six-Legged said. "If you do that, these horses will go away."

Hole in the Sunset rubbed his chin. It wouldn't do to make this person, who might still be a spirit person, take his horse away. The woman could do it, Hole in the Sunset knew from experience. He could feel Uncle watching him from the fire. These horses were making trouble. There were not enough of them, and so everyone was jealous. *Did you send these to us?* he asked Uncle, but Uncle didn't answer this time, either.

Now Wants the Moon was standing before Hole in the Sunset, too, her hands balled into fists on her hips, her chin stuck out. Hole in the Sunset's daughter was shrieking at her husband's other wife over who was First Wife and Most Important Wife, and Porcupine Mother was muttering over her stew kettle, which was full of thin, dried ground squirrel meat and winter nettles. Wolf was throwing bones with Sunflower, and Blue Racer was brushing his hair. Hole in the Sunset had the urge to push them all out of the lodge, tumble them into the snow, and pile boxes in the door.

"I will tell the young men that they are to obey," he said carefully to Six-Legged. "That will settle the matter."

12

The Raiders

HOLE IN THE SUNSET HAD BEEN CLEVER. HE KNEW HE HAD been clever. It was all in how you said things. Uncle had showed him how. When the snow began to melt and everyone was thin and quarrelsome, he told the young men that they were to obey Angry in the Morning.

That made Angry in the Morning happy, and he stopped sulking over White Buffalo. Also, it got Wolf out of Hole in the Sunset's lodge, because Angry in the Morning agreed to take Wolf with him. If Hole in the Sunset was lucky, the People of the Cities would kill Wolf, and he wouldn't come back. The war party left at night when no one saw them go, and Hole in the Sunset and Long Arrow were very surprised in the morning.

The rest of the Buffalo Horn people had only begun to get ready to leave Winter Camp. The snow was still patchy on the ground, and more might fall before the end of the Spring Grass Moon. There were bodies still half frozen on their biers, set on poles above Winter Camp, the last bed of those who hadn't lived through the starving time. It was like living in the Skeleton House, Wants the Moon thought; these people were indecent.

It was still half dark when Wants the Moon woke. The Young Husbands were not there. The sun was just beginning to look over the bluffs to the east, and she fell over a dog in the darkness of the lodge. The dog yipped and ran behind Hole in the Sunset's bed while Wants the Moon peered around her, looking for her husbands. Their bows and quivers were gone, and the box that held their best clothes was open and looked as if someone had rummaged in it with a rake. She stumbled past Lark and Wolf's bed and saw that Uncle Wolf wasn't there, either.

Wants the Moon shook Lark awake by her ears. "Where are they?"

"Whatsit?" Lark said sleepily, but Wants the Moon didn't believe she was asleep. Lark snored, and she hadn't been snoring when Wants the Moon crept up on her.

"Where are my men? Where is your man?"

Lark pushed her away with one hand. "Gone to get horses," she said slyly.

Wants the Moon stumbled across the lodge and down the entranceway and pushed open the double hide that hung over the door. Horse was still where he was supposed to be, tethered outside now that the nights were warmer. His white hide gleamed like shells. She could see Red Horse in the pink dawn light, cropping grass beside him.

But there were tracks in the muddy ground between the lodges. Many tracks, men and dogs, and the marks of travois poles. She thought of the other women last night, the odd smirks she had seen on their faces, the whispers behind hands as she washed her skirt and blanket in the river while they cleaned cooking baskets. *You are dirty,* she thought, *living in hides.* She knew they thought she was prissy and gave herself airs for wearing her cotton clothes and washing them out in the icy river. Now she knew there had been more to it than that. White Buffalo and Wind in the Grass were usually more afraid of her. She went back inside and shook Six-Legged's wives out of his bed. Six-Legged was still there.

"Where are the men?"

"What men?" Six-Legged sat up. "Leave them alone. What men?"

"My husbands are gone. Uncle Wolf is gone. There are tracks outside."

Six-Legged swore and grabbed White Buffalo. "Did you know about this?"

White Buffalo shook her head.

"Yes, she did," Wind in the Grass said.

"Be quiet!" White Buffalo slapped her, and Wind in the Grass grabbed White Buffalo's hair.

"Uncle Wolf told me, and you listened in," Wind in the Grass said, yanking on White Buffalo's hair.

Wants the Moon cuffed them both. "Yah, you are stupid. Where have they gone?"

"To get horses," White Buffalo said sulkily.

"From the People of the Cities," Wind in the Grass said. "Uncle Wolf says there are horses in the rivers there. Now everybody will have one."

"There are fish in the rivers," Wants the Moon said. She looked miserably at Six-Legged. "Now there will be a war. I wish I had never seen your horse."

"We can catch them," Six-Legged said. "On Horse. Hole in the Sunset will come with us and make them stop."

But when they woke him, Hole in the Sunset scratched his head and announced the need to confer with Long Arrow.

"How do you know Long Arrow hasn't gone with them?" Wants the Moon asked suspiciously.

"*If* he didn't go with them," Hole in the Sunset amended with dignity. He heaved himself from his bed and put on his best fringed shirt and buffalo robe while Six-Legged and Wants the Moon danced from one foot to the other with impatience. "I only think Long Arrow hasn't gone because he is a dutiful young man, and his duty just now is to help me lead the people from Winter Camp," he explained. He coughed. The explanation sounded overly elaborate to him, and suspicious. Trickery was complicated. It was not as easy as Uncle made it look.

"We will go and confer with Elk Walker," Hole in the Sunset said. "Come along."

They followed him, stepping over Weaver, who was still there, lying on his back, snoring. Porcupine Mother watched them with a worried look.

Long Arrow was already in Elk Walker's lodge. Besides the shaman, there was no one else there. Maybe all of Elk Walker's young men had gone with the war party, Wants the Moon thought, grinding her teeth.

"The young men have taken the war trail," Long Arrow said solemnly. "They did not tell me this. It is a surprise to me."

"I knew you would stay behind," Hole in the Sunset said. "When this woman told me the men were gone, I knew you would not have gone, too. You are a dutiful young man." He tried to remember what to say next. Long Arrow was not supposed to have said his speech until Hole in the Sunset asked him about it. Now they were all tangled, as if someone had started the wrong pattern in the Dog Dance.

"Yah, you are all fools!" Wants the Moon said, interrupting. "There are no horses there, and now you will make a war for nothing, and those are my people! I am angry, and I am going to take the horses away."

"Where would we take them?" Six-Legged hissed at her in their own language.

"To stop them! And if they don't stop, we will make another storm."

"Oh, no, we won't," Six Legged said to that. "It would come and eat us."

Hole in the Sunset watched them argue. That wasn't how it was supposed to go either, but the river people weren't paying any attention to him. He looked at Long Arrow and then at Elk Walker and nodded his head.

"Hole in the Sunset will send Long Arrow with us," Six-Legged said to Wants the Moon. He hadn't quite finished saying it when someone grabbed him from behind. Long Arrow stuck his foot between Six-Legged's, and Six-Legged sprawled on the floor. He howled with indignation.

Two of Elk Walker's apprentices, who had been hiding behind the bed, jumped on Wants the Moon and held her down while Elk Walker tried to tie her hands. Wants the Moon kicked her legs and bit the hand over her mouth, but Elk Walker got a rope around her anyway. He was surprisingly strong. He pulled her hands behind her back while one of his young men sat on her legs. Wants the Moon thrashed frantically, but she couldn't get loose.

When they had tied her up, they sat her against the lodge wall and propped Six-Legged next to her. He had been cursing steadily, but now he was silent, glaring at them with baleful eyes. Wants the Moon called them all bad names in a low, furious voice, while Elk Walker marched back and forth in front of them chanting and sprinkling them with dried leaves that smelled like skunks.

"The horses will go away!" Wants the Moon spat at them.

"The horses will stay where you are," Hole in the Sunset said. "And the crazy person can feed them. We are very sorry to do this to such important people, but it would not be a good idea for you to go after the young warriors. We will feed you, and when they bring back many horses, we will let you loose."

"We will curse you!" Six-Legged said.

"That is why Elk Walker has made a spell around you," Long Arrow said. He and Hole in the Sunset sounded as if it was important to them that Six-Legged and Wants the Moon understand it all. "So you cannot do that."

"Yah, you are stupid," Wants the Moon said disgustedly. "There are no horses in the rivers there. Your young warriors will get killed, and they have my husbands with them!"

"They will get big reputations on this war path," Hole in the Sunset said. "You should be pleased."

She spat at him and kicked her feet on the floor.

"We will leave you now," Hole in the Sunset said. "Elk Walker has said you may use this lodge until we are ready for Moving On. Porcupine Mother will bring you some food."

"I have to piss," Wants the Moon said.

"Porcupine Mother will bring you a bowl."

They left. Wants the Moon beat the back of her head against the lodge wall.

"Stop it," Six-Legged said. "You are making my head hurt."

"Weaver," Wants the Moon said. "We have to get Weaver to come in here."

"No, we don't."

"He can untie us."

"He is crazy. Someone else will come. We'll just have to see who it is."

Wants the Moon glowered at him. "Do you have a plan?"

"I might if you would be quiet."

"Yah!" Wants the Moon flung herself back against the wall with a muttered curse. He was no help. Six-Legged always wanted to wait and see what happened, but Wants the Moon knew that things happened because you pushed them along. Uncle had told her that.

Uncle watched the war party traveling along the plains, his eyes in a raven that circled over them. Their passing made a great wind, so that something else seemed to be traveling behind them. The grama and the buffalo grass bent under their feet, and the rivers were printed with their shape, leaving holes in the water that could be seen in the right light.

Whatever was behind them made the young men's necks itch, and they kept looking over their shoulders.

"It is our wife coming after us," Blue Racer said solemnly. "I told you so."

"When we have brought her many horses, she will not be angry," Sunflower said. "Anyway, Hole in the Sunset won't let her come after us."

"Something is," Blue Racer said.

With only war gear and journey food to carry, the young men traveled swiftly across the land, until the food was gone. When they stopped to hunt, Wolf and Angry in the Morning argued because Wolf saw the tracks of stranger people who had begun their spring Moving On early, and he wanted to raid them. Angry in the Morning insulted him by saying that they were going to raid the People of the Cities, not fight strangers because Wolf was too lazy to hunt. Blue Racer and Sunflower looked shocked at that—insults were bad luck in a war party. Maybe when they had horses, they would fight them on the way back, Angry in the Morning said, trying to take back the insult. Wolf had to be content with that, but it plainly irked him that he was not in charge.

The raven with Uncle's eyes lit on the end of a dog travois and watched Wolf, head cocked, its polished agate eye gleaming. In a moment it flew up with a dark flapping of wings that made the dogs leap in the air and snap at it, and circled over Angry in the Morning, stumping grimly along in the lead.

The Spring Grass Moon dwindled from a lopsided gourd to a thin sliver before Hole in the Sunset's people were ready for Moving On. Six-Legged and Wants the Moon spent the time in Elk Walker's lodge, cursing Hole in the Sunset and then each other. It was dark in the lodge, with only the fire and the smoke hole to let in light. After the first day, Long Arrow came and untied them and took them up the entranceway, blinking in the sunlight, to let them see the four men with bows standing just outside the door. He left them untied after that.

Porcupine Mother brought them food every day and told Six-Legged that his wives missed him.

"Let them come and stay with me," he suggested.

Porcupine Mother shook her head. "They would let you loose. You would talk them into it."

"You should let us loose," Six-Legged said. "You know this is not good."

"I know it is a starving time, and if we have more of these animals that a man can ride on, then we can catch more food," Porcupine Mother said. "That is what I know."

Six-Legged sighed. "There aren't any more."

Porcupine Mother just shook her head and collected their dirty bowls. She waddled up the entranceway to the door.

Wants the Moon looked at Six-Legged out of the gloom.

"If we could get one of your wives to come in, you could make her help us. They haven't any sense."

"It's a fine thing to insult my wives and ask them to help us."

"I'm talking to *you,* not to them."

Six-Legged sat down on his bed and sighed. He missed his wives, warm on either side of him. They didn't argue with him, and he was beginning to forget that they argued with each other instead. His body ached for them. He looked at Wants the Moon. Neither of them had said anything, and they were still husband and wife by the buffalo hunters' reckoning, but somehow they had come to the mutual knowledge that they wouldn't get in bed together. It would not be forbidden, but somehow it would not be right, either.

Two-leggeds make too many rules for themselves, a voice said from the smoke hole. Six-Legged jerked his head up but didn't see anything. Then a gray spill of smoke seemed to drift *downward* and settle itself in the embers of the fire. Wants the Moon didn't notice; she was making a pot with the river mud that she had convinced Porcupine to bring her, even though there was nowhere to fire it and it would break anyway in the Moving On. She shaped and slapped the clay with single-minded concentration.

Six-Legged looked at the smoke thing.

"That one is right. Those girls don't have any sense," it said.

"I know that."

"Those men are halfway to your city by now. Something is watching them, but I am watching it. When are you going to go after them?"

"Why do you want me to?"

Coyote materialized until he was solid enough to scratch behind his ear. "Something is going to happen. You should be part of it."

"Why? I am tired of being part of things you think up."

"I didn't think it up. I thought I did, but I was wrong. Now we have to be part of it anyway." Coyote stood and disappeared up the smoke hole.

"Did you see him?" Six-Legged demanded.

Wants the Moon didn't look up. "No." She slapped the coils of wet clay with the palm of her hand, flattening them. "I didn't see anyone."

In the morning, Porcupine Mother came and got them. "We are going now. Behave yourselves. I haven't time to look after you."

She bustled off again. Wants the Moon saw that Weaver was riding Red Horse and leading Horse on a rope. He had packs on his back. She stuck her fingers in her mouth and whistled, and Horse turned his head around.

"Stop that," said one of the men with bows. They were grandfathers who walked beside and behind Wants the Moon and Six-Legged. *Yah, they are dodderers,* Wants the Moon thought. But certainly they could shoot an arrow faster than she could run.

The Buffalo Horn women had put their squash seeds in the ground and then loaded all their goods on their backs and on the dog travoises. They looked like a band from the Skeleton House, Wants the Moon thought sadly. Babies too little or sick to walk hung on cradle boards from the women's backs, and thin toddlers staggered after, clutching their mothers' dresses. She supposed she looked like that, too. Six-Legged's face was gaunt, and his arms were bony.

She caught a glimpse of Six-Legged's wives walking with Lark and Porcupine Mother, baskets on their heads. They craned their necks to see Six-Legged, and Lark and Porcupine Mother cuffed them. Wind in the Grass looked back again anyway.

At night the old men tied Wants the Moon and Six-Legged to a tree and lay down to snore on the ground beside them. It was pitch dark. Wants the Moon looked despondently at the vague lump beside her in the darkness that was Six-Legged.

"Watch out," he said, startling her.

She turned her head and saw a shadow bending over them, heard the soft breathing.

"Most Beautiful, your mother will not like your being

here," Six-Legged whispered to the shadow, but he sounded hopeful.

"I saw a coyote," Wind in the Grass whimpered.

"Be careful. They're hungry, too."

"It said my name. This morning when I went to the woods to piss. It came out from behind a tree and said my name. I don't like being alone with it around."

"Of course you don't," Six-Legged whispered solicitously. "Stay here with me." He was glad it was Wind in the Grass and not White Buffalo.

"It's cold," Wind in the Grass said. "And you have *her* here."

"I can't go away," Wants the Moon snapped.

"Take me home with you, then," Six-Legged said to Wind in the Grass. "I won't run away."

"You won't?" She sounded dubious. "Mother said not to. She says Uncle Wolf will bring me many horses."

"I couldn't catch Uncle Wolf now anyway. But this tree is uncomfortable, Most Beautiful. Untie me," Six-Legged wheedled. "We'll leave *her* here at this tree. You know that we have to travel together, so that will keep me in your camp."

"I didn't know that."

"Oh, it's true."

One of the grandfathers made a sudden snort, and Six-Legged stiffened. "We had better go right now," he whispered.

The grass was silent under Horse's hooves. Wants the Moon clung to Six-Legged's waist and felt like a ghost as Horse carried them across it. Maybe they were ghosts already. Certainly they couldn't go back now. They had left Wind in the Grass with a piece of hide stuffed in her mouth, tied to another tree where someone would be sure to find her. She thought Six-Legged was feeling guilty about it.

A raven overhead cawed at them and matched their pace. Wants the Moon saw it flying beside them, beak open. It looked at her, and she buried her face in Six-Legged's back. Six-Legged was sixteen now, his chest bigger and more muscular, old enough to weave a girl a blanket if he didn't already have two wives.

The raven beat its wings about her ears, and she shrieked, waving her arms. It flew up. Six-Legged pulled an arrow out of the quiver at his knee and drew his bow, but the raven had diminished into a speck in the blue sky.

Wants the Moon watched it vanish and wondered if there was any point in trying to catch the young men now. She and Six-Legged had run away only because they didn't know what else to do. But the Young Husbands were with Angry in the Morning's war band. Wants the Moon sniffled at that thought. She imagined them dead, lying in the courtyard of Red Earth City because she had made these people think about horses. If she and Six-Legged had taken Red Horse, too, then they could have run even faster. But Weaver slept with Red Horse, and they had left her alone. Maybe they would get to the cities before Angry in the Morning and keep him and Uncle Wolf and Wants the Moon's Young Husbands from fighting with the Red Earth people, who were Wants the Moon's own first people, over horses they didn't have. Horses had made them crazy, she thought, everyone. Maybe her, too, seeing spirits in the air.

Red Earth City rose out of the river valley like a giants' lodge. Sunflower and Blue Racer gawped down at it from the mesa top. The moon had begun to grow again and hung over the walls like a shell in the dusk.

They stared at the bean fields spreading away from the walls in a pale green veil, the maize fields with their new shoots poking from the brown earth, the curling squash vines and melons. They could see some people moving about the courtyard like ants, driving a flock of turkeys ahead of them with sticks. Others sat on their flat roofs, grinding grain or talking. There were dogs asleep on the still-warm clay of the courtyard.

"They live in hives like wasps," Angry in the Morning said scornfully. "It will be easy to fight people like that." These were bug people, of no account to real people.

Blue Racer watched the bug people apprehensively. There

were many of them. He scanned the open courtyard and the bean fields for signs of horses, but he couldn't see any.

"They will have them inside," Sunflower said. That would make it more interesting. He had always wanted to see the inside of one of the boxes that the city people lived in. He grinned and ran his thumb along his spearpoint.

"Be still," Angry in the Morning said. "We will sleep here, and just before dawn we will attack them."

"You should send scouts ahead," Uncle Wolf said.

"I am not a fool that I need you to tell me that!" Angry in the Morning snapped.

"It is likely that those dogs will bark when we get close," Uncle Wolf said. "We should go fast."

"I will be sure to remember that you told me so!"

The waxing moon washed something through the open windows before dawn, and Uncle Calabash lay awake trying to hear what it was. He thought it had a high-pitched whine, like a mosquito inside his head. He turned restlessly on his bed, hearing the rustle of maize husks in the mattress and the turkeys ruffling their feathers under the window. Bitter Water's tame eagle flapped its wings in the kiva, beating them against the still air.

Yet when they came, he was not expecting them. The raiders from the Buffalo Horn people poured across the footbridge into the courtyard before the Red Earth dogs began to bark, their own dogs snarling at their heels. Uncle Calabash saw one of the Red Earth dogs with a Buffalo dog by the throat, shaking it back and forth, beating it to death against the mud wall by the rain jars.

The Buffalo Horn people had painted their chests and faces with blue mud and red clay, over and around the tattoos that so frightened Red Bean Vine that she ran and hid in the clothes basket rather than fight.

Grandmother Owl Ears fought, waving a broom in their faces, beating away a young man's spear, her teeth bared at him. He backed away, yelling something at her about horses.

The old woman threw a pot at him, and he left her because

she was too old to be worth taking, and anyway Angry in the Morning had said they were not to take slaves, just horses. No one could see the horses. The Red Earth people fought furiously in the doorways to their houses, but the Buffalo Horn men swarmed up the ladders and pushed them through the doors on the points of their spears. Inside, they raged from room to room and threw pots and baskets on the floor, kicking them open as if there might be horses inside. When they could corner a man, they killed him.

Turquoise Old Man's nephew Cat's Tooth found a man spearing Turquoise Old Man, leaving him gasping and dying in the corner of his sleeping room. Cat's Tooth ran at him, driving his own spear clear through the Buffalo man's ribs. He put his foot on the man's chest and yanked at it while the man's eyes grew wide and then rolled up in his head. Blood poured out and painted over the blue mud and tattoos. Cat's Tooth grabbed the Buffalo man's spear and his own and ran across the roof, leaving red footprints behind him.

The Red Earth people climbed higher and pulled up the ladders. They shot arrows at the Buffalo men climbing through the windows below them.

The Buffalo men had kicked their way into nearly all the houses now, howling with fury when there were no horses inside. They caught Green Melons and shouted at her to tell them where the horses were, but she just screamed. A man dragged her into a house and put his hand up her skirt. Swallow beat him over the head with a grinding stone, and then someone grabbed her from behind. A face with spiral tattoos around the eyes pushed into hers, teeth bared. The whine of an arrow went past her ear, and the man fell. The other man ran away. Swallow's father, Armadillo, dropped down from the floor above, his bow in his hand, but two more Buffalo warriors came through the door and killed him before he could draw it again. They grabbed Swallow and left Green Melons screaming on the floor.

Uncle Calabash knelt on his rooftop with Canyon Wren, shooting arrows at the Buffalo men who scurried across the courtyard, carrying things from the houses now, ears of maize

and women's jewelry boxes, embroidered sashes and black
and white pots, their loot wrapped up in blankets. Several of
them were dragging women with them.

Dead men of the city and of the invaders lay in the courtyard, blood soaking into the dust. The turkeys had flown away
into the treetops beyond the city. The Buffalo men returned
the defenders' fire, shooting arrows up onto the roof, before
they went back to rooting in the houses, shouting furious, unintelligible shouts. Uncle Calabash thought of peccaries rooting in a midden, all greed and appetite and snouts. He wanted
to weep. The People of the Cities didn't fight unless they had
to, not even to drive the Outsiders off. They were no match
for these.

Sunflower and Blue Racer climbed through the door of another
house and looked around for horses. Someone else had been
there first. The room was strewn with smashed meal jars and
the wreckage of a broken loom. The brown and white cloth
on the loom was smeared with blood, and blood was caking
on the heddles. The girl Blue Racer had by the arm was shrieking and beating at him with her fist.

"There is a hole in the ground outside, with a ladder in it,"
Blue Racer said. "Maybe the horses are down there."

"If we let go of her, she'll run away," Sunflower said.

They ran toward the hole, dragging the girl with them, while
people shot arrows at them from the roof. They pushed her
down it and went after, tangling their feet in the ladder that
no one had had time to pull inside. In the gloom an eagle on
a perch beat its wings at them and shrieked. Sunflower un-
hitched the eagle's leather jesses from the perch and tied its
feet together with them. Outside they could hear the shouts of
the Buffalo warriors. Blue Racer sniffed the air. Smoke.

Wants the Moon and Six-Legged saw the smoke before they
came to the city. Six-Legged drummed his heels into Horse's
ribs, and they galloped along the stream bank, past the entrance to Old Horned Toad Canyon and the trail to High Up
City. The countryside of their childhood seemed frozen, the

trees still, as if their passing made no mark on it. *We don't live here anymore,* Wants the Moon thought. What would they do when they got there? They could see the city walls now, with the smoke billowing from them.

"There are no horses here!" Angry in the Morning held Uncle Wolf by the throat, flattened against a crumbling wall.

"They must be hiding them."

Flames poured from the doorway behind them. The Buffalo warriors had set mattresses on fire to keep the Red Earth people on the roof. A rain of arrows showered down, and Bull Calf staggered out of the smoke into Angry in the Morning with an arrow in his shoulder. The wind turned and blew the smoke into their faces.

"Come away!"

Blue Racer saw something looming over him as he climbed the ladder. It was the ghost-white horse, with Wants the Moon and Six-Legged on his back.

"Come away before you are killed," Wants the Moon said. An arrow zinged past them in the cloud of smoke. Blue Racer gaped at her as he had at the city walls.

"Yah, you are all fools!" Six-Legged screamed at him. He spun the horse around, beating at the heads of the Buffalo warriors with his bow. A coughing Red Earth man tried to pull him off the horse, and he lashed out with his spear. More of them were coming down off the roof, fighting their way through the flames as the Buffalo warriors faltered. The man grabbed Six-Legged by the shin, and Six-Legged saw that it was Canyon Wren. He kicked him in the teeth, and Horse plunged away. Canyon Wren grabbed at him again. Six-Legged pulled Horse onto his hind legs. The heavy hooves came down on flesh, breaking ribs. Wants the Moon looked down and saw Canyon Wren on the ground with his shirt torn open, gasping as he tried to breathe.

Angry in the Morning gave the signal to pull back. The Buffalo warriors streamed from the city with their loot, dragging their dead and wounded after them while their bowmen kept the defenders on the roofs pinned down. The white horse trotted beside them with Wants the Moon weeping on his back.

Behind them they could hear the howls of other weeping women. The smoke rose from the walls in a black cloud, and the Buffalo warriors smashed the water jars as they left for good measure.

Uncle Calabash waded through the wreckage. Red Bean Vine sat in the ashes with Green Melons, who was rocking back and forth on her knees, sobbing. In between sobs, she would touch the blood on Armadillo's chest and put her fingers in her mouth. Cat's Tooth walked by the door, carrying Turquoise Old Man. He pointed a finger at Red Bean Vine.

"Your son has done this," he said.

"What?"

"They wanted horses," Cat's Tooth said. "Who else would have told them about horses?"

"Why would they think we had any?" Red Bean Vine asked numbly.

"Those people always think other people have what they want," Cat's Tooth said. "And besides, I saw him." He went on across the courtyard with Turquoise Old Man. "That is where your son has gone," he said over his shoulder.

Uncle Calabash put a hand on Red Bean Vine's arm. "I saw him, too."

"Why would he come here? Why is he with those people?" Red Bean Vine's mouth twisted, and her lip trembled. "He knows we don't have any. Why would he tell them we did? I would kill one if I saw it now," she added viciously.

Uncle Calabash sighed. "That is why he is with them, I suppose."

Green Melons sat up, her face slick with tears. "That is why he is with them, people like that! Wicked people! The end of the world is coming. Turquoise Old Man said it, and now he is right!"

Uncle Calabash didn't answer. He took Green Melons by the shoulders and stood her up gently, pulling her bloody fin-

gers away from Armadillo's body. "That is not good. I will
help you get him ready. Red Bean Vine and I. We will help
you wash him."

When they had done that, Uncle Calabash sat on his flat
roof and leaned his back against the smoke-blackened wall.
The air smelled like ashes, and all the pots that had stood in
a neat row on the rooftop were smashed. Someone had kicked
each one of them against the wall. The crows circled overhead
cawing, their black feathers like charred wood in the sky,
drawing burnt trails on the air. Uncle Calabash saw something
else beyond their flight, smudged along the horizon. He had
thought it might be the buffalo hunters going home east, but
now he saw it had a reflection in the west, too, brighter and
more unstable than the buffalo hunters' shadow.

Uncle Calabash tucked his legs under his muddy skirts and
put his arms around them, resting his chin on his knees. The
sky was going turquoise to the west, around pink clouds that
reflected the low sun, brilliant as macaws that came from the
jungles in the south. The People of the Cities knew there was
more world besides their own. They were not ignorant like the
buffalo hunters. They had been places, even if they liked best
to stay home.

Two broken pieces of a pot lay under his feet, shards of
black and white. When the pot was whole, a stream had run
around its middle, with fish dancing above it. Uncle Calabash
tried to fit the pieces together, cupping them in his hands.

Something else was loose in the world, something that
hadn't been there before. Yesterday he had seen a coyote at a
water hole, and he had thought it had been the coyote's voice
he had heard this morning just before the raiders came. Now
he wasn't sure. The coyote had looked west, too, and bared
its teeth and run away.

Uncle Calabash looked across the stream at the four stories
of the Turquoise people's houses. The walls there were
charred, too, and the roof had fallen in three places that he
could see. Already some women had a bucket of fresh mud
and were spreading it on a cracked wall, smoothing it with
clay paddles.

He held the jagged pieces of the pot together. The People of the Cities were builders. They knew how life should be and built theirs around them like a hive. Young Out of Breath had hated that. Uncle Calabash had watched him crawling on the hive, wings whirring furiously in the air, vibrating with the urge to fly away. It had called him, whatever was loose in the world now and taking people away. Maybe as Six-Legged he could wrestle it and subdue it, like the monster-slayers of the old days, but Uncle Calabash was afraid. And whatever it was, Uncle Calabash didn't think that the buffalo hunters had brought it. He thought it might be going to eat them, too.

The Buffalo Horn people put their dead up on biers on the mesa top and scratched spells in the dirt all around them to make the city people afraid to touch them. Angry in the Morning pulled the arrow out of Bull Calf's arm and packed the wound with the medicine Elk Walker had given him to take along. Sunflower and Blue Racer tied their girl to a tree and fed her with their fingers, slapping her when she tried to bite them. Bear Paws and Bull Calf and some others each had one, too. Angry in the Morning hadn't said anything more about the girls. Since there had been no horses, they might as well have these.

"You have to send them back," Wants the Moon said angrily.

"You were not to follow us!" Angry in the Morning said.

"You should be glad we did," Six-Legged spat at him. "They will send a message to the other cities, and then they will *all* come after you. If you want to stop them, send those women back."

"I want this one," Bull Calf said sulkily. He had his girl tied to his good arm with a rope.

"It is only a girl," Sunflower said coaxingly to Wants the Moon. "There is no need for our first wife to be jealous. This one can work for you. I will give you this eagle that I found, too." The eagle sat on a leather pad on his arm, yellow eyes sullen.

Wants the Moon looked at Swallow's swollen, tearful face.

Swallow stared at the men with hatred. "That is this man's mother's sister's daughter." Wants the Moon pointed at Six-Legged and waited while Sunflower worked the relationship out.

"I could trade her for Bull Calf's girl," he suggested.

"No!" Wants the Moon glared at Angry in the Morning. "These are our first people. They are sacred to us. The horses are already angry that you have made war on these people. If you take their women, the horses will curse you. They will run in your dreams. They will eat your children. You will be bones on a bier." She threw the curses at him one after the other like rocks.

"We will make another storm," Six-Legged said between his teeth. "We will make a horse storm this time. Horses are not for such as you. You do not deserve them. That is why you can't find any. Yah! You are pigs! Let these women go!" He strode up to Swallow and pulled out his belt knife without bothering to see if they would stop him. She spat at him while he cut the ropes.

Angry in the Morning looked grim. "I said not to take women," he said between his teeth. Now he was shamed because he had to let them go. He believed the river spirits about the People of the Cities joining together to hunt them, and it was a long way back to the Buffalo country with no horses to ride. "Cut her loose!" he roared at Bull Calf.

Sullenly, the Buffalo men turned their captive women loose.

"You did not obey me about this," Angry in the Morning said, arms folded. "That is why you do not have horses."

Six-Legged and Wants the Moon grabbed the women by the arms and shoved them toward the trail down the mesa. Swallow spat at Six-Legged again, and then they began to run, stumbling wildly down the slope in case the Buffalo Horn people changed their minds.

Bull Calf and the other men shuffled their feet and muttered. Wants the Moon glared at the Young Husbands, who hung their heads.

"We will go now," Angry in the Morning said.

A raven came out of the clear air over the mesa, beating

heavy wings, suspended above them for a moment. Shards of eggshell fell from its beak, and Wants the Moon could see that two smaller birds were harrying it eastward. They dived at its head, wheeling away before it could turn on them, closing again in lightning darts to peck at the black skull.

The raven lifted higher, shook off the small birds, and watched the Buffalo warriors as they limped homeward. It was aware of the gray coyote that slipped through the tall grass beside their path.

The coyote barked from a thicket of mesquite scrub. "Yah, your wing feathers are all pulled out," it said.

Uncle spread himself against the sky, wings roiling the thunderclouds. "Yah, your tail is on fire." He sent a bolt of lightning into the mesquite.

It lit the sky and the rain poured out. The Buffalo warriors slogged through it. The white horse carried the man and woman, its heavy hooves marking its passage on the wet ground.

"It will change everything," the coyote said, holding his singed backside into the rain. "But not the way you think."

"Nothing changes everything," Uncle said. He knew that he could open his beak and swallow the stars. He didn't see why he could not stop this story in its telling.

"Ask Buffalo," Coyote said.

13

Horse Magic

BLUE RACER AND SUNFLOWER WALKED BESIDE WANTS THE Moon while she rode Horse. When she gave Six-Legged a turn on him, they tried to take her hands.

"We didn't really want that girl," they said.

"You took her," Wants the Moon said grimly.

"That is what you do in a raid," Blue Racer said. "Take women. And scalps. But there wasn't time for that," he added regretfully.

"You went for horses," Wants the Moon told him. These people stole anything. They were like the Outsiders.

"The other things are besides horses," Sunflower said. "She could have helped you. Then our wife wouldn't have to do any work."

"She wasn't as pretty as you," Blue Racer said. He patted her arm cajolingly.

Wants the Moon turned a little to look at him. "Do you think I am pretty?"

"Very pretty," Blue Racer said.

When they had put as much distance between themselves and Red Earth City as Six-Legged said would do, they camped

and nursed their wounds. Angry in the Morning got out Elk
Walker's medicine again. Wants the Moon made her bed
where Horse was tethered, but Blue Racer lay down next to
her, dragging his bedding with him and spreading it on the
ground beside hers.

"Sunflower and I drew sticks to see who should come and
talk to you," he told her solemnly. His handsome face was
clouded with worry. She wasn't sure he had noticed anyone
being angry with him before.

"What do you want to say to me?" she asked him haughtily.

Blue Racer smiled slyly. "That we feel shame. That our
wife should come back to us so that we do not pine for her,
and maybe die."

Wants the Moon's mouth twitched. "You won't die."

"How do you know? It might be." Blue Racer put a hand
on her breast, under her blanket.

Wants the Moon took it off again. "Go and sleep with Sunflower, if you are pining."

"We pine for our wife," Blue Racer said sadly.

The stars over them were very far away, and they looked
cold. Wants the Moon shivered in her blanket, wishing for his
hand back again. "I told you there were no horses there," she
said miserably.

"Most Wise, next time we will listen."

She didn't think he would, but she didn't want him to go
away, either. "I thought you might be dead," she said angrily.
"I thought about you being dead and how it might be my fault
for bringing you horses."

"I am not dead," Blue Racer said hopefully. He slid his
hand under her blanket again.

Wants the Moon started to push it away.

"These horse creatures are very magical," Blue Racer said.
"They make men do stupid things, maybe."

Wants the Moon felt salt tears sliding down her cheeks and
into her mouth. She let him leave his hand there. In the morning she woke to find Sunflower sleeping on her other side, the
two of them enclosing her like a cradle.

*   *   *

The warriors found their people at Midsummer Camp, by the Buffalo Trail Water where the white horse had come to them. There had been no midsummer trade fair this year. None of the bands of buffalo hunters had anything to trade, and Hole in the Sunset was afraid someone would steal his horse. The buffalo had come back, he said, but they were fewer this year, and wary. Where were the captured horses?

"They were hiding them," Uncle Wolf said sulkily.

"These men disobeyed me," Angry in the Morning said. "So the horses hid themselves. Otherwise we would have found them."

"There were no horses!" Six-Legged snapped, sliding off Horse's back. "They are not prairie dogs! They do not live in villages! Do you find Great Cat running in herds?"

"They are grass eaters," Hole in the Sunset said. "Grass eaters run in herds." He had been thinking about this since Elk Walker had seen the warriors coming back in his dreams, on foot. "But it may be that these are the First Two, like First Man and First Woman. So in the morning we will make this one mate with the red one."

Six-Legged looked dubiously at Weaver, standing on the edge of the crowd with his hand on Red Horse's hide, his hair full of burrs. Weaver looked even thinner and wilder than he had in the spring, as if part of him were evaporating, leaving only the craziness behind.

"It is important to have more," Hole in the Sunset said. "The Dry River people are hunting our ground this year and leaving us hungry."

"They are hungry, too," Porcupine Mother said.

"That is not for us to be concerned with," Hole in the Sunset said. "I will be concerned for *my* people."

In the morning, Six-Legged went to talk with Weaver. He was often less crazy in the morning, when whatever it was that came with the night had gone away again. Weaver sat cross-legged on the ground in front of his tent, making a little loom out of sticks. Red Horse's rope was in his hand.

"It is time to let my horse make a calf with this one," Six-Legged said.

Weaver looked puzzled. "With my wife?"

"Your wife is a horse now," Six-Legged said, exasperated. "People always do it with the same kind of people they are. This one is a horse now."

"No," Weaver said. "Then she will never get her own skin back."

Red Horse blew down her nose and stamped her feet restlessly. Her dark eye rolled in its socket.

"Maybe she likes this skin," Six-Legged suggested. He had seen bitches in season, and something about the way she moved suggested that mood to him. He couldn't think of anything to do, though, except take her away by force, and who knew what that might cause? Madness was very powerful, and craziness was more dangerous yet.

"Leave him alone," his wives said. "Uncle has that one."

Six-Legged agreed because just now he wanted to placate his wives. Wind in the Grass still had a fading black eye where White Buffalo had beaten her for being tricked into letting him go after the young men, and they were both inclined to feel he should make amends. It had seemed a fine idea at first to have wives, but now he grew increasingly perplexed and secretly felt that they were all playing at some game, like children pretending to be warriors. White Buffalo was very beautiful, and Wind in the Grass did interesting things in bed, which was even better, but outside of bed he didn't know what to do with them.

Wants the Moon had had the long journey back to make her peace with her Young Husbands. Now she sat outside the tent she had been given in the fall, under its running buffalo and bright red sun, sewing new shoes for Blue Racer while he brushed Sunflower's hair. She smiled at them with an odd content. She had never thought to marry, not at home in Red Earth City, and she had only asked for them out of temper. Now they were in her heart somehow, both of them, and she had had bad dreams about their deaths in the horse raid. She felt oddly that she had evaded something, turned something back, because they had not been killed. If Uncle wanted them, he couldn't have them, she thought fiercely.

She knotted the thong in the new shoe with her fingers and teeth and held it out to Blue Racer. She had sewn patterns on the instep, the kind the Red Earth women put on pots. If she couldn't make pots here, she would make shoes and tie Blue Racer to her by the feet.

Blue Racer laid the brush down and tried it on, wiggling his toes. Wants the Moon watched him proudly while Sunflower admired the shoe, too.

They seemed unnecessarily domestic to Six-Legged, who found himself pacing restlessly between the fire pit and the midden, peering at himself in the shallow stream, in a leather breechcloth, his cropped hair growing out like the Buffalo men's, longer than Wants the Moon's. He pulled out his belt knife and hacked at it angrily with the sharp obsidian blade.

Maybe it was Horse's restlessness that transferred itself to Six-Legged. This morning Horse tugged at his tether and whickered down his nose, his big feet pawing up soft clods of dirt. He danced in circles, tail held high like a trophy on a pole.

Red Horse whickered back to him, sidling uneasily at the end of her rope while Weaver frowned and gripped it more tightly.

Six-Legged put the knife back in his belt. He felt a humming in the ground and stood up carefully, looking around to see if anyone else noticed it. Wants the Moon had taken up the other shoe, and the Young Husbands were telling each other some hunting tale back and forth, punctuated with shouts of laughter, the quill brush sliding through sleek dark hair again.

Horse reared, pulling his rope taut. Something hummed in the rope. He neighed, a piercing shriek that flipped the brush from Blue Racer's hand and brought everyone in the Buffalo camp running. Hole in the Sunset gaped openmouthed. Horse's hooves slashed the air. He jerked his head higher, plunging and fighting the tether. The rope, spun of yucca fibers and rolled between palm and thigh on endless winter evenings, snapped, the loose end flying from Horse's head like a snake.

Horse bellowed again, and Red Horse flung up her head, nostrils quivering. Weaver clenched his fingers around the rope, pulling her to him.

"Get out of the way!" Six-Legged shouted at him and started running. He plowed through Bull Calf, who was staring at Horse, and grabbed Weaver. He dragged him away from Red Horse, prying Weaver's fingers open, as Horse shrieked and climbed onto Red Horse's back. Horse swung his heavy head at Weaver, teeth bared, as Six-Legged hauled him away. Then he sank his teeth into Red Horse's neck. Weaver sobbed and cursed in Six-Legged's grip, flailing his arms. Six-Legged grabbed him around the waist, pinning them to his side.

It was like watching mountains mate. Red Horse screamed and bucked, and her heavy hooves came down through the skin of Weaver's tent. Horse rode her back, teeth in her neck, forelegs on either side of her shoulders, pinning her down. They could see his penis, huge and erect, as he straddled her.

Six-Legged felt the magic that shot out of the horses even while Weaver thrashed in his grip. It ran through the earth, waking the bones under the mountains. The grass shimmered as if heat rippled the air and folded it in on itself, making a pocket of magic desire out of which everything would be born. Women swayed a little on their feet as if they, too, could feel the great white weight pressing them down. Men felt their cocks stiffen and looked for their wives. Hole in the Sunset looked at Porcupine Mother and remembered how she had sat naked and brushed magic out of her hair for him when they were young. Wants the Moon let the shoe fall and leaned her shoulder against Blue Racer's chest, feeling the blood beating under the skin. Sunflower put a hand on her shoulder and a hand on Blue Racer's.

The horses rocked back and forth on the ground while Weaver howled and fought Six-Legged. He pulled one arm loose and elbowed Six-Legged in the eye. Six-Legged tried to tighten his grip, but Weaver was like a snapped rope, uncoiling himself, sliding through his hands. He ran toward the horses.

Wants the Moon broke loose from the magic, pulling away from Sunflower and Blue Racer, and ran after him. Six-Legged pounded behind her. The horses had moved beyond the tents, leaving Weaver's in tatters, and were fast together now, beyond the fire pit, Horse's forelegs tight around Red Horse's ribs, his back legs straddling her rump. She stood still, quivering, legs braced in the grass.

Wants the Moon flung herself at Weaver and knocked him down before he got to them. He was bony now, not as big as she was. She sat on his back until Six-Legged ran up and sat on his legs.

"Leave them alone. They will kill you," Six-Legged said.

"Quail!" Weaver wept into the grass.

"Hush!" Wants the Moon said.

The Buffalo Horn people stared silently until the horses separated, White Horse lifting his heavy body off Red Horse. He switched his tail and pranced a few paces, then stopped to crop grass, his penis still swinging ponderously under his belly.

Six-Legged got off Weaver's legs and walked up to Horse quietly. "Are you pleased with yourself, Bigger-Than-Anyone's?" he asked softly, rubbing Horse's nose, getting a grip on his tether. "Come along."

Six-Legged led Horse back to the stake where he had been tethered and cut a new piece of rope. When he looked back, he saw that Wants the Moon had let Weaver go. He was sitting on the ground by Red Horse, her rope in his hands again, weeping and talking to her.

"That one is a crazy person," Bull Calf said disgustedly. He had hoped the horses would do it some more. It was an exciting thing to watch.

"He is jealous," Angry in the Morning hooted. "Even Long Arrow can't compete with that." He pointed at Horse's penis and slapped Long Arrow on the shoulder.

"I don't want to do it with a horse, either," Long Arrow said. "Women are enough trouble."

"Maybe it *is* his wife," Sunflower said. "I would be angry, too, if it was."

Blue Racer looked solemn. "It will not be good if it is. And better not let that one hear the jokes." He eyed Weaver dubiously.

"Now there will be a horse calf," Uncle Wolf said, sidling up to the rest. "Now that horse should be given to me so that the calf will belong to someone who is not crazy. I will tell Hole in the Sunset that."

"Tell him you have your head up your backside!" Angry in the Morning snarled, snapping his head around to glare at Uncle Wolf. "There are horses in the rivers there!" he mimicked Uncle Wolf. "All we have to do is go and find them. Yah!" He lifted his hand as if he were going to hit him, but Blue Racer stepped between them.

"This is not a good idea."

"It is right that the horse should be mine," Uncle Wolf said complacently. "Hole in the Sunset has said so. After all, we are each the father of the river spirit's wives."

"That is Weaver's horse," Six-Legged said quietly from behind them.

Uncle Wolf retreated from Six-Legged, of whom he was a little afraid, without making it seem that he was actually backing away. Angry in the Morning glared after him, his yellow eyes narrowed. Then he glared at Six-Legged, too, and stalked off.

The other men stopped joking about Horse's penis and slapping each other and grew quiet.

"That one will make trouble," Porcupine Mother said to Hole in the Sunset, nodding at Uncle Wolf sitting outside his tent while Lark brought him bowls of stew. The hunters had brought back small game, just enough to feed people, but somehow Uncle Wolf always got extra. Porcupine Mother thought exasperatedly that Lark gave him hers.

The Buffalo Horn people were moving camp every night, converging on the buffalo herds. Wolf had begun to talk of the new horse calf as if it were already his. He told everyone that it was, that it would not be long now before Hole in the Sunset gave him Red Horse. That Hole in the Sunset had not said so did not matter. Wolf had found that if you repeated things enough, then people believed they were true, and then they were true.

He spoke the words around the fire at night, and the words got up and walked into people's ears. He spoke them to the streams, and the water repeated them, murmuring them in its ripples, until all the turtles and the frogs and the fish people knew them, knew the red horse belonged to Wolf, father-in-law of the river spirit. He wore the words in his hair like eagle feathers, and they crawled on his face so that if you looked at him in the right light, you thought that he had been given tattoos, that he had been brave in battle, slain the enemy, stolen horses from the west. People began to believe so.

The words hid in the grass and rustled there like bugs. Angry in the Morning tried to stamp them out. He was to have married White Buffalo, and because he had not, he should be given the horse instead. That was quite clear, but Uncle Wolf's words flocked around like bees swarming and blotted that out, smearing Angry in the Morning's words with dark smudges.

Angry in the Morning watched White Buffalo carrying water on her head from the stream, cooking meal on a hot stone griddle, making a new quiver for Six-Legged, braiding her long hair in the dusk. He thought of the horse he should have had, and of the horses mating, making the air shimmer around them. When the morning climbed up the sky, he saw White Buffalo turn to a red horse, dawn-dusty beside her cookfire, and then back again, her long hair a raven's wing sweep against her face. The eagle that Sunflower had brought back from Red Earth City watched him watch her, sullen on its perch outside Sunflower's tent, pulling its feet at the jesses.

I will give you what is yours. The voice was soft, like the rustle of feathers in his head. Angry in the Morning knew it was Eagle telling him White Buffalo should be his, and the horse should be his. They were the same, as Weaver said, and also not the same, which Angry in the Morning knew because he was not crazy. But they both should be his. Eagle whispered that to him, and Eagle spoke more truly than Wolf, everyone knew that. Angry in the Morning talked to Eagle, crouched beneath the perch until Sunflower came out of his tent and accused him of trying to steal it.

The Buffalo Horn people did not steal from each other. Angry in the Morning balled his hand into a fist at the insult, but the eagle stared into him with its fierce yellow eyes until he unclenched his fingers. "I will buy it from you," he told Sunflower. "I will give you two buffalo hides, one of them painted."

"I don't want to sell it," Sunflower said. Eagles were magical, and their feathers were valuable. It was like growing wealth on a tree to have a tame one.

"I want it," Angry in the Morning said stubbornly. "I want it. I will give you three hides and my best dog. The one with the red hairs on her foot."

Sunflower thought about that. He didn't have a dog, although they were easy enough to come by. But a good one that would run down a rabbit—and pull a travois without upsetting it—that was worth something. And the dog was a bitch, which meant that he could have her puppies, too, to trade for other things. And Wants the Moon would like the painted hide. She hadn't liked the eagle because he had stolen it from her first people, the same way she hadn't liked the girl. "Five hides, and the dog," he said experimentally.

Give him that, the eagle said, and Angry in the Morning said, "Yes."

Sunflower waited until Angry in the Morning brought him the hides and the dog with the red foot, and then he untied the eagle's jesses from the perch. The eagle beat its wings in his face as he lifted it.

"You can take the perch with you, too," Sunflower said.

Angry in the Morning didn't answer. He pulled his belt knife and cut the jesses from the eagle's legs. It clenched its feet for a moment around his hand, talons digging into the flesh, and then lifted into the air with a thin shriek. It beat higher into the blue sky until it was only a small winged shape riding the thermals. Then it winked out like a star when the sun swallows it. A thin stream of blood trickled down Angry in the Morning's hand.

Sunflower goggled at him. "What did it give you?" he whispered, but Angry in the Morning just walked away.

By night the tale was all over the camp that Sunflower's eagle had promised a great magic to Angry in the Morning in return for its freedom.

"What did it say it would give him?" Wants the Moon demanded, but Sunflower just lifted his shoulders and let them fall again. No one knew and everyone knew. It would give him the red horse and White Buffalo. It would give him the horses that the People of the Cities had been hiding. It would give him the magic to fly in the air. It would give him many buffalo in the hunt.

"Now we will see how these horses catch buffalo," Hole in the Sunset told Six-Legged when he was tired of listening to talk about Angry in the Morning and the things the eagle would give him that were Hole in the Sunset's to give, or not.

"That is what he is for," Six-Legged said, hoping he was right about that. It had worked on Antelope.

"If we do not have more meat soon," Hole in the Sunset said, "more of us will die this winter. The women are miscarrying their babies, and old Grandmother Crane has died already."

"Old Grandmother Crane was older than the mountains," Six-Legged said.

"She was not so old before there was no buffalo fat to eat. We are hungry. If these horses do not hunt buffalo, maybe they are good to eat."

"That would make a very bad magic."

"Already there has been a bad magic," Hole in the Sunset retorted, "with everyone wanting one. You will have to stop that."

Hole in the Sunset walked away with a sweep of his buffalo robe. Six-Legged stared after him, aggravated. If Hole in the Sunset couldn't stop his people from quarreling, then he might as well ask a pile of rocks to do it as ask Six-Legged.

"It's Wolf," Wants the Moon said to him. "Anyone can see that. Why doesn't the chief?"

"He sees," Six-Legged said. "He isn't stupid. Wolf is his sister's man. And he keeps the rest from quarreling with each other, since they are all quarreling with Wolf."

Wants the Moon laid her chin in her hand and thought. These people were not so different from her own in that respect. Hole in the Sunset held power in the same way that Squash Old Man and Turquoise Old Man did—because the people thought they were wise. When the people no longer believed Hole in the Sunset was wise, then there would be a new chief. Hole in the Sunset was wise enough to know that that was as it should be, no doubt, but as any man would, he liked being chief. Eventually he would have to do something about Wolf. She could see Angry in the Morning sitting on a stone outside his tent, making arrows, cutting feathers from a pile at his feet. White Buffalo was pretending not to watch him. Wants the Moon got up and went and sat down beside her. The chief's daughter looked at her with suspicion.

"It is flattering to have the young men wanting you," Wants the Moon commented.

White Buffalo narrowed her eyes.

"If only you were not married already. Angry in the Morning has forgotten that, maybe."

"What is it to you if he has?" White Buffalo inquired. She returned her eyes to the rope she had been making and jerked the sinews tight.

"You will put a kink in it that way," Wants the Moon said.

White Buffalo glared at her and loosened her braid.

"Jealousy makes trouble," Wants the Moon said. "It knots people up like that rope you're ruining. Wind in the Grass is talking to her mother's husband too much, too. Angry in the Morning will fight with someone if you're not careful. All these stupid men will try to hurt each other."

White Buffalo looked sulky. "My husband's old wife didn't like us," she said. "Why does she care now?"

Wants the Moon tossed her head. Her hair was growing out and hung loose down her back. The wind flipped it into White

Buffalo's face. "I don't," she said airily. She got up, and
White Buffalo could see the wind rippling her hair like the
grass, like the horse's tails. Most people thought she could
brush magic out of it, little horses, if she wanted to. That was
what Wind in the Grass said that Uncle Wolf said. Wants the
Moon walked away, back to her own tent, trailing magic.
White Buffalo could feel it on her skin. She glared after her
resentfully, then turned so that she couldn't watch Angry in
the Morning anymore and he couldn't watch her.

The trouble Uncle Wolf had stirred up stayed in the air as they
traveled, as if they were all in a big pot with it, beginning to
cook. Hole in the Sunset could almost see the hot rocks dropping through the heavy air. Porcupine Mother felt the sky over
them begin to bubble, and White Buffalo saw it change color,
yellowing like dirty water. At night the horses stamped their
feet and pulled their heads back and forth at the ends of their
picket ropes. Weaver had tied Red Horse to a tree beside his
tent, but Six-Legged had had to take her to graze, because
now Weaver just lay in his tent and cried.

Old Elk Walker looked at the sky and shook his head. It
wasn't rain thickening the air. His apprentices brought his elk-
skin robe and put it around his shoulders. "Will you make a
magic?" they asked him.

He shook his head again. "This is a time when magic makes
itself," he said. "The world is telling itself a new story, and
I am not able to hear the words before they have been spoken." When they did come faintly to his ears, the words were
in a new tongue, puzzling and strange, like stones speaking.
Elk Walker sat down in the dirt and tried to learn that speech,
but it was incomprehensible.

It was easier to understand what Wolf had to say. He talked
of the red horse and its calf to anyone who would listen,
sounding important, talking endlessly of how he would hunt
buffalo from her back. At night the Buffalo Horn people
camped along the edge of a beaver pond, and Wolf talked
some more until Bear Paws and Bull Calf were nodding their
agreement. Behind them Angry in the Morning's hands balled

themselves up into fists without his knowing it. He turned on his heel and stalked the other way into the darkness.

In the morning the sun dribbled over the eastern mountains, sullen as a face with a swollen lip. Six-Legged got up to piss and have a drink and fell over the body of Uncle Wolf stretched flat in the reeds by the pond.

He didn't know what it was at first and sat sprawled in the reeds, rubbing his nose and his shin. Blood from his nose, black in the half light, smeared the back of his hand, and he looked around him for grass to stop it with. The body lay facedown behind him in the reeds, hands stretched out in front as if trying to get a grip on something. Six-Legged forgot his nose and bent over the body. There was a dent in the back of its head that he could see even in this light and that made his stomach heave. He turned the body over and saw after a moment that it was Wolf. It was hard to tell because the face had been battered in with a club.

14

Ghost Wind

THE BUFFALO HORN PEOPLE STOOD AROUND WOLF IN A ring, as if they were waiting for him to get up and dance. "He's dead," Bull Calf said, scratching his head.

Sunflower's face looked chalky, as if he had rubbed it with pale dirt. "Someone has hit him," he said.

"With a rock, maybe," Blue Racer said. He swallowed hard.

"A club," Porcupine Mother whispered.

Angry in the Morning stood on the edge of the circle, twisting between his fingers the knotted thong that held his breechclout. He had stumbled from his tent with the rest when Six-Legged shouted, but no one looked at him. White Buffalo stood by herself, looking at the ground. Wind in the Grass was holding Lark's arm while Lark whimpered.

Wants the Moon shivered between her husbands, trying to soak warmth from them in the chilly dawn. Wolf, dead, seemed to be taking all the warmth away, like cold stone.

Hole in the Sunset stared at the body as if he could make it walk again, as if the morning air would wash the blood away, reshape the smashed cheekbones, the shattered jaw. Elk

Walker sang softly over the broken bones, a chant to hold evil
at bay, if that were possible. Hole in the Sunset, bewildered,
wondered what magic now could lay his ghost. Even the spirit
soul that went to the Lands of the Dead would be reluctant to
go away from this place. The earth soul that stayed behind to
trouble people would be vengeful. Raids on the enemy were
right and proper, but killing did not happen among the Buffalo
Horn people, not among their own. An impossibility had come
among them, splitting open the air, letting spirits loose in the
camp, venomous as hornets.

"Someone has done this," Bull Calf said, speaking the un-
speakable.

Long Arrow glared at him and hissed between his teeth, but
the words had been said.

The others looked at Angry in the Morning now, and then
away, quickly.

"You must find who has done this," Bull Calf said stubbornly to Hole in the Sunset. Bear Paws nodded. Bull Calf
was always the one who said what everyone was hoping would
not be said, who pushed against barriers until they gave way.
Hole in the Sunset knew that he was valuable for that, but he
wished he would be quiet.

"Angry in the Morning was saying bad things to this man
yesterday," Bull Calf added.

The Buffalo Horn people looked at Angry in the Morning
again, and now their eyes lingered on him.

"No!" he spluttered. "No! I did not do this!" He looked
from one to the other of them, yellow eyes narrowed.

"You were angry with him," Hole in the Sunset said
gravely. "It might be that a man who is angry might do a
thing that he wished afterward he had not done."

"I did not!" Angry in the Morning stared back stubbornly
at Hole in the Sunset.

The people murmured among themselves. Lark and Wind
in the Grass wept and pulled at their hair, which was proper,
and Lark had torn her clothes.

"He was not killed here," Long Arrow said, wondering if
that would make it better or worse. Better not to have been

killed so close to the people's tents, maybe, and maybe worse that the killer had carried the body to hide what he had done. But it hadn't hidden anything. Long Arrow sighed. "See, there is one set of prints here." He knelt beside Wolf. "He was carrying something heavy. He came from over there." Long Arrow pointed to the open grass beyond a grove of willows, where Horse and Red Horse grazed on their tethers.

Hole in the Sunset began to walk back along the path that Long Arrow had seen. He could see it, too, now that he looked. Elk Walker stumped beside him, still chanting. It had happened in the long grass. They could see the blood and the trampled, broken stems, the churned-up earth. Afterward someone had dragged the body through the grass and then finally carried it, staggering a little, through the reeds to the pond. At the end he had stumbled under the weight and dragged it again. The horses grazed, oblivious, swishing their tails, while the Buffalo Horn people pointed these things out to each other, following Hole in the Sunset and the shaman. When they had come back along the path to where the body lay, they stopped, staring at it again. It had not gotten up and walked; it had not healed itself; they had not dreamed it.

"Someone has killed my husband," Lark said suddenly, shrilly. It was the first time she had spoken. She pointed a finger at her brother. "You must find out who."

"Someone must be punished," Bull Calf said. He was certain of that at least. It was best to have something to be certain of.

Porcupine Mother's lip quivered, and Wants the Moon went and put an arm around her. White Buffalo was standing with her arms wrapped around herself, as if she was cold. "Hole in the Sunset will know what to do," Wants the Moon said, but she didn't think so. No one knew what to do with this.

"Go!" Elk Walker said suddenly, and one by one the people moved away, uneasy, thankful for someone else's taking charge. Lark lingered, and Elk Walker flapped his hands at her. "Go! I will get him ready. This is fierce magic, not for you."

Lark trudged away with Wind in the Grass at her elbow.

Getting a body ready for the spirit journey was the relatives' job, but Lark was biddable.

The Buffalo Horn people sat inside their tents, putting any doorways they could between themselves and Wolf, while Elk Walker and his young men washed the body and painted it and built a bier on poles. The ground was soft enough to dig, but a death like this one might come up again. Better to do him honor and let the eagles clean his bones.

"How will Hole in the Sunset tell who has done this?" Bull Calf's sister Tortoise said to Young Onion Digger. "A man who would do that would tell lies, too." She ladled hot mush into a hide bowl.

"How do you know it was a man?" Young Onion Digger said. Her eyes slid toward Lark's tent. "He beat her."

"Her old husband beat her, too," Tortoise said. "Some women just let them. It made Porcupine Mother angry all the time."

"You women don't know anything about it," Bull Calf said scornfully. "Where is my breakfast? It was Angry in the Morning, anyone can see that." He stuck his fingers in the bowl and scooped up the mush.

"You should get married," Tortoise said. She had married Long Arrow in the winter, and now Bull Calf was in her tent as often as their mother's, looking for something to eat.

"It was Angry in the Morning," Bull Calf said. "The eagle gave him this death. That is what he asked it for when he let it go."

"He should have asked for sense for you," Tortoise said. "Someone hit that man with rocks. Maybe he lay down and an eagle dropped them on him from the sky?"

Bull Calf looked exasperated. "The eagle doesn't have to have done it to have given it to Angry in the Morning. When you ask for a death, it doesn't matter how it happens. If it happens, it's yours. Besides, he has a temper."

Bear Paws, Young Onion Digger's husband, shook his head, his mouth full. "Angry in the Morning is only in a temper when he wakes up. Old Wolf had been dead since night. I saw

the blood. I think it was Sunflower. Or Blue Racer. Their wife
has been talking against that one since winter.''

"No reason for them to kill him," Bull Calf said. "If everyone killed everyone their wife didn't like—"

"We'd all be bones on a bier," Tortoise said tartly.

"It could have been your husband, too," Young Onion Digger said slyly. "After Wolf told tales about horses in the rivers
and they all went to the cities and were made fools of."

"The fools are the ones who are yammering like magpies,"
Long Arrow said, pushing his way into the tent and frowning
at his wife as if the rest of them were her fault. "Hole in the
Sunset has said we are not to talk of this."

Tortoise shrugged and handed him the bowl of mush. Nothing would stop them from talking about it.

They didn't move camp that day. All afternoon the Buffalo
Horn people's eyes followed Angry in the Morning. When an
eagle was seen riding the thermals high over the windswept
grass, their eyes widened and they dropped their voices to
whispers.

"I did not do this!" Angry in the Morning shouted into
their silence. The eagle floated above him, uncaring.

Angry in the Morning was not the only candidate. Nearly
everyone knew someone that they would have liked to be
guilty or were afraid had done it. Wives looked at husbands,
sisters at brothers, and mothers forbade daughters to walk out
with certain young men. Porcupine Mother narrowed her eyes
at Hole in the Sunset. No one had loved Wolf, except maybe
Lark, and that was only because Lark was biddable and she
had been told to.

Blue Racer and Sunflower looked shamefacedly at Wants
the Moon.

"We need to know—" Sunflower looked down at his
shoes.

"Our wife must tell us—" Blue Racer's lips compressed,
grimly determined.

"What?" Wants the Moon demanded, hands on hips, but
she knew. "I didn't hit him with rocks," she whispered.

The talk slid through the camp like snakes. A sizable faction, gathering around Angry in the Morning, began to talk of its having been Six-Legged. White Buffalo jumped when anyone spoke to her now, and when Six-Legged came toward her and she flinched, Wind in the Grass slapped her, startling even herself.

"Our husband did not kill my father!" Wind in the Grass said. "It could have been anyone. That one didn't make anyone love him." She began to cry. White Buffalo ran out of the tent, and Six-Legged, not knowing what else to do, went on making arrows. Death in their midst would not keep hunger away. Maybe it would call it. There was still the need to eat.

Others whispered that it must have been Weaver, who did nothing now but sit in his tent and who had not come out when the body was found. Others said he was too frail to kill even a little man like Wolf; look how thin he was and how his eyes were hollow—that was the madness, not murder.

At last it didn't matter who had done it. The death circled the camp hungrily, slid down smoke holes and under tent flaps, and left a foul smell in the air. Angry in the Morning's mother fought with Porcupine Mother and other women fought with each other for no reason. Six-Legged broke a good arrow in the feathering and threw the splintered shaft aside with a curse. Old Grasshopper, who had unaccountably survived the winter, sat in his tent with the medicine bundle, praying over it so it wouldn't be defiled.

Six-Legged abandoned the spoiled arrow and got up in disgust. He would ride Horse, he thought, and put some wind between himself and the body that lay on a bier over their heads. Already the vultures were circling patiently, waiting for the people to leave. Six-Legged could see Sunflower's eagle up there, too. Or Angry in the Morning's eagle. It would drive the vultures away and eat what it wanted first.

The horses were on the other side of the camp from where he had left them. Wants the Moon, brushing Red Horse's hide with a porcupine-quill brush, looked up when Six-Legged came through the trampled grass.

"I moved them," she said abruptly. "That was a bad place for them to stay."

Six-Legged nodded and began to untie Horse's rope from the antler stake. "Where is Weaver?"

Wants the Moon snorted. "He's no use. He is sitting in his tent."

"I want to ride. Take Red Horse and come with me."

Red Horse jerked her head up suddenly, looking around, eyes wide, ears swiveling.

"She saw it," Six-Legged said. "She saw who did it. Maybe she will talk in someone's dreams and tell them."

"If anyone dreams her, she will tell them it was Angry in the Morning," Wants the Moon said. She sounded angrier than he would have expected. "Or anyone that that someone wants it to be. Myself, I don't speak horse dream language."

"No one needs a horse to tell them it was Angry in the Morning," Six-Legged said. "Everyone already thinks so. I think so, too."

"It wasn't." Wants the Moon pulled Red Horse's rope loose from her stake and swung herself onto her back. Red Horse danced sideways.

"How do you know that?" Six-Legged looked at her suspiciously.

Wants the Moon was concentrating on not falling off Red Horse, who was bouncing on her back feet and then her front feet. Clinging tightly with her knees, Wants the Moon leaned forward and caught one long ear. Red Horse stopped, rolling her eyes.

"Something's wrong with her," Six-Legged said.

"No more than usual," Wants the Moon said. "If I were Weaver's horse I'd be like this, too, all the time telling her she's his wife. It isn't good." Red Horse shuddered and stood trembling. "I don't know for certain about that one who's dead. I just don't think it was Angry in the Morning. Everyone always wants things to be simple."

"So do you," Six-Legged said. "You want things to be simple." She was telling him he was childish.

"It's men who try to make things simple. They try to beat

on things until they've made them the proper shape.'' She stopped abruptly.

''Someone beat Wolf into the right shape,'' Six-Legged said, finishing the thought for both of them. He pulled himself up on Horse's back and let Horse have his head, as if maybe he could outrun all the things he kept thinking.

Wants the Moon let Red Horse follow them, and they galloped in a wide arc. Six-Legged swung Horse away from the camp and the prairie dog village to one side of it that had left the ground full of holes, and down the broad flat bank of the river below the beaver pond. The wind streamed through Wants the Moon's hair. Could you blow death out of your hair that way? She wasn't sure. In the camp she had felt it clinging to her, greasy and dusted with grit.

Wants the Moon could see their camp in the distance now, full of ant people busy with getting ready to hunt buffalo. She knew that was dangerous work. The hunters drove the beasts into canyon ambushes or off cliffs, butchering the ones who were trapped or fell, but a buffalo herd on the run was like a tornado. There was no stopping it, and it broke human bones like kindling. Every year the hunters lost a man or two under those hooves or gored on the short, sharp horns. It was the price Buffalo asked to feed his people, Long Arrow said.

Wants the Moon wondered how it would be when Six-legged rode Horse. Horse could outrun Buffalo. Horse could change the world, she thought. She wondered if Hole in the Sunset was afraid of that at the same time that he reached for it, like some strange, shiny new thing at the bottom of a hole. Red Horse's muscles worked under her, hooves pounding over the grass, and Wants the Moon imagined driving the buffalo, going anywhere the buffalo went. They ran a long way before Wants the Moon realized that Red Horse wasn't going to stop. She thundered along the grass in a flat-out run, flecks of foam blowing from her teeth. Wants the Moon pulled her back, yanking hard on the rope before Red Horse would slow down.

Red Horse stopped slowly, and once she was still she hung her head, flanks heaving. Wants the Moon let her breathe for a moment, feeling the quick expansion and contraction of the sweat-drenched rib cage. Red Horse's head drooped, but her ears were swiveled toward the horizon. Now that they were standing still, Wants the Moon saw people in the distance, not the Buffalo Horn people but more dark ant shapes silhouetted on the flat skyline, moving along it. She turned Red Horse around, drove her heels into the wet flanks, and raced back to where Six-Legged and Horse were waiting.

"There is someone out there," she said to Six-Legged. "Who is it?"

Six-Legged narrowed his eyes. "Dry River people, maybe. They hunt this country, too. Hole in the Sunset was saying he didn't like it."

"They saw me," she said, nervous. "I want to go back."

Six-Legged was already turning Horse around.

"This is not their country!" Long Arrow said angrily when they told him. "Their hunting grounds are to the east of here."

"Maybe there are no buffalo to the east of here," Wants the Moon said, but Long Arrow and Hole in the Sunset just looked at her as if she were a fish that had suddenly begun to talk. They exchanged a look that said she was a woman and a foreigner at that.

"These people don't give things away the way we do to the other cities when there is a drought," Six-Legged whispered. "At least not to these Dry River people. I think maybe they are like the Outsiders. Not related."

Hole in the Sunset said with satisfaction, "They will be sorry that they came hunting on our ground. We have these horses and they do not. They will look foolish and catch nothing."

Wants the Moon thought that even with the herd still thin and scattered, there were enough buffalo to feed both peoples, but she didn't say anything. She was a woman and a foreigner, and the Dry River people might be too wicked to share with. It was clear that Hole in the Sunset thought so.

That night they danced the Buffalo Dance, the men moving black against the fire, heads crowned with the new-moon horns of the herds. Wants the Moon shivered as she watched. They had drawn Six-Legged into the dance, too, and she saw him horned against the firelight, eyes invisible under the buffalo mask. The Red Earth people danced a Deer Dance, like most of the People of the Cities, but this was different, out under the black sky with the wind coming off the open grass and no walls to block it or anything that might be blowing on its back. Elk Walker danced by her, stamping first one foot and then the next, the tufted buffalo tail wagging behind him, horns swinging from side to side. The firelight shifted a little on his hide, and she saw Buffalo behind him, taller than the sky, dwarfing Elk Walker, enveloping him, dancing on his hind hooves down the spiral of the dance while hide drums beat out his footsteps. The fire ran like water over the horns and the monstrous shaggy head. He stood taller and taller, blotting out the stars, and Six-Legged and then Sunflower and then Blue Racer danced into his shadow. Wants the Moon didn't see them come out again. All the men danced into that great horned shadow and vanished.

Wants the Moon whimpered, but no one was paying any attention to her. Porcupine Mother's hands slapped the skin drums, faster now, and Wants the Moon saw White Buffalo step through the crowd of women, under a horned headdress. She wore a pale robe, the hide of a true white buffalo, and as she danced her way into the spiral of buffalo men, Wants the Moon thought that she, too, changed, became the thing she danced.

She was glad when it was over and the men came around the circle of tents behind which they had disappeared, wearing their own heads now, no tails hanging behind them. There was still something above them in the sky, just under the horns of the moon. Wants the Moon took Blue Racer and Sunflower by the arms and huddled between them, where she could feel the hearts beating under the warm bare skin. She made them come inside the tent with her and lie down, where she could feel them all over and assure herself that the shaggy hide had not somehow covered them over. They laughed and tickled her under the arms, full of the magic of the dance, and would have rolled her over and climbed on top of her if they were not to hunt the next day.

So they lay in a warm heap under buffalo blankets with the dog with the red foot that Angry in the Morning had traded to Sunflower, and Wants the Moon slept and dreamed that Red Horse told what she had to say to Buffalo and Buffalo lowered his huge shaggy head and bellowed the words into the cold morning and the horses ran away across the grass. She woke when she heard Six-Legged shouting after them, and then she was sitting up in a heap of blankets while Blue Racer grabbed the spear and arrows and bow he had laid aside ready for the morning, and everyone outside was screaming and Sunflower pulled the tent flap open and she saw the Dry River people pouring into their camp.

Six-Legged ran past, nocking an arrow onto his bowstring as he went, and Blue Racer pounded after him. What did they want? Wants the Moon wondered, terrified, while Sunflower pushed past her out of the tent. She stumbled to the doorway, holding her robe around her. All the men, some of them still naked, were fighting the Dry River men in a milling mass that spilled through the camp. Four of the invaders raced toward the staked horses. They passed close enough for Wants the Moon to see their faces, cheeks striped and smeared with colored mud, eyes fierce and acquisitive.

The Buffalo Horn women pushed their screaming children inside the tents and blocked the doorways with spears and drawn bows. A Dry River man, painted blue and black, loomed in front of them and caught Wind in the Grass by the arm. Lark took aim and he stumbled, clutching at the arrow. The women fell on him, and Porcupine Mother sat on his chest while his feet kicked and drew her knife across his throat. The children howled. Young Onion Digger's little boy, who had lost his mother, clung fiercely to Wants the Moon's blanket, but she shoved him away. Still howling, he pulled her buffalo blanket with him and stumbled toward Porcupine Mother, stepping on the shaggy fur, clutching it to his chest.

The Buffalo Horn men and the invaders shrieked war cries back and forth at each other. Wants the Moon heard Horse's frantic neighing. She pushed back into her own tent, heart pounding, and burrowed frantically among the travois packs lying ready there. Blue Racer's second spear was lashed to the baggage. She pulled it out and ran through the warm morning after the men. Her feet slipped in blood, sticky on the soles. As she ran she looked over her shoulder, waiting to feel the hand on her arm, the arrow in her back.

Six-Legged had drawn his bow, but he saw that he couldn't shoot without hitting the horses. Red Horse spun in the center of the fighting, hysterically, like a dog chasing its tail. Foam flew from her muzzle. A Dry River arrow went past Six-Legged's ear. *They* could shoot.

"Get in close!" Blue Racer shouted. He and Long Arrow and Bull Calf ran at the Dry River men, howling war cries. Six-Legged chased after them, gripping his spear. Another arrow clipped his ear. He swatted at it, and his hand came away dripping blood. Blue Racer fell under his feet, and he stumbled over him.

Red Horse reared, shrieking. Weaver tried to push his way through the invaders, but they threw him back, tossing him from one to the other, jeering. He crawled doggedly through the trampled grass; another man kicked him in the head, and he lay still.

Two of the Dry River men tried to pull up Horse's stake. Horse reared and lashed out with his back hooves, and one man fell, sprawled in the grass with a piece of his skull caved in. Six-Legged jabbed his spear into the other's belly. The man crumpled, lying on his side, legs churning. Six-Legged tried to pull the spear out again, but it wouldn't come. He put his foot on the man's ribs and pulled backward, terrified. The spear came loose suddenly in a spurt of blood, and Six-Legged swung it wildly, tangling it with another spear shaft, staggering. A Dry River man with white ghost faces painted on his face brought his spear around again, driving it at Six-Legged. Six-Legged ducked. Long Arrow came up beside him and put his own spear through White Face's neck.

There was blood everywhere; the grass was slippery with

it. The Buffalo Horn people's dogs ran in and out through the
bloody grass, teeth bared. One closed its jaws on an enemy's
calf, ripping the tendons, and the man fell, thrashing. Six-
Legged pressed his spear against the man's throat. The man
closed his hands around the shaft, trying to hold it back. Six-
Legged leaned on it, and the hands fell away in a wash of
blood.

He saw Wants the Moon, naked, fighting with a Dry River
man, her black hair flying in a tangle and her teeth bared. He
tried to get to her, but other men came between them. The
battle closed over him like a fierce wind.

Six-Legged had never fought before he had tried to drive
the Buffalo men out of Red Earth City. The men of the cities
didn't fight. Sometimes Outsiders attacked a city or a hunting
band, but that had never happened to him, and he had not
known what it would be like. It had seemed like madness to
him then, men shouting and flailing and all the blood pouring
out while Death poured in, but afterward his heart had
pounded in his chest and he had felt able to run faster than
Horse and jump higher. At the same time he had felt a little
ashamed. And he had secretly wanted to fight someone again.

Now that urge caught him up again. He stabbed his spear
over and over at the Dry River men, at the intruders, the Others. He saw Bull Calf fighting at his shoulder and Long Arrow
beside him. Angry in the Morning threw away his broken
spear, flung a Dry River man out of the way with his hand,
and drove his belt knife into the belly of another. Every blow
was a satisfaction to Six-Legged, a sharp pleasure like sex or
eating meat.

The Dry River men were beginning to fall back; there was
no longer a ring around the horses, only scattered knots of
struggling men. Six-Legged saw Wants the Moon again,
blood-streaked, panting, knock a man backward with her
spear. The horses were pulling at their stakes, eyes white-
rimmed and rolling; there was blood on Horse's white hide.
Sunflower jabbed viciously with his spear at an enemy who
had lost his own, until the man went down. When he fell,
Hole in the Sunset bent swiftly and ran his knife along the

hairline, lifted the bloody scalp, whirled it in his hand. The blood spattered Six-Legged. Sunflower knelt and put his knife through the man's heart. The other Buffalo men howled in approval and fell furiously on the intruders as they staggered back.

Now other women ran from the tents with spears, and the battle spun in a dreadful spiral, like the tornado, until it spat the Dry River men out, throwing them across the prairie. In the Buffalo Horn camp, the women drove their knives into the hearts of the dying enemy and cut away their scalps in a handful of bloody rags.

Six-Legged doubled over and put his hands on his thighs, breathing hard. His stomach churned, and he thought he might vomit. In a moment it passed and he straightened, licking his lips. The men were picking up their wounded. Angry in the Morning lifted Weaver and set him on his feet. Weaver staggered and his eyes were wild, but he didn't seem to be hurt. He tried to pull away toward Red Horse, but Angry in the Morning jerked him back again. Red Horse was plunging at the end of her rope.

"She will trample you. Leave her be." Angry in the Morning pulled Weaver toward his tent and pushed him through the door flap.

Elk Walker peered at the bleeding scalps to see what they had to say. His tufted hair stuck up from his head like wild feathers.

Six-Legged looked to see if anyone had seen him nearly be sick. They were not noticing him. Bear Paws had a deep gash in his arm, and Young Onion Digger was tying a piece of soft hide around it. Porcupine Mother and White Buffalo were patting the weeping children. An anguished wail rose and fell over the bloody grass. Wants the Moon sat on the ground trying to pull Blue Racer's limp body into her lap. She was still naked, her tangled hair smeared with dirt and blood, her forearm bleeding from someone's spear. She sobbed as she tried to shake Blue Racer awake and make him talk to her. The broken shaft of an arrow still stuck out of his chest. The blood had begun to coagulate.

Six-Legged knelt beside them. "He's dead," he said gently. "I saw him fall."

She looked up at him, eyes wide with anger. "Why should he be dead?"

Six-Legged shrugged. How did you answer a question like that? "He just is." He sat down beside her.

Wants the Moon put her face against his shoulder and cried, one arm still clutching Blue Racer. He could feel the tears making her whole body shake. "They wanted the horses," she said through her sobs, face muffled in his armpit.

"What?"

"The horses. They wanted our horses for themselves, because we have them and they don't. Monsters did bring the horses. Monsters gave them to us so we would kill each other." The sobs became a hiccuping wail. She rocked back and forth. "*We* are the monsters. We told lies about spirits and made bad things happen. That's why we keep seeing them. I don't want to see them anymore."

Six-Legged got up, went to Wants the Moon's tent, got the cotton blanket from home that she still carried with her, and wrapped her up in it.

Sunflower came and sat down on her other side. "Go away," he said to Six-Legged. "This is *my* wife." But he looked bewildered, too, staring at Blue Racer the way everyone had stared at Wolf, trying to make him be alive.

Wants the Moon pulled the blanket closer, putting it between herself and both of them. Six-Legged stood up and went away, leaving Sunflower patting her arm.

The Buffalo Horn people's camp was a ruin of broken tent poles and scattered trash. Elk Walker was still talking to the scalps that now hung on a pole outside Hole in the Sunset's tent. Things that had just died knew secrets and could tell them. Six-Legged wondered what Blue Racer knew, and if he would tell it to anyone. He felt light-headed, as if he might be sick again.

White Buffalo bustled up to him, her medicine bag in her hand. "Come into the tent, Husband." She clucked her tongue. "You are bleeding."

Six-Legged peered at himself, craning his neck, trying to see what she was talking about. The air beside him was suddenly still, as if it were made out of something solid. *I told you this would happen,* a voice said.

"Go away!" Six-Legged swatted his hand at the empty air. White Buffalo dragged him into the tent, it spun around his head, and he toppled over.

15

Weaver and His Wife

WHEN SIX-LEGGED OPENED HIS EYES, WHITE BUFFALO WAS smearing salve on his leg, which hurt now. His ear stung as if a bee had bitten it.

Wind in the Grass was slicing strips off a soft hide that she kept for bandages. "You will have a nick in your ear," she said. "Like an old dog that's been fighting." She smiled at him sunnily. "And Hole in the Sunset says that now you may have Old Grandmother Locust prick patterns on your skin."

Six-Legged closed his eyes. He would look like a buffalo hunter, like a wild person who lived in a tent. His mother would say it was uncivilized.

"And me, too," Wind in the Grass said importantly. "Because I am your wife."

White Buffalo made a face. "Also that other old wife of yours, because she fought the Dry River men, naked like a slut, and because Blue Racer was brave." White Buffalo, a chief's daughter and tattooed already, was not eager to share her distinction with Wants the Moon.

"It was a mistake for Hole in the Sunset to give her two husbands," Wind in the Grass said, shaking her head. She tied her strips of bandage around Six-Legged's thigh and clucked her tongue. "This is not so bad. You will be ready to hunt in three days. Hole in the Sunset says we are to wait that long. Otherwise the buffalo will smell blood and run away."

Six-Legged felt them packing up their salves and bandages, but he didn't open his eyes. He was sleepy, and there was an odd taste in his mouth. White Buffalo had given him some curing tea. Curing teas always tasted like poison; he wondered why that was. Outside he could still hear Wants the Moon crying as the women made her help get Blue Racer's body ready for the bier. She wasn't like Weaver. She knew he was dead.

Six-Legged remembered how he had felt when he was fighting the Dry River men, how he had liked that feeling, and he felt ashamed now. Human people were monsters, Wants the Moon had said, as wicked as whatever shiny strange creatures had brought the horses. Maybe that was true.

Let them go, a voice suggested out of the fog of the curing tea. *Let the Dry River people have them. Then they can be sorry, too.*

"I am not sorry," Six-Legged said stubbornly, opening his eyes halfway, which was as far as they would go. "I am only sad."

"Two-legged people are like that," Coyote said, materializing at the end of his bed. White Buffalo and Wind in the Grass didn't see him. White Buffalo was drawing designs with paint on Wind in the Grass's face, trying on her promised ornamentation. Coyote turned around three times and settled on the bed.

"You aren't a dog," Six-Legged said crossly. He wondered why he kept seeing him. Maybe Wants the Moon was right about that. If you said things, maybe you made them true— Wolf had tried that, and it had been true enough to kill him.

Coyote nosed in the furs on Six-Legged's bed. "I don't suppose you can give the horse things away now anyway," he said. He sounded only mildly regretful. Coyote doesn't worry about things for long. It is one of the reasons he gets killed so often. "It is a time of change, these days. And that is human people's fault, not mine. Two-leggeds were made out of changes in the first place, so no wonder they can't sit still.''

"I thought *you* made human people," Six-Legged said accusingly. He didn't know if he believed that either. Some people thought so.

"Oh, true. I did that." Coyote seemed happy to take the responsibility. He bit at a flea at the base of his tail. "I'll tell you in a minute," he said, chewing, but the story didn't wait. It came up out of the curing tea like steam, so Coyote began to tell it before it could run away from him. He had found that stories did that if you didn't watch them. Six-Legged listened sleepily.

"It was after I found the dirt under the water and made the world with it," Coyote said. "Everyone was arguing about how to make people . . .''

When Coyote had made all the other animal people and all the rocks and trees and plants and things they would need to live, he called a big council of every animal to see what they should do to make men. He built his council fire by the riverbank and gathered everyone around it. The grizzly bear lumbered out of the forest and took his place, and the black bear sat next to him, and then the mountain cat and the wolf and the badger and the fox and then, carefully and at a little distance, the rabbits and ground squirrels and horned toads, and the snakes and lizards. Deer and Antelope and Elk came to give their advice, along with Buffalo. Hawk and Eagle perched in a tree, and old Grandmother Owl lit on a dead branch and watched with eyes that were as round and yellow as the moon.

"Well!" Coyote said. "We're going to make man."

"What will he be like?" Black Bear asked.

"Well, first of all, he will have to have a voice to make everyone afraid of him," Mountain Cat said. "And claws to kill his prey with."

"Only a fool would go squalling around, scaring off his dinner," Grizzly Bear said. "What he needs is great strength so that he can move silently and knock his prey senseless with

a blow. That is the sensible and proper way to do it.''

Black Bear nodded in agreement.

"He ought to have antlers," Elk said. "How will anyone know he's important? And I personally find that good ears are more useful than being a big lumbering lout. What he needs is good big ears." He wiggled his.

"Antlers will get caught in the brush, and then he will look like a fool," Mountain Sheep said scornfully. "What he needs are horns that curve downward usefully, so he can batter things with them."

"It is better to live under the water," a trout said, lifting his head above the stream. "He ought to have scales and fine, delicate fins to swim with."

"He needs claws to catch fish with," the eagle said, and the trout disappeared under the water with a plop.

"He needs good eyesight," a lugubrious voice said from a dead tree. Condor was sitting over them. "To find lunch."

Grandmother Owl hooted at him. "Night vision. Carrion will make him sick. Mice are better." The field mice all ran into a hollow log.

"Well, wings, anyway," Mockingbird said. "How can anyone get along without wings?" He sang a three-note trill and flashed his feathers.

"He will bump into the sky," Mole said. "Anyone with any sense lives underground."

"Why not just make him big and strong?" Bull Buffalo asked. "What else would he need then?"

"Yah!" Coyote yelped, snapping his teeth at them. "I am about to go to sleep listening to this nonsense. You all want to make man just like yourselves. Why not just pick one of your cubs and call it man and have done with it? Yah!"

"Well, what do you suggest?" the beaver asked sulkily. He had been just about to point out the advantages of a nice flat tail.

"Has anyone thought of a brain, to start with?" Coyote looked at them all with exasperation. "Buffalo is big and strong, yes, and he's as stupid as rocks. But Bear is strong, *too, and better yet, he walks on his hind feet, which is useful, so we will give man that.''*

The bears looked pleased.

"However, it isn't enough. Bear also has no tail, which is only a place for fleas to live, so that is good, too. But it still isn't enough. The fish is naked and has no fleas at all, and furthermore he can keep cool in the summer. So we will give man just enough fur to keep his brains warm. And good claws, like Eagle's, except even more flexible, so he can make things with them. But none of this will be any good without a brain, so I will give him that, because I am the only one of you with the cunning he will need.''   -

"But tails are good," the beaver said, interrupting. *"Give him a nice flat one so he can carry sand and mud on it.''*

"Then he won't be able to get off the ground," Eagle said, *"if he's dragging a great heavy thing like that around. Give him feathers in his tail, and wings.''*

"Bump into the sky," Mole said again, bumbling into the log. *"Just bump into the sky. Get burned up by the sun. Asking for trouble. He should burrow in the nice cool dirt and be happy.''*

"Fins," the fish said, leaping out of the water.

"Long legs," the deer said.

"Whiskers," the little mice squeaked.

"Yesss. Whiskerrrrs.'' Great Cat stuck his neck out toward them, his whiskers twitching. The mice ran inside the log again.

"Tough hide," Horned Toad said.

"Speed," Hummingbird whirred.

"Beauty," sighed the butterfly.

"Flat tail," the beaver said stubbornly.

Eagle glared at Beaver. Bear and Cat began to argue between themselves, and Coyote lost his patience and snapped at Horned Toad, taking a good bite out of his scaly hide. The council degenerated into a row. Owl flew down and hooked her claws in Coyote's scalp. Hawk flew at Owl. Snake coiled up and bit Badger, who hadn't said anything at all, and Deer stamped his pointed hooves at Mole until he burrowed into *the dirt. Bear and Cat were rolling around on the ground biting each other, and all the little mice shrieked at them from their log.*

"All right! All right!" Coyote shouted. "All right, if you think you can do so well, you can all go and make your idea of man yourselves. I'm tired of the lot of you. Go and make him how you think he ought to be!" He shook Owl off his head, swatting at her with his front paws.

The animals separated grumpily, and each one went to make his own idea of man from the clay by the river.

Bear made a squat heavy thing that stood on its hind feet. Deer made a long-legged graceful thing with twigs for antlers. Beaver made a thing with a broad flat tail. But it was dark now, and the tail and the antlers kept breaking off. Bear's man fell over, and one of its front paws looked strange afterward. Deer's man had trouble with his thin legs.

"Oh, it's too dark," Deer said fretfully. Bear yawned. Beaver pushed his man aside and waddled down to the river. Cat was asleep already, his whiskers twitching.

Coyote grinned. They were all tired from arguing with each other and brawling. The little mice were snoring in a pile in their log. Only Mole was working stubbornly, since he couldn't see anyway and didn't care if it was dark.

Coyote, wide awake, went on with his man. He made his man standing up, with long arms that had fingers on the ends to grasp with, just as he had said at the council. He gave his man no antlers or fangs, or fins or scales, or tails, but he gave him soft lips and a tongue that could make words, and a voice to make them with. In his man's head he put his own adaptability and cunning and wit. He gave him just enough hair to protect his head and his sex organs, and just to amuse himself he made the man be interested in sex all the time, not just in certain seasons like the other animals. (He didn't know how much trouble that was going to cause, or he might not have done it.) He made his man a wife and made her interested in sex all the time, too, and gave her teats that stayed swollen even when she wasn't nursing, so the man would have something to play with. He thought they looked very good.

*When Coyote looked up again, even the mole had gone to
sleep, leaving his mole-man outside his tunnel. Coyote walked
over to it and nosed it. He snorted with derision, lifted his
back leg, and peed on the mole-man so that it melted back
into the mud. Then he went around and peed on all the other
clay figures and spoiled them.*

*By that time, Morning Star was starting to dim. Coyote held
up his man and woman and breathed life into them. As they
opened their eyes and stretched their arms, Coyote sang a
morning song about how happy he was with his creation. His
song woke everybody up. They came, rubbing their eyes, to
look at man.*

"I never saw anything like that before," Grizzly Bear said.

"That's the point," said Coyote.

"So you can't help wanting new things," Coyote said to Six-
Legged. "You are made out of change."

"Most people don't like that," Six-Legged said. "They
don't like things to change."

"Doesn't matter," Coyote said. "I'm sorry about that now,
I think. But I can't help it. I asked Grandmother. She said so,
too."

Six-Legged groaned and closed his eyes. His head felt
swimmy from the wound in his thigh, or from talking to spirits. "Please go away," he said, and when he woke again in
the evening, Coyote had gone. But Blue Racer's dead body
was still there on its bier, and the horses were still there, too,
in the cloud of flies and envy that the Dry River people had
left behind them.

Six-Legged got out of bed and went to see Wants the Moon,
ignoring his wives, who said he was too sick, and Sunflower,
who said Wants the Moon wasn't Six-Legged's wife.

Wants the Moon looked sick, too. Porcupine Mother had
been there and brought her a curing tea. It was something for
women that smelled like swamp water, but Wants the Moon
closed her eyes and drank it.

Six-Legged limped over to her bed and sat beside it, stretching his bad leg out in front of him. The dog with the red foot

was asleep on her feet. "I came to say again that I am sorry about your husband." He touched her hand awkwardly.

Wants the Moon nodded. There were dark circles under her eyes. She closed them, and two tears ran out from under the lids. Six-Legged patted her again and went away, not knowing what to do. He wasn't used to Wants the Moon being like this. He went to check on the horses and found Weaver sitting beside Red Horse. She was still in her mating season and restive, and Weaver jumped up and drove Horse away with a stick every time he got near her. When Six-Legged came close, Weaver stood up and shouted at him, waving his fist.

"Go away! Stay away! Go away!"

"They need to be moved to better grass," Six-Legged said, untying Horse and keeping his distance from Red Horse. "Bring her along yourself, then."

Weaver shouted something angry and unintelligible at him and sat back down. Six-Legged took Horse down to the beaver pond to drink, and when he got back, Weaver was still sitting there. Six-Legged pounded in Horse's stake with a rock and went up to Weaver. "You have to feed her."

Weaver's skin shirt and leggings were torn and dirty, and there were burrs in his hair. It looked greasy and lifeless. Six-Legged felt as if he weren't seeing Weaver but someone new. This person was thin as a blade of grass, and his bones stuck out. Weaver picked up a rock and threw it at Six-Legged.

Six-Legged looked at him suspiciously, thinking of Uncle Wolf. But Weaver wasn't strong enough to have beaten Uncle Wolf's head in with rocks, and he had never hurt anyone before. Six-Legged brought a basket of water for Red Horse. Then he took out his knife and cut an armload of grass for her. He put it down on the edge of the circle she had grazed, out of range of Weaver's rocks.

On the third morning the Buffalo Horn people left that camp, looking over their shoulders to make sure the spirit of Wolf wasn't following them. The women and dogs carried everything on their backs and travoises now, tents and packs and food, while the men went ahead, burdened only with their bows and spears and their hunting robes of buffalo hide. The buffalo herd was near, and they had to move quickly, Sunflower had explained while Wants the Moon scowled at him. She had spent the night cuddled against him, her face stinging from Old Grandmother Locust's needles, dreaming that Blue Racer had come back to them. But he hadn't. He was on a bier, too, beside Wolf.

"You will catch up to us in a few days, when we have killed the buffalo," Sunflower said. "That is how it is."

Wants the Moon compressed her lips in a thin line. That was how it was among the cities, too—women didn't hunt. But she had been in the wild and knew things she hadn't known before. She had lines like the river current pricked into her cheeks now, and she had fought the Dry River men.

She saw Weaver trying to get on Red Horse's back while Red Horse danced and edged away from him. "You are ill," she said to him. "Let me ride her. You know I can."

Six-Legged was sitting on Horse nearby, watching. Hole in the Sunset had fallen off Horse several more times at Winter Camp, and he had not said anything else lately about riding.

Weaver shook his head. "That would not be right."

"I will only drive the buffalo," Wants the Moon said. "I will not hunt. Ask Elk Walker if that will do any harm."

"No." Weaver bent down, his expression earnest now, trying to explain something. "This is my fate. It is what I am to do. She has told me."

"Who has told you?" Wants the Moon asked. Six-Legged raised his eyebrows. That was more words than Weaver had spoken to anyone lately.

"My wife has told me," Weaver said.

Wants the Moon started to say, "That is not your wife," but she wasn't sure anymore. Words were powerful. Maybe Weaver *could* put the spirit of Quail in a horse by saying so.

Weaver turned and tried to climb on Red Horse again, and this time Wants the Moon held Red Horse's head for him so she stood still. When Weaver was on her back, Red Horse rolled her eyes and twitched her ears, but she didn't try to throw him off.

The hunters set off at a trot with the two riders at their head
and a pack of dogs behind. Even the dog with the red foot
had left, following Sunflower. Wants the Moon thought the
hunting dogs gave the pack dogs the same look the men gave
their wives. She tightened the straps of her bundled tent, kneeling in the shadow of Blue Racer's bier. Except for the bier,
the ground was empty where all the tents had been yesterday.
The bier was decorated with feathers and bright strips of cotton cloth, torn from her blanket, that fluttered in the wind.
Shouldering her tent on her back, Wants the Moon scrubbed
her hand across her eyes and followed the other women. The
poles dragged on the ground behind her, trying to pull her
back.

The first night the hunters camped under a tangle of grapevines
that festooned the windblown trees by a small river. They
danced the Buffalo Dance in the moonlight. They had not
brought the buffalo masks, but it didn't matter. Buffalo was
near enough to smell. Six-Legged followed their steps, dancing his way into this new world. The night before, Old Grandmother Locust had pricked spiral designs like the whirl of stars
into his cheekbones and three dotted lines between his brows.
The lines still stung; he could feel the pattern on his face.
Wind in the Grass had been given markings, too, a sunburst
between her eyebrows and cupped new moons on her cheeks.
Six-Legged wondered what his mother would think if she saw
him. Maybe it was too late to go back, now that he was marked
as a buffalo hunter. Maybe they would throw rocks at him the
way they had at Weaver.

The dancers swayed around the fire, singing the buffalo
closer. Weaver danced with them, but Six-Legged wasn't sure
he was really there. Often these days he thought Weaver was
somewhere else. *It is my fate,* Weaver had said to Wants the
Moon, and then again to Six-Legged tonight, even though Six-
Legged hadn't asked him. Six-Legged wondered uneasily what
he meant by that, or if he knew.

Six-Legged tipped his head back as he danced. The stars
sparkled across the black sky like the dew on a spiderweb,

and he wondered if Grandmother Spider watched them from it, the way she watched everything. He began to dance for her, because now he had the stars on his face. The buffalo dancers swirled around him, and he found himself making a new dance to go with theirs, a Horse Dance of the wind in his mane and the grass under his feet, running faster than the buffalo. They began to run before him, hands at their heads to make horns, stamping buffalo hooves in the flattened grass. Six-Legged danced after them while the horses watched them from beyond the firelight, eyes glinting enigmatically.

When the dance was over, it hung an instant in the air above them like the net of stars, then winked out. Men who had quarreled with each other over Wolf's killing found that they had danced next to each other and backed away now. Angry in the Morning snarled something at Bull Calf, and Long Arrow stepped between them. Sunflower looked bewildered, as if he had just remembered again that Blue Racer was dead.

Six-Legged wondered how magic could be that short-lived. He didn't see Weaver, so he went to look at the horses and found him tugging at Red Horse's lead. They had been tethered apart because Horse was still trying to mount Red Horse, although she wasn't interested anymore and usually kicked him. Now Weaver has been trying to make Red Horse lie down next to where he had spread his bedroll. Red Horse pulled her head back and showed the whites of her eyes.

"Let her be," Six-Legged said. "She will roll over on you in the night or kick you."

"No." Weaver wrapped himself in his blanket and lay down at her feet.

"She will step on you," Six-Legged said.

Weaver shook his head.

"Yah! Let her step on you!" Six-Legged said, suddenly angry. He stalked away.

Bear Paws shook his head as he passed. "It is not good for that man to have a spirit wife."

"I didn't give her to him," Six-Legged said.

"He must have done something to call her back," Bear Paws said. "It isn't good. Dead is dead."

"I will be certain to tell him that," Six-Legged snarled.

*   *   *

In the morning Long Arrow told Hole in the Sunset there were fresh tracks. The herd was near, and the hunters might catch up to it in a day. Even Sunflower was cheerful at that. "We will see how this horse chases buffalo," he said to Six-Legged, running his hand along Horse's hide. He held the other hand out the way Wants the Moon had taught him and smiled when Horse nibbled the small green grapes off his palm.

"When we are in camp again, I will teach you to ride him," Six-Legged said. After he had said it, he thought that would make trouble, but he wanted to give Sunflower something, the way he wanted to give Wants the Moon something, because Blue Racer was dead.

Sunflower smiled. He went away, eating grapes, and Six-Legged swung himself up on Horse's back. Horse whickered interestedly at Red Horse, and Six-Legged jerked the reins.

"No! Let her be." Horse scuttled sideways resentfully and Six-Legged leaned down and cuffed his nose.

The other hunters eyed them with suspicion. No one was sure what the horses would do now, and Angry in the Morning was already muttering that if it hadn't been for the horses the Dry River raiders would never have come. Angry in the Morning was looking for things to be someone else's fault because nearly everybody still thought he had killed Wolf, and he was bitter over it. Now he was arguing with Long Arrow over who should lead the buffalo drivers. Everyone took a side in that, except Weaver, until Hole in the Sunset shouted at them to be quiet.

Weaver wouldn't have noticed if a fish fell out of the sky and led the hunters, Six-Legged thought. Weaver was talking softly to Red Horse. Now and then she flicked an ear backward at his voice, but Six-Legged couldn't tell if she was really listening. It wouldn't matter to Weaver. When he stopped talking, he held his head very still as if *he* was listening to something—Six-Legged didn't know what. Red Horse didn't seem to be saying anything. Six-Legged hoped nobody else was.

When the sun was at the top of the sky and they stopped

to eat, Horse waited until Six-Legged slid off his back and then tried to mount Red Horse again. Weaver screeched at him, and Six-Legged smacked Horse's nose and dragged him off. "Put that away," he said furiously to Horse, but Horse didn't. It hung impressively under his belly, waiting for something to put it in. Six-Legged tied Horse's reins around his waist and sat down.

Bear Paws lumbered by and stopped to disapprove. "That is bad luck," he said.

"He's a horse. He doesn't know anything," Six-Legged said.

Sunflower joined them. "He knows how to copulate," he said, chuckling. He sat down next to Six-Legged and smiled gently up at Bear Paws. "Our—my wife told me the story of how First Man had to teach the Mudheads how to do it. It is a funny story—they couldn't do anything right. At least these horses can do that."

"And run. He knows how to run," Six-Legged said. "So that is two things."

Bear Paws growled at them and stumped off. Six-Legged grinned at Sunflower. He thought maybe they were going to like each other now. He wasn't sure why. Maybe Wants the Moon had made that happen.

At night they camped at the foot of a butte where a scree of rock tumbled down to a crystal stream. There were crayfish in the stream, living under the rocks, and Six-Legged and Sunflower took off their shoes and waded into the water with a cooking basket. Six-Legged turned the rocks over with a stick, and Sunflower held the basket to catch the crayfish when they shot backward in surprise. Bull Calf laughed at them and called them women and turtle hunters, but they caught a handful to boil in the basket and then wouldn't give him any.

When they had eaten, Six-Legged tethered Horse where he could watch him, well away from Red Horse. Sunflower lay down next to him. The other hunters were spread out on the grass, rolled in their blankets under the full moon. The fire was nearly out, just a faint drift of smoke rising in the silver air, pale against the dark outline of the rocks behind them.

"I want to learn to ride the horse," Sunflower said quietly in the dark. "Do you think that if there had not been horses, the Dry River people would not have come and my brother would be alive?"

"I don't know," Six-Legged said. "The Dry River people have raided your camp before, when there were no horses. My wives said that. They say the Buffalo Horn people have raided the Dry River people, too, and it has all been going on for a long time."

"How else is a young man going to make a reputation?" Sunflower didn't expect an answer. There wasn't one. That was how things were.

"I don't know." Six-Legged thought about it. "My people are different." But he remembered the feeling he had had while he was fighting the Dry River men and wondered if they really were. He had always thought so. "I don't know," he said again. He kept saying that, over and over—like a whippoorwill, he thought in disgust. Six-Legged looked at Horse again, to be sure he was still at the end of his tether, and closed his eyes. Horse didn't worry about things like that. Worrying was another thing Coyote had given human people.

Weaver had been hearing the voices all day. Quail wouldn't talk to him, although she flicked her red ears back when he spoke to her. But the spirits in his head spoke to him about her, and about the white animal who had copulated with her. That wasn't good, they said. A woman might give birth to monsters that way, to children with hoofed feet and hairy heads. Weaver knew what had to be done to banish these monster offspring and lure Quail back into her own body again. The spirits had told him.

Quail was cropping grass with her horse teeth, her dark eyes luminous in the moonlight. Weaver put his blanket aside and went to her. She tossed her head nervously, and he stroked her nose, running his hand down the hard bony ridge and the soft, whiskered nostrils, feeling the warm horse breath on his fingers. He untied her tether from its stake, quietly.

The voices told him where to go. Weaver led Quail out of the camp full of sleeping men, careful to go away from the white horse, not even to look at it or let it call her name. The path was easy to see, almost as light as day under the full moon. The light dappled Quail's back like water. Weaver knew that he could fall through the water, sink into Quail's world, but it would be easy to drown. Better to bring her up through the water into his, shrugging off the horse skin like a blanket. She would hang it up on a tree, and they would preserve it for their children to see and play with.

Weaver led Quail through the scree of rock that littered the foot of the butte, picking his way carefully across the uneven ground. The sandy path rippled ahead, dotted with moon-washed stones and pale grass, the shadow of the butte cutting across it like a knife. He saw a coyote sitting on one of the high stones, watching them as they passed, its eyes reflecting the moonlight, but it didn't say anything. Red Horse snorted at it, and it jumped down and ran away into the shadows.

Weaver crooned to Quail, calling her Most Beautiful, Most Wise, Not-Dead, Wife Come Back, while Red Horse rolled her eyes and swiveled her ears. They crossed into the warm darkness under the edge of the butte, where its height blotted out the moon. There were more stones here, strange undulating shapes cut away by the wind and fallen from the crest. Thistles and sumac grew up between them. Weaver stopped. He could feel Quail's breath in the darkness, the warm grass smell of her. He tied her lead to a sumac bush and scrambled up a stairstep of stone behind her.

"Most Beautiful," he said. "Beautiful Quail." He laid his hands on the warm red hide.

It was hard to tell how it happened. Maybe Weaver flailed his arms for balance as the stones shifted under his feet and the harsh buzz erupted beneath them. Or maybe Rattlesnake rattled his tail, and then Weaver stumbled. It didn't matter. Rattlesnake, coiled underground, heard the heavy footfalls and lifted his wedge-shaped head. The vicious warning vibrated from his tail: *Go away. I am Death.*

Weaver heard Rattlesnake and froze, teetering, but Red

Horse, who was always afraid and only lived in Now, swung around, pulling at her tether, her feet clattering, sending a rain of pebbles into Rattlesnake's house. Rattlesnake's brothers hummed in the rocks, all of them vibrating the stones with their anger. Weaver backed away, stones scattering under him. Red Horse reared, panicked, plunging in the rubble, fighting her tether. Weaver's foot slid into a cleft, and he lost his balance. Thrashing, he pitched forward down the slope, hands clutching sumac branches. The snakes' harsh rattle filled the rocks. He fell beneath Red Horse's feet. His touch terrified her. Things were twining about her ankles; the snakes were biting her. She reared and brought her front hooves down hard, again and again, pounding the stones. Her hooves came down on his chest, on his head, in terrified fury.

The snake people slid away through the rocks, but Red Horse didn't stop pounding her feet. She could still feel them, their sinuous shapes and the burn of their fangs, the dry whisper of their scales. She stamped and stamped at the things in the rocks until she was exhausted. Then she stood, quivering, her neck extended, her tether stretched taut, the rope still caught in the sumac bush, waiting for someone to find her.

16

Buffalo

Six-Legged found Weaver in the morning, when he and Sunflower went to look for Red Horse. His face was unrecognizable. They knew it was Weaver because no one else was missing.

Rattlesnake's children had come back, and one of them buzzed at Six-Legged as he touched the body.

"I'll take him away from here, Brother," Six-Legged said, trying not to shift the stones.

Sunflower came gingerly to help him.

"Good fortune come to you and your children," Six-Legged told Rattlesnake, easing backward. They set Weaver down in the grass. Red Horse didn't seem to notice him now.

"Maybe snakes bit him," Sunflower said, but he could see that Red Horse's hooves were caked with dried blood. The rocks and the butte face were quiet now, the snake people waiting to see if the two-leggeds were going to come in their house again.

Six-Legged didn't answer.

"Why would he come here?" Sunflower asked him, as if he thought Six-Legged might know. "The snakes would frighten her." He touched Red Horse's nose gently.

"He thought she was his wife," Six-Legged said. *He* knew she wasn't, now. What else she might be, he wasn't sure.

"Was he going to—?" Sunflower looked dubious. There were stories in legend about men with animal wives. Those men mated with their animal wives and had strange, magical children. Maybe it wasn't as easy to do, though, in now times.

"I don't know what he was going to do. He was crazy," Six-Legged said. Anyone who tried to mate with a horse was crazy. Sex might be dangerous at any time. It was always dangerous with spirits. It stood to reason it would be dangerous with a horse. He picked up Weaver—he didn't weigh anything—and started back to camp.

Sunflower got on Red Horse and rode her back without asking Six-Legged, although Six-Legged took note of that. When they got to the camp, Six-Legged told Hole in the Sunset he didn't know what Weaver had been doing, but that rattlesnakes had scared Red Horse.

They buried Weaver in a hole in the ground because there were no good trees around and also because he had not died a death that had earned recognition. Six-Legged didn't object. Red Earth people put their dead decently in the ground, not up on poles. He didn't want anyone putting *him* up on a bier in the air when he died. They put Weaver's hide shirt on a stick on the grave, so the women who were following them would see it and know who was dead. No one knew whether the buffalo would smell this death or not.

"Get on Red Horse and ride with me," Six-Legged told Sunflower. "I will have to teach you things before we come to the buffalo."

Angry in the Morning glared at them and stalked off to find Hole in the Sunset. "Why does he have the horse?" Angry in the Morning demanded of Hole in the Sunset.

Hole in the Sunset sighed and walked back to the horses with Angry in the Morning. He wasn't the one who had decided this. Six-Legged had just given Red Horse to Sunflower. Hole in the Sunset looked as if he might be about to decide something else.

"Why does he have the horse?" Angry in the Morning demanded again.

"Because she is still when he is on her back," Six-Legged said truthfully. He thought Sunflower could handle Red Horse, but she would only catch Angry in the Morning's anger. Sunflower was talking to her, not the way Weaver had, but in the way Wants the Moon did.

"This horse is dangerous and has killed somebody," Hole in the Sunset said.

"All the more reason to give it to me." Angry in the Morning glowered at Sunflower. "I am stronger than Sunflower. And I was supposed to have married the chief's daughter." He reached for Red Horse's lead. She tossed her head up, baring her teeth, her eyes rimmed with white.

"This horse is not a chief's daughter," Six-Legged said. "She is not anybody's daughter, or anybody's wife. She is a horse. Go marry something with two legs."

He and Angry in the Morning glared at each other while Hole in the Sunset watched Sunflower on Red Horse. Angry in the Morning's yellow eyes were slitted like the snakes'.

"For today," Hole in the Sunset said, "Sunflower will ride this horse because she is not afraid of him. Afterward, we will see."

Angry in the Morning compressed his lips in a tight line, but he didn't argue. Causing strife before a hunt was bad luck, and there were hunting chiefs to keep order and see that no one did that. This time they were Bear Paws and Bull Calf, who watched Angry in the Morning with their arms folded across their chests, waiting for him to do something.

While the hunters walked half the morning on the fresh buffalo trail, Six-Legged taught Sunflower to turn Red Horse with her leads and hold on with his knees and the muscles in her thighs when she trotted. Ahead of them, the ground was torn up with the hooves of thousands of buffalo, a trampled swath stretching two hours' walk from one side to the other. They galloped a little way, in a circle around the hunters, and Sunflower didn't fall off. As they circled back toward the hunting band, a coyote ran through the grass with a hide shirt in its mouth. Long Arrow shouted and threw rocks at it, but it disappeared in the brush.

Everyone looked warily over their shoulders. Now Weaver's spirit might go into that coyote, and that was not good. The coyotes were following the hunters because they knew there would be carrion left. A ghost inside one of them would be a bad thing.

"The ghost still wants that horse," Bull Calf said. "Better turn her loose and let it have her."

"That is my horse!" Angry in the Morning said.

"Then you can have the ghost, too," Bull Calf said. "I wouldn't want it in my tent."

Horse tossed his head up and snorted, ears pricked. Six-Legged couldn't see anything, but the dogs were doing the same thing.

"Buffalo," Long Arrow said. "Over that ridge."

They looked ahead to where the land rose in a slow slope to a ridge dotted with bent trees. The dogs were whining now. Horse danced backward, snorting.

Six-Legged kicked him. "It is only buffalo, stupid." The horses didn't know things. Their magic was only in being themselves. Weaver hadn't understood that. "It will not eat you," Six-Legged said, stroking Horse's white neck.

"Take the horse away from here," Long Arrow said, "before it frightens the buffalo."

Six-Legged frowned. Sunflower motioned to him, and he walked Horse over to Red Horse.

"We'll go around the herd now," Sunflower said, "and make a pen to take them over the cliff."

"I know that," Six-Legged said. "I am not ignorant."

Sunflower smiled. "If the horses make a noise, the buffalo may hear it and run too soon."

Six-Legged said, "Ummm," but he followed Sunflower. Long Arrow led them, flanked by Bear Paws and Bull Calf. These three would lead the hunt now. Hole in the Sunset would follow Long Arrow. That was Long Arrow's job.

When the hunters topped the ridge, Six-Legged stared openmouthed. The buffalo covered the plain. He remembered the herd that he and Wants the Moon had seen in their wanderings, but they had not been this close. From here he could smell them and see the light glinting off their dark eyes and short, curved horns. There were as many as there were stars in the night sky or stones on the riverbank. They were humpbacked and mysterious, creatures from a world that the People of the Cities never saw. City people saw buffalo robes and cups and slow-burner boxes made of their horns. They saw hoof rattles and hide tents. But they never saw Buffalo, in his endless herds, blackening the plains.

It took until sunset to circle around them. At dusk they made camp where the ground dropped sharply to a river, to the north of the grazing buffalo. It was the river where he and Wants the Moon had found the Buffalo Horn people, Six-Legged realized. The trail they had taken down to the water was only a little way away.

The buffalo hunters would drive the herd over the cliff instead. When they had eaten, they began working in the deepening dusk to pile river stones and brush into a pen with a mouth that widened as it spilled southward and narrowed as it neared the river. It would turn the buffalo away from the trail to the precipice beside it. Six-Legged could tell the Buffalo Horn people had used this cliff before. The remains of an old pen were still tumbled on the ground. The brush had rotted away, but the stones were there.

Long Arrow called a halt only when it was black dark, and they started again as soon as the moon rose, stacking stones to Long Arrow's satisfaction. In between and atop the stones they laid cut brush.

"A buffalo could knock this down," Six-Legged said, squinting at it.

"They don't," Sunflower said. "They don't try to knock down walls. They just keep running."

"Widen the mouth here," Long Arrow said, coming by.

Six-Legged grunted and heaved up a stone. He tipped it onto a hide, and he and Sunflower lifted it together to the top of the wall.

At dawn the pen was no more than half finished. Six-Legged was giddy with weariness, and the scab on his half-healed leg ached. When Long Arrow stopped the work, Six-Legged collapsed in the dirt by the half-built wall. When he opened his eyes again, the sun was high in the sky. He pulled himself up and staggered to where the others were asleep in the shade of the narrow end. Angry in the Morning was getting ready to take the trail down to the river to look for fish. Six-Legged untethered the horses and went with him. Sunflower was still asleep on his back, his mouth open, so Six-Legged took both horses.

"Will we finish the pen today?" he said to Angry in the Morning's silent back.

"We don't work in the daytime," Angry in the Morning said without turning around. "The buffalo would see us and be frightened. Or come to see what we are doing before we are ready for them. You are ignorant."

"I wish to learn," Six-Legged said mildly.

Angry in the Morning made a snorting noise through his nose. When they got to the bottom of the trail, he said, "Take them down there to drink, or they will frighten the fish. They frighten everything. I don't know what they are good for."

"Then why did you want one?" Six-Legged asked him, goaded.

"Because I was supposed to marry the woman that you have!" Angry in the Morning snapped. "Because I was made to look foolish. That is why!" His knuckles whitened as his fingers clenched around his fish spear.

"I can see how that would be," Six-Legged said. He could, too. "I didn't ask for her."

"Yah! She didn't ask for you! She asked for me."

Six-Legged thought that over. White Buffalo had been moody lately. He wondered if she were regretting her father's gift. She had seemed happy enough with the idea at first. He wondered, too, if now she thought Angry in the Morning had killed Uncle Wolf. Six-Legged thought so less and less himself.

Angry in the Morning's yellow eyes narrowed. He had

wide, dark bands tattooed on each temple and looked more
like a snake than ever. "We quarreled," he said to Six-
Legged. "If not, she would not have gone with you."

"Did she have a choice?"

Angry in the Morning ground his teeth. "No. And yes. She
could have argued. Hole in the Sunset would not have forced
her. You can't force a woman to marry if she doesn't want
to. Unless you steal her from somewhere else."

"Oh." Six-Legged thought. "Do you want help catching
fish?"

"No," Angry in the Morning growled. "You will frighten
them away."

"Mmm." Six-Legged looked downstream. "I will go and
water the horses down there."

When they had scrambled back up the trail, he tied the
horses in the small shade that the pen afforded and sat down
beside them. The others were waking up, talking and laughing
softly with each other, and some of them went down to fish.
Long Arrow came along and told Six-Legged to go back down
the trail and cut brush.

At night they started on the pen again. They built it a long
way out into the plain and as high as a man's shoulders. They
could just see the buffalo in the distance, a dark blotch across
the pale grass. Six-Legged thought he could hear them, chewing grass and thinking silent buffalo thoughts, unknowable as
shooting stars or underground streams. He was beginning to
be a little afraid of the buffalo.

It wasn't quite dawn when they finished the pen and lay
down to sleep again, and not dawn yet when Long Arrow
woke them. They got up sleepily, complaining, although
mostly for form's sake, and gathered around Long Arrow.

"Bull Calf will stay here," Long Arrow said. "With Angry
in the Morning and two more that he picks. Bear Paws will
come with me and Hole in the Sunset and the rest."

They nodded. The hunters at the pen would try to draw the
buffalo in, pretending to be buffalo themselves. They would
put buffalo robes over their heads, bending low as they

walked, and see if the herd would come toward them. The rest
would circle back to the other side of the herd, hidden under
hides that would disguise scent as well as silhouette. The people of the plains had learned that Buffalo was curious but not
very smart.

Buffalo was unpredictable, though. Long Arrow said so and
said to the hunters to remember it. Six-Legged thought about
it carefully as he and Sunflower rode in opposite directions
along the bluff, circling to the back of the herd to wait for
Long Arrow's signal. Buffalo's weapons were his horns and
his size, and his numbers. With those he didn't need brains
very often. Except when someone was trying to run him off
a cliff. But then he might turn on the hunters, and someone
would die on those horns or go over the edge with him, falling
surprised into nothingness. Six-Legged imagined tumbling
head over feet with the lumbering buffalo, flying out of the
air into death.

Six-Legged circled the ridge on the far side of the herd and
came up it again from the back. Near the top he dismounted
and eased his way, holding Horse by his lead. Horse's nostrils
opened wide, and Six-Legged put his hand over them before
he could whinny. "No," he whispered. He crouched under a
sumac bush and waited while the buffalo-robed hunters fanned
out through the grass, working their way around both flanks
of the herd.

Six-Legged held his breath while they crept closer, skins
drawn around them. The buffalo were ambling as they grazed,
slowly, pulling grass from the earth, tails swatting flies from
their great backsides, teeth slowly chewing. The bulls were on
the outside of the herd, with the cows and their calves in the
center.

Sunflower was to the west, waiting with Red Horse for
Long Arrow to call them out. Their job was to drive the buffalo, to run faster than men could and turn them toward the
pen and the cliff. Then they were to shoot from the horses'
backs and bring down buffalo on the edges of the herd. Six-
Legged had said they could, but now he wondered. Buffalo
was not a deer. And he thought Sunflower would fall off.

It seemed a long time while Six-Legged watched the hunters edge closer. From this distance they looked like odd, misshapen buffalo, spiders under buffalo robes, scuttling on hands and feet. The dogs trotted behind them. The buffalo didn't seem to mind those. Six-Legged couldn't see Angry in the Morning and Bear Paws in the far distance where the pen began.

Below him, Long Arrow stood up, raised his hand to his mouth, and whistled, a sharp screech like a hawk's. The buffalo threw their heads up. They stared at the shouting men and lumbered away. Six-Legged put his heels to Horse's flank.

He nocked an arrow to his bowstring as they galloped, clinging to Horse with his knees. In the distance he could see Red Horse running with Sunflower on her back. Sunflower reached over his shoulder for his quiver and lost his balance. As he slid sideways, the quiver flopped, strewing arrows. Sunflower righted himself and clung to Red Horse's mane. Six-Legged grinned. He drew his bow as they closed on the buffalo.

The wind turned, and the buffalo smell enveloped Horse. He skidded to a stop, his front hooves dug into the grass, and Six-Legged nearly went over his head. Horse danced backward on his hind legs while Six-Legged swore at him, fighting his head down, the bow tucked under his arm. Nostrils flaring, Horse tried to run away from the huge things that made that smell. Six-Legged pulled his head around and kicked him hard. Horse began to run again, terrified, but now the huge, bad-smelling things were lumbering beside him. He ran faster.

Six-Legged loosed an arrow into the racing herd. He wasn't sure what it hit. The hunters were driving them, running behind, shouting, but the buffalo on the flanks didn't notice them. They had smelled Horse, and now they ran faster, tails high, snorting in terror. They began to turn, legs churning.

On the other side of the herd, the buffalo who had seen Red Horse lumbered frantically on, foam flecking their mouths, not toward the cliff but along its side, while the buffalo hunters shouted and waved their spears, trying to turn them, and at last flung themselves out of the way.

Sunflower clung to Red Horse's back, the fingers of both hands knotted in her mane, afraid to let go to catch her reins. She raced beside the buffalo, and he could feel the salt sweat soaking her hide. His bow was gone, his quiver bounced wildly on his back, and he knew if he fell off, the buffalo would trample him. If they turned on the horse, they could trample her, but instead they ran away from her, their wild eyes ringed with white.

Angry in the Morning ran along the walls of the pen, his heart pounding in his chest. The herd thundered toward him, but they were going to miss the pen. The leading edge of the herd burst through the pen walls in an explosion of stones and brush. Two fell under the hooves of the others, while Angry in the Morning and Bear Paws scrambled over the walls, flinging themselves into the dirt on the other side while the buffalo thundered around them. The noise of the stampeding herd was like an earthquake, and the ground shook under their feet. The rest of the pen walls came down.

Angry in the Morning scrambled to his knees and found his bow. He nocked an arrow and let it fly into the herd streaming past, and then he dived over the edge of the bluff, clinging to the stunted brush that grew on its lip, while the buffalo went by a handspan from his head. He felt their hot breath and the spittle from their lips.

The ground shook, vibrating as if some hulking beast were working its way up from the depths. The bones in the earth heard it and quivered in the stone. The woodrats who lived in the little ravines cowered in their dens while dirt fell from the ceiling. Panicked, they ran outside to be crushed under the feet of the buffalo. The raven beat his wings through the dust cloud, his yellow eye glowing in the darkness. The gray coyotes who had followed the hunters ran back up the ridges and sat on their haunches to see what would be dead when it was over.

Sunflower clung to Red Horse's back, his arms wrapped around her neck, while the buffalo hurtled by him. He had made a wild grab for the reins and had brought her to a shuddering stop by main force, and he was afraid to set her moving again. She stood quivering, rolling her eyes wildly. The ground trembled under the buffalo, and a cloud of dust rose over them, dark as smoke. The dog with the red foot, who had followed him, was gone, lost in the dust. The buffalo spilled over the plain and the ridges and the ravines that broke the ground before the bluff's edge. The dust was choking, too thick to see.

The dog with the red foot ran yelping through the grass. She was coming into her season and hadn't wanted to follow Sunflower, but he had shouted at her and she had come, tail between her legs and looking over her shoulder at the males. Like Weaver, Sunflower had thrown rocks at them. Now she ran in blind panic, the males forgotten, terror of the buffalo overpowering her. She scrabbled through the scrub of a ravine, splashing through the trickle of water at its bottom. Above her, yellow eyes gleamed through the dust, and a gray muzzle sniffed interestedly.

Hole in the Sunset stumbled through the choking dust as hooves thundered around him. The drivers were not trying to run the buffalo now, only to get out of the way of the careening herd. His spear was gone, his bow trampled. The dogs had all scattered in terror. A buffalo ran by him so close he could see its red tongue, hanging from its foam-flecked lips. He backed away, and another buffalo came at him from the other side. Hole in the Sunset saw a man loom out of the dust and then vanish, rolled under the pounding hooves.

The buffalo didn't see Hole in the Sunset. Terror-driven, they lumbered on through the dust. The ones in the middle of the herd didn't know what they were running from. It didn't matter. All that mattered was that buffalo on the edges had seen something dreadful. Now everyone would run until the leaders slowed from exhaustion.

* * *

The buffalo smell filled Horse's nostrils. It was all around him, and the great shaggy bodies and curved horns surrounded him, monsters, dark, terrible monsters with humps on their backs. He tried to run away from them, but Six-Legged pulled his head around. Horse reared, backing up on his hind legs, while Six-Legged clung to his mane. Horse plunged down, head below his knees, back feet kicking the air, defending himself from the monsters. A huge head loomed at him out of the dust. Horse swerved, breaking from the edge of the herd, careening blindly across the trampled grass. The horrible thing pursued him, thundering on his heels.

He stumbled on the edge of a small ravine, and Six-Legged slipped sideways on his back. Horse righted himself and plunged on again, headlong through the dust, through the roar of uncounted, uncountable hooves, afraid of everything now, including the thing that clung to his back. He fishtailed, twisting as he ran, careening up a ridge and down the other side.

Six-Legged's grip loosened, and he slid across Horse's withers, one leg dangling. The fingers of his other hand scrabbled in the flying mane, at the leads now trailing free on the ground. Horse leaped, twisting his spine, and Six-Legged flew from his back. The sky upended itself, and Six-Legged came down on his head. The blow compressed his neck and cracked his skull, and the thunder of the buffalo folded itself into the ground like a stream running out.

17

The End of the Story

THE WOMEN HAD MADE THEIR CAMP ON THE NEAR SIDE OF the ridge. From the top of it they could see the buffalo herd and the walls the men had built to pen them on the bluff's edge. After the buffalo had been run, then the women would move up and butcher the kill. So Porcupine Mother said. Wants the Moon sat by the fire and thought about Weaver while she waited.

They had found the grave with coyote tracks all over it, and all the women had begun wailing at once because that was a bad sign and because no one knew who was in it. Wants the Moon had stood on the grave and thought, and the more she thought, the more she knew it was Weaver. But there was no way to prove it, so she had kept her mouth shut until the next day, when they had found the chewed pieces of Weaver's hide shirt. Then she told Porcupine Mother what she thought.

"Poor man," said Porcupine Mother, relieved that the shirt hadn't been her husband's, and inclined now to be charitable. "Maybe he's happier now."

Wants the Moon looked back the way they had come. She couldn't see anyone. Weaver had gone away.

"That one was crazy," White Buffalo said to her.

"He was one of my first people," Wants the Moon said. The world felt empty without him now. Blue Racer was dead; Six-Legged and Sunflower had left her. Even the dog with the red foot had gone, leaving her here with strange lines like black water on her face.

"My husband was one of your first people, too," White Buffalo said. "Maybe you are all crazy." She looked as if she might want to say something else but didn't. She compressed her lips.

"He was my husband first," Wants the Moon said, feeling surly.

"Angry in the Morning was mine," White Buffalo snapped. "My father decides these things."

"Don't you like your husband anymore?"

"He is very important."

"That is more important than liking him," Wants the Moon said in disgust. "Of course."

White Buffalo glared at her. "Nobody *asked* me what I wanted. You asked for your husbands."

Wants the Moon's eyes stung. She could ask for Blue Racer now, and he wouldn't come. Maybe Weaver had been right. It might be better to be crazy and think your dead husband was in a vulture or a prairie dog.

Porcupine Mother bustled up with Lark behind her. "They are running the buffalo," she said. "Can't you hear that? You can feel it in the ground. Come along, come along." She shooed them ahead of her with flapping hands. Wants the Moon got her bundle of skinning and fleshing knives and went obediently. White Buffalo stood for a moment with her fists clenched, then ran after the others.

When they cleared the ridgetop, they could see what had happened. Porcupine Mother's hands flew to her mouth. Wants the Moon stared, unsure. She had never seen a buffalo run before. The ground below was dark with dust, chaotic, and she could tell that the buffalo had turned from the cliff's edge. They were a heavy cloud in the northwest. The women began to stream down the ridge.

A rider came out of the dust—Sunflower on Red Horse.

"What happened?" they cried out to him.

Sunflower was gasping for breath. "They turned. They frightened the horses and the horses frightened them. They turned and we couldn't hold them. I think we killed some, but I can't find anyone."

Wants the Moon clutched at his foot. "Where is Horse?"

"I don't know. I saw him running loose. I don't know where he went. There were too many buffalo."

"Loose?" Wants the Moon could hear the hooves in the distance, drumming on the earth, flattening everything underneath them.

"Where is my husband?" Wind in the Grass shrieked.

Porcupine Mother cuffed her, gently but enough to make an impression. "Where are any of our husbands? Be quiet."

Wants the Moon dropped her knives in the grass and ran. The air was still thick with dust. She had seen a forest fire once, and this felt like that. She plunged through it anyway, choking. Hooves drummed after her.

"Come back!" Sunflower shouted at her from Red Horse's back.

Wants the Moon stopped. "Give me the horse."

"Get up behind me," Sunflower said. "I'll take you back."

"No, give me the horse." In her mind Wants the Moon saw Six-Legged on the ground, body broken the way Weaver's had been, with Horse lying trampled beside him. The red blood soaked Horse's white hide like a sunset.

"You won't find anything," Sunflower said. "I couldn't. Come back with me."

Wants the Moon turned and ran into the grass again. Sunflower shouted at her, but she didn't turn back. She climbed down a ravine, put her fingers in her mouth, and whistled. Nothing answered her. She climbed up the other side, Sunflower following on Red Horse, telling her to come back. She found a trampled dog, its blood soaking into the churned earth. Beyond it was a buffalo calf with its rib cage caved in, and a cow with an arrow in her chest. Her eyes were slitted open, her tongue between her teeth, black with flies.

She saw movement—men coming back through the wreckage, marking the dead buffalo and counting their own numbers.

"Where is Six-Legged?" she shouted at Bull Calf. Bull Calf shrugged.

"Let his wives find him!" Sunflower shouted angrily from Red Horse's back.

"Give me the horse!" she said again.

"No." Sunflower was less biddable than he had been.

Wants the Moon climbed a hillock and looked around. She clambered down again and went on.

Angry in the Morning saw her, with Sunflower behind her, waving his arms and talking to her back. Angry in the Morning had almost been trampled, but he had seen through the dust to the thing that had been important. "The buffalo are afraid of the horses!" he shouted to her, his eyes bright. Sunflower ignored him, but Wants the Moon turned toward him for a moment. She nodded, then ran on.

There was nothing in the grass. All the grass people, the lizards and field mice and horned toads, had run away under the ground, flat as stones, waiting for the thunder to pass over them. The earth above was battered, the broken walls of the buffalo pen scattered on it like welts. Wants the Moon stopped to catch her breath, ignoring Sunflower, who was still telling her to come back. When she could draw air into her lungs again, she put her fingers in her mouth and whistled. This time something answered. It might just have been bugs in the brush.

"All right. Get up on the horse with me and I will take you," Sunflower said. "I will take you to find them."

Wants the Moon spun around. "Yah! Go away! Be quiet!" She whistled again and listened.

Horse whickered and trotted through the scrub to her, his leads trailing on the ground.

He butted his head against her chest and kept it there, like a child hiding its face. "Yah, you are a coward," she said soothingly into his ear. "The buffalo came and you were afraid. What have you done with Six-Legged?"

Horse rolled his eyes. Wants the Moon took his leads in

one hand and wrapped her fingers in his mane, low on the withers. Sunflower was still berating her. She swung onto Horse's back and straightened up, tucking her skirt around her knees.

Sunflower stopped talking. When Horse trotted off, he turned Red Horse after them, jolting over the rough ground. "I am your husband. Let his wives find him!" He bit his tongue as Red Horse broke into a trot.

Six-Legged was lying on the ground, not dead, he thought, but with lights in his head. One of them seemed to be Buffalo. A huge shaggy head with curved horns and dark eyes looked at him out of a shower of sparks.

"You have changed the world," Buffalo said.

Six-Legged nodded.

"You won't be able to stop it now," Buffalo said angrily.

"I don't want to." Six-Legged thought he wasn't dead. Being dead should be different from this. There was a spot on his head that hurt when he touched it. He had been told he was supposed to change the world.

"You will want to one day," Buffalo said. *"We will all want to."*

Six-Legged saw Horse standing beside him now. His white coat shone like milk. Horse and Buffalo looked at each other for a long time. Six-Legged could see them acknowledging each other.

Horse spoke. His mouth didn't move, but Six-Legged knew Horse's voice, though he hadn't heard it before. "We have just found a better way to hunt you," Horse said. "Those other things are not our business."

"Not your business, no," Buffalo said. *"But they will come to you anyway."*

Horse's white head blotted out the sparks that came from Buffalo. It was cool in his shadow. His voice sounded like the grass growing.

"I will learn not to be afraid of you," Horse said. *"Then*

Man and I will hunt you together. That is what we do. That is why we are.''

''For a while,'' Buffalo said.

''For always,'' Horse said.

''What is always?'' *Buffalo's huge head swayed from side to side, shooting sparks. ''I have seen always in a clay pot. A mouse ate it.''*

Six-Legged's head hurt more, and he put his hand to it again. Someone else's hand was already there. He opened his eyes to find Wants the Moon bending over him and dripping tears on his nose. Sunflower was standing beside Red Horse, his arms folded over his chest in disgust.

Horse swished his tail, cropping grass a little way off. He lifted his head from the grass and looked at Six-Legged, but he didn't appear to have anything else to say. The sun was low over some hillocks in the west.

''He talked to me,'' Six-Legged said.

''You hurt your head,'' Wants the Moon said.

''You fell off,'' Sunflower pointed out. *He* hadn't fallen off. Six-Legged sat up. His head throbbed violently with the motion.

''Be still,'' Wants the Moon said.

''I can't sit out here all night.'' Six-Legged winced.

''We can put you over this one's back.'' Sunflower jerked his thumb at Red Horse. He looked as if he liked that idea.

''Not that horse,'' Six-Legged said.

Sunflower shrugged. ''I didn't fall off her,'' he observed.

''And you weren't facedown on her,'' Six-Legged said. ''I will walk.'' If he fell down, then it wouldn't be so far to go. ''That horse killed Weaver,'' he said to Wants the Moon, forgetting not to name him. Maybe Weaver dead couldn't be more trouble than Weaver alive had been. Anyway, Six-Legged thought he had gone away by now. What Weaver wanted hadn't ever been here. ''I don't know what he was doing.''

''I do,'' Wants the Moon said. ''But it doesn't matter. She would have killed him anyway. She killed Wolf, I am sure of

it now. I told Porcupine Mother, and she will tell Hole in the
Sunset that it wasn't Angry in the Morning.''

Six-Legged tried to think about that. His head pounded.

Sunflower looked skeptical. ''Someone hit Wolf with rocks.
And carried him. That wasn't a horse.''

''That was afterward,'' Wants the Moon said. ''Weaver did
that because the horse killed Wolf. He was afraid someone
would find out. He thought she was his wife.'' She didn't seem
afraid of his ghost.

''How do you know this?'' Six-Legged demanded.

''There was blood on her hooves.'' Wants the Moon looked
at Red Horse. ''I washed it off. I didn't know what he would
do next. Someone might have hurt him.''

''You should have told me,'' Sunflower said.

''I didn't know you were going to ride the horse. I told him
he should let me ride her.''

''You should have told me because I am your husband,''
Sunflower said.

''You should have told *me*,'' Six-Legged said. ''You should
have told us both.'' They looked at her disapprovingly.

''Then you would have done something to him.'' Wants the
Moon inspected Six-Legged's head, trying to abandon the sub-
ject. ''That needs salve.''

''Leave it alone,'' Six-Legged said.

Wants the Moon ignored him.

Six-Legged batted her hand away and thought. Weaver
wouldn't have had to hit very hard to mask the hoof marks,
if Wolf was already dead. He supposed Weaver could have
dragged the body, too. Wolf wasn't very big. And Six-Legged
had never thought it was Angry in the Morning. He looked at
Red Horse appraisingly. Maybe she was crazy from living
with a crazy man.

Wants the Moon followed his eyes. ''She is dangerous,''
she said quietly.

You could give her to me.

The suggestion formed itself hungrily in Six-Legged's head.
From Wants the Moon's expression, he thought she had heard
it, too.

"She's the only one we have," Wants the Moon said.

Sunflower watched them. He had ridden a horse now. That made him one with the horse people. If his wife wanted to talk to her horse husband, he supposed it was all right. She was still Sunflower's wife, and all she ever did with Six-Legged was argue with him. "You can ride on the white horse," he said to Six-Legged. "I will catch you if you fall."

White Buffalo and Wind in the Grass were dragging butchered carcasses toward the fire with ropes. Wants the Moon rode Red Horse toward them while Six-Legged slumped on Horse's back, behind Sunflower, arms around his waist, head dropped to Sunflower's shoulder.

Wind in the Grass's eyes lit up when she saw them. She dropped her rope. "Husband!" She raced across the ground, mouth stretched in a wide smile. She put her foot in a hole and nearly fell, arms flailing. She kept going until she was panting at Six-Legged's side. "Angry in the Morning told us all about it! He told us how you shot the buffalo! I was afraid you were dead!" She wrapped her arm around his leg and laid her head on it.

Wants the Moon lifted a hand as if she were going to cuff her, then let it drop.

Six-Legged smiled foggily at Wind in the Grass. He touched her cheek.

"Come back here and help me!" White Buffalo shouted at her. She yanked furiously at the rope, but the dead buffalo wouldn't budge. "Yah, you are a worthless, lazy slut!" Her voice broke. She stamped her foot and scrubbed her hand across her eyes.

Wind in the Grass turned and ran back while Wants the Moon looked thoughtfully at White Buffalo. Six-Legged didn't seem to notice anything amiss. Wants the Moon kicked Red Horse in the side, and they followed the women and the buffalo carcasses.

The coyotes on the hillock watched them go. Their eyes were bright and curious, and their tongues lolled out. Those were strange new animals, and they had made the buffalo run

very fast. There were two dead dogs down there, trampled by
the herd. At dusk they would go down and eat them. The dog
with the red foot had left already, to go back to her people.
They might have eaten her, too, if there had been more than
three of them and she hadn't been so fierce. As it was, there
would be half-coyote puppies in the people's camp.

It was hard to say if the world looked different. Hole in the
Sunset thought it did. There was a faint shimmer to the grass,
like mica. Elk Walker was down by the river, talking to it,
seeing if anything else was going to come out of its enigmatic
waters.

The Buffalo Horn people had made camp on the butte's
edge just above the trail. They had found Long Arrow on the
ground where the herd had passed, and Tortoise was weeping
over his broken body while Bull Calf paced back and forth
beside her, trying to think of something comforting to say.
The other women chased him off finally, and Porcupine
Mother put her arms around Tortoise.

"It's the price Buffalo takes," Porcupine Mother said.

"It was the horses!" Tortoise wailed.

"It wasn't. Often enough there is someone killed. Two
years back it was Elk Walker's son. Ask him what Buffalo
takes."

Angry in the Morning stood on a rock that had fallen from
the walls of the buffalo pen. His eyes were bright with excitement. "And we drove the buffalo, and Six-Legged raised
his bow and let fly an arrow, and a buffalo bull fell down."
He spoke with the cadence of a storyteller, rolling his words
over the crowd. The children listened to him wide-eyed, and
women whispered and looked sidelong at Six-Legged and
Sunflower. The two had drawn rein and sat on Horse's back
together, tall, dark silhouettes against the low sun. Wants the
Moon sat on Red Horse beside them. There was enough meat
now to feed the people for a year, and hides for tents and
clothing. Next year there would be even more, and the Buffalo
Horn people would grow rich.

"We drove the buffalo hard to the cliff edge, but they feared the horses, and so they turned. In the turning they trampled their own kind, and the horses ran faster then, and our men loosed their arrows." Angry in the Morning's eyes gleamed. Hole in the Sunset had been told who had killed Wolf, and the red horse's calf had been promised to Angry in the Morning. Next year or the next, Angry in the Morning would ride a horse and shoot down the buffalo from its back, and people would tell about him long after he had died.

His voice washed over White Buffalo, and she laid her skinning knife down and went to where Six-Legged had dismounted and was standing with Sunflower and Wants the Moon.

"It is good that my husband is not hurt," she said.

"Yes. I am all right." Six-Legged nodded to her, puzzled. She stood stiffly, in some sort of formal posture, looking oddly ceremonial to him.

"It is difficult to have a spirit husband," she said.

Six-Legged felt even more puzzled. "I suppose it is."

"And Wind in the Grass is jealous. She is only a chief's niece," she added with elaborate kindness. "It would be nice for her to be First Wife instead."

"Oh." Six-Legged watched her walk away, back into Angry in the Morning's voice.

"Three wives is too many," Wants the Moon said. "Two is too many, too." She leaned her head against Sunflower's, resting her shoulder on his.

Six-Legged felt angry, abandoned. Then Wind in the Grass came up to them and took his hand. "Elk Walker will have something to put on your head," she said. "And then I will make up your bed." Her voice was a whisper in the shadows, promising soft skin against his and round breasts to put his head on.

Bear Paws and Bull Calf listened to Angry in the Morning and nodded at each other. That was immortality. They eyed the horses consideringly, wondering how many calves a horse could bear at a time. Elk Walker had thought only one, but you never knew. The three riders had gone away now, but the story went on, humming in the air where they had been, more real than they were.

Angry in the Morning told it into legend: how the buffalo had been so close to him that he had smelled their breath and seen their wild, dark eyes. Excitement radiated from him; his arms curved in a great arc, describing the vastness of the buffalo herd. His voice was more powerful than the ghost of Wolf or the ghost of Weaver, and it was louder than the voice of Tortoise wailing for Long Arrow.

The horses nosed at the trampled grass. A small girl brought a handful of berries and offered it to Horse. He nuzzled them from her hand. The shadows came down the riverbank on the opposite side and flowed over the ground. Angry in the Morning was still talking, still telling the tale from his rock. His voice rose over the hum of the dusk people, the insects. His shadow lengthened and blurred with the horses'.

Elk Walker saw it as he came up the trail from the river with a skin of water in his hand. Wind in the Grass and Six-Legged were waiting for him, but he looked past them at the shapes of the horses on the grass, and the man's shape across those. The hair rose on the skin of his arms.

18

Next Time

"AND THAT IS THE WAY IT ALL HAPPENED," COYOTE SAID. He stretched. You could see the stars through the brim of his hat and, maybe, through his shirt now.

"Did they raise many horses?" a girl asked.

"Oh, I don't know. They stole some, or someone else did. They bought some, when they had to. It took a long time."

"And then they were a horse people?" The girl had heard the stories that everyone had, about the days of the buffalo and the spotted horses on the plains.

"For a while," Coyote said. "For a while they were."

"And is it all true?"

"No," Coyote said. "None of it is true, but a lot of it is true."

"Then what happened to Six-Legged? And Wants the Moon? Did they stay with the buffalo hunters?"

"White Buffalo married Angry in the Morning after all, and they and Six-Legged and Wind in the Grass and Wants the Moon and Sunflower all had many children, and their children's children were horse people, and maybe some of them even came home to Red Earth City and lived there." He said it fast, as if he were bored, but the child seemed satisfied.

The trail guide came back with the red roan that had got loose and put her back on the picket line. The fire was nearly out.

It was cold, and the stars looked a little like bits of ice in the black air. Someone put more wood on the fire, and they watched the little horse shapes running in the flames.

AUTHOR'S NOTE

THE STORIES OF NATIVE AMERICAN TRADITION HAVE AS many variants as there are tellers to tell them. That is the way story is, and what it is for, to stretch reality over possibility. The old tales I have retold in this book have their origins in fables recorded by others, and I owe them my gratitude. How Coyote taught man to hunt is a Zuni story. The tale of Uncle, Coyote, and the prairie dogs belongs to the Kiowa, and how Coyote made man is a Miwok legend from California. The story of Coyote, Duck, and Rattlesnake has had many variants, including one told in the 1930s by a Mexican coyote trapper in the valley of the Rio Grande, to which I have added my own new ending, as well as taking it back to an earlier time. The originals of all these may be found in *The Voice of the Coyote*, written in 1949 by J. Frank Dobie. I recommend this book as well to anyone who would like to know more about the habits of *Canis latrans*, the little yellowy-gray wolf of the Southwest who is far more like his magical counterpart than we might suspect.

In addition, I owe thanks as always to those who have given help and encouragement along the way: to Elizabeth Doolittle, reference librarian at Hollins University; to my editors, Elizabeth Tinsley of Book Creations and Lucia Macro of Avon; and to the attendees at the International Conference on the Fantastic in the Arts, on whom I tried out parts of this book in its early stages.

And finally, my deep gratitude goes to Ursula K. Le Guin, for kind words kindly spoken, and to the late Eleanor Cameron (whose friendship and encouragement made all the difference) from her fan club.

THE HORSE CATCHERS

— TRILOGY —

by

AMANDA COCKRELL

Continues in March 2000
With the next installment
of this unforgettable series

Six-Legged and Wants the Moon are legend now, connected to their great grandchildren by people who remember knowing them in a far-off time. It is the Buffalo Horn people themselves who are six-legged now, riders and hunters from horseback. Stories still exist of how First Horse was found, and someone brave enough—or crazy enough—might find more. So the tribe selects Blue Jay, great grandson of the legendary horse-bringers, and Spotted Horse, son of Eldest, to travel west and bring back horses.

This is their story...

SUE HARRISON

"A remarkable storyteller…
one wants to stand up and cheer."
Detroit Free Press

"Sue Harrison outdoes Jean Auel"
Milwaukee Journal

MOTHER EARTH FATHER SKY
71592-9/$6.99 US/ $8.99 Can

In a frozen time before history, in a harsh and beautiful
land near the top of the world, womanhood comes
cruelly and suddenly to beautiful, young Chagak.

MY SISTER THE MOON
71836-7/ $6.99 US/ $8.99 Can

BROTHER WIND
72178-3/ $6.50 US/ $8.50 Can

SONG OF THE RIVER
Book One of The Storyteller Trilogy
72603-3/ $6.99 US/ $8.99Can

CRY OF THE WIND
Book Two of The Storyteller Trilogy
97371-5/ $24.00 US/ $31.00Can